Pordan.

...your ...no rules.

Ma... of the Nibrilsiem is the fourth book following the adventures of the imaginary races who dwell here.

After completing the Karrak trilogy, Robert was overjoyed by how many loyal readers had entered his world, but they wanted more!

This is a prequel to his trilogy, but there are even more in the pipeline.

Robert attends as many events and fayres as possible amongst his busy schedule. Who knows, you may get to meet him one day.

Follow him on The Ascension of Karrak Facebook page.

Or, check out his website: www.robertjmarsters.com.

Acknowledgements

To my wife, Jane, my best friend in both of my worlds.

To Scott Stitcher, artist and tattooist extraordinaire, for the original cover artwork of this book. Instagram Scott_Stitcher, and Facebook. Thank you, brother.

To my existing readership. Your loyalty and support is priceless. Thank you to you all.

Other titles by Robert J Marsters:

The Ascension of Karrak

The Bane of Karrak

The Cessation of Karrak

Robert J Marsters

Robert J Marsters

Mark Of The Nibrilsiem

Robert J Marsters

Copyright © Robert J Marsters (2019)

The right of Robert J Marsters to be identified as author of this work has been asserted by him in accordance with section 77 and 78 of the Copyright, Designs and Patents Act 1988.

All rights reserved. No part of this publication may be reproduced, stored in a retrieval system, or transmitted in any form or by any means, electronic, mechanical, photocopying, recording, or otherwise, without the prior permission of the publishers.

Any person who commits any unauthorised act in relation to this publication may be liable to criminal prosecution and civil claims for damages.

A CIP catalogue record for this title is available from the British Library.

ISBN 978-1-7122222-1-8 (Paperback)
EBook

CHAPTER 1

As Ballorn stared across the village square, he shook his head in frustration. He didn't hate, or even dislike the villagers, but he wasn't overly fond of them either. Not a single one had done anything in particular to deserve his cold demeanour, just the opposite, in fact. They knew he had been orphaned as an infant and tried to include him in any celebrations that arose in the village. Throughout the years, many had tried to befriend him, to no avail. Somehow, he would always manage to come up with an excuse or simply slip away undetected. As Ballorn grew into adulthood the villagers became less concerned, resigning themselves to the fact that it would be best to allow him to lead the solitary life with which he seemed content.

He had reached the age of fourteen before finding something which he not only enjoyed, but also helped to drown out the incessant chatter of the villagers. Within a few short years he had become an accomplished blacksmith. The nemilar, as a race, hated getting their hands dirty and frowned upon Ballorn's chosen trade. However, they never frowned upon the quality of his work, something that had now given him an innate sense of pride for over twenty years.

Focussing his attention on his forge, he pulled the handle of the bellows. The sound of the roaring flames was home to him. He raised his hammer, grunting as he brought it down heavily, creating a shower of sparks that lit up the failing light of dusk. It was nothing new for him to work late into the evening, in fact it was the most pleasurable time of the day for him. No pesky questions from annoying villagers who had placed orders for horseshoes or garden tools would delay him once night fell. They were everyday harmless nemilar he could easily dismiss.

Dannard however was one nemilar he could have happily flattened as soon as look at. He was the local cooper and always complained that the barrel hoops that Ballorn had forged were somehow lacking in quality, then attempted to haggle for a better price. Ballorn never wavered and, in return, always flatly refused. He knew that his workmanship was worth far more than he actually charged, his way of repaying the villagers for their kindness to him as a child. Above that, he also had the smug pleasure of knowing that the nearest blacksmith to him was almost a hundred miles away.

Hammering loudly, Ballorn did not hear the approaching footsteps until they were right behind him. He wasn't startled and turned slowly to face the nemilar who was nervously edging closer. The blacksmith was huge for a nemilar. Standing over five feet tall and with a deep barrel chest and muscular arms, he could be most intimidating to the average nemilar who stood not much above four.

"Evening," said Ballorn, gruffly.

"Good evening," replied the stranger, "I wonder if I could place an order?"

"Aye," replied Ballorn, "What do ye need?"

"Well, that's the thing," began the stranger, "I'm not sure. I was hoping that you could suggest something."

"I can try," said Ballorn. He looked the stranger up and down. He was slender and wiry, a farmer, was Ballorn's guess. *How could he not know what he needed?* "What's it for?" he asked, tossing his hammer aside with a sigh.

"I need something sharp enough to cut through…" he replied with a nervous laugh, "this will sound silly, I'm afraid."

"Come on, spit it out," said Ballorn, impatiently. "I'm not here all night. Sharp enough to cut through what?"

The stranger leaned closer to Ballorn, "Erm… dragon hide," he whispered.

Ballorn raised his eyebrows and leaned on the counter, "Dragon hide?" he asked with mocking disbelief.

"Exactly," replied the nemilar. "So, I'm not sure whether I need a sword, or perhaps an axe, or something like a really large scythe. Either way," he urged, "it has to be razor-sharp."

Ballorn had had some strange requests in the past, but this was the most unusual by far. "I'm guessing you're a farmer?" he suggested.

"Yes, that's right. So, you see, I'm not sure what type of weapon I may need." He was looking at Ballorn, hoping that the blacksmith could provide an answer that he, himself could not, "Or do you think a selection would be best?"

Still leaning on the hatch, Ballorn beckoned the farmer forward, "What's your name?" he asked.

"Lonny," replied the farmer, stepping toward the counter eagerly.

"Listen to me carefully, Lonny," Ballorn said quietly, grabbing the farmer by his collar and almost lifting him from the ground with one hand. "I've not got time for your jokes and japes. So, tell whoever sent you that the next time someone comes here trying to make a fool of me, he'll be going away from my forge with his head in a sack. Got it!" He pushed the nemilar away, turned and picked up his hammer.

"Ahem, excuse me."

Ballorn dropped his chin to his chest and closed his eyes. *Why were there always interruptions? Couldn't he just be left in peace to get on with his work?* He turned slowly, looking over his shoulder. Lonny was still standing there patiently. Physically shaking but determined to place his order, he smiled nervously at Ballorn. Ballorn sighed and placed his hammer gently onto his anvil. Opening the hatch, he stepped out from behind the counter and stood before the farmer.

"Before you do anything, sir," Lonny pleaded, taking out a coin purse and showing Ballorn the gold coins inside. "I am neither joking nor mocking you. I have seen the beast with my own eyes. For the sake of my family, forge me a weapon with which to protect them. I'll pay in advance, simply name your price."

Ballorn shook his head, "It wouldn't be right," he muttered. "You're obviously off your bonce. I won't take money from a loony, however easy it is."

Mark of the Nibrilsiem

"I assure you, sir, I am quite sane. I have seen the monster, black scales, huge teeth, sparks flying from its body as it walks. Please sir, I implore you, take my order."

"There's no dragons around any more!" bawled Ballorn. "They've been gone for over a thousand years. If there were any left, don't you think others would've seen 'em?"

"I cannot speak for others, sir, only myself," Lonny replied, grabbing his arm. "Please Ballorn, even if you think me insane, forge me a weapon." The farmer began to pour coins onto the hatch. Ballorn had never been swayed by money, but what now lay on the counter was easily as much as the humble blacksmith could have made in a good year.

Ballorn dragged his hand across his face, smearing the black soot and mixing it with the sweat on his brow. He threw his hands into the air, "Alright, I give in. What do you want?" he sighed.

"What would you suggest?" asked Lonny, eagerly.

"Well, if it was me, and if there was a *real* dragon, I suppose a broadaxe would be my first choice."

"Excellent," said Lonny with relief. "A broadaxe it is then."

Ballorn looked Lonny up and down, gauging his height. The length of the handle had to be right if he was to wield the axe properly. Although exactly what he would be wielding it against, was a mystery. *Dragon indeed*, he thought.

Advising the farmer to return in a week, Ballorn watched as he hurried away. He raised his hand to his neck, rubbing the silver pendant that had belonged to his father. He wondered how things would have turned out had his parents lived long enough for him to remember them.

***

His thought strayed to the tale he had been told as a child. His father, merely wanting to provide for his family, had taken him and his mother into the forest on a hunting trip. The forest was vast and teemed with wildlife. Deer, rabbit and glamoch were aplenty. Add to that the many species of fish that swam in the Rebnar river and you had the ingredients for a banquet suitable for any table. Ballorn's father was a carpenter, not a big game hunter. So, once his hunting trips were done, it was not surprising that his bounty was somewhat lacking. His greatest achievement was that he caught a deer, once.

Alas, the glorious day they had spent together, would be their last. They were on their way home, Ballorn's father carrying a brace of rabbits and some fish and his mother, carrying him. He was less than a year old and therefore had no recollection of that fateful day.

His parents were in high spirits and had almost cleared the edge of the forest when his father lost his footing. Rolling down a steep embankment, he crashed through the bushes below. Slightly winded but luckily uninjured, he scrambled to his feet. He brushed himself off, laughing at how stupid he must have looked as he went head over heels down the bank. Holding his hands out to his sides, he waited for his wife to begin teasing him and glanced up lovingly at his young family. But his expression quickly changed as he saw the horror on his wife's face. Dumbstruck, she pointed behind him. He turned slowly, terrified at what he might see. The horns and wet, black skin of the glamoch glistened. During his fall he had not heard it emerge from the river behind him, but it was there now. Its dark red eyes glared at him, steam rising from its back as the noon-day sun beat down. Shaking its' head from side to side, it snorted. *Was this a warning or a challenge?* Ballorn's father began to back away slowly, not wanting to startle or antagonise the beast that towered above him. But as he took a step, so did the glamoch. His wife was calling for him to run, but he was almost petrified with fear and struggling to move his feet. His wife placed Ballorn on the ground, pushing him under the roots of a nearby tree. Her thoughts, to keep her son safe until she could retrieve him. Half walking, half stumbling, she hurried down the embankment, calling for her husband to grab her hand. But in her haste, she too lost her footing!

Many hours later, a few of the villagers noticed their absence. The whole village knew one another's business and very quickly banded together, heading into the forest to find the missing family. It did not take long for them to discover where Ballorn's parents had met their grisly end. The glamoch had moved away but could still be seen in the distance. "They must have fought hard," said one of the village elders. "I don't know what he used, but he put a few good gouges into the side of the beast."

The nemilar were in a state of shock at what had transpired, but suddenly their hearts leapt as Ballorn began to cry. Dashing over to where Ballorn had been hidden, a young girl reached down and scooped him up in her arms, staring up in disbelief at the rest of the villagers, "He's alright!" she cried, stroking his cheek. "There's not a mark on him." But then the realisation that Ballorn was now an orphan, dawned on her. A single tear trickled down her cheek as she gazed with pity at the baby, "Oh, the poor little mite," she cooed.

***

It was not yet light as Ballorn fired up his forge. It had been many years since anything had brought him even a glimmer of excitement. *I'll get all of the nonsense jobs out of the way early, then I can spend the rest of the day working on that axe for Lonny*, he thought. He knew that it was impossible to complete the axe in a single day and looked forward to working on something that would test his skill as a smith.

By mid-afternoon, the head was taking shape and he barely noticed the inquisitive looks he was being given by the villagers as they tried to work out what he was making. He shook his head as thoughts of Lonny ran through his mind. *Would the farmer even have the strength to lift it, let alone wield it against his imaginary foe?* he thought. As the day drew to an end, Ballorn shut down his forge and headed into the woods. *No good producing a masterpiece and then sticking it on a crap handle.* Selecting a suitable branch, he began chopping it from the tree. He made his living as a blacksmith but was also a competent carpenter, a skill he must have inherited from his father. It was getting dark and Ballorn placed the branch across his shoulder, content that he had done enough for one day. "You've paid for perfection, Lonny, so that's what you're going to get," he said quietly as he headed home.

The following day he began work even earlier. He had barely slept and feverishly fired up his forge. He had become fixated, determined that the axe would be a work of art. He worked long hours shaping the axe-head, honing and polishing it to a mirror-finish. But that was only the first step. Taking some of the gold coins he had been given by Lonny, he dropped them into a melting pot and watched as they began to liquify. He had engraved the axe and began spooning the molten gold into the patterns. Many times the villagers tried to interrupt him but he would not allow them to break his intense concentration and rudely ignored them. Unblinking, he peered closely as he intricately shaped the gold until each side of the axe was adorned with a fire-breathing dragon. For some reason, he had even chosen to lay runes that spelt out Lonny's name.

Ballorn was not yet finished. He began to carve the handle with a precision that had never been witnessed, inlaying even more gold into each notch and groove. The final stage, three coats of wax, which he polished and buffed to a brilliant shine. Joining the pieces together, he gazed at them smugly. He had used at least half of the gold with which the farmer had paid him, but he did not care. His chest swelled with pride. "Oh Lonny," he chuckled quietly, "you mad old bugger! I've created a weapon that any warrior would be glad of. I hope your imaginary dragon's worth it."

CHAPTER 2

The week passed quickly. Ballorn was excited, but a little impatient as he regularly scanned the village square waiting for Lonny to collect his axe. He wondered if the farmer would be as impressed with it as he was himself or would simply view it as another tool. He pottered around finding menial tasks to occupy his time but was completely guilty of neglecting any pressing work that needed doing. Throughout the day, various nemilar would enquire about work they needed doing or enquire as to whether their orders were ready. Ballorn would give a lame excuse as to why an item would take more time than usual, or, was already overdue. *Tomorrow*, he'd say, *come back at noon, I'll have it ready by then*. All he could focus on, was the axe. All day he waited, but there was no sign of the farmer. He had seemed so desperate when he placed the order. *Why had he not collected it?* He'd even stressed that he needed it to protect his family. *Maybe I was right*, thought Ballorn. *Maybe he was just a nutter.*

The square was emptying as the hour grew late. Ballorn, realising that the mad farmer would not be collecting that day, began packing his things away. Leaning beneath the counter, he took out the axe he had carefully wrapped in an oilcloth. Opening it, he tapped his finger against the handle thoughtfully. *What to do*, he thought. He had never felt this way before. Usually he dreaded customers returning to him for any reason, because it meant he would have to talk to them. For the first time ever, he decided that he would find out where Lonny's farm was, and hand deliver it. After all it was paid for, and it shouldn't take too long. *It'll probably do me good to get away from this place for a while anyway*, he thought.

He spent the following day quizzing the villagers about Lonny.

Who was he?

Did they know him well?

Had he ever shown any signs of eccentricity?

But mostly: *Did they know the whereabouts of his farm?*

Although most of the villagers were unfamiliar with the farmer, there were a few who knew him well and where his farm could be found. They told Ballorn that it was located to the south of the village. "Mind you," warned one of the villagers, "it's half a day's walk and you'll have to go through the Garlann forest to reach it." It seemed that Garlann was plagued by ferocious beasts, the worst of which being wolves. A few of the older villagers took delight in relating tales of mysterious disappearances that were thought to be the result of unfortunate meetings with monsters and mythical beings. Ballorn ignored the fanciful tales. "Flaming superstitious nonsense," he mumbled to himself after they had left.

He would wait one more day and, if Lonny did not show, he would set off. That day came and went and as Ballorn closed up, he reached beneath the counter and took out the sign that he had prepared earlier. Placing it on the counter, he huffed. *That'll give 'em something to moan about*, he thought as he looked at his handiwork.

CLOSED ALL DAY
URGENT BUSINESS

Ballorn chuckled, if anyone wanted to complain, they would have to wait until his return.

The following morning, Ballorn pulled the strap on his shoulder a little tighter as he wriggled to get the axe to sit squarely between his shoulder blades. Leaving the village he hadn't ventured from for more than a few hours at a time in many years, he headed down the trail as the sun began to rise. He paused, staring around the woods with a sense of freedom. He was devoted to his work and always felt a little lost when he was away from his forge. Yet today felt strangely different. Ballorn was actually enjoying the clean air as he listened to the birds singing and breathed in the fresh smell of the dew-covered grass. Clutching his home-made map, he turned along a smaller dirt track and followed it downhill. *A nice morning stroll by the stream*, he thought, *that'll make a change from the smell of smoke and molten metal.*

It was roughly mid-day and Ballorn, beginning to feel more than a little peckish, plonked himself down on a convenient tree stump. *Fresh air has given me quite an appetite*, he thought. Reaching into his pack he pulled out a loaf and a small lump of meat he had left over from the night before. *It can't be much farther now*, he thought. *I should be there within the hour.* Glad that he had had the foresight to bring some lunch with him, he wolfed it down with relish. It could have been quite embarrassing trying to explain to Lonny the fine detail he had so lovingly applied if his stomach was rumbling. He was a businessman after all and, although he could at times be a little blunt with his customers, he always tried to uphold a sense of propriety.

It was then that he noticed how quiet the forest had become. He was some distance from the stream now, so it was no surprise that he could no longer hear the trickling water. The thing that he found most strange of all was the fact that he could no longer hear the birds singing.

He shrugged his shoulders. *Ah well, what do I know?* he thought, getting to his feet. *Maybe this is what the countryside is like now.*

As he walked, he started to notice even more things that, to him, seemed a little odd. Up ahead, there was a break in the trees that seemed most peculiar. A patch of ground roughly a hundred feet across was completely barren. Not so much as a blade of grass could be seen on the ground that seemed scorched as if a huge fire had raged there. *What in blazes could have done this?* he thought. He started to chuckle to himself, *scorched ground, blazes, I made a funny.* He had made light of it but, truth be told, for some reason it gave him a sense of unease. He dug his heel into the ground.

"You shouldn't be out here alone, you know. It's not safe."

Alarmed by the voice, Ballorn spun around, "Who's there?" he yelled. "Show yourself!"

"Why?" came the reply. "Is it necessary for you to see me for us to converse?"

"No, but it's difficult to trust someone if they choose to remain hidden. I warn you, I've got an axe that could cleave you in two, so if you're looking for trouble, you'll get more than you bargained for."

The voice laughed gently, "I'm sure I would, but trust me, I have no intention of harming you, stranger," it said. "As for you hurting me… well, let's just say that would not be as easy as you may think."

"You must be up to some sort of mischief or you wouldn't be hiding!"

"Oh, I have a good reason for remaining hidden," came the reply. "A reason that you would not understand I'm afraid. My anonymity will keep our conversation amicable I assure you."

Ballorn's eyes darted from tree to tree, hoping to catch sight of who was speaking. They were sparse, leaving very few possible hiding places. He even considered that the stranger could have concealed himself behind the rocks at the foot of the mountain to his right but dismissed the idea immediately. They were too far away for him to be able to hear any voice clearly from that distance. "Do you know anything about the ground being burned over there?" he asked tentatively. "Did you do it?"

"No," came the abrupt reply. "But I know who did, and I would suggest you leave this place lest he return."

"Can't do that," said Ballorn, bluntly, "I've got some business to take care of and I won't be leaving until I'm done."

"Business?" asked the voice, obviously intrigued by Ballorn's statement. "What business could you have…?"

There was a brief pause, "Ah, you're looking for the farmer, aren't you?"

Ballorn took a step back, "Farmer? What farmer? I never said anything about a farmer!" he spluttered, unconvincingly.

"In that case I can only surmise that you came to see me. How pleasant, I've not had a visitor for years!" mocked the voice.

"Why would I have come to see you? I don't even know who you are!" exclaimed Ballorn. "And my business is none of your concern, *so I suggest you keep your nose out of it!*"

"My apologies, stranger, I did not mean to pry. It's just that you look to defend yourself with an axe which is still firmly strapped to your back. That tells me that it does not belong to you and that your intent is to deliver it to another. Add that to the fact that the farmer, apart from myself of course, is the only one within many leagues of this place and it is the only feasible conclusion that anyone could make. *The farmer commissioned you to make an axe for him and you are dutifully delivering it!*"

"So, you think you're clever, do you?" spouted Ballorn. "Well, like I said, it's none of your business!" Ballorn spun on his heel and began to march away. "I've wasted enough time with this nonsense!"

"Where are you going?" called the voice, laughing again. "The farm is the other way."

Ballorn scowled as he wheeled around. It was pointless trying to hide his destination, whoever was watching him obviously had a vantage point from which they could see him. "If you try to follow me, there'll be trouble!" he growled.

***

Although still some distance away, Ballorn slowed his pace as the farm came into view. Something was dreadfully wrong and he stared in confusion at the fields. The ground was churned up so badly in places that it looked more like a quarry than a farm. Making his way around the potholes and trenches, he approached the pile of rubble he suspected had once been the farmer's house. Large blocks of stone lay on the ground with random timbers poking out amongst them. Ballorn rubbed the back of his head as he tried to make sense of it. Close by, numerous planks of wood protruded from the ground as if they had been placed there deliberately. *Oh*, thought Ballorn, *that must be all that's left of the barn!* Deciding to investigate further he approached the remnants of the barn. Stumbling on the uneven ground he stared down at his boots, frowning. Only then did he notice the dirt beneath them. It was scorched, charred almost. *It looks just like that patch of ground I passed earlier today*, he thought.

He was feeling more uncomfortable by the second and called out, optimistically, "Hello, is there anybody here?" He turned his head, listening intently, but no-one answered.

He crouched down, taking a pinch of soil and inspecting it. "Hello!" he called again, "It's me, Ballorn, the blacksmith. I've brought your axe."

Mark of the Nibrilsiem

Should I just leave it here, he thought. *I could place it near the ruined farmhouse for Lonny to find when he returns.* He looked around at what remained of the farm. *Return to what?* he thought. *There's nothing left of the place!*

He sat down on a pile of rubble, unsure of what to do next. It was late in the day, his journey having taken far longer than he had anticipated. If he was to head back home now, he would undoubtedly end up walking through the woods after dark. He shuddered at the thought and decided to make himself a small camp for the night. *Perhaps the farmer would return before he left in the morning.* But, deep down, he knew that Lonny had no good reason to return. After all, there was nothing to return to.

It was a restless night for Ballorn. He was tired, that he could not deny, but each time he dozed off terrible nightmares filled with monsters, wild beasts, raging fires and explosions haunted him. He would wake with a start, his wild eyes searching for terrors in the dark. But everything was as serene as it had been when he had first closed his eyes. The only sound to be heard was the gentle breeze that produced faint whistling noises as it whipped around the small piles of stone surrounding him. Unfortunately, for him, his sleepless night would undoubtedly make his homeward journey far more arduous. Nonetheless, he was ready to set off as dawn broke. "I'll be glad to see the back of this place," he chuntered quietly.

***

He breakfasted on dry biscuits and laughed at himself for being so childish the previous night. "Like a big kid!" he chuckled to himself as he set off for home.

With the axe still firmly strapped to his back, his mind wandered as he walked. *Such a shame*, he thought. *Lonny paid a hefty price for this.* But, glancing back at the devastation, Ballorn feared that he would never see it, let alone wield it. Optimistically, he believed that there was still a slight possibility that the farmer would suddenly appear and hurry after him. *Doubtful*, he thought as he quickened his pace.

The morning was pleasant. The sun shone and a light breeze cooled Ballorn as he ambled his way home, kicking at small tufts of grass as he went. Distracted slightly by the shrill chirping of the birds, he failed to notice that he was nearing the scorched patch of ground he had discovered the day before. A small plume of dust erupted from the toe of his boot as he stopped dead in his tracks.

Realising where he was, he called out. "Are you still here?" He glanced around but was happy when nobody answered. Moving forward warily, he approached the treeline. "I'm just passing by, I don't want any trouble."

He paused again, sensing that something was different. The scorched area seemed far bigger than it had been the previous day and even the side of the mountain seemed blackened. He carried on, trying his best not to make a sound as he virtually tiptoed closer to the trees. His heart skipped a beat when he heard the sound of splintering wood, but it was far louder than a small twig snapping or even a thick branch breaking. It sounded more like a tree exploding. Ballorn was not easily startled but his heart was racing and he began to hurry toward the comparative safety of the trees. Reaching them, he darted behind one. All he could hear was his own heartbeat as he craned his neck to listen. Sweat began to trickle down his temples as he saw something move ahead of him. Whatever it was, was big, very big!

Now in a blind panic, he ran. He had no idea what he had seen but he was sure he didn't want to see it up close. Dashing amongst the trees, he sprinted away as if his life depended on it. His blood ran cold when he heard the first roar. Glancing quickly over his shoulder he saw trees being smashed by the gargantuan shape that was now charging after him. He could hear it getting closer and tugged at the straps holding the axe. His father's pendant becoming entangled in his fingers as he frantically tried to free the weapon from his back. He wheeled around, hurling the axe with all his might and cried out as he saw that the beast was almost upon him. The forest was ablaze with a strange glow. It was as if lightning were striking both trunk and bough of every tree. There could be no escape! Ballorn lowered his head and braced himself. He could not see clearly what it was that was about to take his life, its form hidden amongst the dust cloud and splintering trees as it fell upon him. He was hurled into the air as his attacker slid to a halt, his poor body bouncing off numerous branches as he soared uncontrollably. Adrenalin surged through his veins, staving off most of the agonising pain he would have otherwise felt. But his pain was fleeting as the side of his head slammed mercilessly against a tree. Suddenly everything went black.

Ballorn opened his eyes, amazed that he was still alive. How long he had lain there was uncertain. His blurred vision was of very little use to him as he tried to focus in the dim light. Then the pain hit him. He grunted loudly as he clutched at his leg. At his forge he had caught himself many times as he wielded his hammer and had scars on his hands and forearms from sparks that had landed on them, but he had never had to endure an agony such as this. He leaned back as he gasped, realising that his leg was broken. He tried a few times to scramble to his feet, hoping that his good leg would support him long enough to escape the pit into which he had fallen, if indeed it was a pit. He knew not whether it was day or night as he shuffled around in the dark. Feeling the walls around him revealed that they were not solid, but damp earth covered in many thick, gnarled roots. Using these as handholds he dragged himself toward the pale light that seeped through to one side of his tomb. His muscular arms were a blessing, making it easy for him to pull himself up to the hole that he had noticed above him. The roots were thicker now and strong enough to hold his weight but as he inched closer toward freedom the searing pain got the better of him. He rolled to one side and began retching, panting loudly before wiping his mouth on his sleeve. *Not far now*, he thought. *Come on Ballorn, you can do this*.

Breathless and exhausted after his arduous climb, he managed to pull himself free and rolled onto his back in the cold night air. To be out in the forest at night was not safe, even for someone in perfect health. For Ballorn, exhausted and lame as he was, it could possibly be a death sentence. Shuffling backward he leaned against the tree, reaching up and patting it gently. "So, *you* protected me," he said quietly. Luckily, his limp body had rolled down the hill right into the hollow and tumbled into the pit directly beneath it. "I don't know what it was…" whispered

Ballorn, "... but it would've had me if you hadn't kept me safe. I thank you for that."

He glanced around, "I hope you'll forgive me," he mumbled, "I think I might need to borrow a couple of bits of you, but only the bits you don't seem to want any more." He was referring to the fallen branches that lay on the ground. He needed a splint for his leg if he were to have any hope of escaping the forest. The straps that held the axe in place were still entangled around his body and would be perfect to hold the branches in place. He scrambled around picking up any of the fallen branches he thought might be of use, discarding many before finally choosing some that he thought would be suitable. Glancing at the night sky, he guessed that it was not long after midnight. It would be at least five hours before he would have the safety of daylight. He was in a wretched state. Covered in bruises, cuts and scrapes, Ballorn took comfort in the fact that his luck could have been much worse. But it was about to be!

He heard a rustling as something moved in the undergrowth. Whatever it was quickly grew closer and it was not long before he could hear its rasping breath. He had lost the axe and all he had to defend himself with was the branches he had just collected. He picked at the end of one, trying desperately to make it into more of a stake. His strong hands tore at the bark as he peeled both it and a few splinters away from the edges. Bracing himself against the tree, "Come on then you evil buggers," he shouted at the darkness, "I'm ready for you! You won't be getting a taste of me without a fight!"

The hazy moonlight was enough for Ballorn to be able to see the bushes twitching, and what was prowling through them. *Gemnars!*

Smaller than a wolf but far more dangerous, gemnars also hunted in packs. If uninjured, Ballorn would have been able to fend them off quite easily. But injured and unable to stand meant that there was no way he could defend himself. They edged forward, an entire pack, drooling and snarling as they circled him. One suddenly charged, its jaws snapping at Ballorn. He swung the branch with all his might, sending the beast yelping in pain as it tumbled across the ground. "You're not getting me that easy," he roared. They grew closer until Ballorn could see the vapour from their breath as their black eyes flashed in the moonlight.

Suddenly the ground between them erupted in flame, then again to the left and once more to the right. Ballorn, now shielded by a wall of flame, was as confused as the gemnars who bayed and howled, enraged at having been deprived of their easy meal. One was undaunted and leapt through the flames, but it was dead before it landed, an arrow deeply embedded in its skull. The remainder of the pack were not as eager and turned, vanishing into the darkness.

Ballorn was startled as the slender figure landed beside him. The stranger glared at him as he reached down and snatched up the dead gemnar.

"Thank you," sighed Ballorn. "You saved my life."

The stranger sneered at him, "You thank me, for this!" he exclaimed, thrusting the carcase toward him. "You people do not belong out here, now one of the forest creatures has lost its life because you dared to venture into their home!"

"But... but they would have torn me apart!"

"Perhaps I should have let them! They were only doing what comes naturally to them! If you had stayed in your village, climbed into your nice warm bed and hidden beneath the covers, none of this would have been necessary!"

"Now you listen here," Ballorn protested. "As much as I appreciate your aid, I didn't ask for it! It was your own decision to help me and if you're regretting it, it's tough. Just push off, I'll be fine on my own! If them blighters come back you can watch 'em eat me, maybe that'll make you feel better!"

The stranger pointed at Ballorn's leg, "Is it broken?" he asked.

"Yeah," grunted Ballorn, reaching out to retrieve the branches that lay a short distance from him. "But I've got these and a couple of leather belts, it'll be fine once I've strapped it up."

"Your courage is admirable," snorted the stranger. "It almost outshines your stupidity!"

"Keep it up, skinny," grunted Ballorn, unfastening the belts. "See if you still want to insult me when I'm on my feet."

"Why, what will you do?" laughed the stranger. "Call me names, hurl abuse at me whilst you try to hobble after me?"

"You'll see," warned Ballorn, "I'll put you on you're ar…"

"What are you trying to do?" interrupted the stranger as he watched Ballorn's pathetic attempt to construct a splint. "You're doing it all wrong! Here, let me do it for you."

He knelt beside Ballorn, who immediately grabbed him by the collar with both hands. "Now insult me if you dare," he hissed. He felt a rhythmic tapping against his chest and slowly looked down to see the tip of a large hunting knife resting against it.

"I have saved your life this night, nemilar," smiled the stranger. "Are you really that keen for your stay of execution to be so short?"

Ballorn released his grip and held his hands up. "My apologies," he said quietly.

"Oh, I wouldn't apologise just yet," advised the stranger. "Trust me, this is going to hurt me far less than it will you."

A short while later, not without much yelling, groaning and foul language, the stranger had expertly braced Ballorn's broken leg.

"You weren't bloody kidding when you said it was going to hurt!" gasped Ballorn.

"Ah but the good news is, I never felt a thing," smiled the stranger.

Ballorn frowned, "What's your name?"

"People just call me Hunter," replied the stranger.

"Why?" asked Ballorn as he rubbed his leg. "Haven't you got a proper name?"

"Of course I have."

"So, why do people call you Hunter?"

"Because it's what I do, in fact, it's what I am."

Ballorn studied the stranger. He could tell that he was a nemilar who was unused to a comfortable bed or soft living. His bare arms were slender, but the muscles were sinewy and strong. Perhaps he was indeed a hunter. "Alright, so you're a hunter, but what's your name?"

"Why?" asked the stranger, confused as to why it was so important to the nemilar he had rescued.

"Just wondering. I'm Ballorn, by the way. Sorry about earlier, it's just that, well, with the pain and those…"

"Malgruth," said the hunter, raising his voice and cutting short Ballorn's attempt at an apology.

"Oh!" said Ballorn with surprise, "I thought it was a pack o' gemnars!"

"My name is Malgruth… and it's *gemnar*, not *gemnars*."

"Oh… right, sorry, I just thought that…"

"Are you always like this?" asked the hunter, seeming agitated.

Ballorn looked puzzled, "Like what?"

"Blathering on and apologising all the time. Do you realise how annoying it is?"

"Of course not!" exclaimed Ballorn. "I don't usually do anything that warrants an apology! And, I don't 'blather on'! Then again, it's not an everyday occurrence for me to be indebted to someone for saving my life either!"

"What happened to you?" asked Hunter. "How did you manage to break your leg?"

"I didn't!" snorted Ballorn. "Something else did!"

"Something?" asked Hunter, intrigued by his answer.

"Yeah, *something*," repeated Ballorn. "But I didn't get a good look at it before I was knocked clean off my feet. Next thing I knew, I woke up in the hollow of this here tree."

"How big?" asked Hunter. "As big as a glamoch, perhaps?"

"Hah, a glamoch! Trust me, a glamoch would only be the size of a florrip compared to this thing."

"So, you have no idea where it went, I mean, in what direction it was headed?"

"Not a clue," replied Ballorn. "All I know is that I woke up with a broken leg and a lump on my head you could build a house on."

Hunter suddenly seemed alarmed, "We should leave this place," he urged.

"Easy for you to say," replied Ballorn, his eyebrows raising as he looked at his leg.

"Don't worry," Hunter assured him, "I'm not about to abandon you. Here, take my arm. The sooner we leave, the better."

"But it's still dark, let's hang on a couple of hours. We'll make better progress once it's light."

"No," replied Hunter, adamantly. "We're leaving now."

CHAPTER 3

Hauling Ballorn to his feet, the two of them set off. Hunter had done an excellent job with the splint and Ballorn felt hardly any pain as he limped along with his arm around Hunter's shoulder. As daybreak came, and despite Ballorn's disability and the rough terrain of the forest, they had covered roughly five miles. Although Ballorn had never met Hunter before, he was surprised that he knew the way to his home village of Krevick.

"How do you know where it is?" he asked.

"I have conducted business many times in your village, Ballorn. I have also seen you many times. However, in my line of work, I have very little need for a blacksmith."

"So how come I've never seen you?"

"I am a hunter, Ballorn. My business is conducted mainly with the fletcher and the butcher, and I only deal with them if there is no other option."

"I get it, they're both on the other side of the village. That's why I never saw you."

Hunter laughed, "Do you ever see anything when you're at your forge, Ballorn? Every time I saw you your head was down and you practically ignored anyone who spoke to you."

"That's what you'd do if you had 'em around you all day. *They're just so damned annoying!*"

Hunter sighed, "Yes… I'm beginning to understand that."

Ballorn shook himself free of Hunter's grasp. "If you think I'm annoying, just sod off!" he snapped, "Go on, I'll manage on my own!"

"Stop moaning, you stupid nemilar. I'm staying with you whether you like it or not. Come on, put your arm back around my shoulder and let's get moving."

Ballorn scowled at Hunter and held his tongue for a while, but he had questions. Small doubts about Hunter niggled at him. "That trick with the fire…" he asked, "Do you use that a lot?"

"Very rarely," Hunter replied. "I only use pomlay sap to light a campfire usually, but it can be used as a coating for my arrows should the need arise."

"It was very good of you to protect me like that, I am truly grateful."

"I wasn't protecting *you*," laughed Hunter, "I was trying to protect the gemnar."

Ballorn laughed with him, but his laughter was cut short as he realised what Hunter had just said, "Good grief, you're serious!" he exclaimed.

"Of course," replied Hunter, "I told you before, they belong there, *you don't.*"

Ballorn pouted, "Anyway," he continued, "have you had to use it recently? I mean before you rescued me, say, in the last few days?"

Hunter frowned, "I haven't had to use it for years, it's not often one finds a clumsy blacksmith with a broken leg dragging himself around in the forest."

Ballorn felt deeply offended and made no attempt to hide those feelings, "I am not clumsy!" he said, tipping his head closer to Hunter.

"Why are you so interested in the pomlay sap?" asked Hunter with a smile.

"Oh, no reason," replied Ballorn. "Just thought it was quite impressive, that's all." He paused, "I suppose you could make a far bigger blaze with it if you needed to?"

"What are you getting at, Ballorn? There's something rattling around in that thick skull of yours, so why not just get to the point?"

Ballorn let out a deep sigh, "Well..." he began, "... the reason I'm so far away from Krevick is because I came out to make a delivery to a farm not far from where you found me."

"You mean Lonny's farm?"

"Yes," replied Ballorn with surprise. "Why, do you know him?"

"I've known him and his family for over a decade, but I've not seen them for close on two years now."

Ballorn suddenly felt very uncomfortable, "So, he's a friend of yours then?" he asked tentatively.

"Not as such," replied Hunter. "More a business acquaintance… but one of the nicer ones," he added with a smile.

"Oh," said Ballorn, quietly. He was unsure of how to tell him that the farm no longer existed. "I need to rest for a moment, if that's okay with you."

Hunter lowered him to the soft grass and stood with a concerned look on his face. "Something's bothering you, Ballorn. Come on, out with it."

"The farm," began Ballorn, "it's gone. Nothing left but piles of rubble and a few scorched timbers sticking out of the ground."

"And you think I may have had something to do with it?"

Ballorn held up his hand, "I just needed to be sure. You do understand that, don't you?"

Hunter stared at him, his lower lip firmly between his teeth, "Yes," he said slowly. "But what could raze an entire farm to the ground?" He stroked his chin thoughtfully. "This delivery…" he asked, "… what was it?"

Ballorn cleared his throat nervously, "Ah, yes… the delivery. Now before I go any further just let me say, I thought he was a bit cracked! You know, long hours out in the hot sun baking his brain. So, of course when he came to me and asked…"

"What… were you… delivering…, blacksmith?" growled Hunter.

"An axe," replied Ballorn, his voice tailing off almost to a whisper.

Mark of the Nibrilsiem

"An axe? Surely a farmer would already have an axe of his own? Why would you come all the way out here simply to deliver an axe?"

Ballorn looked up sheepishly, "Because he commissioned me to forge it especially."

"There are plenty of merchants around who could have sold him an axe. What was so special about the one he had you make for him?"

"Well, the one I made him was not a mere wood-cutters axe, it was a broadaxe. One that could be used in battle."

"In battle!" exclaimed Hunter, "Against who?"

"Not who, *what*. And it's *whom*, by the way. You *should* say, against *whom!*"

"Ballorn, *what was Lonny afraid of?*"

"He said he'd seen it! I didn't think for a minute that he had, but he was adamant! He paid up front and was supposed to collect the following week. Of course, when he never showed up, I thought it only fair…" Hunter glared at him. "… Lonny said he'd seen a dragon!"

Hunter dropped to the floor and sat cross-legged in front of Ballorn. "So, the rumours are true," he whispered staring deep into the ground.

"What!" breathed Ballorn, "You think there really is a dragon?"

Hunter leaned forward and grabbed Ballorn's arm, "Think about it! An entire farm destroyed; scorched timbers from an inexplicable fire; you, hunted down and lucky to be alive after being thrown through the air by a colossal beast. It's the only explanation. *The dragons have awoken.*"

"What do you mean, *awoken*? They're all dead, and have been for an age."

"Tell me, Ballorn, have you ever heard any stories of anyone finding the remains of a dragon? If they were extinct, surely the bones of at least one would have been discovered by now."

"Stone me!" Ballorn replied, wild-eyed. "You're right! The old tales and drawings show them to be forty feet tall, some even bigger. But no trace of them has ever been found."

"We need to get back to Krevick and warn them," said Hunter, dragging Ballorn to his feet.

"They won't believe you. They'll think you're a loony…" Ballorn's voice became quieter, "… same as I thought about Lonny."

"I'll have a better chance of being believed than any other, Ballorn. After all, who would know what lives in the wilds better than I."

"Right, let's go then. But leave me behind if you must. Get to the village and warn them. You can come back for me later." Ballorn grinned, "Not that I'd want to inconvenience you."

"I have a better idea," Hunter rummaged through his many pockets. "Chew these," he said handing Ballorn some pale-green seed pods. "Do not swallow them whatever you do, just keep chewing them. They'll help ease the pain."

Ballorn winced at the smell of them. "What are they?" he asked.

"They're pollum pods," Hunter informed him. "Normally we only use the leaves, but this is an emergency and we don't have time to boil them anyway."

"What happens if I swallow them by accident?"

Hunter shrugged, "I'll hide you under a bush and come back for you next week," he said, thoughtfully. "You might have woken up by then."

"Nice," replied Ballorn as he popped them into his mouth and started chewing. "Ooh, they're quite tasty aren't they!" He wobbled his head, "Ooh look..." he said giggling, "... the trees have gone all wibbly wobbly."

Hunter groaned. He knew all too well how Ballorn would react to the pollum pods. *Oh well*, he thought, *at least he'll be in a good mood for the rest of their journey... and possibly the next few days as well.*

Hunter tried his best to hurry Ballorn along. His leg was no longer a problem. However, his fascination with everything around him, *was*.

"Look, Hunter, a purple tree! I've never seen a purple tree before. Have you, Hunter, have you ever seen a purple tree? I suppose you have, you've been out here for years wandering the forests... oooohh look, there's a bear over there... a green one... and it's dancing! Why's it wearing a dress?"

"Ballorn, that's a bush, not a bear! Come on, you're doing fine, just keep following me."

Further along the trail, Hunter was actually glad that Ballorn was... *confused,* by the pollum pods. With luck, the blacksmith would be oblivious to the sight of huge boughs that had been sheared from the mighty trees around them. Many had been torn from the ground, their withering, scorched roots bared to the daylight. The ground in which they had proudly stood was nothing but ash, dust rising from it with each step they took. Hunter began to fear the worst as they eventually neared the outskirts of Krevick. His heart sank at what he saw. It was late, and sunset would soon arrive, but what lay ahead would make anyone believe that it was already the dead of night. Plumes of black smoke billowed into the air, it could be coming from nowhere else but the village. They were too late, *the dragons had already attacked Krevick.*

They entered the ravaged village that had been home to Ballorn and his fellow nemilar for many generations. The few buildings that remained were now charred and ugly, their thatched roofs gone. It was silent save for the crackling of timbers that still glowed red. Unrecognisable corpses lay strewn in every direction, the flesh seared from their bones. Hunter shuffled forward in disbelief. He turned to Ballorn, wrapping his fingers gently around his jaw and looked deep into his eyes. "Swallow the pods, Ballorn," he whispered. "Swallow the pods... you should get some rest."

CHAPTER 4

Settling Ballorn into one of the lesser damaged buildings, Hunter prepared himself. He began by scouring the village, hoping to find anything that may help with his gruesome task. Finding a broken handcart he repaired it and, after wrapping a scarf about his mouth and nose, began the removal of the corpses from the village streets. It would have been impossible for him to bury them all singlehandedly and he chose to lay the bodies out in one of the larger buildings. It took almost the entire day, but eventually, three of the derelict structures in Krevick were now occupied by the dead. Hunter gathered beams and planks and sealed the doorways, it was all he could do to protect their remains from scavengers.

Occasionally he would check on Ballorn, who slept peacefully thanks to the pollum pods. Hunter sat beside him on the ground wondering whether it would be best to load him onto the cart and wheel him far away from Krevick, or wait until he awoke and allow him to witness the horror that had befallen his home. For two days Hunter toiled, making sure to check beneath the rubble for any victims. He had no friends or family here, but it was the decent thing to do. Not even Ballorn was truly a friend. After all, they had only just met. But something stirred within him. He felt that the blacksmith was somehow different, somehow… *important*.

Hunter frowned as he watched Ballorn. He himself was exhausted, but he was sure he had seen Ballorn's eyes open briefly. He leaned forward. *No, that would be impossible*, he thought. The nemilar had swallowed three pods! There was no way he would awaken for at least another three days and even then it would take another two for him to shake off the effects of the pollum.

But he was wrong. Ballorn suddenly sat bolt upright and immediately grabbed his leg. "Soddin' buggery and blast it all!" he roared.

Hunter jumped to his feet. "Take it easy, Ballorn," he urged. "Give yourself a minute."

"Get stuffed!" bellowed Ballorn. "Give yourself a minute! Stuffin' 'eck… me leg."

Hunter frantically searched his pockets, "I'll give you something for the pain, Ballorn. Just give me a second."

"You can shove your pods and crap! Where am I? How long have I been out?"

"Just relax, my friend, you're safe."

"Up yours!" shouted Ballorn. "I'll decide whether I'm safe or not, and I ain't your friend. Tell me where I am!"

"You're home, you're in Krevick," Hunter said, trying to calm him.

"Krevick ain't my home, you idiot!" Ballorn ranted. "It's where my forge is! My home's over a mile away. What did you bring me here for?"

"You were in pain. The pollum made you… *drowsy* and I thought this would be the safest place for you."

Mark of the Nibrilsiem

Ballorn stared into space as he tried to recollect his thoughts, then it dawned on him, "You, you slimy git, YOU DRUGGED ME!" he exclaimed.

Hunter squirmed, "Well, yes I did, but it was only to help you cope with the pain," he said quickly. "Don't you remember? You were in agony."

"So what! You don't give a person..." His voice tailed off. "Whose house is this? I don't recognise it." He gave Hunter a piercing glance, "Did you get permission to bring me in here? I don't want to be in debt to one of those sanctimonious village dwellers! They'll be expecting me to do work for 'em for free for the rest of my life!"

Hunter lowered his head, "That's not going to be an issue," he said quietly. "You see, there was nobody here to seek permission from."

"Oh, that's alright then!" exclaimed Ballorn. "There was nobody to ask, so I'm guilty of trespassing as well!"

"That's not what I meant, Ballorn," sighed Hunter. "Whoever the owner was, is probably dead."

"What!" exclaimed Ballorn. "What do you mean, the owner's dead?"

"Look up, Ballorn. There's no roof on the building. There are no roofs on any of the buildings, the ones that are still standing, that is."

Ballorn glanced up, "Hunter..." he asked slowly, "...what happened here?"

"It seems we were too late," whispered Hunter. "It also seems that the dragons we thought were a distant memory are, in fact, real. There was a trail of devastation leading straight to Krevick, Ballorn. The dragons reached here a long time before we did… and it looks as if everyone was killed."

Ballorn's mouth was agape, "Surely… surely some must have escaped?"

Hunter shook his head, "I'm not sure," he replied. "Perhaps, but I wouldn't hold out much hope. If any did, they knew there was no safety to be had amongst the carnage here. I lost count of the dead I cleared from the streets."

"Were there that many?"

Hunter nodded, "I'm afraid so, my friend." He held up his hand, "Oh, I forgot, my turn to apologise. We aren't friends, are we?"

"Take no notice of what I said. I'm a bad-tempered sod at the best of times. We can be friends if you're happy to have me as one."

Hunter glanced sideways at him, "We'll see."

Ballorn rubbed his leg, "I need to stand," he groaned. "Let's have a walk about, see what we can find. I'd like to see if there's anything left of my forge."

Hunter helped him to his feet. Leaving the ramshackle building they headed to the forge. Hunter hadn't paid it much attention as he had cleared the dead from the streets. From a distance the damage didn't look that bad. The buckskin canopy was slightly singed, but other than that, it seemed to be in perfect working order. Ballorn stared in disbelief, but then noticed something strange. His tools were strewn about the floor and he looked to his tool chest expecting to see it destroyed. Strangely enough, it was perfectly fine, sitting against the back wall where it had always been. He limped forward, cager to investigate the mystery. Leaning down, he grasped the iron handle and began slowly lifting the lid. To his surprise the handle was suddenly torn from his fingers and the lid slammed shut. Ballorn frowned. "*What the…?*" he muttered.

Hunter had witnessed the strange event and now stood directly behind the blacksmith holding his knife.

Ballorn shrugged his shoulders as Hunter nodded toward the chest. Leaning down, he once more began to raise the lid. Again, it was ripped from his grasp and slammed shut. *Third time lucky*, thought the blacksmith as he gripped the handle.

"No," came the voice from inside as the lid closed again. The voice gave no hint of alarm or fear, but there was an adamant tone to it. Whoever was inside was determined that they were not going to allow anyone to disturb them.

Ballorn wiped his hand across his face, "Oh, no," he moaned. "Please no, not him. Anyone but him."

Hunter smiled, "Friend of yours?"

Ballorn rolled his eyes and tapped the chest with the toe of his boot. "You can come out, it's safe," he sighed.

"No thank you, I'm fine. Go on about your business. Just pretend I'm not even here. Do it quickly though, I don't want you to draw any attention."

"Attention?" asked Hunter. "Attention from who? We're the only ones here!"

"Just go away!" came the exasperated voice. "Here..." it said as the chest lid opened by an inch, "... take this. That's more than a fair rent for such a small space. Now please take it and leave me in peace!" Two gold coins were shoved through the gap, jingling as they hit the floor.

"I don't want your money!" exclaimed Ballorn. "I just want you out of there!"

With no reply, two more coins were pushed through and landed with the others.

"Oh, I've had enough of this," growled Ballorn as he grabbed one end of the chest and began to lift it. "Out!" he demanded as he shook it.

The lid flew open and a small, tubby nemilar rolled out onto the floor. He was about to protest but then saw Hunter, who stood brandishing his knife. Although unnerved, he still seemed more concerned about what else might be watching them. "Quick, hide!" he urged. "It could be lurking anywhere."

"We've been here for days," Hunter informed him. "I can assure you, there is nothing lurking anywhere!"

"Ah, see. That's what it wants you to think and then it'll pounce." The nemilar suddenly noticed his surroundings, "Oh, my word!" he sighed. "It's gone! The whole village has been destroyed." A horrified look swept across his face, "M m m my shop, my beautiful shop," he stammered.

"Beautiful!" exclaimed Ballorn. "You haven't spent a penny on it for years! It was the most dilapidated building in the whole village! Who knows the last time it had so much as a lick of fresh paint!"

"How dare you, sir. My establishment is one of the most respectable businesses in Krevick. There is not a tailor in the whole village who can produce garments as fine as mine."

"True," admitted Ballorn. "Then again," he added as he glared at the tailor, "that's because there *are* no other tailors in Krevick. Come to think of it, the nearest to you is fifty miles away."

"Let's not start making this personal, Ballorn," suggested Hunter. "We may have to rely on one another before long."

"Suppose so," grunted Ballorn, staring at the tailor. "This is Hunter. Hunter, this is Twitch the Stitch."

The tailor gave Ballorn a scathing look as he turned to face Hunter. "Actually, it's Portwitch... *Felidan Portwitch*," he announced. "Pleased to meet you, sir. May I enquire as to your given name?"

"Hunter's just fine," he laughed. "Would you mind answering a few questions? Such as why you were hiding inside a tool chest?"

A look of dread came upon the tailor's face, "I couldn't see," he replied staring into thin air with a distant look. "The fire, the smoke, the screaming. The monster, you see, it was huge, wrapped up in some kind of unnatural storm. We had no warning before it descended on the village. Fires erupted around it as it trampled everything in its path, lightning bolts and howling winds following its every step. I panicked and ran the same as everyone else, but I fell as I tried to get away and found myself hidden behind low walls. These walls to be precise, the ones around Ballorn's forge. I was in a right kerfuffle and wasn't thinking straight so I clambered inside the chest, still expecting to be crushed or burnt alive at any moment. Then everything suddenly went quiet. I'll admit, I was too terrified to come out. I'm a tailor not a warrior, what was I supposed to do against a dragon? I'm a bit of a coward to be honest, so that's where I've been hiding ever since, until you found me, of course."

"Did any of the villagers escape?" asked Hunter, placing his hand on the tailor's shoulder, sympathetically. "Did you see anything before concealing yourself?"

"The monster… the way it moved," whispered Felidan. "It was strange. It never rampaged through the village, it took its time as if it were revelling in the mayhem and panic. It never gave chase to anyone who fled into the trees. At least, I don't *think* it followed them."

"So there's a good chance there were survivors," said Ballorn. "That's a relief."

"How many lived here?" asked Hunter, slowly.

"Over five hundred now," replied Ballorn. "Lots of young ones born recently."

"Six hundred and seventeen," sighed Felidan. "I know the village clerk. He keeps records of all the villagers."

"Why?" asked Ballorn, knowing that Hunter would not have asked the question without good reason.

"Whilst you were asleep," began Hunter, "I removed the bodies of the villagers from the streets." He lowered his head. "I lost count, to be honest. But I'd say there were at least three hundred."

CHAPTER 5

The days that followed were difficult for the three nemilar. Stitch was a nervous wreck and quivered at the slightest noise that came from outside the village. Ballorn was angry and had fired up his forge, despite Stitch's pleas. The smaller nemilar begged him not to run the risk of drawing any unwanted attention toward the village. However, it was neither the flames from his forge nor even his hammering with which they should have been concerned.

The smell of death hung in the air, a subtle scent that went unnoticed by the nemilar. The sensitive noses of the scavengers and predators that dwelled in the woods, however, were a different matter... and it was not long before they ventured closer to investigate.

Hunter coped easily with driving off the smaller ones with his flaming arrows. The larger ones unfortunately were far bolder and would soon follow. Packs of wolves skirted the treeline, venturing closer as they realised that the flames would not harm them if they kept their distance. They too were driven away at first, startled by the roaring figure of Ballorn throwing rocks and anything else he could lay his hands on.

The immediate threat dealt with, he returned to his forge and flicked the lid of his tool chest open. "You can come out now," he grunted at the shaking Stitch. "They've gone."

"They'll be back," called Hunter.

"I know," Ballorn replied quietly. "We'll deal with it when it happens."

Hunter was intrigued. He knew that Ballorn was in no mood for conversation, but he simply had to know. "Why are you at your forge, Ballorn?" he asked. "What are you making?"

"Can't go anywhere on a busted leg," he replied gruffly. "Making a brace for it, so I can travel."

"Travel?" enquired Hunter. "Travel to where?"

"Lonny's farm," grunted the blacksmith.

"Lonny's farm? Why do you want to go back there? You said all that was left of the place was rubble."

"I lost something and I want it back."

Hunter watched as Ballorn bent and shaped the iron bar on his anvil for a minute before thrusting it back into the fire. "It looks sturdy enough," he said.

"Wouldn't be any good as a brace if it wasn't."

"How will you fasten it to your leg?" asked Hunter with a faint laugh, "You can't exactly nail it in place."

Ballorn was in no mood for humour and gave Hunter a look that conveyed his lack of amusement. "I've got some rope, I'll just tie it in place."

"You can't do that," said Stitch, quietly. "It'll take the skin off your leg before you've gone a mile!" He thought for a moment, "If one of you could go to my shop, there's a few scraps of hide in the back room, presuming they survived the fires of course, the shop didn't look in a good state the last time I saw it. I could make some strapping to hold that brace to your leg as if it were a part of it."

Hunter shook his head, "What are we talking about!" he suddenly exclaimed. "Whether it be rope or straps, you can't head into the wilds in your condition. It would be far too dangerous!"

Ballorn slammed his hammer down and turned to face him, "Firstly, I didn't ask your permission, and secondly, how are you going to stop me?" he growled.

Hunter shrugged his shoulders, "I have no intention of trying to stop you, Ballorn," he replied. "It's your life to risk if that's your intent. I'm simply warning you of the perils that may await you."

Ballorn pointed at the remains of the village, "And what have I got to lose?" he asked, his hands shaking in anger. "Whatever did this took my life away as much as it did the nemilar who lie in those buildings. Why should I fear death when everyone I knew has already gone before me!"

Hunter sighed as Ballorn resumed his hammering, "My apologies, Ballorn. You are correct, of course. You must have had a deep affection for many who lived here."

Ballorn paused as he glanced at Hunter, "Affection?" he asked with a surprised look. "I couldn't bloody stand them, not a single one! But that doesn't give anyone or *anything* the right to slaughter them."

Hunter shook his head in disbelief. He turned to Stitch, "I'll see if I can find those scraps of hide for you," he said. "But, you'll need to show me where your shop is."

Stitch shook his head vigorously, "No, I'm staying here with him," he said adamantly, nodding toward Ballorn. "There could be anything hidden around a corner waiting to grab me as I pass."

Hunter smiled, "So it's alright for you to risk my life, but not your own?" he asked, quite amused by the terrified tailor.

"You're a hunter, Hunter," replied Stitch. Realising how silly it sounded, he paused, then continued regardless, "You have a bow, a knife and a… whatever that thing is strapped to your thigh," he added, waggling his finger at the scimitar at Hunter's side.

"Well I'll lend you them all if it makes you feel safer," Hunter laughed.

"No, I won't need them," smiled Stitch. "As I said, *I'm staying here.*"

Hunter reached forward and grabbed the back of the tailor's collar. "No, you're not, come on," he laughed, as he hoisted Stitch to his feet. "See you shortly, Ballorn."

Ballorn grunted, paying little attention to Hunter, which was a shame. The sight of Stitch trying to wrestle free from Hunter's grip as he was unceremoniously marched away was most amusing. He continued with his work, glancing occasionally at the twitching bushes at the edge of the forest. Whatever was there, would not stay hidden for ever.

Hunter and Stitch were not gone long. As they returned, Stitch scampered ahead and crouched down near to Ballorn. Logically, the forge would have afforded him no more protection than anywhere else in the village, but he was a creature of habit and seemed content as he sighed loudly and wiped his brow with a small handkerchief.

"Find what you were looking for?" asked Ballorn.

"I did," replied Stitch, "and a few other things besides."

"I still don't get it," smiled Hunter. "What was wrong with the coat you had on?"

"Nothing," replied Stitch. "But this one has always been my favourite," he grinned, stroking the lapel of his pristine garment.

"Well, I hope it's warm," mumbled Ballorn. "Chances are it won't stay like that for long. It gets cold out in the forest once the sun sets and everything gets dusty or muddy, however hard you try to keep it clean."

"Well that's something I won't have to worry about," Stitch sniffed. "You won't catch me out in the forest at night. You won't catch me out there during the day either, come to think of it."

Ballorn stared at him for a while, "Fair enough," he said, shrugging his shoulders. "You can stay here by yourself then. We'll only be gone a couple of days, you should be alright 'til we get back."

"What!" exclaimed Stitch. "You can't leave me here by myself! You've seen the wolves and things, they'll come into the village and…" he gulped, "… *eat me!*"

"I'm sure they won't," laughed Hunter. "Wolves are very particular about what they eat. Stay inside the chest though, just to be on the safe side."

Stitch glared at him, "I'm glad you think it's funny," he snapped. "Don't you think enough nemilar have died? Now you want to abandon me so that I can be added to the list!"

"Oh shut yer face, Stitch!" sighed Ballorn. "Nobody's leaving you behind! You're coming with us, whether you like it or not."

Stitch pouted and began searching the shoulder bag he had returned with. He pulled out the pieces of hide that he had retrieved from his shop. Then he withdrew a large pair of tailoring shears, a ball of twine and a pack of thick needles. "Show me the brace," he grumbled. He studied its shape for a moment, lowered his head, and set to work.

Hunter watched Ballorn and Stitch as they each worked on their individual parts of the brace. He felt a little awkward. He was unused to his hands being idle as others toiled. "I'm going to have a scout around," he announced. "We'll need more food for our journey. I'll see if there's any game to be had just inside the forest."

Ballorn looked up, his eyes showing concern. "Be careful," he said, slowly.

Hunter nodded, "Always am," he smiled as he jogged off toward the trees.

He could still hear the clanging of Ballorn's hammer as he entered the forest. Whatever had been lurking there must have been spooked by his approach. Warily, he entered the shade of the trees. It was unusually quiet and he was surprised that he could hear his own footsteps, not something that would aid him if his hunt were to be successful. Slowing his pace, he listened carefully to the forest sounds. Birds were singing in the distance, but nothing nearby was stirring.

"Ain't got any cake have you?"

Hunter raised his bow, his head snapping from side to side as he searched for the owner of the voice.

"You can put that down," said the voice calmly. "I ain't got no weapons or nothing." Hunter looked up. Above him, clutching a branch, sat a scruffy-looking nemilar. "I's been up here for days and I is starving hungry," he added, forcing a weak smile. "Anything you might have spare'll do. I ain't fussy." He began to rifle through his pockets, "Here, look, I'll pay you for it."

Hunter lowered his bow, "Come down from there," he said gently. "You're quite safe. But I have no cake," he added with a smile.

"Oh, alright then," sighed the nemilar. "Well, sorry to trouble you. You'd best be on your way afore them wolves come back."

"The wolves will not be a problem, friend. Come down. I'll take you to the village where we can get you cleaned and fed."

"I's fine where I are, thank you. I don't want to be no trouble. Now you get off out of harm's way, young fella. I don't want you getting hurt for the likes of me."

"Don't be ridiculous!" exclaimed Hunter. "I'm not leaving without you, so I suggest you come down. Or should I remain here until the wolves return? Is that what you want?"

The nemilar shook his head, "Of course not," he said quietly. "Problem is, I don't think I *can* get down! My legs is weak and if I let go, I'll probably fall to my death."

"Do it then," Hunter urged him. "Let go, I mean. Don't worry, I'll catch you."

"No, I can't do that!" replied the nemilar, his voice rising until it was virtually a squeak. "You might get hurt. Nice young fella like you getting hurt to save me, it wouldn't be right."

"Well how's this for an idea then? I shoot you in the leg, you fall out of the tree anyway, and I still catch you."

The nemilar laughed at Hunter's plan, "You is not going to leave is you, whatever I says?"

"I've always been a little stubborn," sighed Hunter. "What's it going to be then, the first plan or the second?"

"Well I don't fancy you sticking an arrow in my leg, so I suppose I'd better just let go and hope you're strong enough to not get hurt."

Hunter moved closer to the tree, "Don't worry about me," he said, reassuringly, "I'm a lot stronger than I look."

The weary nemilar gave Hunter a dubious look, "Alright then," he warned, "Here I come. Brace yourself!"

***

Ballorn was so engrossed working on his brace that he did not notice Hunter as he approached. Stitch of course could see nothing at all as he cowered behind the hatch in the forge.

"How's it coming?" called Hunter.

Ballorn glanced up, and his mouth fell open, "Oh, no!" he groaned. "No. It's not possible. Why? Why him? Of all the nemilar you could have discovered, you had to find *him*!"

The exhausted nemilar smiled at the blacksmith, "Hello, Ballorn," he said quietly.

Stitch recognised the stranger's voice and leapt up from behind the counter, "Dannard!" he cried with glee. "It's you, you're alright. I thought you had been roasted or gobbled up by that monster, but you're here!"

The smile on Dannard's lips widened as he saw Stitch, "I've been better, I has to say," he replied. "But yes, somehow I was lucky enough to escape the beast."

"Typical!" moaned Ballorn. "*Absolutely typical*! As usual, someone else gets all the good luck and I get all the bad!"

Hunter eyed him with confusion, "I take it you all know each other?"

"Oh yes," groaned Ballorn, resuming his hammering. "Well done! You've rescued the most miserly, tight-fisted skinflint in the whole village, *Dannard the cooper*!"

"What was I supposed to do, Ballorn, leave him in the forest to die of starvation? Or would you have preferred he fell from the tree in which he was hiding, to be devoured by wolves?"

Ballorn slammed his hammer onto the anvil beside him. "Do me a favour would you, Hunter? *Stop saving people*! Honestly... this mission is..." His voice tailed off.

Hunter stared at him for a moment. "Stop saving people? You mean the way I saved you?" He paused, "What... *mission*?" he asked slowly.

Ballorn suddenly looked uncomfortable, "It doesn't matter," he said quietly as he turned to his forge. "I'll go alone when I'm ready. You can stay here and take care of these two."

"To Lonny's farm?" asked Hunter. "You're going to travel there by yourself, with a broken..."

"*He's not a skinflint!*" Stitch suddenly blurted out, interrupting Hunter. "He's one of the kindest, most generous nemilar I've ever known!"

Dannard waved his hand frantically at Stitch, "Shush up, Stitch," he urged. "Be quiet, that's quite enough."

"*Generous!*" roared Ballorn, beginning to laugh. "He'd want a discount on something if it was free!"

"That's because he needs the coin to pay for other things!" protested Stitch. "If it wasn't for him, those people..."

"Enough, Stitch!" shouted Dannard. "None of that matters now! We must be dealing with the bother what we is in *now*. Ballorn's not interested in what happened before!"

But, to the contrary, Ballorn was most intrigued by Stitch's outburst. "What *people*?" he asked.

"There's them little orphans for a start," Stitch said quickly. "And the old lady who lost her husband in that accident, and the chap who lost his arm when he was chopping lumber in the forest. If it weren't for Dannard, they'd have all gone hungry and been without a roof over…"

"*Stitch!*" cried Dannard. "*Will you please stick a sock in it?* My business affairs is not summat you go spouting off about to people what ain't involved. Now shut your gob!"

Hunter intervened, "Let's get you something to eat, Dannard," he said. "You need feeding up. I could almost lift you with one arm."

Dannard frowned, "I does not need feeding up," he mumbled. "I've always kept myself fit and slim. We're not all like him you know," he added, gesturing to Ballorn. "And afore you start thinking that's an insult, Ballorn, it ain't. I don't mean you is a fatty, but look at you. You isn't the normalist nemilar is you? You has *got* to be over five feet tall and you has a chest bigger than one of my barrels."

"It's true," agreed Stitch. "You are *freakishly* tall, and then there's your muscles. Arms like tree trunks, legs thicker than…"

"Have you quite finished?" growled Ballorn, glaring at them both.

"Oh, Ballorn, do lighten up a little," sniggered Hunter. "Let them feast their eyes upon the nemilar mountain! They'll be the founder members of your fan club before you know it."

CHAPTER 6

The following day, Ballorn rose at dawn. His brace strapped tightly around his leg, he began to pace gingerly around his forge. Initially there was the occasional sharp intake of breath and a good deal of muttering as he cursed his misfortune, but after a while he resigned himself to the fact that he there was no way he would be completely comfortable. Reaching under his counter, he took hold of a small sack and began placing a few scraps of food in it that were left from the previous night.

"You were serious then?"

Ballorn glanced up at Hunter, "I don't say things I don't mean."

"And you were going to leave without telling anyone?"

"Why wouldn't I?" asked Ballorn, frowning. "Dannard's too weak to travel, Stitch is an idiot and they're both scared of their own shadows! As for you, well, you just want to mother 'em. So yes, I was going to leave without telling anyone."

"Is we all ready to go then?"

Ballorn hadn't seen Dannard behind Hunter, or Stitch for that matter. For the briefest of moments Ballorn wondered if they had heard him insulting them. Not that he really cared. After all, it was the truth.

"Almost," replied Hunter. "Just waiting for Ballorn to get himself sorted."

"Just out of interest," asked Dannard, "where is we going, and what is we doing when we gets there?"

Ballorn limped past them as he headed toward the edge of the village. "*I'm* going to Lonny's farm, and what *I'm* doing is none of your business," he replied gruffly.

"You are right of course," said Stitch, who had hurried to be by Ballorn's side, "I *am* scared of just about everything, that's why I'm not staying in the village alone. The safest place to be, for now at least, is with you and Hunter."

"You wasn't going to be alone, Stitch. I would have stayed with you if Ballorn told us we wasn't to go with him."

Stitch smiled at Dannard, "I know you would have my friend. Let's face it though, neither of us is what you'd call aggressive. We aren't giants like Ballorn, or hunters like him. No, folk like us are meant to be looked after by others, let them do the fighting and the dangerous stuff."

***

Their pace was slow. Ballorn's breathing was laboured and the sweat soon poured off his brow as the pain grew worse. Despite pleas from the others, he would not stop. His stubbornness and determination drove him on. Many times he stumbled, too proud to accept help from anyone who tried to assist him. As the light began to fail they had only covered half the distance to where the stream was located.

Hunter called them to a halt, "We'll make camp here," he said. "We cannot travel at night, it would be far too dangerous." He lit a fire and they sat close to it, more for protection than warmth. Ballorn lay flat on his back with his eyes closed, glad to finally rest his leg. Although he would never have admitted it.

"Here," said Hunter, "take these."

Ballorn opened his eyes to see Hunter offering him a few of the familiar pollum pods. "No thanks," he snorted, "I remember what happened the last time you gave me some of those. I've things to do, no time for sleeping for days on end!"

"If you don't swallow them, you'll be fine. Just chew them, it'll take the edge off the pain."

Ballorn stared at Hunter defiantly.

"Go on, stupid. If you don't, we is going to be out here for weeks. Take the nice pods, whatever they is, and have a bit of a kip. It'll do you good," Dannard urged.

"I'm sensing that whatever it is you intend to do is important to you, Ballorn. Therefore, there must also be an urgency that drives you to suffer such pain," whispered Hunter, offering the pollum once more. "Take them, you can thank me later."

"I is starving hungry. Has we got any grub? Did anyone bring some cake?"

Hunter laughed, "No, Dannard, we are still without cake. There are edible plants and roots out here in the forest, I'll see what I can find." Tapping his bow, he leaned down to the two gentle nemilar. "You never know, we may even be luckier still."

Before long, Hunter returned carrying three tondy (a large breed of rodent), and two gebblar (a flightless bird slightly larger than a chicken). He gutted the tondy and wrapped them in mud before placing them into the flames. The gebblar were then plucked and placed on a skewer above them. The nemilar watched in fascination as Hunter placed leaf-wrapped roots and bulbs at the edge of the fire.

"You is really good at this cooking lark, Hunter," said Dannard in admiration. "You is good at catching and digging up things too. My belly is grumblatin' something rotten I is so hungry."

"Well I hope you enjoy it, Dannard," replied Hunter grinning. "Sorry, still no cake I'm afraid."

"Not wanting to pick fault or anything, Hunter, but why are you cooking so much?" asked Stitch. "There's only four of us and there's enough there for double that at least."

Hunter nodded toward the snoozing Ballorn, "He'll eat at least one of the tondy and a gebblar by himself," he replied. "Those pollum pods do give one an appetite. Any less than this and we three would have to stay hungry."

"Ah, you is saying he's a greedy guts!" said Dannard, nodding.

Hunter laughed, "No, that's not what I'm saying, but he's had a much harder day than any of us. He'll need his strength if he's going to survive tomorrow."

A look of dread swept across Stitch's face, "Why, what's happening tomorrow?" he asked, nervously.

"Nothing," replied Hunter, reassuringly. "I simply meant that the route we shall follow is more difficult. Today we were mostly on level ground, but tomorrow is mostly uphill."

"What!" exclaimed Dannard. "We isn't going up no mountains is we? I's had enough of being up in the air. I was stuck in that tree…"

"*No*, Dannard, *no mountains,*" Hunter assured him. "Just a slope. Easy enough for us, but not for someone with a broken leg."

Hunter was correct when he had suggested that Ballorn may have an appetite when he awoke. They watched in disbelief as he devoured his food. He scoffed it down as if he hadn't eaten for a week, before turning to them, "You going to finish that?" he asked, expectantly.

The two smaller nemilar did not have the nerve to refuse and handed him what was left of their meals. They too disappeared as quickly as his own.

Wiping his mouth on his sleeve, Ballorn promptly lay back and immediately fell asleep.

Hunter produced the rest of the food he had hidden from Ballorn. Sharing it equally between Dannard and Stitch, he winked, "I think you were right, Dannard," he whispered, "he is a bit of a greedy guts."

***

The following day was much easier for them all. Ballorn, chewing gratefully on the pollum pods, marched on almost as if his leg was perfectly fine. This left the others to concentrate on their own footing, relieved to not have to watch Ballorn in fear that he may take a tumble from which he would not recover.

"Does you hear that?" asked Dannard, tilting his head. "That tricklatin' noise? We's near water we is."

"There's a stream up ahead," Hunter informed him. "We should be at the farm before nightfall."

"You mean, where the farm was?" Ballorn's expression changed to one of deep concern. "Hunter..." he asked slowly, "... when you found me at the foot of that tree, was that the first time our paths had crossed?"

"Well, as I said..." began Hunter, "... I had seen you in the village, but we had never been formally introduced. Why do you ask?"

Ballorn shook his head, "No reason... just wondering," he said dismissively. "My memory, it's not what it used to be." But there was nothing wrong with his memory, nothing at all. He was remembering the voice that had spoken to him the last time he had visited Lonny's farm, remembering the warning it had given him regarding the dangers that may surround him. *Would the stranger still be there and, if he was, would he reveal himself now that Ballorn had company? Only time would tell.*

They halted briefly at the stream, filling their water skins and washing their faces in the crystal-clear water. Well, three of them did.

"We isn't supposed to be all wet. I isn't no fish! Water is bad for my skin, makes it all wrinklified and stuff. I doesn't mind drinking a bit of it, but it's only good inside a nemilar like what I is, it spoils my outsides something rotten."

"Good choice of words!" exclaimed Hunter. "I was trying to think of a good term for your fragrance… *something rotten* sums it up perfectly."

Dannard wasn't offended, in fact he seemed quite proud of his pungent, stale odour. "Good honest sweat that is," he announced. "Comes from hard work, something most folks ain't got no clue about."

"Well, to be fair," said Stitch, quietly, "you can't count any of us amongst the work-shy, and *we* all find time to bathe."

"You isn't like me though is you? My skin is delicate, I isn't going to wash away the natural oils what's in it just to keep you happy."

"Delicate or not," began Ballorn with a sinister tone, "get that coat and shirt off and clean yourself up. If you don't, I'll give you a bath myself. Or should I say *a dunking*? The biggest question you should ask yourself is *would I be kind enough to pull you back up once your head's underwater?*"

"That's nice!" squeaked Dannard, "I come out into the dangerous woods to help you and what does you do? You threatens me, that's what! *What has I ever done to you?*"

"Oh, I don't know! Perhaps it's the fact that you've picked fault with every bit of work I've done for you for the last five years, and by the way it wasn't a threat, more a premonition," said Ballorn as he glared at the cooper.

Dannard hurriedly began pulling at his coat, trying his best to remove it before Ballorn could follow up on his promise. "I's doing it, I's doing it," he said, nervously.

To be fair, Ballorn really didn't care whether Dannard smelt of roses or dung, but he hadn't been able to resist the chance to wind him up when that chance had presented itself so perfectly. He turned away, smiling to himself as he listened to the panic-stricken babbling of Dannard behind him. The smile left his face quickly as he eyed up the trail ahead of them. "Five minutes," he announced. "Then we need to push on, and make sure he cleans behind his ears."

***

"Stay right here," urged Hunter as he steered Dannard and Stitch behind a tree. "We'll come back for you shortly but don't come out until we return." Glancing up, he grabbed hold of the lowest branch and began to climb.

"Why's he stuck us in here?" whispered Dannard.

"To keep us safe," replied Stitch, quietly.

"Keep us safe from what?"

Stitch shuddered, "I don't know," he said. "In fact, I'd rather *not* know."

Hunter travelled swiftly through the trees above them until he was above Ballorn. They nodded at each other and Ballorn walked on. They had come to the scorched ground and, strangely enough, it was Ballorn himself who had suggested that the others be hidden.

It was not long before he heard the familiar voice, "You came back," it said with faint surprise. "Either you are very brave, or very stupid. Which one is it, my little friend?"

Ballorn glanced around. The stranger had chosen, yet again, to remain hidden. "Where I go is none of your concern," he replied politely. "Who are you?" asked Ballorn. "There's very few in these lands who would refer to me as little."

"Perhaps not," laughed the stranger. "Forgive me, I meant no insult nor offence."

"None taken," sighed Ballorn. "But you didn't answer my question."

"Ah, yes. Difficult one that, I suppose you mean my name."

"Of course I mean your name," smiled Ballorn. "Or do you have a title? Perhaps you prefer to be called your majesty."

"Ooh, that would be nice," replied the stranger, "but not at all justified. No, the problem is that my native tongue is somewhat different to yours and I'm afraid you would not be able to pronounce my name properly."

"Give me a try," suggested Ballorn, "I might surprise you."

"No, I have a better idea," said the stranger. "Why don't *you* give me a name? Think of all your favourite names and I shall answer to the one you choose."

"What!" exclaimed Ballorn. "I can't just give you a name!"

"Why not?" asked the stranger. "Your kind do it all the time. You call your friend *Hunter*, but that is not his name, it is what he does."

Ballorn's nerves were beginning to show as he tried to choose his words carefully, "I, I don't know..."

"Don't know what?" asked the stranger. "You don't know that your friend is in the treetops above you, shadowing your every move? There is no need to worry, Nibrilsiem, you are quite safe. You, the hunter and the tiny ones you have hidden have no enemies here."

"Then why don't you come out of your hiding place? If you're not our enemy, show yourself!"

"Firstly, you must continue on your quest," replied the stranger. "Find the answers you seek, and we shall speak when you return. For now, that is all I will say."

"How do I know you're alone?" called Ballorn. "You might wait until we're all out in the open and then attack us." He waited a few seconds but there was no response. "Hello... hello, are you still there?" Glancing up at Hunter, he raised his arms out to his sides before pointing back the way they came.

Meeting back at Dannard and Stitch's hiding place, Hunter climbed down to join them. "What was all that?" he exclaimed.

"You heard him," replied Ballorn. "He won't come out until we get back."

"Heard who?" asked Hunter, frowning. "All I heard was your voice and a lot of growling and snarling. "Oh, I did catch one word that was not spoken by you, *Nibrilsiem*, whatever that means! It sounded like you were having a conversation with some ferocious beast!"

Ballorn stared at him, his face expressionless. "Do you have problems with your hearing?" he asked seriously.

"How long do you think I'd survive out here if I had?"

"But you never heard a word the stranger said?"

"Whoever this stranger you keep referring to is, never spoke!" exclaimed Hunter. "He, or *it*, just growled! The only discernible word spoken other than by you, was Nibrilsiem, and I've never heard it before!"

Ballorn was, understandably, a little confused. He sighed loudly and shrugged his shoulders, "I don't know what to say," he announced shaking his head. "Let's just carry on and we'll see what happens on our way back. Dannard, Stitch, come on, let's get a move on."

Stitch smiled at him, "Erm, no thanks," he replied. "Dannard and I have been having a little chat and we've decided to stay here. We heard that thing growling and what- not all the way back here so, we're fine where we are. You can get us on the way back."

Dannard wagged his finger at Ballorn, "You never said nothing about no snarly things being involved," he said in a slightly trembling voice. "I isn't out here to get gobbled up by some kind of beastie."

Ballorn lowered his head and thought for a moment, before glancing up at the two nemilar cowering behind their tree, "Whoever, or *whatever* it is, knows you're here," he whispered. "But, if you prefer to remain here by yourselves, that's your decision. Hunter and I will look for you on our return," he glanced at Dannard, "providing, of course, you haven't been gobbled up in the meantime."

Dannard and Stitch stared wide-eyed at one another before quickly turning to face Ballorn.

On second thoughts…" began Stitch, "… it wouldn't be right to allow just the two of you to continue alone, you may need our help. What if you split a seam or something awful like that? Who would sew it for you? No, we're coming with you. No, there's no need to thank us, it's only fair that we stay together."

Hunter grinned at Ballorn, "Imagine," he said, stifling his laughter, "splitting a seam! The world would surely end after such a tragic event!"

"Let's not go directly past the scorched ground," suggested Ballorn. "We'll skirt around it." He seemed distracted, "Can you remember where that tree was when we first met?" he asked.

Hunter nodded, "That way," he said pointing. "Why?"

"Something I need to check," replied Ballorn.

Hunter lead the way. "That one over there," he said as they neared the tree where he has rescued Ballorn.

Ballorn turned away and began to follow the trail of devastation that would eventually bring them closer to Lonny's farm. His head was down as they walked, his eyes scanning the ground searching for something.

"What is it you're looking for?" asked Hunter.

"The axe I made for Lonny," Ballorn replied. "I have no idea what it was that came after me, but in a blind panic I hurled it as hard as I could at the beast. Something tells me it survived, don't ask me why or how I know, I've no idea."

Hunter was intrigued, "Why are you doing this, Ballorn?" he asked. "What is it that you hope to gain by coming back here?"

His answer surprised Hunter, "I don't know," he said. "It's as if I have to. But I don't know exactly what it is I'm doing... or what it is I'm *supposed* to do."

Hunter rubbed his head, "Oh well, as long as we know."

"Nobody asked you to come along," snapped Ballorn. "You can leave if you like. I..." He took a deep breath, "... I *have* to do this," he said calmly. "You do not."

Hunter laughed, "You don't get rid of me that easily, blacksmith. I love a good mystery and I haven't enjoyed myself this much in many years," he said. "Come on, let's find this axe."

It wasn't long before the hunter spotted a glint of metal partially hidden beneath the churned ground. Trotting across, he unearthed the remains of the axe. The handle was no more and the steel of the head was now simply a malformed clump. The gold inlays of which Ballorn had been so proud were now unrecognisable blobs. *But the silver was perfectly preserved.* The intense heat that had reduced the work of art to nothing more than globs of base metal had somehow been ineffective against the precious metal. Hunter handed it to Ballorn.

"Seems I was wrong," snorted Ballorn. "What a mess! Shame really, I was really proud of that."

"No," Hunter disagreed. "You were right. Admittedly, most of it is ruined, but the silver survived. Perhaps that is what you were supposed to discover?"

Ballorn pondered over their findings, "So this beast could be defeated by a weapon made from silver," he said quietly. "But it's impossible to hone a blade made from silver, it would never be sharp enough. Then there's the problem of getting close enough to use it even if it *were* possible."

"Easy," Dannard said suddenly, "you makes some armour from silver and you doesn't get frazzled by the monster."

Ballorn and Hunter stared at one another. The annoying cooper was spot on.

"Then again…" continued Dannard, "… it wouldn't matter anyway. If you was that close, it'd just stomp on you and squidge you, I s'pose."

Unfortunately, Dannard was right again.

They proceeded to the farm. Nothing had changed since Ballorn's last visit and, after a brief look around, they turned back. Even as they did, Ballorn still appeared to be searching for something.

"Was there something else you were hoping to find?" asked Hunter.

"A couple of things to be honest," replied Ballorn.

"Tell us what they are and we can help you look for them," volunteered Stitch.

"Well, there was a silver pendant that belonged to my father, but I managed to tear that from my own neck just before I hurled the axe at the dragon, so that could be anywhere."

"And what was the other thing?" asked Stitch.

"A hammer," replied Ballorn.

"Why did you bring a hammer?" asked Stitch.

"I take it everywhere with me," replied Ballorn. "It's the one I use most so it's always tucked in my belt."

"So, you wasn't hoping you might be offered a few more jobs by the farmer then? Always handy when you has a bit more coin in your purse you wasn't banking on."

"No, Dannard, I was simply carrying it out of habit."

"What's it look like?" asked Stitch.

Ballorn frowned, "Seriously?" he asked. "It's a hammer! It looks like a hammer!"

"I know that!" exclaimed Stitch. "But if we find one, how do we know it's yours?"

Ballorn shook his head in disbelief, "How many discarded hammers do you think there are out here, numbskull? If you find one, it'll be mine!"

Hunter took Ballorn's arm and steered him away from the others. "I was wondering," he said, "are we going back the way we came? To be honest with you, I'm a little concerned. I know this area well, and the lack of predators is unnatural. There are no wolves, no gemnar, nothing that you'd normally encounter out here."

"Well surely that's a good thing, isn't it?" replied Ballorn. "We have enough to contend with without having to fight off wolves and things every step of the way."

"Ordinarily, I'd agree with you," said Hunter. "My concern, however, is with whatever you were chatting to on the way here. It was no nemilar or man you were talking to, Ballorn. If we retrace our steps, we could be in grave danger."

"We were in danger the moment we left Krevick!" hissed Ballorn. "What if we are in even greater danger out here in the wilds? What is it that is so precious that we are looking to keep? Our lives! As far as we know, we are the only survivors, the only ones to have escaped the terror of this beast, this *dragon*! I've told you before, if you want to leave, then go. Take that pair with you as well! I'm out here to get answers, and I intend to get them with or without you! So what if the stranger kills me! At least I'll have tried to get some justice for our people!"

Hunter lowered his head, stepped aside and stretched out his arm, "Lead on," he instructed as he gave a slight bow.

Dannard began to chuckle, "Yeah, come on," he said. "Let's go and get chobbled on by a beastie."

CHAPTER 7

They stood together, Stitch latched firmly to the back of Hunter's waistcoat.

"We've returned," called Ballorn. "Time for you to prove your word and reveal yourself."

"About that," came the stranger's voice, apprehensively, "I just need to clarify something."

"Another excuse," sighed Ballorn. "Very well, but there are to be no more bargains. I'll agree one last time, after that, we're leaving!"

"I want you to make me a promise," said the stranger. "That you will behave in a civilised manner. There is to be no screaming or silly behaviour, and under no circumstances must you attack me, or I shall be forced to defend myself and neither of us want that."

"Why would we attack you?" asked Ballorn, flummoxed by the stranger's request.

"Promise?"

"Yes, alright!" exclaimed Ballorn, impatiently. "We promise we won't attack you! Now show yourself."

There was a faint rumbling sound. The nemilar felt the ground beneath their feet tremble and shake violently enough to cause dust to fall from the nearby rock-face.

Mark of the Nibrilsiem

Stepping back, they watched as it seemed to pulsate, a shape beginning to form clearly deep within it. Alarmed, they fell back as they were suddenly covered with silt that had erupted as a huge leathery wing stretched out above them. A body shook itself free and immediately towered over them, its neck stretching high into the air before lowering its head to reveal deep, ochre eyes that burned brightly within the dust cloud that surrounded them. A second wing now appeared as a deep rasping breath left the body of the beast as it stretched to its full height. It shuddered, freeing itself of the remnants of its rock-formed shroud. Leaning forward, it lay down before them and lowered its head. "Welcome, Nibrilsiem," it breathed.

Ballorn stared deep into the dragon's eyes. Strangely, he felt no fear. Despite its fearsome appearance he felt a calmness sweep over him as if they were connected in some way, as if it had always been his destiny to face this kindred spirit. He smiled.

Hunter had tumbled backwards and lay sprawled on the ground. He had heard many tales throughout his lifetime, but not a single nemilar had ever managed to convince him that dragons actually existed.

Dannard watched open-mouthed but never said a word.

Stitch too had toppled over. Chuntering to himself, he rose with his back to dragon, totally oblivious of what was happening behind him. All he cared about was that his beloved jacket was now covered in dust as he frantically attempted to brush it away. "Look at the state of it!" he whined. "It's going to take ages to get this cleaned properly. Ballorn, look!" he said, glancing over his shoulder. He smiled briefly, "Ooh look, it's a dragon," he giggled, not even realising what he had said. It took a few seconds, but it soon sank in. A look of horror descended immediately. He spun around, his eyes wide in terror. "It's... it's... it's... A DRAGON!" he bellowed. "RUN FOR YOUR LIVES... IT'S A DRAGON! WE'LL ALL BE KILLED!"

He had only taken three steps before Ballorn grabbed the back of his jacket. However, his legs were still pounding frantically as he tried to make good his escape. Within seconds his heels had created a groove and a dust cloud that rivalled the one that had enveloped the dragon only moments before. The sweat poured down his brow as he heard the growling behind him, terrified that he would be burnt to death or eaten at any moment.

"Brackin' 'eck, e's right you know," whispered Dannard. "It is, it's a brackin' dragon."

Hunter frowned at him, "Yes, it is," he said quietly. "And you're not going to give a very good impression of us using language like that in front of it!"

"But it's a brackin' dragon! Well I'll be grabbled!"

"Now you're doing it on purpose," growled Hunter.

"You promised there would be no nonsense," sighed the dragon.

"To be fair, no I didn't," replied Ballorn, dismissively. "However, you must admit that only one out of four losing his nerve at the sight of you isn't bad. I don't think so anyway."

"Is it upset with us?" asked Dannard. "Only it don't sound best pleased."

"What makes you think he's upset?" Ballorn asked, turning to face him.

"Well I'm sure he don't growl and roar like that when he's in a good mood, do 'e?"

"Dannard, what are you talking about? He's speaking as plainly as you and I. On second thoughts, perhaps not you, but definitely as clearly as the rest of us."

"You has gone completely bonkers you has," snorted Dannard. "Ain't a single word come from it, ain't that right, Hunter?"

Hunter gave a slightly embarrassed smile and nodded gently, "I'm not sure how you're able to understand it, Ballorn, but you're on your own. We can't make out a single word."

Ballorn gave the dragon a quizzical look, "How come they can't understand what you're saying?"

The dragon snorted, "Because they're imbeciles," it replied. "They're nothing like you, Nibrilsiem, and never shall be unless I deem them worthy."

"Of course they're not like me. We're all different from one another! Different skills, different trades, the only thing we have in common is that we are all nemilar."

"Oh how right you are," groaned the dragon. "Perhaps I should have introduced myself earlier. How's the leg by the way?" he asked, suddenly changing the subject.

"It'll be alright soon enough. I made a brace and Stitch..." his voice tailed off. "How did you know about my leg?" he asked slowly.

"Oh, please," moaned the dragon. "I'm not blind. I can see that it is braced, so you must have injured it fairly recently."

Ballorn peered at the dragon, "No... you knew. You knew my leg was injured before we even came here earlier. Was it you?" he asked pointedly. "Did you chase me down and attack me?"

"Certainly not!" protested the dragon. "How could you even think such a thing? Do I look like the type of dragon who would terrorise innocent travellers? I find your accusation thoroughly distasteful, Nibrilsiem."

"Why do you keep calling me that?" Ballorn asked, seeming slightly agitated. "What does it mean, is it your word for stranger or something like that?"

The dragon drew back its head and stared down at the blacksmith, "I know you are small..." he said, "... but I never realised that your miniscule stature would directly affect your memory."

Ballorn was now completely lost, "My memory? What is it that you think I've forgotten?"

"Why, your rescue of course. The day your..." he thought for a moment, "... *parents*, yes, that's the word I was looking for. The day your parents died."

"Well I can't remember it, but I was told some of the other villagers found me bundled up in some bushes or under some tree roots."

"And who put you there?" asked the dragon, leaning his head right down to the ground to face Ballorn.

"My parents did, to protect me from being trampled."

"No," whispered the dragon. "It was I who placed you there. And I stayed with you until you were found, Nibrilsiem. If I had not granted you *the dragon's sigh*, you would surely have perished."

Dannard tugged at Hunter's sleeve, "I don't know what that thing just said to him, but 'e don't look too happy about it," he whispered.

Peering around Ballorn, the dragon tilted its head. He knew that the nemilar could not understand what he was saying. He however, clearly understood every word that passed their lips and could bear it no longer. Opening his jaws, he let out a rasping breath. A yellow mist surrounded the nemilar and they waved their arms frantically, trying to disperse the vapour before it melted the flesh from their bones, or worse. Stitch grabbed his nose, fearing that the smell of the dragon's exhalation would be even more rancid than it looked. To their surprise, they neither melted nor were harmed in any way and were totally amazed that the dispersing mist actually had a faint fragrance of lavender about it. The dragon glared at them, "Now perhaps I may continue..." it said, sternly, "... without interruptions or commentary!"

The three nemilar were shocked, *they understood every word the dragon had said.*

The day wore on and soon the light began to fail. Hunter, Dannard and Stitch had moved away and built a fire, allowing Ballorn and the dragon a little privacy. Hunter and Stitch thought it best, but poor Dannard was beside himself at not being included in their conversation and one ear or the other was always cocked in the hope of overhearing what was being said.

"Come and sit down!" hissed Hunter. "If there's anything we need to know I'm sure Ballorn will tell us later."

Dannard stared wide-eyed at him. "What's wrong with you pair!" he exclaimed. "A brackin' dragon appears, blows snot all over us so we can understand what it's saying, and then buggers off to have a conflab with a nemilar it reckons it saved when he were nowt but a bundle of rags under a bush! Is I the only one who don't think it's quite right?"

Stitch shrugged his shoulders at Hunter, "He's got a point you know," he sighed. "If you were to tell this story in any inn, they'd take your ale away and show you the door, thinking you'd gone barmy."

"What's more…" continued Dannard, "… how does we know this ain't the beastie that destroyed Krevick and murdered all of our friends."

"We don't," snapped Hunter. "But if it was, do you think it would introduce itself and have a cosy little chat with Ballorn? No, it wouldn't, it would have slaughtered us as soon as it saw us. I'll admit that it's an unusual state of affairs, but there's more to this than we know. Ballorn will fill us in on the details later, of that much I'm sure."

***

"Alright, so you're saying that it wasn't my parents who protected me from the beasts, but you."

"Your mother tried, Nibrilsiem. If I had not checked that you had survived the attack, those beasts would have surely sealed your fate."

"Did you see it happen?"

The dragon lowered its head. "Yes, I'm afraid I did, but there was nothing I could do to stop it."

"You couldn't do anything! Look at the size of you, nothing could ever stand against you. You should've saved them!"

"We are not allowed to interfere in the lives of others, Nibrilsiem. It is our way."

"Your way! How can it be your way? How do you explain *me*? You say you saved me, but you weren't allowed to save my parents? What sort of creature are you?"

"One who, ordinarily, obeys the laws of my lord," replied the dragon.

"Lord! What lord? Your lord would stand by and watch as simple village folk are trampled to death?"

"That... and far worse, I am sad to say," replied the dragon, quietly.

"Your village," he whispered, "it was the crystal lord himself who destroyed it and took the lives of your people."

"So, it *was* one of your kind," roared Ballorn. "Murdering piece of filth! I'll gut it like a fish, and mark my words dragon, if you intend to stand in my way, you'll be first!"

"You are a very... *excitable*, fellow, aren't you," the dragon said, calmly. "Now settle yourself, I have no intention of standing in your way. Quite the contrary, *my intention is to help you.*"

Ballorn stepped back, "You want to help?" he asked, suspiciously. "I've just told you I'm going to kill your dragon lord, and you want to help? What's in it for you? Do you get to take his place?"

"You really do have a very low opinion of me, don't you?"

"Why would you expect anything else?" growled Ballorn. "The only one of your kind I've encountered tried to kill me! But that wasn't enough, it decided to destroy my whole village as well!"

"Ah well, that was your fault, I'm afraid."

Ballorn stood agog, "How is it my fault?"

"When I say, your *fault*, I do not mean you are to blame," the dragon assured him. "Only, he had not intended on heading in that direction until you came along. You see, he followed your scent and it took him straight to your home."

"So that's my fault!" roared Ballorn. "How was I to know there was a murderous dragon skulking around, it's not like it came out and introduced itself before it attacked me!"

"No, his manners are lacking somewhat of late," groaned the dragon. "I blame the crystal."

Ballorn glared at him, "This conversation is going nowhere," he growled. "I'm done with you and your nonsense! Tell your dragon lord, when you see him, that I'm coming after him," he pointed at the dragon, his arm

Mark of the Nibrilsiem

shaking in anger. "You tell him, when I find him, I'm taking his head as a trophy!"

"No, Nibrilsiem. When you find him *he* will kill *you*," the dragon sighed, looking to the other nemilar, "and any who accompany you."

"He might, but rest assured, dragon, I won't go down without a fight, and neither will they!"

"You could defeat him you know. Now don't interrupt," said the dragon, holding up a claw. "You already have the clues that would provide you with an advantage. However, I am surprised that the stupid one has come up with the most sensible suggestion so far."

Ballorn glanced over to where the others were seated around the campfire. *Could the dragon be referring to Dannard's idea of the silver armour? How would he know? Surely, he could not have heard them? They were at least two miles away when they had spoken of it.*

"Ah, there it is," laughed the dragon. "It's all coming together for you now isn't it? It is the crystal lord's only weakness, alas it will not protect you fully. Magical attacks can be nullified, but physical attacks cannot."

"Silver," said Ballorn. "You're talking about silver. I've already told this lot, you can't get a good enough edge on silver. There's no way it would cut through a dragon's scales. In fact, I can't think of anything that would be sharp enough to cut through them!"

"That's because there *is* nothing that could cut through them," replied the dragon.

Ballorn stared at him. It was a little unnerving, and he wasn't completely sure that he was correct, but the dragon seemed to be smiling. "So, I can get close, but what then? How do I beat it?"

"Please, Nibrilsiem, I implore you! Use the brain inside that disproportionate head of yours! If something cannot be cut, then…"

"You have to smash it!" exclaimed Ballorn. "I don't need anything sharp, I need something blunt, and heavy… *very heavy*!"

The dragon's smile grew wider, "See, not so difficult was it?"

"So, you're saying…"

"No, no… I'm not saying anything!" interrupted the dragon, nervously. "I would be guilty of treason were I to impart upon you information that would lead to the harm or death of another dragon."

Ballorn's eyes widened, "You're scared of him," he breathed.

The dragon lowered his head, "Yes, I will admit, I am. Even we, his own kind, are not safe from his cruelty and wrath. Several of my friends have met their demise at the claws of the crystal one, for he is above our laws and free to murder at will if he so chooses."

"That's… that's… *dreadful*!"

"Yes, Nibrilsiem, it is. Once, he was beloved and admired by all dragons. But the light from the crystal has begun to blacken and, with it, so has his heart."

"So, he's gone nuts then!"

Ballorn glared at Dannard, who quickly lowered his head.

"You must rest now, Nibrilsiem, but before you do…" the dragon lowered his head and, once more, exhaled a vapour that surrounded Ballorn. "When you awaken, your leg will be fully healed. Return to your village, craft what it is you need to enable your revenge. There is ample time so do not rush and skimp in its construction. Return to me when it is complete, and I shall bestow upon you one final gift."

***

They rose early the following day. Ballorn tapped gingerly against his leg. The pain was gone. Removing the brace, he clambered to his feet and stamped on the ground a few times. His leg, as the dragon had promised it would be, was completely healed.

"Full of tricks, your dragon friend," said Hunter, smiling as he handed Ballorn some food. "It's only nuts and berries, I'm afraid. Very slim pickings around here this morning."

Ballorn grunted and nodded. "Better than nothing," he mumbled.

"You never said much last night, Ballorn, did the dragon tell you something that we should be concerned about?"

Ballorn looked up at Hunter and smiled, "Him? No, he never told me a thing," he replied, chuckling. "However, I have had an idea. Do you know of any silver mines around here?"

"Silver?" asked Stitch. "What do you need silver for?"

"I've got some," said Ballorn as he glanced at the tailor. "But not enough to make a full suit of armour, and I'm going to need a lot more than that for something else I've got in mind."

"Why not go all the way and make a shield to complete the set," laughed Hunter. "May as well while the forge is hot."

"How much silver will you need though, only Dannard…?"

They looked at Dannard, whose eyes were as huge as dinner plates. He was glaring at Stitch and shaking his head vigorously, "No, no, no… shut your brackin' face! Ignore 'im, it's only a few coins I was keeping for a rainy day. You know, a bit o' savings in case times gets a bit lean," he laughed nervously.

Hunter grinned, "How many is *a few*?" he asked.

"Ooh, he's got hundreds of 'em. I remember when you asked me to help you count them, Dannard." Stitch laughed, "We kept losing track, remember, but it was typical that it was always after we'd gotten past six hundred."

Ballorn raised his eyebrows, "You miserly little oik!" he said, his voice higher than usual, "You always said you were broke, when you had all that stashed away! You should be ashamed of yourself!"

"I isn't a miser, I uses it to help other folks what ain't got much, them as really needs it! I doesn't keep it for myself and never has done! Ain't my fault that most of 'em is doing alright lately and don't need no help!"

"Perhaps not!" exclaimed Ballorn, "But it never stopped you pleading poverty and complaining every time you wanted the hoops making for your poxy barrels!"

"My barrels is not *poxy*!" exclaimed Dannard, "They is the bestest quality barrels what money can buy, so there!"

"I swear, if…"

"There's one near Cheadleford," announced Hunter, raising his voice. The others looked at him confused, having forgotten what started the argument. "There's a silver mine about ten miles from Cheadleford. It's a bit of a jaunt, three or four days to be precise."

Stitch shook his head, "How is *three or four*, precise?" he asked.

"If I were by myself, it would be three," replied Hunter. "If Ballorn's leg holds out, it would still be three. However, for the gentile members of the nemilar, it would probably be four."

"So, you think me and Stitch is a couple o' feggers, that we'll slow everything down?" snorted Dannard.

"All I'm saying…"

"Yes!" exclaimed Ballorn, "You'll slow us down!" He pointed at Dannard, "You're the only nemilar I've ever seen sitting down to make a barrel, and Stitch *has* to sit down to do his tailoring. Your legs aren't strong enough to keep up with us, simple as that!"

"I'll try my best," Stitch assured him. "But I do understand. I couldn't possibly stand up to work, my seams would be all over the place if I did that."

"It's only a day!" exclaimed Hunter, "Stop making such a fuss."

"But it's another day out here waiting to be gotted by a beastie what wants us for dinner, ain't it? Another day as we could fall off a cliff or down a big hole as we can't get out of, so we starve to death. No, I isn't doin' that!" Dannard glanced sheepishly at Ballorn, "You can have loan of my coins," he muttered. "But I wants 'em back," he added, wagging his finger at the blacksmith, "When this is all done, I wants them back, do you hear me?"

Ballorn stared at Dannard in disbelief. "So, I melt down your coins and make armour from the silver, Then if we survive the encounter with the crystal dragon, which I very much doubt we will, you want me to re-forge the silver back into coins?"

"Well it don't have to be *exactly* the same, but as long as it's coin-shaped and about the same size."

Ballorn glanced at Hunter. Rubbing his eyes, he sighed, "That settles that then, *we're headed for Cheadleford.*"

"What!" exclaimed Dannard. "But why? I just said as you could have my coins, what more could you want?"

Ballorn waved his hand in dismissal of Dannard's questions. "Hunter, do you know where this silver mine is?"

"It's past the village itself, about ten miles, as I said. But, it's tough going, Ballorn, the rock-face it's set in is a perilously steep climb."

"Excuse me, Ballorn," said Stitch, "I was just wondering. If we travel to Cheadleford, how are you going to pay for the silver? What's more, how are you going to transport it back to Krevick?"

"I'm not going to pay for it!" replied Ballorn, shrugging. "They're going to give it to me. And, they're going to help me bring it back."

Dannard burst out laughing, "Oh yeah, they're gonna do that ain't they! *S'cuse me, can I have a couple of hundred pounds of silver for free? Oh, and while you're at it, sling it on your back and carry it home for me will you?*"

Hunter nodded his head. "He does have a point, Ballorn. You're going to need a heck of a lot of silver to make a full suit of armour, you're not really expecting them to just hand it over, are you?"

"That's exactly what I'm expecting, Hunter, *and more,*" replied Ballorn. "Come on, we may as well just carry on from here. There's nothing worth going back for in Krevick, anything we collect in the form of provisions will be used up by the time we get back here anyway."

"Ooh no, we can't do that!" protested Stitch. "I've not got my travel cloak and I'll need it if we're going that far. My lovely jacket will be ruined if it rains."

"You'll have to survive without it, I'm afraid," smiled Ballorn. "It's not cold and I doubt we'll have any rain for a while, you'll be fine. Trust me," he added, squeezing the tailor's shoulder.

CHAPTER 8

Dannard and Stitch surprised Ballorn and Hunter. Other than the occasional concerned whining from Stitch about his *poor jacket*, they complained very little and managed to reach the outskirts of Cheadleford at the end of their third day.

Dannard curled his lip, "Bit crappy lookin' for a village, ain't it."

Hunter stood next to him, "It was never meant to exist, that's why. It was only supposed to be a settlement until the silver in the mine ran out, but there was far more than anyone had expected. The settlers began to build permanent homes, that meant there was an opportunity for them to open various businesses and trade with the miners. They've only been here a couple of years, Dannard, so don't be too hard on them."

"If you say so," replied Dannard. "But look at 'em all, look at the way they is all glarin' at us! They don't look too friendly to me."

"They've had to put up with a lot," sighed Hunter. "Every vagabond, thief and bandit headed here when they heard that silver had been struck. They've fought off every insurgent who tried to take what was theirs by right. I doubt that there is a single person who has not lost at least one family member to the scum that was drawn here."

"Good evening," came a sudden cry from a nemilar who approached them. He was rather portly to say the least and Stitch covered his face to hide the smirk as the stranger waddled toward them. "Hunter," he continued, "how nice to see you again, and with friends! What brings you to our humble little village, do you have fresh meat and pelts to trade perchance?"

"No, not this time, Senn," replied Hunter. "Our business here is far more important, I'm afraid. Allow me to introduce my friends, Ballorn, Stitch and Dannard," he said gesturing to each in turn. "My friends, this is Senn Pinom. He was chosen by the villagers to be the head of the town council, here in Cheadleford."

Dannard scratched his head, "What's one 'o them?" he asked.

Senn leaned forward slightly and smiled, "Sorry?"

"What's a *cows... thingy*, what he just said?"

"Ah, you mean a council!" laughed Senn. "It's a group of nemilar who gather together in order to decide what is best for the village and all who dwell in it."

"Bit thick your villagers then?" snorted Dannard. "Can't decide for themselves what's good and what ain't?"

Senn looked a little uncomfortable at the slight on the villagers, "Hunter," he said, deciding not to go any deeper into the subject, "you look worn out. Would you care to join me in the tavern? My invitation is extended to your friends as well, of course. The village may not look much, but our hospitality will, one day, be legendary!"

They followed Senn toward the tavern. Stitch could not resist and mimicked his waddle, making sure that none of the locals were watching, of course.

"Funny lookin' ain't 'e," whispered Dannard as he nudged the tailor.

Stitch wasn't really paying attention, far too amused in perfecting his impersonation of Senn. "Who?" he asked quietly.

"Lord Gutbucket there," replied Dannard. "Wonder if he smiles like that all the time? I don't care what Hunter says, I think he's a bit nuts!"

"What's wrong with someone being nice for a change!" exclaimed Stitch. "He's obviously been chosen to lead these people because he *is* nice. If the village is going to grow and be successful, they'll need someone like him to make everyone feel relaxed and happy. In a way, he's like you, you're nice, well, most of the time. You always help people who need it!"

"I'm nothing like him!" hissed Dannard. "I don't go around with a big stupid smile on my face all the time!"

Stitch closed his eyes and shook his head, "I didn't mean… look, can we talk about this later?"

As they neared the tavern, Dannard glanced up at the sign above the door. "*The Hangman's Noose,*" he read slowly. "Well that's really going to make visitors feel welcome ain't it!"

Senn turned and smiled at him, "It is not meant to intimidate… well I suppose it is, in a way."

"Do you always talk such crap?" asked Dannard, placing his hands on his hips.

Stitch nudged him sharply in the ribs, "Don't be so rude!" he exclaimed. "Now apologise!"

"For what?" asked the bewildered Dannard. "How can something not be a warning, but on the other hand *be* a warning?"

"It's alright," chuckled Senn. "I understand what he's getting at." He studied Dannard closely before attempting to explain, "You see, the idea of the name is to show that we'll stand no nonsense or lawlessness. The noose shows the law-abiding citizens that they will be protected from those who are not."

Dannard shook his head slowly and pouted, "Well I think you is just inviting trouble giving the inn a name like that."

Senn smiled again, "Trust me, my dear nemilar, it is as friendly an inn as you would find anywhere. Come inside, you'll see," he said opening the door.

They had taken no more than a few steps inside before Stitch grabbed the back of Ballorn's jacket and tried to hide. "He didn't say there'd be monsters in here!" he whispered. "Look at the size of them, Ballorn! Quick, let's leave before they see us!"

Ballorn glanced around the inn, "What monsters?" he asked with confusion.

"Over there in the corner! Are you blind?" hissed Stitch.

Senn patted him on the shoulder and laughed, "Not monsters," he whispered, "*Men.*"

"Men?" asked Stitch, nervously. "What are *men?*"

"They're much like you and I," Senn assured him. "Only, a little bigger."

"Well I don't like the look of them," replied Stitch, dubiously. "Come on, Ballorn, we need to go before they decide we look tasty and eat us!"

Ballorn wriggled free from his grip, "We aren't going anywhere yet," he grunted. "We have business to conduct, or did you forget about that? Anyway, after three days on the road, I doubt anyone or anything we encounter would want to eat us. Especially him!" he added, pointing at Dannard.

"Is you sayin' I is stinky again?" asked Dannard, glaring at him. "You made me wash just the other day, how could I possibly be pongin' again?"

Ballorn lowered his head in disbelief, "Senn…" he began slowly, "… we should sit and talk."

Senn steered them toward a table, Stitch doing his best to keep as far away from the men as possible.

"I needs an ale," said Dannard, clicking his tongue in the roof of his mouth. "I is as dry as an old stick."

Senn ordered drinks for them all, and they had barely touched the table before Dannard grabbed a mug and slurped noisily from it. "Ooh, that's better," he gasped, ignoring the looks of embarrassment from the other nemilar.

Ballorn turned to face Senn, "We need silver," he said bluntly.

"You've come to the right place then," smiled Senn. "How much do you need?"

Ballorn tilted his head to the side, "Roughly… 150lbs."

"That's a lot of silver, Ballorn," replied Senn. "Why do you need so much?"

"To save the world," said Ballorn, quietly.

"Ha, to save the world!" laughed Senn. "Are we in danger then?" he added, smirking.

"More than you would ever know," replied Ballorn. "Can you help us?"

"But of course we can," grinned Senn. "But tell me, what are you offering in exchange for the silver? Precious stones perhaps, or something even rarer?"

Ballorn locked his fingers together as he leaned on the table and looked deep into Senn's eyes, "Nothing," he replied. "You're going to give it to us, providing you want to live of course."

Two men listening in on their conversation suddenly took more interest in what was being said and sat forward.

Ballorn held up his hand, realising that they had misconstrued his meaning, "I offer no threat, Senn, you have no need to fear us. We have grave news, news that you may find hard to believe."

Senn looked at the men who were now watching them closely and nodded. They sat back, but still watched them intently.

The smile had gone from Senn's face, "Tell me more," he said. "But I warn you, Ballorn, this had better not be a trick. We deal swiftly with swindlers and the like who try to take advantage of our generous nature."

Dannard slammed his empty mug on the table noisily, "I knew it wouldn't be long before he started on about that noose," he sighed. "All they wants is someone to…" he jerked his head to the side, holding his fist above his head and allowing his tongue to hang from the side of his mouth.

***

They spoke for almost an hour before Senn leaned forward and placed his elbows on the table, "Well, I must say, Ballorn, it is a convincing story. But you admit that you can offer no proof of its validity. How can I be sure that once you leave here you would ever return to compensate us?"

"You shouldn't concern yourself with that," grunted Ballorn. "If I don't return, it means that I'm dead. If I die, so will you. The only thing that remains to discover is in which order our deaths will occur."

Senn drummed his fingers on the table, "So, if I don't give you the silver, we will both definitely die. But if I give you the silver, then there is only a chance that both of us will die?"

"Precisely," replied Ballorn. "And no amount of silver has any worth to a dead nemilar."

"Or man," added one of the men.

"I have a suggestion, Ballorn," said Senn. "If what you say is true, does it really matter where you forge the armour? You could make it here and simply wear it on your homeward journey."

Ballorn shook his head, "That's a lot of weight for one nemilar to carry," he sighed. "It would be far more manageable for the four of us to transport the silver between us, but even then, it would be no easy task."

"If, once it is forged, it would be too cumbersome for a lone nemilar to bear on a simple journey, how would he expect to cope with that weight when facing a dragon?" asked Senn with a wry smile.

Ballorn shrugged, "I've asked myself that very same question," he replied, "I was hoping that the dragon may have the answer."

"Ah, you think that the dragon you are hoping to slay is going to give you advice on how to defeat it then?" suggested Senn.

"No, not that dragon," sighed Ballorn. "The other one. The one that's helping us."

"Ah, now it's starting to make sense," sniggered Senn. "One dragon is going to help you to kill another dragon. How silly of me of me to not understand that!"

"I know how it sounds, Senn, but you have to trust me," Ballorn implored him. "There is an honesty in its voice that cannot be mistaken. We can trust its word."

"Or could it have cast a spell on you to make you believe its sincerity? You say you can trust this dragon, but it was reluctant to even give you its name!"

"Not reluctant, only that it would be difficult for me to pronounce!" Ballorn rubbed his hands over his face. "We're going around in circles," he sighed, "it's obvious you're not going to help us. We'll just go. We've wasted enough of your time, and ours."

The four stood, ready to leave, but so too did the men. Their hands rested on the hilts of their swords, it seemed that the four nemilar and the villagers would not be parting on good terms. Before the first man's hand had even fully gripped his sword, he was facing an arrow.

Hunter's movement had been so swift that the man had not even seen him raise his bow, "Take your hands away from your weapons," he said quietly.

The men did as they were instructed.

Senn glared at them, "How dare you treat my guests thus!" he roared. "Get out, both of you."

The second man began to speak, "But, we thought that…"

"You thought? Really? You thought? No, you didn't think, that's your problem, George, *you never think*! Now get out before I have you put in the stocks for harassing our visitors!"

The two men hurried from the tavern. Senn immediately began to giggle, "Don't be too hard on them, Ballorn. They really are lovely chaps, just a bit dim that's all."

"But they were…" began Stitch.

"Mistaken," said Senn, finishing the tailor's sentence, but not as Stitch would have.

Ballorn glanced at Senn, "We'll be off then," he said quietly.

"Aren't you forgetting something?" asked Senn.

Ballorn glanced around, "No, I don't think so," he replied.

"What about the silver?" asked Senn.

"I don't have time for any more discussion, Senn. You've made your decision and I thank you for your time, but we must hasten and rethink our plans if we are to continue with our quest. We'll have to make do with what we have."

"Who said I'm not willing to give you the silver?" laughed Senn.

"You will?" asked Ballorn in surprise. "All it took was a show of arms and you hand it over. So much for the noose being a deterrent!"

"Oh, don't be stupid!" exclaimed Senn, "I decided ages ago that you could have the silver you needed. That little misunderstanding was just... *unfortunate*."

"You'd already decided! So why keep us here all this time?" asked Stitch.

Senn rolled his eyes, "Have you ever had a conversation with a miner? Even worse, with a guard? They're so boring! Bless them all, they are wonderful at what they do but..."

"You is sayin' we can have the silver then? Why? What's the catch?"

"There's no catch!" replied Senn, enthusiastically. "You can have the silver, I'll let you have a couple of carts and ponies to transport it, and I'll even assign those two men as guards to protect us on the way to your home!"

Ballorn's eyes widened, "That's very generous of you, Senn. I, I don't know what to say. Thank you, thank y…"

"Us?" said Dannard, suddenly.

Ballorn stared at him.

"He said *us*. There's your catch, Ballorn. *Fatty wants to go with us… don't you, Fatty!*"

Senn beamed at them, "Oh, absolutely. You don't think I'm going to miss out on an adventure like this do you?"

CHAPTER 9

Their return journey to Krevick was far more difficult than they had envisaged. Many slopes and tracks they had so easily clambered up on their outward trip were far too steep or rocky for the carts to traverse. Time after time a halt was called. They would huddle together, studying the terrain and trying to figure out the best way to steer the ponies so that they, and the carts carrying the silver, could continue safely. As night fell at the end of their first day, they had barely covered half the distance they would have. The carts were slowing them far more than they had anticipated.

"I estimate that the way we is going, it will take us more than a week to get home!"

Ballorn rolled his eyes before staring at Dannard, "Work that out all by yourself, did you?" he sighed.

"Well, we has climbed bigger hills than these before we got to here on the way up."

Ballorn had learned to tolerate Dannard when they were in the village. But out here, in the wilds, there was no escaping the annoying cooper. Turning his back, he wandered away and flopped down behind a boulder where he could no longer hear any of the conversations being held within the camp.

"You too?"

Ballorn glanced up at Hunter. A brief smile flickered on his face, "Yeah..." he chuckled, "... me too."

"I know he's annoying, Ballorn, but he means well."

"I understand that," replied Ballorn holding up his hands in surrender. "But does he have to speak every word that comes into his head? He never shuts up!"

"I thought you'd be immune to his ramblings. You must have known him for a long time. Did you both grow up in the village together?"

Ballorn shook his head, "Good grief, no. I'd have killed him by now if I'd had to put up with him for that long," he laughed. "No," he repeated, "he moved into the village about five years ago."

"And before that?" asked Hunter.

Ballorn shrugged his shoulders, "No idea," he replied. "Never asked him. Then again, we're not exactly what you'd call friends."

"You're not exactly *friendly* with anyone, Ballorn," smiled Hunter. "I just thought you may have heard rumours from the other villagers."

"Oh, I don't listen to tittle-tattle and gossip from all those busy-bodies," snorted Ballorn.

"You must admit though, Ballorn, it is a little intriguing."

"What is?"

"I find it a little odd that a half-decent cooper would choose to set up shop in a village such as Krevick. Admittedly, there were a few individuals who had coin to spend, but surely it would make more sense to open a shop where there was more commerce. He could have made a fortune in Cheadleford, or even that new village where men live."

"What new village?"

Hunter scrunched up his eyes and tapped his brow, "Oh, what's it called?" he mumbled. "Burble! No, that's not it… Bremble…" He paced as he tried to remember, gently slapping his forehead. "Borell!" he suddenly exclaimed, "Yes, that's it… Borell!"

Ballorn snorted, "What a stupid name for a village! Wonder what dumbbell thought that one up?"

"The same man who brought them all out here," replied Hunter. "Dunbar is his name. Very polite man, but you can see in his eyes that you wouldn't want to upset him. And when I say *village*, that's a bit of an understatement. It's huge, there must be at least a thousand people living there."

"And they all look to this Dunbar chap for guidance?"

"Indeed they do, my friend. And rightly so. He's as willing to muck out the pigs as he is to pass judgement on a criminal."

"And I suppose he demands taxes from all the others for his leadership skills?"

"I don't know about that," replied Hunter. "But it seems that the people who live there are his main concern. You should see the size of the fences he's building to keep them safe!"

"Fences are made of wood, Hunter, and wood burns. If the crystal lord gets a sniff of the place it'll be the biggest pyre you've ever seen."

They were interrupted by the sound of footsteps. Stitch eyed them suspiciously, "If you're hungry, Senn has started making everyone some supper. Apparently, he likes to cook."

Hunter smiled at Ballorn, "Well that explains a lot," he snorted, unable to contain his laughter.

"Someone should tell him he doesn't have to eat everything he cooks, and if he does, he should cook less," chuckled Ballorn.

Stitch scowled at them, "How rude!" he exclaimed as he marched away.

As he accompanied Ballorn back into camp, Hunter could not resist the urge to question Dannard about his past. He tried to hide the fact that he was watching him before ambling over and taking a seat on the ground next to him. "How are you coping, Dannard?" he asked with a smile.

Dannard eyed him suspiciously. Very rarely did anyone ask about his wellbeing and when they did he immediately went on the defensive, "I'm fine," he snapped. "Why wouldn't I be? What's it to do with you anyway? Pokin' your nose into other people's business is not polite!"

Hunter's eyes widened, "Well, forgive me for being friendly!" he laughed. "Just making sure you're okay. You know, no blisters on your feet or aching legs. It's a hard trail and you're not used to it."

"How dare you!" exclaimed Dannard. "You can't just walk up to someone and talk to 'em about their legs! My legs is my own concern, not yours. Leave me alone!"

"Ah, but you're wrong, Dannard. Your legs are my concern. If you end up falling behind because of a muscle strain or a turned ankle, you'll slow us all down. Krevick is nice and flat and you're not used to hills like these. I'll bet that your homeland was the same," he sighed. "Where did you say you were from originally?" he asked, trying his best to make his question sound innocent.

Dannard glared at him, "Keep... your... nose... out!" he growled. "Where I is from is also none of your business." He clambered quickly to his feet and stormed away.

Hunter glanced over at Ballorn, "Think I hit a raw nerve there," he said smiling. Ballorn shrugged his shoulders and returned the smile.

Senn joined them and flopped heavily onto the ground, "How's your supper?" he asked. Ballorn and Hunter complimented him on his culinary skills, which was a shame really, because they were both lying when they said it was delicious. The only thing they were convinced of was that it was supposed to be some kind of stew. As they poked around, neither of them recognised any of the ingredients. There were green blobs of what were originally vegetables, but the brown chunks they thought to be meat were a complete mystery. "Oh good," smiled Senn, "remind me to give you the recipe before I leave."

"Leave?" asked Ballorn with surprise.

"Don't worry," laughed Senn, slapping Ballorn's thigh. "I'm not going anywhere yet. I'm intrigued by how my silver will look when it's forged into armour and, to be honest, I had to agree to the villagers demands that I witness it."

"They don't trust us then?" grunted Ballorn.

Senn sat back and folded his arms over his potbelly, "Would you?" he grinned.

Ballorn screwed up one eye and rocked his head from side to side, contemplating the question, "Not really," he replied. "No, I wouldn't."

"Then of course, there's the other thing," whispered Senn.

Hunter frowned, "Other thing?" he asked, sounding surprised. "What other thing?"

Senn's face lit up, "*I get to see a dragon.*"

Ballorn and Hunter glanced nervously at one another. Whilst barely moving, Ballorn could see that Hunter was trying desperately to shake his head. Ballorn held up his hand behind his leg to allay his concerns. "Senn, you do realise how arduous the search for the crystal…"

"Oh don't be so stupid!" laughed Senn, "I'm too old and fat to join you on your quest! I never meant *that* dragon… I meant the other one. The one that's been helping you, the one that told you to make the silver armour!"

"What makes you think we'll be seeing the dragon again before we set off?" asked Ballorn.

"Because he told you to take the armour to him once it was forged." Senn smiled at him. "Don't worry, Ballorn, I got that little nugget of information from your chatty little friend. He never stops talking, blurts everything out as he chunters to himself. I swear he doesn't even realise he's doing it." He leaned forward, "Are you sure it's safe to have him tagging along? If he lets slip what you're up to in front of the wrong people, he could cause you a lot of problems."

Hunter sighed, "We have no choice," he admitted. "We can't leave him to fend for himself, he wouldn't last five minutes."

"I could take him back to Cheadleford with me," suggested Senn.

Ballorn laughed, "If you took him back there with you, he wouldn't last *three* minutes! You've seen how annoying he can be, those miners would probably drag him down a shaft and he'd never be seen again!" He mused over his own statement. "Perhaps that might not be so bad after all," he joked. "No, he's far safer with us, at least we can keep an eye on him."

"Well, if you change your mind, let me know. In the meantime, I'm shattered. I'm going to get some sleep and I suggest you do the same."

"Just one thing," Ballorn said as Senn walked away, "Keep the secret about the dragon to yourself, will you? We don't want to spook your guards."

"Oh them!" shrugged Senn, "Don't worry about them, they already know. As I said, *your friend's a blabbermouth!*"

***

The sweat ran into Ballorn's eye, stinging him like an angry wasp. He balled up his fist and screwed it into the socket, trying his best to contain the rage that was building within him. The breastplate on his bench was beginning to take shape. He tapped as gingerly as he could for fear of repeating his mistake, a mistake he had already made twice. His reticence was clear to see as he faced his third attempted creation of the silver armour. Holding his breath, he brought his hammer down. There was a faint clink. Ballorn roared as he hurled the breastplate, sending it over the counter and out into the street. "STUPID BLOODY IDEA!" he screamed. "HOW IS THIS GOING TO PROTECT ME AGAINST A DRAGON WHEN IT WON'T EVEN WITHSTAND A TAP FROM A HAMMER?"

Stitch watched him with interest. Sitting on the counter, his feet crossed as they dangled, he tentatively spoke to the blacksmith, "Perhaps it needs a lighter touch," he suggested.

"A LIGHTER TOUCH?" shouted Ballorn. "Any lighter and I may as well stroke it with a feather!"

Stitch spoke even quieter than before, "That's the thing, Ballorn, your lightest touch, compared to anyone else's is a bit like… ooh, I don't know how to put this. It's the sort of force a *normal* nemilar would use to knock in a fence post… or a glamoch would use when stamping on your face, or a tree would have when falling on your head."

Ballorn glowered at him, "A *normal* nemilar?"

Stitch was beginning to look nervous, "I don't mean it as an insult," he said hurriedly, "but perhaps someone with a more delicate touch would have more success in shaping the armour."

Ballorn placed his elbows on the counter and leaned closer to Stitch, "So, what you're saying is that we need a *puny* blacksmith to make this armour?"

Stitch shuffled slowly along the counter away from Ballorn, "Not exactly," he replied, grinning, "We couldn't find a better blacksmith than you, Ballorn. If there *are* any other blacksmiths still alive around here, that is. No, what I'm suggesting is that you tell someone else what needs to be done and let them do the hammering."

"You think it's that easy, do you?" Ballorn asked with a grunt. "Do you know how long it takes to learn exactly how to beat metal into shape without destroying it? Well I'll tell you, shall I? HALF YOUR LIFE! And even that's not long enough, because all of a sudden some nosey git suggests you'd be better off clad in a silver suit of armour to protect yourself against a blasted dragon!"

Stitch held up his hands in an attempt to calm Ballorn, "Let's face facts, Ballorn," he said, lowering his voice. "What harm would it do to try? Three times you've shaped that breastplate, and three times you've managed to split the silver."

Ballorn stared at him thoughtfully, "You're not suggesting that the person who might be able to help is you, are you?"

Stitch suddenly became very enthusiastic, "I've worked with every kind of leather and hide you could care to mention," he said reassuringly. "I doubt that working with as soft a metal as silver would offer any difficulties." He smiled, "With the right teacher by my side of course," he added.

Ballorn grabbed Stitch's wrists and turned his hands palm up. The skin on the tips of his fingers was as thick as the leather he had mentioned previously. Although not as strong as the hands of the blacksmith, it was obvious that the tailor was no stranger to hard or difficult work. "You're going to need some gloves," Ballorn muttered, "I've seen babies with tougher skin than yours."

Stitch could not hide the smile on his face, "Where do we start?" he asked.

Ballorn glanced around him, "Well, if you're going to be my apprentice, you get all the crap jobs as well as trying to be the hero by shaping the armour. So there's your first task, go and fetch that breastplate. It landed over there somewhere, I think."

Stitch scurried away.

Many hours later, as night fell, the pair were still hard at work. Hunter passed them a few times during the afternoon, and each time would catch snippets of their conversation before smiling and going on his way. He expected Ballorn to be bawling and shouting at Stitch, but it seemed the blacksmith was as keen to teach the tailor his craft as the tailor was to learn it. But it would be at least a few days before they would complete their task. Hunter would provide their meals, resisting Senn's protestations and reminding him that he was a guest in the village. The truth that his meals tasted dreadful was never mentioned by Hunter or the others, although the relief could be seen on the faces of the guards.

Mark of the Nibrilsiem

On the second evening after arriving in Krevick, they all sat enjoying a much-needed meal. Dannard stood immediately after finishing and headed toward the woods.

"Where are you going now?" exclaimed Stitch, "I'm starting to think we've upset you! Or do you just not like us?" he laughed.

Dannard turned and sniffed, wrinkling his nose as he looked at them in turn. "What is you... *my gaoler*?" he asked. "Has I done something wrong that I does not know about and been made a prisoner by you lot?"

"Of course not," replied Stitch. "But it's dark and you're headed off into the woods again. It's not safe in there during the day, but it's ten times worse at night!"

"I doesn't need anyone holding my hand, thank you," Dannard said slowly. "I can look after myself! I doesn't need someone with a bow like his," he added, pointing at Hunter, "nor a big bag o' muscles with no brain like him," he continued, looking straight at Ballorn.

"Well off you go then," sighed Hunter. "If you get attacked by animals that want you for dinner, give us a shout, will you?" A huge smile appeared on his face, "We'll come and watch."

Dannard snorted and walked away.

Senn shook his head, "He can be a most disagreeable fellow at times, can't he," he sighed.

Ballorn glanced at Hunter before replying, "Oh, you're right there, Senn," he said. "But only on the good days. Most of the time he's an absolute git!"

"Oh, come on!" protested Stitch. "He's not that bad, he just gets a little cranky at times. We all have our good side and bad side."

"Perhaps," said Hunter. "It's just a shame that Dannard only has a backside, and his own head is shoved firmly up it!"

"Where do you think he's going?" asked Ballorn.

"Don't really care," replied Hunter. "But if it means we don't have to listen to his whinging and moaning for a while, he can stay there as long as he likes."

"He just likes his privacy, that's all," mumbled Stitch. "He's always been the same, as long as I've known him anyway."

Ballorn winked at Hunter, "How long have you known him, Stitch?"

"Same as you, I suppose. About five years. Since he moved to the village and set up shop."

"Where's he from, has he ever told you?" asked Hunter.

"No idea," replied Stitch. He glanced up, realising where the conversation was headed, "And *no*, I haven't asked him, it's none of my business. Prying into someone's private affairs would be downright rude!"

Ballorn shrugged his shoulders, "No need to get on your high horse. I just thought that, as you two are so close, you might be able to tell us a bit more about him. You know, things that would help us understand him so that we could make him feel more comfortable and welcome amongst us."

Hunter hid his smirk behind his hand.

"Are you having us on!" exclaimed Senn. "I gave you a load of silver and what did Dannard do? He complained that it was too heavy! That's the sort of person he is!" he laughed.

Stitch was cross with them all, "Just leave him alone!" he exclaimed. "He's done nothing wrong to any of you! Stop picking on him!" He shuffled down and closed his eyes.

CHAPTER 10

Watching the faint orange glow from the cave high above, the cloaked figure drew the hood tightly around his face. The nights here were cold and silent, for the wind, combined with the sub-zero temperatures had rendered the area lifeless. No race nor beast had ever managed to survive the harshness of the terrain.

The stranger continued to study the mouth of the cave. With the slightest twitch of a finger, he disappeared. A split second later he stood watching the occupants of the cave as they slumbered in the relative safety the rock provided. To most they would appear as a most insignificant race, but not to him. When standing they were no more than two feet tall, had spiky hair of various colours with tiny horns poking out of it and cute little tufty beards. Well, the males did. Walking silently, he lowered himself and sat close to the welcoming flames. He meant no harm to anyone within and waited patiently. Whether it would be minutes or hours before any knew of his presence was, to a degree, of no concern. However long it took, it would be worth it. One way or another he would have to be patient if he were to inevitably achieve his goal. He must present his gift, a gift that would ensure the survival of an entire race! Gently rubbing his hands together, he glanced at his surroundings. *How desperate could anyone be for them to seek shelter in such a place?* he wondered.

Looking back at the fire, a glint of light caught his eye. It was the reflection of the flame in the eyes of one the people before him, eyes that were now fixed on *him*. He smiled as he spoke gently, "Do not be alarmed, my friend. I mean you no harm. The night is bitter, and I hoped that you would not mind me warming myself by your fire."

"We're doing no harm, and have nothing worth stealing," replied the resident, cautiously. "I'm just trying to keep my family safe, that's all. Leave us in peace, we're no threat to you nor anyone else. We'll be gone in the morning, I promise. If we're trespassing, I'll rouse my family now and we'll leave straight away. If you're looking to hurt someone, choose me. Just let them go."

The stranger smiled again, "As I have already said, friend, I have no intention of hurting anyone. As for what I wanted from you, well, that you would be willing to allow me a brief respite from the elements." He shuffled slightly closer to the fire, "Although I must say that I am surprised to find anyone here. Why would you choose to be in such a place?"

"Survival," replied the resident.

"Out here in this wasteland?" asked the stranger. "Forgive me, friend, but the climate alone could be the death of you and your family. There must be a fierce calamity awaiting you if you would risk their lives in this barren landscape. There is nothing here."

"Nothing," repeated the resident, solemnly. "Nothing. That's the reason we're out here, sir, because there is *nothing*. We are *alone*. At least, we hoped we were. It seems we were wrong."

The stranger shook his head, "Me, you mean? Oh no, friend, you are wrong. I am just a visitor to these parts, as are you, I deduce."

The resident nodded his head. "Only for tonight though," he whispered. "Tomorrow, well… who knows?"

"So, you're not actually headed anywhere?"

"No, sir, we're not. We just keep moving, hiding, staying as safe as we can."

"Safe from what?" asked the stranger.

"From *them*," replied the resident, his eyes now fixed firmly on the entrance to the cave. "Just seems there's more and more of them. Only a matter of time before they catch up with us, I'm just hoping it'll be a long time before that happens. If I can hide my family somewhere safe and draw them away, they might give up once they get *me*."

"Who are *they*?"

The resident locked eyes with the stranger, "*The dragons*," he whispered.

The stranger looked shocked, "Dragons?" he asked. "There are dragons here?"

The resident looked up at him, "Well, I'm hoping there *aren't*, that's why I brought my family out here. I know the scent of a dragon once it's visited a place, and I don't smell it here."

"But why would a dragon hunt you and your family? No offence but you're not exactly the largest of prey."

"Nothing to do with size, it doesn't see us as food as far as I can tell," growled the resident. "To be honest, I don't know why it wants us. Just a few days ago there were a lot more of us, until the attack." The stranger could hear the anger in his voice beginning to grow as he continued. "It found us. Husbands, brothers, mothers, children, it didn't care. They were trampled, burnt to a crisp by its fiery breath or mercilessly torn apart by its claws and gnashing teeth."

"My dear fellow, that's dreadful!" breathed the stranger. "However did you manage to escape?"

"Sheer luck," replied the resident, lowering his head. "We were in a blind panic. The night was pitch black, but the dragon fire was behind us so we ran as hard as we could. Before we knew what was happening, we were rolling down a huge bank of rock. It was covered with moss and, now I think about it, it must have cushioned our fall. We reached the bottom relatively unharmed, oh, a few bumps and bruises and scrapes and the like, but nothing serious. We hid until daybreak and crept away as quietly as we could. Luckily the dragon never came after us. We just kept moving and luckily, we found this cave and took shelter here."

"And you've obviously managed to evade it since."

The resident nodded, "Know what the strangest thing is?" he asked.

The stranger shook his head.

"Strangest thing is why I'm telling you about it," he said.

His unexpected guest smiled, "I can understand your confusion. People have always seemed to confide in me, it's never been any different. Whenever anyone has a problem or simply needs to bend an ear, they tend to seek me out."

"Why would they do that?" asked the resident, warily. "Who are you?"

The stranger held out his hand, "How rude of me," he chuckled, "Barden," he replied, "Barden Oldman... and I have a gift for you."

***

"Nearly there, Stitch, nearly there," said Ballorn, enthusiastically. "Just a few places that need thinning out a bit and we'll be done. You'll need to use that small mallet over there, grab it for me, will you?"

Stitch reached across, but immediately drew back his hand, "No, I can't pick that up. Not a chance!" he said emphatically.

Ballorn frowned at him, "What do you mean, *you can't pick it up*? You've been using tools twice that size all morning."

Stitch looked sheepishly at him, "No, I didn't mean it's too heavy," he said quietly, "I meant *I can't pick it up.*"

Ballorn looked confused, "Why not?" he asked, impatiently.

Stitch lowered his head, "There's a spider on it!" he whispered.

"What!" exclaimed Ballorn.

"I can't help it!" Stitch squeaked apologetically. "I don't like spiders! All those legs and their beady little eyes." He shuddered, "Ugly, horrible, creepy-crawlies. I can't stand 'em!"

"So, you're alright with chasing after a fifty-foot dragon, but you're scared of a tiny spider!" exclaimed Ballorn.

"Tiny?" protested Stitch, "It's nearly as big as my hand! Look at it! It's just waiting for me to reach for that mallet so it can sink its fangs into me!"

"Then squish it with a different mallet and it won't be able to!"

"What! You mean *kill it*? I'm not going to kill it! It hasn't done anything." He paused, "Alright, it probably would given half a chance, but you can't just kill the thing for something it *might* do!"

Ballorn sighed and lowered his head as he walked toward Stitch. Leaning down, he eyed the spider, "'Scuse me," he said as he flicked it away, "Work to do." Looking over at Stitch, he pointed at the mallet, "Happy now?" he asked. Stitch nodded. "Good!" said Ballorn with another sigh. "Perhaps we can get this finished. Now, the mallet if you would be so kind."

"But, you're right by it. Why don't you just pick it up?"

"Because you're the apprentice, and I said that it was what you would need for us to continue before all this nonsense with the spider. Now, *pick up the mallet.*"

Ballorn would never have admitted it, but he and Stitch made an excellent team. Less than an hour later, the armour was complete. Laid out on the ground were a breastplate, backplate, gauntlets, greaves, and a very impressive helm. Stitch was eager to begin the stage that only he could complete, *the strapping*. He had already prepared the thick leather that would secure the armour to Ballorn. Wielding his needle with a dexterity that impressed the blacksmith immensely, he tested each seam by trying to tear it apart, confident that he would not be able to. He doubted that even Ballorn, with his freakish strength, would have any better luck.

Ballorn had wandered off a few times. There was nothing he could do to help the tailor and knew first-hand how annoying it was to have someone standing over you as you worked. Each time he thought to come back to enquire how Stitch was getting on, he thought better of it and walked away without uttering a word.

"Ballorn," Stitch suddenly called excitedly. "Over here, come and try it on."

Unfortunately for Ballorn, everyone else heard Stitch beckoning him. As he approached the tailor, he was flanked by them all.

"You'll have to help me," Stitch said apologetically, pointing at the breastplate, "I can't lift it on my own. But if you put it on, I'll make the adjustments so it's comfortable."

Ballorn wasn't so much concerned about how comfortable he would be when wearing the armour, he was concerned as to how *uncomfortable* he felt right now. "No need for that," he said clearing his throat, "I'm sure it'll be fine."

"Alright," replied Stitch as he reached down and grabbed the helm. "Look, I've lined it with wool, so it'll be not only comfortable, but warm as well if we end up somewhere cold." He then grabbed the gauntlets, "I've used the softest hide I had for these so they don't chafe your hands, you can't face a dragon if..."

"*Put... it... on.*"

They all turned to see a very serious Senn staring at them. His arms were folded and rested on his ample stomach, an indication that his words were no mere request.

Ballorn disliked being the centre of attention. Declining to try the armour when Stitch suggested it was only due to embarrassment, *but would the same refusal insult their benefactor?* "I made it, Senn. I know it's going to fit me when the time comes to wear it properly."

Senn lowered his head and looked up at him, "I don't like having to say this, Ballorn," he said quietly, "but either you try the armour on, all of it, or I have my guards throw it all on the back of a cart and we haul it back to Cheadleford. This is not about you, this is about all of us. I have chosen to believe in you, and your friends for that matter, but you're more concerned about feeling daft in front of us. Imagine meeting up with this dragon you've told us about and not being able to cover yourself quickly enough because that armour isn't properly adjusted. You're as likely to become a pile of ash as the poor villagers who once filled this village, Now, be a good chap and let the tailor do his work."

Ballorn shrugged and held out his arms in submission, "Alright," he sighed. "If you insist." He marched over to

Stitch, "Come on, I'll be your tailor's dummy," he said, placing the plate against his chest.

Stitch called Senn's guards over, "Could you be so kind as to hold the backplate in place whilst I attach the straps, please?" he asked politely.

"Bloody dragons… armour… silver… standing like a right wally with everyone watching me like it's some sort o' sideshow."

"Oh, do stop chuntering, Ballorn," chuckled Stitch. "This won't take long."

Soon, Ballorn was fully adorned, "Satisfied?" he grunted as he lowered the helm onto his head. He had been almost spot-on with his prediction, as very little adjustment had had to be made for his creation to fit perfectly. Had it been broad daylight, the armour undoubtedly would have gleamed. But, as the sun sank below the horizon, it glowed fiery red, giving it an impressive, yet menacing appearance. Although very plain, there was still a magnificence to it.

Senn smiled, "That's some grand work that is, Ballorn. You and Stitch should be proud of yourselves."

"Thank you," replied Stitch with a beaming smile.

"Whatever!" grunted Ballorn.

"Hmph," snorted Dannard. "All this 'cause a dragon told him he is this *sebrinilim* thing."

"*Nibrilsiem,*" said Hunter correcting him.

Ballorn's head began to swim. He stumbled and fell to one knee. *What was happening to him, what was the voice in his head trying to tell him?* He could hear it but the words it spoke made no sense. It was a language unlike anything he had heard before. All he could decipher, and even that was a shock to him, was one word that the voice repeated over and over... *anvil*.

"Ballorn? Are you alright?" asked the panic-stricken Stitch.

Ballorn looked up, "Yes," he said breathlessly, "I'm fine. What happened?"

"You just keeled over," replied Hunter, helping him to his feet.

"Just keeled over, my arse," yelled Dannard. "What was all them strange words he was saying then? That ain't like what no speech I has ever heard."

Ballorn was still swaying slightly. Hunter wrapped the blacksmith's arm around his shoulders, "Ignore him, Ballorn. Let's get you sat down."

"It's the armour!" exclaimed Stitch. "It's too heavy for him! He only had it on ten minutes and look what it's done to him. How can he face a dragon, well, anything if he can't even stand up in it?"

As Hunter sat him down, Ballorn grabbed Hunter's shoulder and pulled him close, "The voice?" he asked shakily, "Did you hear the voice?"

"All I heard, and regrettably so did everyone else, was your voice, my friend. However, you were speaking in a tongue that none of us recognised."

Ballorn stared at the ground, shaking his head occasionally whilst trying to regain his thoughts. "Not possible," he whispered, "I don't know any foreign languages." He smiled weakly, "Unless of course you count Dannard."

"Ah, you must be feeling a bit better," said Hunter with a sigh of relief.

"Is that what the problem is, Ballorn?" asked Senn with genuine concern. "Is the armour too much for you to bear?"

"It's nothing to do with the weight of the armour!" yelled Ballorn. "This is... *something else.*"

"So, when the dragon gobbles us all up, we doesn't have to blame the armour. All we has to say is that it was *something else* what caused it. We can die knowing that all of this wasn't just a big stinkin' waste o' time!"

Hunter glared at Dannard, "Remember when we first met, Dannard? I still have that arrow if you want it."

Senn wagged his finger at Ballorn, "It must have something to do with the dragon," he said slowly. "It all makes sense if you think about it. It told you that you needed to make the armour and that you must use silver. Everything was fine until you put it on, wasn't it? Do you think it knows that you have completed your task and is somehow trying to communicate with you?"

Hunter raised his eyebrows, "He may be right, Ballorn. Who knows what powers those creatures hold, besides breathing fire and tearing people apart, of course?"

"Not me, that's for sure," replied Ballorn. "There's one thing I do know though... I'm knackered. Help me get this lot off, Hunter. I'm going to have an early night."

CHAPTER 11

They set off early the following morning, but not before Ballorn had caused a bit of a stir with his unusual request.

"What do you want to take that for?" shrieked Stitch. "You can't use it up there! You've seen the place, what use would it be to you? I've heard of people taking their work with them, but this is ridiculous!"

"I don't *want* to take it with me, I *need* to take it with me, I *have* to take it with me. I don't know why!"

"Oh, that's alright then, it's much clearer to me now," replied Stitch, mockingly. "It makes no sense, Ballorn!"

"It makes as much sense as trolling across the wilds for weeks to find a pile of silver! It makes as much sense as turning that silver into a suit of armour. To top it all is that it makes as much sense as a brackin *dragon* telling us to do it! So, let's just get some ropes and get it loaded onto the cart!" Ballorn ranted.

"You're sure about this?" asked Hunter. "We couldn't just come back for it if we need to?"

Ballorn leaned in and whispered, "All I know is that the voice in my head kept repeating one word… 'anvil'. It said it over and over as if it didn't want me to forget. I know it's a lot to ask, you've just got to trust me."

Hunter smiled at him, "Okay then, let's get it loaded. You tie it off and I'll go and fetch the cart and Senn's guards. We're going to need them to lift it."

There was much grunting, groaning, and a few choice phrases directed toward Ballorn, that were far from complimentary, as the anvil was eventually secured on the back of the cart. Once it was loaded they set off in the direction of Lonny's devastated farm. Many things made the trip far easier than the last time they had visited, what little remained of, the missing farmer's family home. They had a cart and were therefore relieved of the burden of having to carry anything they may need, the party had almost doubled in size giving them the strength to fend off any animal attacks and, more importantly, Ballorn's leg was now perfectly healed allowing him to set a brisk pace as he marched ahead of the procession.

"This might be a stupid question…"

Ballorn rolled his eyes, not even looking back at Dannard as he awaited his next gem of observation. "You don't say!" he sighed.

Dannard seemed oblivious to Ballorn's tone as he continued, "Why is we bothering to go back to see the dragon again? We has the armour now. Alright, it's a bit dull and boring, but it'll do the job won't it? Stop you being frizzled and all that."

"Because he told us we need to," called Stitch. "He has more to tell Ballorn that could help us win against that horrible monster that's killing everyone. If we can find it, of course."

"There's no *if*," said Ballorn, correcting him, "*When*. When we find it."

Dannard's eyes widened, "Ooooh," he gasped. "What if it isn't alone? What if it's got some other dragons to go with it and they is all attacking villages together?"

"Then I'll slay them too!" Ballorn growled. His show of bravado was impressive, but Dannard's question was a valid one. The mere suggestion that anyone would think that they could face a dragon and survive would, without doubt, cause others to question the sanity of that person. The fact that Ballorn was now contemplating that he may have to face multiple dragons would have him branded as a lunatic by any nemilar, present company excepted.

Hunter appeared suddenly behind Dannard and slapped him on the back, startling the cooper. "If it's not alone we'll just join in," he announced with apparent glee. "After all, they'll only be fire-breathers or ice dragons. Just remember not to engage them head on and you'll be quite safe," he added, laughing. He caught up with Ballorn, turned his head, and winked at him.

Dannard frowned, "Oh really!" he exclaimed, calling after them. "And what if they decides to stamp on me and squidge me?"

"Well," smiled Hunter, briefly glancing over his shoulder and looking him up and down, "you're only a little chap. You wouldn't leave much of a mess, we'd scrape you up in no time."

Dannard glared at him, "That isn't funny!" he exclaimed. "Talking about me getting…"

His objections and complaints continued for many miles.

***

It was mid-afternoon when Ballorn eventually announced, for the benefit of the newcomers, that they were nearing the dragon's resting place. Senn's nerve began to faulter. "Perhaps…" he said apprehensively, "… you should go on alone," he gulped. "After all, it knows who you are. It wouldn't do to startle it, who knows what it might do if it feels threatened."

Ballorn surveyed him through half-closed eyes, "Firstly…" he said slowly, "… it's *him*, not *it*. Secondly, *he already knows we're here* and how many of us there are. Thirdly, and most importantly of all, *he would not feel threatened if there were ten times as many in our group!*"

Senn's eyes darted from side to side in panic. He spoke, his voice barely a whisper, "You mean, *he's watching us? He's watching us right now?*"

"Of course he's not watching us, you fool!" Do you think he has nothing better to do? He just *knows*." A mischievous grin appeared on Ballorn's face as he turned away. "Well, he won't be watching *us* anyway… however… he might be keeping an eye on *you*."

Senn backed away and took refuge behind his guards.

Ballorn sighed, "Fine!" he said loudly. "You'll probably start asking stupid questions anyway." He walked away, followed closely by Hunter, "You don't have to tag along if you don't want to," he announced.

"Raging storms and rockfall wouldn't keep me from your side, Ballorn. We started this little adventure together and I intend to remain by your side until it is done."

"How very noble of you," said Ballorn, a hint of scepticism in his voice.

"Me?" laughed Hunter. "Oh no, it's not nobility. Well, maybe a bit. I'm just naturally inquisitive."

"You mean you're a nosey git?"

Hunter smiled widely, "Yeah… that's the one."

They slowed their pace and Ballorn began to call for the dragon, "We have returned," he announced loudly. He waited momentarily but there was no reply. He glanced at Hunter and shrugged his shoulders, "We have constructed the armour as you instructed."

"I'm not deaf," yawned the dragon as he moved toward them. "Nor am I blind. I know time is not on your side, little one, but all you had to do was sit and wait a few moments. Instead you choose to let the whole mountain know of your presence."

"If you didn't keep hiding, I'd know where you were and wouldn't have to shout!" protested Ballorn.

Hunter caught his eye and shook his head. He felt that getting into an argument with a dragon would not be the wisest decision one could make. "Our apologies," he said, his voice taking a gentle tone as he turned his attention to the dragon. "We weren't sure if you were still here. Our task took far longer than we had anticipated and feared that you may have had more pressing matters to contend with and moved on."

The dragon lowered his head, the pupils of his enormous eyes narrowing as he peered at Hunter, "More pressing matters?" he asked. "What would be more pressing than the eradication of all life on our world?"

Hunter tilted his head to one side as he gazed up at the dragon, "I hadn't given it much thought until now," he replied slowly.

The dragon snorted, tiny wisps of smoke drifting from his nostrils, "Evidently."

"Can we stop picking faults with each other?" Ballorn asked, impatiently. "You gave us instructions and we followed them. I've made the armour and now I've…" he glanced at Hunter, who had raised his eyebrows at Ballorn's use of the singular description, "… *we* have returned."

"But only with the aid of our new-found friends," added Hunter. "One of them is quite fat, so if you fancy a snack, he'd be the one I'd choose."

"Hunter!" exclaimed Ballorn.

"I'm joking!" Hunter laughed. "I know our friend here wouldn't really eat him." He paused, "He'd want something with more muscle than fat… *you'd* be first on the menu." Both the dragon and Ballorn were now staring at him. He lowered his head and cleared his throat. "I suppose we should get on," he announced, his voice taking a more serious tone. "Shall I fetch the armour?" he asked, looking for any excuse to escape the uncomfortable situation he had placed himself in.

"No," replied the dragon. "That must wait until nightfall. Go back to your fellows and wait until you are summoned. Ballorn and I have much to discuss."

***

"Why me?" asked the vikkery. "Why *us*, in particular?"

"The reasons are many, dear friend. None of which, I'm afraid, I am at liberty to divulge. Simply know that you are the only ones who can end the reign of terror with which the dragon is tormenting our world."

"We do not lack courage, Barden, of that you can be assured! Neither do we lack intellect. The dragon is a colossus and we are small and few. How could we possibly defeat such a gargantuan enemy?"

Barden peered at him, "What if I were to give you the ability to be more than you are? Would that give you the courage to face the one responsible for the deaths of scores of your kin?"

The vikkery stared at Barden, the flickering of the firelight enhancing the look of rage in his eyes, "If I had something that I thought would give me even half a chance," he said shuffling forward, "I'd face it head on and consequence be damned!"

"Good!" growled Barden, "That's the mindset I've been looking for. Strength is measured by the heart, friend, not merely physical ability."

"You seem very sure of yourself, Barden, and even moreso of us. Do you have a weapon with which we could kill the dragon?"

"Indeed I do, my friend, indeed I do. Something far greater than a cumbersome tool or weapon that one can wield wildly and be lost or broken on the battlefield." He pointed at the resident. "I have you, I have... *the vikkery.*"

The vikkery looked confused, "Help me understand," he began. "You are saying that you will not present us with a weapon, but that we *are* the weapon?"

"Not yet, but I can make it so," replied Barden, calmly. "I must be honest, however, you must agree to my terms before I can hand you this great gift. No less than a solemn promise will suffice before you can receive it."

The vikkery sat forward, "Name your terms, Barden," he growled. "If you can offer us anything that gives us the power to destroy that filth, you'll have my promise."

Barden stroked his beard thoughtfully with one hand whilst drumming the fingers of the other on his thigh, "What is your name?" he asked.

"Gelbran," replied the vikkery.

"And I trust that you are allowed to speak for the rest of your clan?"

Gelbran nodded his head, "I am," he replied. "I cannot see behind me, but I would think that by now they are all awake and listening to what's being said."

Barden smiled, "They are," he confirmed. "And it speaks volumes that you have not taken your eyes off me since our meeting began. You were, and possibly still are, unsure whether I am friend or foe, but I can assure you that it is not the latter."

"Well I can assure you, Barden, that if I or any of my people thought that was so, this discussion of ours would have been over long ago."

"Good," said Barden. "That means that I was correct in my estimation of the vikkery. You are indeed worthy of the gift."

"What is this gift going to cost us?" asked Gelbran. "Sacrificial offerings, perhaps? A share in any valuables or profits in future ventures? Perhaps my unborn child?"

Barden laughed loudly as he shook his head, startling the vikkery who were behind Gelbran. "Oh, no, no, no," he chortled. "Dread the thought."

"Good," said Gelbran. "Ask what you will but my kin must be protected, as must my little Grubb."

"Little *what*?" asked Barden.

"My unborn child," replied Gelbran. "It's what me and the missus call him, or her, until we choose a proper name."

"Well, there will be no offerings or sacrifices involved," Barden assured him. "Your oath to me will be made up of two parts, Gelbran. Firstly, you must promise that, whenever and wherever you encounter *any* dragon, you must slay it without mercy. Secondly, and this is the most important part, when you find the one responsible for the murder of the rest of your kin, *you must remove the crystal embedded in its brow and present it to me.*"

Gelbran's face wore a grim expression, "Give me what I need to defeat it and I'll present you with its entire mangy carcass," he hissed. "You have my word."

Barden nodded slowly. Opening his palm, he blew gently. A faint, pale pink mist began to fill the entire cave, enveloping the vikkery. One by one they became drowsy. Then, succumbing to the mist, each of them fell into a deep sleep.

***

"The armour is strong, dragon, but I fear that it will be of little use."

"You need not fear, Ballorn. I am sure it will be up to task."

"Of that I have no doubt," replied Ballorn. "That is not the issue. I'm no weakling, dragon, but I can barely move in it because of the weight! I haven't mentioned it to the others, but I'd struggle to repel any attack if I was wearing all of it."

"It'll be fine," the dragon assured him. "It's not finished yet."

"What do you mean, *it's not finished yet*? Of course it's finished! I made it!"

"You'll understand later," sighed the dragon dismissively, "We have other things to discuss. "What about my name?"

"Sorry?" said Ballorn.

"*My name,*" repeated the dragon. "You were going to give me a name."

"Oh that," replied Ballorn, quietly.

"Yes *that,*" said the dragon. "Or had you forgotten?"

"Oh no, I hadn't forgotten," replied Ballorn. "I just hope that you like the name I've chosen, that's all."

The dragon lowered his head and peered at the nervous nemilar, "Well?"

"Kel…" mumbled Ballorn.

"What? Speak up, I can't hear you."

Ballorn took a deep breath, "Keldenar," he said clearly.

The dragon thought for a moment, "Yes," he said approvingly, "I like that, I like that a lot. It has a certain ring to it, an air of nobility. What does it mean?"

"Raging fire," Ballorn replied, "Well, it's made up of two words, *keld* means rage and *denar* means fire. Mashed up together they just seemed to fit you perfectly."

"But how would you know?" asked the dragon. "You've never seen me in a rage. Come to think of it, you've never seen me so much as cross."

Ballorn placed his hands on his hips as he glared at the dragon, "It was a guess!"

The dragon lay flat on the ground as he studied Ballorn, "Well you guessed correctly," he said, his smile unnerving Ballorn who was now viewing two rows of intimidating, razor-sharp teeth. "I have been known to be a little tetchy on occasion. Thank you so much, Ballorn, it's perfect."

"Happy to help," said Ballorn with a sigh of relief. "Now, what else did you want to discuss?"

"*Keldenar,*" said the dragon quietly. "*Keldenar,*" he repeated more confidently. "*I am Keldenar*!" he finally announced aggressively, raising his head for effect.

Ballorn rolled his eyes, "*Yes*!" he said impatiently, "Your name is Keldenar. Now can we get on?"

"Terribly sorry, Ballorn," said Keldenar, "I've never had a new name before. It's very exciting!"

Ballorn folded his arms, raised his eyebrows and began tapping his foot, "Well?" he asked bluntly.

"Yes," said Keldenar, lowering his head back to the ground. "You are about to embark on a very dangerous quest, Ballorn, of that I am convinced."

"Get on with it!"

"As time passes it will become increasingly dangerous and some of your friends may not survive."

Ballorn wobbled his head, "Well, there's one I'm not particularly bothered about," he said honestly, "but I'll do my best to keep the others out of danger."

"Perhaps," said Keldenar. "However, regardless of what you may encounter, you must promise me one thing."

"Which is?" sniffed Ballorn, a little disinterested by Keldenar's request.

"There is no doubt that you will come across more than one dragon on your travels, Ballorn, but you must not kill them! In fact, you must do them as little harm as possible if you are to eventually find and destroy the crystal lord."

Ballorn frowned, "Seriously!" he exclaimed. "You're telling me that if one of your lot attacks me I can't defend myself! What am I supposed to do, have a nice chat with it while it's chewing on me?"

"I never said you can't defend yourself, Ballorn," replied Keldenar. "I only said that you must not kill them. If you are forced to engage them in battle, you must restrain yourself and not deal a fatal blow. After all, they will be nowhere near as strong as you!"

Ballorn's mouth fell open, "Am I hearing things?" he asked in amazement. "I've just told you I can't even take a step in that armour without falling flat on my face! If I don't even have the strength to do that, how could I possibly be stronger than one of you lot?"

Keldenar closed his eyes and shook his head, "I know you're not strong enough now," he sighed, "but you will be soon."

"Oh that's alright then!" exclaimed Ballorn. "What am I going to do, grow some more muscles overnight? Or perhaps I'll sprout extra arms and legs to help me get out of the way when a dragon tries to flatten me?"

"Now you're just being silly," snorted Keldenar. "Just wait until tonight and all will become clear."

Ballorn did as he was asked. He headed back to the others and suggested that they make camp a short distance from Keldenar.

"Charming!" said Dannard in a high-pitched voice. "We is good enough to trek all the way to Cheadleford for him, we is good enough to find enough silver for you to have your armour and we is good enough to haul it all back here, but we isn't good enough to be in his company! *What a cheek*!"

Ballorn rolled his eyes, "He said he needed to be alone to prepare himself," he sighed. "It's nothing to do with not wanting us nearby... well, I suppose it is but only because he needs to concentrate without any distractions."

"That's what he says! We could be quiet, he wouldn't hear a peep out of us, at least not from me anyway."

"You?" laughed Hunter. "You're about as distracting as anyone *could* be."

"How dare you!" exclaimed Dannard, "I'll have you know..."

"Calm down, Dannard!" Stitch urged him. "He just means that you like to be informed, and you do ask a lot of questions."

"And you wouldn't want to run the risk of upsetting a dragon, would you?" suggested Hunter. "One swipe of his tail or a misplaced step and... *splat*!"

Dannard's eyes widened, "Well..." he gulped, "I wouldn't want to get in the way whilst he, erm... preperates himself. I think right here would be just dandy for a campsite."

Hunter smiled, "Good idea," he said, "I'll grab some firewood."

Time went slowly as they waited. Endless times Ballorn glanced up at the sky, but each time he did, the sun seemed to have barely moved, "How long is this going to take?" he groaned, the frustration clear in his voice.

"Until it's dark," mumbled Senn. "You did say nightfall, didn't you?"

"I know what I said! It's just, it's just... oh, shut your face, Senn!"

"Why don't you try to get some rest, Ballorn?" suggested Stitch. "After all, I'm sure that the dragon's preparations will have something to do with you."

"His name is *Keldenar*, and why would what he's doing have anything to do with me?"

"That's any easy one," said Hunter. "Allow me. All of this has something to do with you, you fool. *You* were the one who was attacked; *you* were the one he healed with magic; *you* were the one he told the secret of the silver armour to and finally, *you* are the one who'll be wearing it! Why would you suddenly be excluded from anything?"

Ballorn stared at him thoughtfully, "Alright, smarty pants, what do you think he's up to?"

"Ooh, I know!" exclaimed Stitch. "Maybe he's going to give you some of his magic so that you can breathe fire like he does."

"Or you'll grow scales like his so you can't be frizzled," smiled Dannard.

Ballorn shook his head in disbelief, "So why would I need the poxy armour then?"

Dannard opened his mouth, thought for a second, then closed it again, "Hadn't thought about that," he mumbled.

Ballorn sat up and wagged his finger, "I've just remembered," he said quickly, "He said the armour wasn't finished yet!"

"So it's something to do with the armour?" suggested Hunter.

"It must be," replied Ballorn, "It's the only thing that makes sense."

"So that's why you had us drag the anvil all the way here?" asked Senn.

"I suppose so," said Ballorn.

"You *supposes* so!" exclaimed Dannard. "You mean you doesn't know? You never asked it, I mean *him*?"

Ballorn shook his head, "Never even thought about it," he admitted.

"Well we'll find out soon enough," said Hunter winking at him. "Just keep your fingers crossed that it doesn't hurt too much."

Once that thought had entered his mind, the time seemed to pass far more rapidly for Ballorn. He had managed to snooze for a while, much to the relief of the others, whom he berated constantly as his mood began to change. He had become anxious, but the angst soon turned to agitation. It reached a stage where his companions were reluctant to move, speak or even look in his general direction and all were grateful when he began to snore gently. Even Senn's guards, despite being much larger than the bad tempered nemilar, breathed a sigh of relief.

"Thank goodness for that," whispered Dannard, glancing over nervously at Ballorn to make sure that he *was* definitely asleep.

"Wouldn't you be a little unsure if the weight of the world rested on your shoulders?" asked Senn.

"But we is here to help him! Honest," insisted Dannard. "Why would I be here if I doesn't want to?"

Senn placed his hand on Dannard's shoulder, "The only way that any of us can help him right now is to keep our voices down and let him sleep," he smiled.

Ballorn was actually relieved when he was awoken from his troubled dreams. He saw raging infernos and heard deafening roars. He saw nemilar fleeing desperately before they were engulfed by flames, their screams piercing through his very soul as he stood there powerless to save them. He woke with a start, his eyes wild.

"Are you alright?" asked Hunter.

"Course I am!" snapped Ballorn. "What do you expect when you shake someone awake like that!"

Hunter had barely touched his shoulder to rouse him but had not spoken. "Sorry, Ballorn, I can be a little heavy-handed at times," he lied.

"What do you want anyway?"

"It's getting dark, Ballorn," Hunter informed him, "I thought it might be time to see what the dragon's next instructions are."

"Keldenar," Ballorn reminded him.

"Yeah," smiled Hunter, "*Him.*" Reaching down, he grabbed Ballorn's arm and pulled him to his feet.

The others were trying to make themselves look busy, not wanting to make eye contact with Ballorn.

"Sorry, you lot," called the blacksmith, "Must have been a bit tired, I always get tetchy when…"

"You doesn't say!" exclaimed Dannard. "We never would have noticed!" He gently tapped the hindquarters of the pony pulling the cart and it began to trundle up the hill toward Keldenar.

"Ballorn, you're not on your own," said Hunter, quietly. "You do realise that don't you?"

Ballorn looked into his friend's eyes, "Oh, really," he replied, smiling. "Where's your silver armour then?"

"Come now, Ballorn. How could I climb trees and give cover if I was encumbered by a cartload of silver?" laughed Hunter.

Ballorn raised his eyebrows, "Come on, let's catch up with the others before Dannard gets himself eaten."

"Ah yes," replied Hunter, "But not too quickly, there's no rush."

CHAPTER 12

Barden's eyes moved from vikkery to vikkery. He had studied them for some time before making his decision. Yes, they were small in stature, but there was something about them that gave him hope. Since their encounters with dragons their number was significantly depleted, and their diminutive stature and insignificance would hopefully render them inconspicuous. They had a natural distrust of strangers since becoming the prey of dragons and would stay hidden from prying eyes, perfect agents for him as they hid in the shadows. Should they succeed they would bring him his prize. Should they fail, the result, for them at least, would be the same. They would be eradicated. His gaze fell on the form of one of the female vikkery. Her stomach was swollen and Barden thought back to what Gelbran had said earlier... his unborn child. "Not you, little one," he said quietly. "You need something else." Placing his hand gently on the tiny vikkery's stomach, he closed his eyes. A bright blue light pierced through the pink vapour that still lingered in the cave. "We can't have all of you on the battlefield," Barden whispered. "There must be someone left to care for the wounded. You and your mother will be the healers amongst the warriors of your kin." Moving to the entrance of the cave, he looked down at Gelbran sleeping peacefully. A glint flashed in his eyes as he spoke one word, "Remember."

It was daylight when Gelbran awoke. His head was swimming as he turned to see his people still sleeping. He rubbed his eyes, trying his best to remember the events of the previous night. He stumbled to his feet, walked to the entrance of the cave and looked over the edge. *Was the stranger real or had it all been a dream*? His head was beginning to clear, but for some reason there was a strange voice in his head, a voice that kept repeating a single word, *remember*. Venturing back inside, he sat down.

Looking across, he saw his wife. "Has he gone?" she asked.

"So I wasn't dreaming then?"

His wife shook her head, "No, my love, you weren't dreaming. We all saw him."

Gelbran stared at his feet, trying harder to remember. Holding out his hands, he stared at his palms. His eyes grew wider as they began to change shape. His fingers began to knit together as fur sprouted from them. His fingernails became claws and his arms thickened. He looked up at his wife, his eyes were different, but panic stricken nonetheless, and she began to scream.

The rest of the vikkery, awoken by the screaming, scrambled to the back wall of the cave. Gelbran was horrified. The stranger had tricked him, he was somehow cursed, turned into a beast of which his people were now terrified. He tried to speak, wanting desperately to assure them that it was still him, but instead of words leaving his lips, he let out an enormous roar. He clamped his hands

Mark of the Nibrilsiem

over his mouth. *How could he tell his family that he meant them no harm?* He fell to the floor and began to sob.

Then the strangest thing happened, *the cave fell silent.* Gelbran looked up, but now it was his turn to be afraid. The vikkery were gone and in their place stood many huge brown bears and an entire pack of wolves. Gelbran breathed a sigh of relief, *he was still dreaming.* He had to be. If this were real there was no way that even this many bears and wolves could devour his kin so quickly, and there was no blood either. Despite the peculiarity of his dream, Gelbran began to laugh. He looked at his paws. "This is fantastic!" he said aloud.

"I'm glad you think so!" shrieked his wife. "Look at us! Why would the stranger do such a thing?"

Gelbran laughed even louder, "Oh, this is hilarious. I can't wait to tell you about this when I wake up!"

"Oh really?" said his wife, looking down at her stomach. "Well you tell me this then clever-clogs! Have you ever had a dream this realistic before?"

Gelbran looked at the bump, "But you're… even in a dream?"

"It's not a dream you fool, that stranger's turned us all into forest creatures, carnivorous ones!"

"No, no, no," scoffed Gelbran. "You watch this then." Closing his eyes, he whispered, "I'm a vikkery, I'm a vikkery." Opening them he looked at his hands, yes, *hands*. "See, if this wasn't a dream, how could I do that?" However, he was still looking at bears and wolves who were still growling and roaring. "It's a dream, I turn you back into vikkery," he shouted, but nothing happened. *How strange*, he thought.

Suddenly, his wife began to transform until she was, well, his wife. She stared at Gelbran. "It's real," she mouthed. "We can really change shape!" She became very excited, "Gelbran, think of something else, a different beast you can change into!"

Gelbran was confused, "Like what?"

"Erm…a horse, turn into a horse!"

"Calm down!" yelled Gelbran, "Think about the baby."

"Never mind the baby, turn into a horse!" she ordered.

It only took a few seconds. When he looked down again, there were the long legs and hooves. He had transformed into a horse. His wife had a beaming smile on her face. "He was telling the truth, my love. He gave us something that can help us destroy those dragons."

Gelbran had changed back, "I'm starting to remember even more now!" he said. "We have to be careful, we're not all the same!" He added with urgency, "If we turn into anything too big, *we could all go pop*!"

***

Keldenar sat up as Ballorn approached, "Ah, good," he said. "You're ready."

"*I'm* ready?" exclaimed Ballorn. "I've been waiting all day because *you* told me to!"

Keldenar collected his thoughts, feeling the need to expand on his statement, "I meant that you are now mentally prepared," he said.

"Or just mental," mumbled Stitch. Ballorn gave him a hard look. "Well you must admit that this isn't normal," added the tailor. "You have no idea what he's got in store for you, but you're going to let him do it anyway!"

"Surely if I meant any one of you harm, you would have known it by now?" sighed Keldenar.

"Just ignore him," grunted Ballorn, his eyes still fixed on Stitch. "Let's get on with it, whatever *it* is."

Senn tugged gently at Hunter's sleeve, "Doesn't any of this bother you?" he whispered. "That dragon's growling and roaring and they're talking to it as if it's normal!"

"That's because we can understand what he's saying," replied Hunter. "Keldenar gave us the gift before we set out for Cheadleford."

"Really," said Senn slowly, intrigued by the thought. "Do you think he'd be willing to share the gift with me?"

Hunter looked him up and down, tilting his head to one side as he considered the question, "Erm, well... no!" he said adamantly.

"Lay the armour on the ground before me," ordered Keldenar. Each piece was carried and arranged at his feet. "Now, Ballorn, kneel behind it facing me." He leaned down and scrutinised the workmanship, "You've done well," he said slowly. "I feared that you may be a little heavy-handed to skilfully shape so soft a metal."

"Now that you mention it," admitted Ballorn. "I did have to rely on some help with the more intricate parts."

Stitch puffed out his chest.

"Oh I know that," said Keldenar, "I never said it was perfect, I can see the faults. But never mind those, you'll never notice once I'm done. And before you start fretting, it won't affect the strength either."

"FAULTS?" shouted Stitch, loudly. "FAULTS! How dare you! I'll have you know that my skills as a…"

Keldenar turned to face the enraged tailor and blew gently. A fine wisp of smoke shot from his left nostril and immediately disappeared up Stitch's. The tailor instantly stopped shouting as a dreamy look swept over his face and a silly smile raised the corners of his mouth. It happened so quickly that none of them had a chance to feel alarmed by what had happened.

Senn, once again, tugged on Hunter's sleeve, "Do you think he'd teach me that one then?" he sniggered.

Keldenar beckoned toward Hunter, "Stand behind Ballorn," he instructed.

Hunter stepped forward warily.

"Come along," Keldenar said gently. "There is nothing to fear."

Hunter took his position. Any good reason to follow the direction of the dragon seemed to be eluding him, but he had promised Ballorn that he would stand with him through thick and thin, and it was a promise he would not abandon lightly.

"Now, both of you, close your eyes and relax," continued Keldenar.

"Easy for him to say," Hunter mumbled to Ballorn. "He knows what's going to happen."

Keldenar opened his jaws. An eruption of flame surrounded the two nemilar, unbeknownst to them, but they remained unharmed. Senn panicked and was about to rush forward, when Stitch grabbed his arm, smiled and pointed, "They're alright," he said dreamily, "look, the fire's not so much as scorching them."

"Good grief!" whispered Senn with excitement, "Look at the armour!"

Neither Ballorn nor Hunter had ever felt more alive. The warm breeze enveloping them was invigorating. They felt strong, refreshed in a way they had never felt before. It was as if they were floating, unrestricted by gravity or even the weight of their own bodies. In their minds they could see one another, surrounded by an aura that made them glow. Their thoughts were as one as they basked in the freedom of, what could only be, their shared hallucination.

What the rest of the party was witnessing, however, was slightly different. The two guards had sought shelter behind the cart, but Senn, Stitch and Dannard watched with open mouths. They were transfixed by the sight of their two friends suspended in mid-air, whirling around like spinning tops.

The golden aura that surrounded them illuminated the entire area, mesmerising the onlookers. The eruption of flame from Keldenar had only lasted a few seconds but had obviously been a catalyst to set the whole scene in motion.

The spectator's eyes were so wide that any onlooker would have been forgiven for believing that they would fall out of their sockets at any moment. This was the result of, not only their friends' suspension, but that of the armour that eerily rose from the ground and hovered before Ballorn. It hissed and smoked, small arcs of energy sparking from one piece to the next as it began to re-form. Its bland appearance changed, it was as if an eminent sculptor had been allowed to work on it for months, if not years. The smooth breastplate now had the clear markings of the pectoral and abdominal muscles of a perfectly honed athlete. The bulbous helmet narrowed, the clear shape of a raptor's wings appearing on each side and the gauntlets and greaves were now grooved instead of plain.

As the transformation of each piece was completed there was a loud crack, like the sound of a bullwhip penetrating the silence of the night. A rune, now blatantly clear, could be seen glowing white-hot on both the breastplate and the helm.

"*The Mark of the Nibrilsiem,*" whispered Keldenar, "*May you wear it well.*"

***

"Now you will be careful won't you, my love?"

Gelbran smiled as he gently stoked his wife's cheek, "Of course I will," he assured her.

The vikkery had spent weeks practising their new skills, each finding a particular form that came more naturally than others. Well everyone except for Gelbran. No matter what beast or monster he pictured in his mind, his replication of it was perfect. For some strange reason his kin seemed to struggle when it came to imitating larger beasts, but Gelbran actually felt stronger the more adventurous his transformations were. A few vikkery seemed more comfortable transforming into raptors, which was most beneficial to them all. Owls and eagles regularly flew from the cave and later returned with fresh fish from a lake many miles away. Some were lucky enough to snatch a rabbit or two on occasion, but a young vikkery named Torson was the most celebrated when he returned clutching the carcase of a young deer in his talons. As they soared high above, it was also a good way of keeping watch for any danger nearby.

The vikkery had feasted almost every night and were feeling refreshed and strong, but it was evident to Gelbran that they must leave the relative safety of their cave and make good on their promise to the wizard. His eyes grew dark as he recalled the horrors that his people had endured and thoughts of revenge clouded his mind. The wizard had bestowed them with a gift that would allow the vikkery a chance to destroy their enemy, a chance that burned deep within Gelbran as his yearning for it grew more intense as time passed.

"Remember," said his wife, "no charging into caves and dark places by yourself, I know how headstrong you can be."

"Yes, my love," sighed Gelbran.

"The others can have a bit of a fly around to make sure it's safe for the rest of you before you sneak into anywhere."

Gelbran wrapped his arms around her, "I won't take any chances," he said. "You just make sure you stay wrapped up and look after our little Grubb."

It would have appeared as the strangest sight to anyone who had witnessed their departure from the cave. Some turned into goats and stealthily bounded from rock to rock, others resembled large apes and clambered down easily. The cleverest of them all, however, simply waited patiently and were carried down by the eagles.

Now in their natural form, they marched forward. There was a strange determination that showed as they moved. They had no idea where they were going or what they would face, but not a single ounce of fear could be detected. Their goal was to find the dragon who had cruelly slaughtered so many of their friends and family and kill it. That single thought drove them on.

"Where are we headed?" asked one of them.

"We're going back," replied Gelbran.

"Back where?"

Gelbran pointed to the top of the mountain. "Up there."

"Why?"

"That's the last place we had an encounter with that beast," growled Gelbran. "We might be able to pick up its trail and follow it."

"And, if we find it?"

Mark of the Nibrilsiem

Gelbran turned and sneered, "Then we kill it!"

His friend shrugged his shoulders and smiled, "Sounds like a plan," he said winking at Gelbran as he strolled past him.

Gelbran stared up at the cave that had been a safe haven for them, and still was for his expectant wife and the children who remained there. The longing to kill the dragon gnawed at his mind, but he could not allow his rage to consume him so much as to make him reckless. He must survive to protect his family and the families of the other vikkery should any of his comrades be lost.

The days that followed were hard on the vikkery. The biting winds and harsh terrain took their toll, but not as much as they could have. Their new abilities allowed them to transform into fur-covered beasts, a protection from the cold that they would not have formerly had. The eagles would occasionally fly high above and scout the area ahead until, eventually, they reached the site where so many of their brethren had fallen.

Spreading out, they studied the ground. The earth was scorched, blackened by the intense heat of dragon fire, but no clear signs of tracks had been left by their elusive prey. The results of its frenzied attack, unfortunately, lay everywhere. Incinerated corpses were strewn about, their jaws agape as testament to their agonising deaths and the heads, limbs and torsos of others were scattered amongst them. The reactions from the vikkery were mixed. Some wept openly, whilst others went into a rage and began swiping at what remained of saplings and bushes.

Gelbran simply glared at the scene, "Let's move on," he said quietly. "We must not linger amongst death."

"Move onto where?" roared Asdor. "We have no idea where it's gone, or do we trust to hope that we have chosen the path that will lead us to our quarry?"

Gelbran looked sympathetically at his friend, "We shall concern ourselves with our direction later, Asdor," he whispered, glancing at the other vikkery. "For now, we must leave this place."

Asdor understood what was being said to him and let out a long sigh. Approaching a sobbing vikkery, he placed his arm around her shoulders, "Come," he said, "Gelbran is right, we can do nothing for them." He steered her away, embracing others as he moved along, driving them on ahead of him.

Barden watched the actions of the vikkery with interest. It seemed a little help would not go amiss. *Time to set them on the right path*, he thought. Lowering his head, he waved his hand. It was dark and Barden had maintained a distance so as not to be discovered by the vikkery, therefore he could not see the results of his spell. The vikkery however, would soon discover the bait and follow it blindly. The dubious actions of the wizard meant that he only had to wait a few short moments before the vikkery discovered his lure.

"Gelbran, quickly!" called Asdor, excitedly. "Over here, I've found something."

Gelbran hurried across to his friend. No questions were necessary. Before him lay deep impressions in the ground. The size of the three-toed tracks could only have been made by one creature, *a dragon*!

Gelbran spat at the tracks, "Now we can find it and kill it," he growled.

Asdor smiled at him, "Yes, but let's hope that's not too soon, I think we need a little more practice in honing our new abilities. By the way, have you any thoughts of what we could transform into that would be effective against a dragon?"

CHAPTER 13

Ballorn opened his eyes. Raising his hand, he rubbed his head vigorously. "What happened?" he asked aloud. A puzzled look appeared on his face. *Had he actually said that?* He didn't recognise his own voice. Perhaps the question had simply been a thought. His body felt stiff and he stretched his arms out in front of him. That was when the panic began to set in. His arms were huge! Bulging biceps and triceps seemed to have torn through the sleeves of his jacket, leaving them shredded. He sat up, his jaw dropping as he saw his own legs. His trousers matched the sleeves of his jacket perfectly, for they now, were also in tatters. Glancing up, he saw Hunter lying on his side smiling at him.

"Good morning," he said jovially. "Sleep well?"

Ballorn tried to climb to his feet, but as his legs were so immense and he was unused to them, he fell flat on his face. "WHAT'S GOING ON?" he bellowed. "What's that bloody dragon done to me?"

Hunter laughed, "He's given you a gift, Ballorn. Trust me, it may take a little getting used to."

Ballorn scrambled around clumsily before managing to control his unusually large limbs. Unfortunately for him, he did it with a bit too much vigour. Instead of merely standing up, he launched himself at least fifteen feet into the air.

Crashing unceremoniously into the ground, he was amazed that it didn't hurt. Not even a twinge of pain! "He's made me into a freak," he yelled. "What use will this be if I can't even stand up?!"

Hunter was in hysterics, "Calm down, Ballorn, you'll be fine. Just give it a little time to sink in."

"Easy for you to say!" snapped Ballorn. "You're not the one who's all puffed up like an overfilled water skin!"

"No, I'll give you that," sniggered Hunter. "My gift was somewhat different to yours."

Ballorn decided to stay on the ground. "He did something to you as well?"

Hunter picked up his bow. "You could say that," he replied. "Watch." Raising his bow, he let an arrow fly into a distant tree.

Ballorn did not look impressed, "So you can shoot a tree? So what? You could do that before."

Hunter's hands became a blur until, less than three seconds later, his quiver was empty. Every arrow had followed the trajectory of the first perfectly, piercing the shaft of the previous one and splaying it. Lowering his bow, he sighed, "But I couldn't do that," he said, raising his eyebrows.

"And what use is that!" exclaimed Ballorn. "We're going up against a dragon! It doesn't matter how fast you fire them, arrows will just bounce off it!"

"Those will," admitted Hunter. "But the special ones won't."

Ballorn was intrigued, "What… special ones?" he asked slowly.

"The ones Keldenar made for me," grinned Hunter. "The arrowheads are made from silver, but blunt so they don't do any permanent damage."

Ballorn frowned, "Let me get this straight," he sighed. "You get special arrows to basically distract and annoy the dragon! Then what am I supposed to do, run up behind it and tie it up whilst it's not looking?"

"Don't be stupid, Ballorn," groaned Hunter. "You knock it unconscious, *then* you tie it up!"

Ballorn balled up his fist, "Somehow, I don't think, even with these," he said, wiggling his sausage-like fingers, "I'd be capable of knocking a dragon out!"

Hunter smiled, "Come with me," he said, "I've got something for you. But take it slowly this time, we don't want you flying into the air again."

Warily, Ballorn rose to his feet, cursing quietly under his breath. "Brackin' dragon, puffing me up like a…"

He followed Hunter, tentatively sliding his feet instead of taking normal steps. He wobbled a few times, looking around, hoping that there may be something to grab on to so that he could steady himself. "This is ridiculous!" he growled, "I can't even walk properly, how am I supposed to face a dragon? A famper kitten could knock me over!" Then he noticed the furrows he had ploughed with his feet. "And I'll dig up half a ton of dirt wherever I go!"

"Time," Hunter called back to him. "That's all you need, Ballorn, a bit more time. You'll see. Come over to the wagon, your surprise is over here."

Ballorn was glad to reach the wagon and grabbed at the board on the side, which promptly came off in his hand. He looked sheepishly at Hunter as he tried to replace it, but even that did not go well. He slapped it as gently as he could but ended up knocking the wagon three feet sideways. He cleared his throat, trying his best not to make eye contact with Hunter, which would have been difficult as he was now watching Dannard and Stitch who had been concealed behind the wagon and were now fleeing to a new hiding place.

Hunter held up his hands, palms facing Ballorn, "Just drop it on the ground," he suggested, "I'll deal with it later."

Ballorn shrugged and let the board fall. "What's this surprise then?" he asked.

Hunter pointed.

Ballorn gazed in awe. What looked like an anvil with a sapling for a handle stood on the ground ahead surrounded by a suit of magnificent armour. Strangely, he felt more stable and focussed than he had since his awakening. He walked slowly toward the fascinating display, feeling more confident with each step. Getting closer, he realised it was a hammer, but it was the most immense hammer he had ever seen and even the handle seemed to have been forged from pure silver. He turned to face Hunter.

"All for you!" his friend smiled. "Everything you need to defeat a dragon. More importantly, everything you need to ensure your survival."

Reaching the centre of the circle, Ballorn stared at the hammer. The head was polished to mirror-like perfection, the handle as smooth as satin with ancient runes carved deeply into it. He wrapped his fingers around it. Despite its size it seemed as light as a feather as he lifted it from the ground with one hand. He stroked it lovingly, fascinated by the magical bond he never even knew existed.

Something seemed familiar to him. He glanced over at the cart and then at Hunter. "Where's my anvil?" he asked.

Hunter looked a little uncomfortable.

"Hunter, is this my anvil?"

"Keldenar said it would be perfect for what you needed."

"But where's the bick?"

Hunter looked confused, "The what?"

"The bick, the horn?"

"The pointy bit on the side," shouted Stitch, quite proud of the fact that he knew what Ballorn was talking about.

"Oh that!" said Hunter. "Keldenar said he couldn't possibly leave that on there, you might kill one of the dragons by accident hitting it with that! You shouldn't have a problem with the weight though, the handle is only a silver-covered sapling."

"But look at it!" exclaimed Ballorn. "The hardy hole and the pritchel hole have been filled in, it's useless now!"

"But look at it, Ballorn, it's beautiful," shouted Stitch. "Much nicer than that ugly old anvil."

Ballorn thought for a moment as he stared at the hammer. He bared his teeth as he held it aloft and roared, "NIBRILSIEM!"

***

"They're gone! What do you mean, they're gone? How can they be gone?"

"They just stopped!"

"It must have changed direction, try looking somewhere else!"

"I've searched everywhere, there's nothing there!"

"Well search harder, they can't have just disappeared!"

"I want to find this thing as much as you do, Gelbran! I've been tracking the foot and hoofprints of beasts for nigh on sixty years, do you really think I could miss ones that are ten feet long and six inches deep?"

Gelbran looked at Asdor, stamping his foot in frustration, "We were close!" he raged, shaking his fist. "I know we were close and now the trail has gone cold! It may take weeks or even months before we find another one to follow!"

"If at all," added Asdor. "You do realise these things can fly, don't you?" he said, flapping his arms. "That's why the trail ended so abruptly."

"You think it took to the air?" asked Gelbran.

"I don't think," replied Asdor, laughing. "I know. The last prints were deeper than the others, must have been caused by it launching itself from the ground. If you look up there…" he pointed at the trees ahead, "… you'll notice there are a few of the smaller branches broken from those trees, and it happened recently. I've inspected them and the stumps are still clean. It must have clipped them as it flew past."

"Wonderful!" exclaimed Gelbran, "How are we supposed to follow it now that it's taken flight?"

"Well we do have one thing that we never had before," replied Asdor.

"Which is?" Gelbran asked, sceptically.

"Have you tried turning yourself into a hawk yet, Gelbran?"

Gelbran raised an eyebrow, "Your point being?"

"You can see for miles, much farther than you can in the form of anything else."

"So what are you suggesting, we all turn into birds and fly around until we find the dragon?"

"Kind of," replied Asdor, "I'm suggesting that those of us who can, because somehow we are all limited as to what we can transform into, search for *a* dragon*, any* dragon. I know we all want to find the one that killed our people, but it's possible that that may not be feasible. When it attacked it didn't choose which ones of us to slaughter, it killed all within reach. I suggest we treat their kind with the same contempt. Let's kill any we encounter, better still, *let's kill them all.*"

Gelbran stared long and hard at his friend, thoughts of revenge whirling through his mind. "Agreed," he said quietly. *"We kill them all."*

The next few days were... *interesting.* The vikkery camped where the dragon had taken flight, occasionally glancing at the deep prints made by its claws as a reminder of why they were doing what they were doing. They were *practising.* They huddled around discussing what would be the best form to take if they were facing a dragon and their progress was remarkable.

Bears and wolves and the like, were ruled out. In fact, anything with fur was not an option. If they met with a fire breather, the fur would ignite far easier than a thick hide or scales. Four of the vikkery had perfected the form of a glamoch, surpassing even that by changing into one double the size of a real one.

"We can charge at their legs and bring 'em down for the kill," growled one of them.

"And if we fail," laughed another, "at least the survivors will have a nice roast dinner!"

Asdor screwed up his face but could not help laughing, "You're sick!" he chuckled.

"Alright, that's enough," said Gelbran, quietly. "Any other ideas?"

A young female raised her hand nervously, "I have *one* idea," she said quietly. "It's not brilliant, but it might help."

"Go on then, Fellis, what is it?"

Fellis lost her nerve, "No, it doesn't matter. It was a silly idea anyway. Forget I said anything."

Gelbran smiled at her, "Now you listen to me, young lady," he said. "There can be no thought, plan or idea suggested in this meeting that *isn't* silly. We're talking about slaying dragons, who's to say your idea won't the best of the silly?"

Fellis smiled shyly at Gelbran, "Alright then," she said. "But it'll be easier to show you than to tell you. I've got a couple of ideas you see."

"This is going to be dreadful," muttered Asdor.

Gelbran nudged him hard in the ribs with his elbow. "When you're ready, Fellis," he smiled.

Fellis backed away and closed her eyes. She began to change shape and grow. Feathers sprouted all over her body and her arms became huge wings, which she flapped a few times before drawing them in to her sides. She shuddered slightly for a moment, and her transformation was complete. Before the rest of the vikkery stood a ten-foot tall falcon complete with razor-sharp talons and a beak that looked capable of tearing the toughest flesh.

The vikkery were dumbstruck.

"I told you it wasn't a very good idea," said Fellis as she changed back. "I should have stayed quiet, only I heard you talking about dragons being able to fly and I thought I could move faster and bring one to the ground if I was quick enough. Sorry. I'll shut up now." A little tear appeared in the corner of her eye.

The vikkery began to applaud and cheer.

"That was incredible!" shrieked Asdor. "Talk about inventive, nobody else thought of that. Fellis, you're a genius!"

Fellis wiped away the tear and stared, wide-eyed, at the reaction from the group. "Really?" she asked.

"Absolutely!" exclaimed Gelbran. "What was your other idea?"

Fellis laughed excitedly, "Well, it's a bit similar to the first one, but without the feathers," she giggled. "Would you like to see?"

Cheers rang out from the crowd.

"Alright," said Fellis, "but this one's easier if I start like this." She got to her hands and knees and, once again, closed her eyes.

The transformation started as before, only this time there were no feathers and her skin began to turn green until the distinct shape of scales could be seen appearing all over her body. She grew and grew, until she was even larger than when she had changed into a falcon. Her hands and feet became three-toed claws and with a final shudder, leathery wings erupted from her back. This time, *she was a dragon*. Opening her jaws, she revealed huge fangs and the black forked tongue struck dread into the hearts of the vikkery observing the spectacle.

She changed back and waited for the reaction from her friends and family, who simply sat open-mouthed in awe.

"I tried to breathe fire the first time I did that one," she said, slightly embarrassed, "but I just made myself sick."

Gelbran walked toward her, hands outstretched. "You are a marvel, my dear," he sighed. "I am confident that not a single vikkery would deny that you are the most gifted amongst us."

Fellis allowed him to take her hands, "You're just being nice," she said quietly. "But thank you for letting me try. I bet everyone else has much better ideas than mine."

"Well I haven't," Gelbran confessed.

"Nor me," called Asdor.

"Oh, Gelbran," laughed Fellis, "I bet you've got loads of ideas."

"No, just the one," he admitted. "And it's nowhere near as good as either of yours."

"Let's see it then," shouted Asdor. "What was that you said about silly ideas?"

"No, no," protested Gelbran. "We are here to make sure everyone else is safe, we'll concentrate on them first," said Gelbran, trying to avoid putting on his own display.

"Ah, but that's the point, we protect each other," said Asdor, enjoying teasing Gelbran, perhaps a little too much. "Your efforts could help save someone else's life. I'm sure everyone is beside themselves with anticipation and longing to see the shapeshifting abilities of our leader."

Gelbran smiled at him through gritted teeth, "I'm gonna kick your backside for this, Asdor. You just wait!" he whispered.

The crowd began to cheer his name *Gelbran, Gelbran, Gelbran.*

He held up his hands, nodding to them, then took a deep breath. He began to grow but did not change shape. Now fifteen feet tall, he looked down at them. Reaching across he gripped one of the smaller trees, tearing the roots from the ground. His voice boomed as he spoke, "Would any dragon dare face me now?" he bellowed. *"I'll crush it's skull with a single blow!"*

The gathering erupted in cheers and applause once more. Many displays were put on that evening, admittedly some more successful than others. The changeling game continued for some time, but it gave them a brief respite from the memories of the horrors they had already seen and, perhaps, the thoughts of the ones they were still yet to witness.

CHAPTER 14

"Is it comfortable?" Stitch called from a distance.

"It's alright," replied Ballorn, raising his voice slightly.

"No, that's not good enough," said Stitch. "It has to be comfortable! I'll make any necessary adjustments, just tell me what you need."

"I just said it's fine!" Ballorn yelled, testily. "Will he ever shut up about this blasted shirt?" he asked Hunter in a quiet voice.

"I have to give him his due," chuckled Hunter. "He did put in a lot of time to make sure it was finished before you had to wear your new armour."

"But, *a padded shirt*. It doesn't seem right to me."

"Perhaps not, but it has to be better than bare metal rubbing against your skin."

"Hunter managed to collect a load of gombin feathers, that's why it's so soft," called Stitch. "Don't worry, I washed them all first in hot water, so they're nice and clean."

Ballorn turned to face Stitch, "Why don't you stop shouting and come over here?" he asked.

"Ooh… no, I don't think so," replied Stitch, nervously. "I think I'll hang on a bit, you know, until you're used to your new… erm, arms, and things!"

"In other words, *you're scaring the crap out of him, you freak,*" yelled Dannard.

Hunter smiled, "Charming to the last, as always," he sniggered.

"Do you know," said Ballorn, "for the life of me, I can't remember why I thought it would be a good idea to bring him along."

"Because you're a good person, Ballorn, that's why. You know he wouldn't have lasted a day without us to protect him."

"Too good for my own good, that's my problem," snorted Ballorn.

"I know," laughed Hunter. "But the skill with which you hold that frown and gruff manner is something to behold, knowing it encases that big, soft heart of gold!"

"Oh, shut it!" mumbled Ballorn.

"Why don't you give Stitch some praise? It might relax him a bit. Tell him the shirt's wonderful and the most comfortable thing you've ever worn."

"Why?" grunted Ballorn. "It's only a shirt!"

"He worked on it for three days, Ballorn!"

"Three days!" exclaimed Ballorn. "How could he have worked on it for three days?" He thought for a moment, "Hunter," he asked quietly, "How long was I asleep?"

"Five days according to those two."

"What! That's not possible."

"It is," replied Hunter. "Apparently, we were twitching and mumbling all the time we were asleep as well, and before you ask, neither of them understood a word we were saying. They stayed a safe distance from us the entire time."

"We've wasted almost a week, Hunter!" Ballorn began pacing, "We must leave at first light tomorrow, that wretched dragon could be anywhere by now!"

"I know," replied Hunter, sympathetically. "So, it's execution is stayed for a while. Don't worry, Ballorn, we'll catch up with it eventually."

Ballorn shook his head, "Execution?" he asked slowly. "You are mistaken, my friend. There will be no execution. I do not mean to slay the dragon, *I mean to capture it*!"

"What! But you said…"

"I know what I said, Hunter, but it's the deal I made with Keldenar. He gave me, well…" he waved his hand toward Hunter, "… us, these gifts, but only if I gave my solemn word that we would not kill any of his kind."

"Which makes perfect sense, because no dragon could possibly want to kill us!" Hunter exclaimed sarcastically.

Ballorn grinned, "I know," he said, "but I didn't say I wouldn't knock the living crap out of 'em!"

***

They set out the following morning as planned. Senn had graciously left them a pony and the smaller of the two carts, which now trundled behind them as they discussed what to do next.

"The only way to find out anything will be to head to the local villages," suggested Stitch. "Perhaps one of the locals will have seen or heard something."

"And what if all the villages has been burnded to the ground?" sighed Dannard.

"Then we'll know we're on the right track," replied Hunter.

"You know the land better than we do, Hunter," said Ballorn. "Where do we start?"

"Gendrim," said Hunter. "It's about twelve miles from here and the way is easy enough. Shouldn't take more than a few hours."

"Gendrim it is then," said Ballorn. "Are you two happy with that?"

Stitch shrugged his shoulders, but Dannard as usual, couldn't keep quiet. "Happy? Happy! How is we supposed to be happy? We has been stuck out in the wilds for over a week! Most of which you two was sleeping! We has had to fend for ourselves! We is gentle folk what is used to the finer things in life, not beasts what lives in the woods! Now we has to go into a village what is full of strangers what might want to hurt us, if the village hasn't been squished by a plonking-great dragon... and you asks us if we's happy? No, boulder bonce, *we is not happy!*"

173

"We could leave you behind," suggested Hunter. "We'd leave you the pony and cart of course," he smiled.

"That's just typical!" exclaimed Dannard. "We watches over you while you is asleep to make sure nothing nasty happens to you, Stitch makes you a lovely shirt so your armour doesn't scratch you, and you wants to abandon us out here in the…"

"I'm happy!" squeaked Stitch. "Gendrim sounds lovely to me! I'm happy to tag along with you. Ignore Dannard, he just gets a little agitated when he hasn't eaten for a while!"

"I has only just had my breakf…"

"Shut up, Dannard!" pleaded Stitch. "For goodness sake, just this once, please… shut up!"

***

Many heads turned as they entered Gendrim. The locals had seen many strange things in the past, but none as strange as this, it seemed. Dannard and Stitch rode on the cart with Hunter walking beside it. Ahead of them, Ballorn was the main attraction with his armour gleaming in the sunlight and the glint from the silver hammer catching everyone's eye. The crowd ahead of them stopped whatever they were doing and just gawped at them. Ballorn eyed them, unsure of what to do or say to get them to move.

Dannard could not resist. Leaping from the cart, he ran in front of Ballorn. "MAKE WAY!" he bellowed, "MAKE WAY FOR THE *SEBRINALIM!*"

Ballorn's head dropped and he shook it slowly. Hunter placed his hand over his mouth to stop himself laughing and Stitch just tutted.

"Didn't you hear me?" continued Dannard, "*MAKE WAY FOR THE BRENISALIM!*"

Ballorn grabbed the back of his collar and marched him back to the cart, "Shut up and get on!" he hissed.

The crowd had suddenly lost interest and went about their business.

Ballorn whispered to Hunter, "See if you can find an inn. If we want to hear any local gossip, we'll hear it there."

Hunter nodded and began to walk away. As he did, three men stood in his path.

"And what might four strangers be wantin' in our humble village?" asked one of them.

"Just passing through," said Hunter, politely. "We mean to take sustenance in your inn, if you have one, and then we'll be on our way."

"Oh, we've got an inn, a really good un an' all. Not interested in our livestock then?" the man asked.

The question threw Hunter a little. "Erm, no, not really," he replied shaking his head.

"What about giants, you interested in giants? Got any giant friends?"

Hunter smiled, "Giant friends? No! What sort of a question is that?"

The villager screwed up his eyes and peered at Hunter and the others. "Oh, nothin' just askin'. Enjoy your time in Gendrim." He turned and ambled away, followed by his two accomplices.

Hunter turned to face Ballorn, who shrugged. "Not a clue," he said, bewildered.

The villager paused for a second, "Oh," he said, pointing, "the inn's that way."

***

Stepping through the door, the nemilar were overwhelmed by the smell of stale ale and pipe smoke, as well as the odour of many a villager who was sorely in need of a bath. The inn was busy, but not crowded, allowing clear visibility across the room. Well, the parts that weren't obscured by the smog, at least. Strolling to the bar, Ballorn ordered two jugs of ale and waited patiently whilst the innkeeper drew them from the barrel. Hunter found a table that was free and sat at it with Stitch. Dannard, however, grabbed a tall stool and decided to sit at the bar. Ballorn shook his head, poured some ale into a tankard for him, and joined the others at the table. Dannard immediately leaned over the bar to get the innkeeper's attention, "Excuse me," he said politely, "Does you have any cake?"

The innkeeper laughed, "Sorry friend, this is an inn not a bakery."

Dannard pouted, "Where's the bakery then?" he asked.

"Other side o' the village," replied the innkeeper. He stared at Dannard for a moment. "I could get my lad to go and fetch you some cake if you like, but I'd have to charge you a bit extra."

A beaming smile appeared on Dannard's face, "Oh yes, that'll be perfect," he said. "I does like my cake, and by the way, my friend's paying. Him in the shiny armour."

His unusual request had attracted the attention of two young men on the other side of the room who were now leaning close and whispering to one another. They waited until the innkeeper was busy with other customers before getting up from their table and approaching Dannard. Taking a stool each, they sat either side of him.

He looked at them in turn, "Afternoon gentlemen," he said politely.

"Hmmm," said one of them. "What do you think he's up to, Emmy?"

"Not a clue, Yello. Nothing good I'd guess."

Dannard looked nervous, "I doesn't want any bother gentlemen," he said. "I has just come in with some friends for a bit of ale and some cake."

"Cake?" asked the young man named Yello. "We know someone who's very partial to cake."

"Nothing strange about that!" said Dannard. "Lots of folk like cake... 'cause it's nice."

"Nice?" said the young man named Emmy. "He always says that too... It's nice."

"What are you up to?" asked Yello. "Why are you talking like that? And, not wanting to be insulting, why the ridiculous disguise?"

"You gentlemen seems to have me mixed up with somebody else," said Dannard, now more nervous than ever. "If you'll excuse me, I think I'll join my friends."

Dannard began to rise but Yello placed his hand on the nemilar's shoulder and pushed him gently back onto the stool. "Friends?" he chuckled. "You? Since when did you have friends?"

"Moreso," asked Emmy, "when was the last time you bathed? You've never had any friends, and you never will smelling the way you do."

Dannard glared at the young man, but not because of the insult. "Go away, Emnor," he hissed. "You're interfering with things you would not understand."

"Come now, Barden, you don't know that. Why don't you try us?"

"You and Yellodius should leave now! It's taken me years to get this right and you're going to ruin everything. The dragons are rising and if someone doesn't step in this will end badly for us all."

"All the more reason for you to allow us to help," said Emnor. "You know that our powers are much stronger than yours, and always have been."

"It's not about power this time, Emnor. It's about timing, having the right players in place for when they are needed most!"

"I could help you there, Barden. I have been experimenting with time magic for a few years now, it may come in handy."

"I know that, Yello, but you are attempting to manipulate time. These events have to be allowed to occur naturally."

"Events?" asked Emnor. "How curious. What *events*?"

"Events that have been foretold for centuries. I've read the scrolls!"

"This is becoming more fascinating by the second, Barden. Why don't you come with us and we'll discuss the situation, in detail."

Ballorn was watching the men. As annoying as Dannard was, he felt a duty to protect him. "Everything alright, Dannard?" he called.

Dannard smiled, "Yes, fine, fine. We is just discussing cake. This chap thinks seedcake is better than carrot cake and won't admit he's wrong."

"Who's your shiny friend?" asked Emnor.

"None of your business," growled Barden, covering his mouth so that Ballorn and the others could not see his lips move. "Now will you go away and leave me in peace?"

"Ordinarily," began Yello, "there's nothing more we'd like than to get away from you. Unfortunately, we have taken… *employment* here, so we won't be going anywhere for a while."

Emnor grinned, "You know what he's like, Barden. Not only are the villagers offering payment in gold, *we get all the free wine and ale we can drink.*"

"All for sorting out a minor problem they have with giants pinching some of their livestock," laughed Yello. Gold to spend and lakes of wine to swim in. *I may just stay here forever."*

Ballorn watched with interest. "Why are they speaking so quietly?" he asked.

"Probably just being a bit wary," replied Stitch. "You know, strange place, strange people. Who knows who you could disturb."

Hunter gave him a look of disbelief, "You do realise who that is, don't you?" he asked. "That's Dannard. Quite probably one of the most outspoken and obnoxious nemilar to have ever walked these lands. I hardly think that he would be concerned about disturbing *anyone.*" He peered at Dannard, "No…" he said thoughtfully, "… there's more to this than a discussion about cake, of that I'm certain."

"Agreed," said Ballorn. "Perhaps he knew them before he moved to our village?"

"It's possible," said Hunter, "They seem to dislike him as much as anyone else who makes his acquaintance."

"Don't be so horrible!" whispered Stitch. "He's alright is Dannard, he just gets a bit grumpy at times."

"At times?" chuckled Ballorn. "In the five years I've known him, not once has he…"

"So how long have you known this little stain?" called one of the young men at the bar. It was Yello, of course.

Ballorn placed his elbows on the table and glared at the wizard, "I'd mind my manners if I were you," he warned. "That's our friend you're talking about."

"Not long then?" laughed Yello. "Give it time, sir. You'll realise soon enough that this one has no friends. He only has acquaintances, whom he quickly discards once they have served his purpose."

Ballorn stared at the two men either side of the cooper. He had known Dannard long enough and, ordinarily, would have agreed with the statement made by the young man. But now was not the time to be siding with strangers. Then he noticed the look on Dannard's face. It was more than anger, it was rage. *How close to the mark had the young man's statement been to invoke such a response? What did he know about the cooper that they did not?* "I think you're confusing him for someone else," he said quietly.

Yello screwed up his nose and glanced at Dannard, "Perhaps," he said slowly. "But you have to be careful of the company you keep in the wilds. People are not always what they appear to be."

"You leave my friend alone!" Stitch shouted suddenly, pointing at Yello. "If you've got a problem, perhaps we should take this outside!"

Hunter grunted as he stifled a laugh, "What are you going to do?" he sniggered. "Sew him to a cart or something?"

Yello rose slowly from his stool. Emnor leaned across and touched his arm. Yello pouted, shook his head and waved his hand in dismissal, "No need," he said quietly. "Forgive me," he began, turning his attention back to the table. "I did not mean to upset you, friends. Allow me to buy you a drink and let us forget this nonsense."

"You should apologise!" protested Stitch. He glared at Yello, then nudged Ballorn, "Make him apologise."

"He just did, you imbecile! Didn't you hear him?"

"Not to us!" exclaimed Stitch. "To Dannard."

Ballorn shrugged, "Well he has got a point," he whispered.

Hunter had heard enough, "Thank you," he said smiling at Yello. "I think a jug of ale would be welcome."

Yello nodded and signalled to the innkeeper, who seemed most relieved that their quarrel had progressed no further than a few harsh words. Yello carried the jug across to the table and placed it in front of Ballorn. "So what brings you to this boil on the backside of a glamoch known as Gendrim then?"

"Ballorn is the sinrilbem and we is…"

"Be quiet, Dannard!" said Ballorn, raising his voice slightly. He looked up at Yello. "We're merely travellers," he smiled. "Wandering the land in hopes of adventure and riches."

Emnor raised his eyebrows, "Really?" he asked dubiously. "Bit overdressed in that armour to be a simple adventurer, aren't you?"

"Oh this old stuff?" he asked looking down at himself. "Just a musty heirloom," he sighed. "Been in my family for generations."

"You've kept it in very good order," said Yello. "What's that thing there, that mark on your breastplate?"

"Erm, oh that… family crest," he replied, having to think quickly.

"I'm sure I've seen that before," said Emnor. "Or something very similar. What does it mean?"

"Ah... well..." began Ballorn, trying to think of a convincing answer. "... It's lost something of its translation over the years, but it means strong arms."

The wizards glanced at Ballorn's biceps and then at one another.

Yello sucked the air through pursed lips, "No..." he said, "...I disagree. I don't think it could be any more accurate a translation than that."

"I've got an idea!" Emnor suddenly exclaimed, "If you're looking for adventure and riches, why not give us a hand to sort out the village's 'giant' problem? There'd be a bit of coin in it for you as well."

Ballorn leaned forward on the table, "We'd like to help, we really would, but we have urgent matters to attend to elsewhere. We'll be moving on once we're rested."

"Oh, that's a shame," sighed Yello. "I would have liked to have seen what you were capable of with... well, you know," he said, gesturing at Ballorn's arms.

"Come on, Yello," called Emnor. "We have business of our own to attend to. Time to go."

The two wizards bade them farewell and left the tavern, but not before both managed one more scathing look at Dannard.

"Nasty buggers!" muttered the cooper.

CHAPTER 15

The moonlight cast an eerie glow across the fell. Gelbran lead the way, followed closely by Asdor and Fellis. The three had unknowingly formed a bond and now rarely left one another's company as they continued their hunt. Months had passed without so much of a trace of anything that might reveal the presence of a dragon. Those vikkery most adept at transforming into winged creatures took flight each day, but returned with their search proving futile. But four days prior, *their luck had changed.*

Quite by chance, one of the vikkery had landed on a pile of rocks. His wings were aching and his intention was merely to a rest for a few minutes before taking to the air once more. He stretched his arms, arching his back and tilting his head from side to side. *It was then that he noticed the carcases on the ground.* There were eight of them, all had been burned to a cinder. They had no signs of predation on them, so it was clear that they had not been hunted as a food source. From what he could tell it had been a wolf pack, or something similar. It was hard to tell as even the teeth had been disfigured by what must have been an intense heat. Eager to report his discovery, he headed back to Gelbran.

Excitement travelled through the vikkery camp like wildfire. At last their search was over, they could reap a modicum of revenge on the dragons. The hum of chattering voices grew louder as the excitement turned to anger and bloodlust. Although Gelbran wanted this more than most, he felt that he must quell the emotions of his kin. If they were to face a dragon, and survive, rational thought would surely be the key to success. "SILENCE!" he bellowed.

He paused as a hush fell around him. Looking from one to the next of his kin, he raised a hand. "I know what you feel," he said slowly. "And do not think for one second that I feel any different. We have searched and waited for this moment, and now it is upon us. Fear not, *we will defeat this enemy!*" Cheers erupted from the crowd.

Waiting for the noise to die down, he continued, "Despite our new abilities, we will be severely outmatched. But we will use something that our foe is incapable of." Mumbles ran through the crowd.

"We will use stealth," he whispered. "How many have charged headlong toward these beasts, only to be incinerated in the blink of an eye? How many have faced them honourably, challenging them to a fair battle, only to be lured into a cowardly trap? How many have attempted to flee, knowing that they have neither the skill nor the bravery to face them, only to be sadistically chased down and trampled?" The crowd were suddenly not so enthusiastic.

"But what if one of them were not given the chance to strike first? How would it react if suddenly *it* were the victim as its enemy dealt the first blow? Our abilities will mean nothing if we face a dragon head-on... but if we were to strike from behind, or from the side, it would have no time to defend itself. It may seem cowardly when said aloud... but is that not the way *they* would normally behave?

Gelbran had rekindled the fire within the vikkery and searches over the next two days lead to the discovery of a cave not far from where the carcases had been discovered. It did not appear to be huge, but the mouth was sizeable enough for a dragon to enter and the gloom beyond proved that it was certainly deep enough to conceal one.

The vikkery produced sketches of the cave and the surrounding area, scoring images into pieces of wood and creating a map of sorts. Back at camp, they laid them out for all to see. Discussions were had and a battle plan drawn up. If they were to succeed, everyone must play their part and follow the plan to the letter. Although all were slightly unsure of their own abilities, they agreed wholeheartedly on one major aspect of the plan. *They must attack after dark.*

That same night the air was still. The distant howling of a wolf pack did nothing to ease the tension of the vikkery, who had already begun to transform. Much thought had gone into their strategy of what to choose as a suitable opponent for a dragon. Now beasts who had excellent night vision surrounded the cave. Wolves and gemnar amongst others crept around, determined to stay hidden and wary of any movement from within.

Gelbran, however, did not transform. Taking a deep breath, he marched toward the cave, "GET YOUR MANGY, FLEA-BITTEN CARCASE OUT HERE YOU PIECE OF FILTH!" he bellowed.

There was a brief flash of light from inside the cave, and a rumbling could be heard as something stirred deep within.

"SHOW YOURSELF, SLIME. I HAVEN'T GOT ALL NIGHT!"

The entrance to the cave lit up and a roar echoed from within that turned Gelbran's blood cold. "No going back now," he mumbled under his breath. "Wish my hands would stop shaking!"

The huge silhouette almost filled the cave mouth, illuminated from behind by the flames that now obviously filled it.

"OH, YOU HAVE GOT SOME GUTS THEN!" roared Gelbran. "COME ON... COME AND FACE ME! COME AND FACE THE ONE WHO'S GOING TO PUT YOUR FLAMES OUT FOR GOOD!"

As the dragon moved forward, Gelbran began to transform. The dragon paused, it had not seen anything like it before and seemed a little wary of its unknown challenger.

"Aaah, what's wrong?" taunted Gelbran. "Bit scared when you're facing someone who's not half the size of your fetid claws!"

The dragon tilted its head back and roared, its fiery breath illuminating the surrounding area. Gelbran could see the others closing in behind the dragon. Luckily, *it* could not.

He stepped forward, "WHAT'S WRONG, DRAGON, AFRAID TO LEAVE THE SAFETY OF YOUR CAVE?" he screamed. "DO SOMETHING!"

The dragon moved further forward, spitting fire and roaring even louder. But it was angry and still confused by the challenge as it swayed from side to side.

"NOW!" shouted Gelbran as loudly as he could.

Before the dragon realised what was happening, four glamoch charged into its hind legs, unbalancing it and bringing it crashing to the ground. Claws and hooves tore and stamped as it rolled helplessly amid the confusion. A giant wolf sprinted toward it, the vikkery's intention, to tear out its throat. But at the last second, *disaster struck!*

One of the glamoch charged forward, striking the dragon full force in the side of the head. The dragon's jaws opened as it gasped for breath and flames erupted, engulfing the wolf. Its fur immediately caught fire and it yelped as it rolled on the floor and fell into a ditch. As horrific as it was, none of the other vikkery could risk relenting their attack until the dragon was dead. It seemed that there was to be more than one death this night.

The dragon was defenceless, now doomed as the final blows rained down on its battered body. Then a rumbling began. The dragon twitched slightly, but never again would it slaughter any innocent.

The vikkery eventually backed away, but the rumbling began once more. Now as themselves, they looked at one another. *Where was the rumbling noise coming from?* Their answer came almost immediately as, erupting from the ground, *rose another dragon!*

They were unprepared and began to flee. Charging past Gelbran, the vikkery pleaded and implored him to do the same. But he could not. His eyes were fixed on the dragon they had not known was there. *Had it been buried in the ground?* The dragon reared up on its hind legs as it clawed at its own head and horns. It roared and bellowed as if in great pain, but there were no signs of any physical wounds.

Then the strangest thing of all happened. It caught sight of the dragon they had just slain and began to tear it apart. It was as if it were making sure it was dead! *Was this the way dragons existed? Was it territorial?* It suddenly dropped flat and began to howl. Turning its head, it looked Gelbran directly in the eyes.

Gelbran transformed, "WELL WHY NOT!" he bawled, "WE TOOK ONE OF YOU DOWN, MIGHT AS WELL MAKE IT TWO!"

The dragon stared at him with soulful eyes and lowered its head. Climbing slowly to its feet, it headed toward the cave. Glancing back briefly, it went inside, its wails echoing mournfully from within.

***

The vikkery sat around the fire in silence. Nervous glances passed between them, but all were lost for words. Tears had been shed as, in dribs and drabs, friends and loved ones returned to the camp. None could bring themselves to ask the obvious question. *Where was Cordain?*

Cordain was the vikkery who had transformed into the huge wolf. Many had witnessed his terrible fate but also hoped that somehow he had survived. To them, the fact that any of them was still alive was a miracle in itself.

Gelbran was the last to return. The vikkery gathered around, praising him for his heroism when facing the dragon. Their words felt hollow. His mind was in turmoil over what had happened, or what he thought may have happened. He was not prepared to discuss it with anyone else. Not yet anyway.

Asdor approached him and took his arm. Raising it, he placed a small wooden bowl in his hand, "Tea," he said. "Drink it, you look exhausted."

Gelbran gave him a weak smile, "Thank you, my friend," he said quietly.

"What news of Cordain?" whispered Fellis as she appeared behind Asdor.

Gelbran sighed and shook his head. "Not good I'm afraid. Give me a few minutes, I need to speak with you both." He glanced around, "Alone," he added, and shuffled away toward the fire. Flopping down, he rubbed his face in his hands. *They'll think I've gone mad*, he thought. *But somehow, I know I'm right!*

He lay back and closed his eyes, reliving the events of the night. He could still hear the roaring of the dragon clearly and see the flames vividly. Although completely spent, he knew that sleep would evade him for some time. Perhaps that was a blessing. He drank what was left of the tea that Asdor had given him, having spilt most of it as he collapsed beside the fire. It would do no good for him to dwell over what had happened. Within minutes, he rose and beckoned his friends to follow him. They wandered a few yards away from the others and sat on a fallen tree at the edge of a clearing.

Gelbran stroked his beard as he considered what he was about to say, "I don't think Cordain is dead," he said bluntly.

"Oh, thank goodness," sighed Fellis.

Asdor leaned forward, "That's impossible!" he exclaimed quietly. "You saw what happened and so did I! He was engulfed by dragon fire, Gelbran! Nobody could survive that!"

Fellis slapped his arm impatiently, "Hush up, Asdor. Let him finish!"

"Well if he's not dead, he's bound to be in a bad way," Asdor groaned. "I'll get everyone ready and we'll mount a rescue mission immediately!"

"Just... hear me out, Asdor," Gelbran hissed, gesturing for Asdor to resume his seat. "It seems that... well, the Cordain that *we* knew is gone... but Cordain himself is not."

"Oh, that makes perfect sense!" scoffed Asdor. "He's dead... but he's not dead!" he shook his head. "What are you talking about!"

"Keep your voice down!" Gelbran urged him. "I wanted to hear what you two thought of my idea before I spoke to the others."

"Well so far it's as clear as mud!" exclaimed Asdor. "You might want to practise a bit, work on your presentation and all that," he added.

Gelbran stood up and was about to walk away, "Forget it!" he growled. "I wish I hadn't bothered now!"

"Just tell us!" squeaked Fellis, grabbing his hand. "Whatever you've got to say can't sound any stranger than us being able to turn into beasts!"

Gelbran snorted, "That second dragon!" he said.

"What about it?" asked Fellis.

"Don't you think it's strange that it rose from exactly the same place as Cordain fell?"

"Him falling there is probably what disturbed the thing."

Gelbran shook his head, "No, Asdor, I don't think so," he said stooping down to face them, "I think that the dragon *was* Cordain!"

Asdor's eyes widened and he blinked a few times, unable to believe his own ears. "Have you gone barmy?" he laughed. "Or did that dragon bang you on the head when we weren't looking?"

Gelbran stayed stone-faced, "Do I look like I'm dazed, confused… or joking?"

"Ooh, my word," gasped Fellis. "You're serious!"

Gelbran nodded slowly, "That wizard told me that the power he gave us was a gift. I now believe it to be a curse. I trusted him because I was consumed with having my revenge on the dragons. I'm beginning to think he never told me all the facts about the spell he performed on us."

"Go on!" Fellis urged.

"I think that if one of us is struck by dragon fire, *we actually become a dragon!*"

"What!" exclaimed Fellis, "You mean, for good?"

"Ah, but all dragons aren't fire-breathers," said Asdor, quickly. "There are ice dragons as well! And then there's that big one that attacked us, the one that uses lightning!"

"True," agreed Gelbran. "But it's my idea that, whatever you get struck with, determines what type of dragon you become."

"Well I suppose it's better than it killing you," suggested Fellis.

Asdor shook his head again, "Sounds a bit far-fetched to me, Gelbran. Anyway, what on Pordan gave you such an idea?"

"After you lot ran away, I lost my temper a bit, fool that I am," he confessed. "I actually stood there and challenged the dragon by myself."

"I was right!" laughed Asdor. "You did get a bang on the head!"

Gelbran rolled his eyes. "Anyway, the dragon didn't even look angry. In fact, it looked rather sad. I thought it was going to cry at one point, if dragons are capable of crying that is."

"So, what did it do?" asked Fellis, excitedly.

"Well," answered Gelbran, "it just, kind of, whimpered… then went into the cave that the other one came out of."

"We have to investigate, just the three of us for now!" Fellis said adamantly. "If Cordain *has* been turned into a dragon we need to find out for definite!"

"And then what?" asked Asdor. "Are we going to bring him back with us?"

"So, what should we do?" asked Fellis, glaring at him. "Should we just abandon him?"

"I never said that," replied Asdor, quietly. "All I meant…"

"What if he's changed by the time we go back?" suggested Gelbran. "What if this is how dragons have always been made? Maybe in the past, there were others like us who were tricked into the same deal by wizards? Perhaps it's only a matter of time before the rage takes hold of someone who has been changed, making them forget who they once were?"

Asdor frowned, "That's a lot of questions," he groaned. "And ones I may not like the answers to."

"Questions we *won't* get answers to if we just sit around here!" Fellis protested. "Cordain is our friend and if you're right, Gelbran, he's out there alone. He's probably more scared of what he has become than we are." She moved closer to Gelbran, "Assuming you're right of course," she whispered.

CHAPTER 16

Barden was livid. Still disguised as Dannard, he had gone into the woods alone before changing into his true form. *Damn Yello and Emnor*, he thought, *they could ruin everything*. It had taken years for him to implement his plan and now he was close, so very close, to seizing the one thing that could bring order to the chaos that existed all over Pordan. Villages and towns were sprouting up, spreading filth and disease across what was once an idyllic world. He would not rest until he brought it to an end. He would find his prize and wait, wait for the one who would have the power to wield it properly. Once *he* had it, the end would be swift. However, he had not anticipated the interference of Keldenar. Aligning himself with Ballorn was simply an act of self-preservation. Only hints of one who would come to aid the dragons had appeared in the scrolls, but the word 'Nibrilsiem' had never been written. He had searched for years before finally discovering Krevick and even as he neared the village sensed that there was a nemilar there far different from the rest. He was convinced that the blacksmith was unaware of the power within him. Disguised as the cooper, he watched and waited.

Spying on Ballorn consumed him during his time in Krevick. Five years, to a wizard at least, was the mere blink of an eye and passed quickly for Barden. Each day was the same as the last for so long, *until Lonny came*. Barden had followed him with interest and studied him for days until, inevitably, he witnessed the farmer and his family being slaughtered as his farm was razed to the ground by the rampaging dragon.

Skulking amongst the trees he watched as the dragon charged after Ballorn, but somehow the robust blacksmith had even managed to survive that. Barden had seen him disappear into the hollow of the tree and was still there when the blacksmith emerged. He frowned at the resilience of Ballorn, but the frown changed to a twisted grin as he saw the gemnar pack approach. *To survive an attack by something so formidable only to be torn apart by such insignificant beasts*, he thought. *Oh, the irony.* Then, the hunter appeared. Ballorn was saved yet again!

It seemed the blacksmith lead a charmed life. *If his demise cannot be left to chance*, he thought, *perhaps I should interject and affect the outcome myself*? Despite his frustration a flash of inspiration drove him to hide in the tree. What better way to gain someone's trust than to appear as the helpless victim?

Then of course there was his manipulation of the vikkery. Once he had cast his spell over them each had the possibility of becoming a dragon. With luck, rumours of dragons would spread, keeping the Nibrilsiem busy. Barden would then be left unfettered, free to pursue his ultimate reward. He would find the crystal alone and keep it hidden until the day came when he could hand it to… *him*.

***

Ballorn and Hunter were loading the cart, carefully selecting only the essentials they may need. They knew that sooner or later they would have to abandon it. However, Ballorn realised that much of their supplies would be used up as they travelled, but they would still need a goodly amount to keep them going. He had tasked Stitch to make him a large bag fitted with straps that would secure it to his back. He could carry far more than the others and having his new backbag would leave his hands free to carry his hammer.

"I've double-stitched it, Ballorn, so it shouldn't split as long as you don't put anything too heavy or sharp in it," the tailor had said proudly.

Ballorn tugged at the seams, "I can see that, Stitch," he said, admiringly. "Cracking job, my friend. Well done."

"And I've waxed the cloth the best I could given the time allowed, it should keep the rain out easily enough. I can't promise it'll work if you drop it in a river or something though."

"Water?" The question came from Dannard, who had suddenly appeared now that the loading of the cart was almost done. "Why has we got to worry about water?"

Stitch rolled his eyes, "If you'd have gotten up a bit earlier, you'd know, wouldn't you?" he sighed. "The way Ballorn wants to go will eventually lead through the marshes, you can't really find a place that has more water unless you go to the ocean."

"The marshes!" Dannard said nervously. "Oh, no, no, no, we doesn't want to be going through no marshes!"

The others weren't taking much notice of Dannard. He scurried in front of them and stared up, seeming almost panic-stricken, *"The woodles!"* he whispered, glancing around to make sure no-one was watching.

Ballorn leaned against the cart and folded his arms, "The *what*!"

"The woodles!" hissed Dannard. "They is like giant frogs, *but they eats people.*"

"Most things that live in the wilds eat people," said Hunter, "what's so different about these... *woodles*?"

"They doesn't kill you like the other beasts!" exclaimed Dannard. "They has these really long tongues what shoot out and snaffle you up. Then they drags you into their mouths and pulls you under the water, and you is never seen again!"

"I'm sure we can defend ourselves against a couple of frogs," laughed Ballorn.

Dannard shuffled in front of Ballorn, grabbing his shirt with both hands, "That's what everybody thinks, until it's too late!"

"Tell you what," said Hunter, "if we see one of your woodles, I'll shoot it and skin it so you can wear it as a hat. Would you like that?"

"That's the thing, you won't see it!" pleaded Dannard. "The singing makes your brain go funny and you just walk up and lets them take you. Them what it snatches don't even put up a fight!"

Stitch looked at him sceptically, "How do you know?" he asked, slowly.

Mark of the Nibrilsiem

"I has seen it with my own eyes!" replied Dannard.

"You've seen it?" asked Ballorn.

Stitch nodded, "So why didn't *you* get lured in and eaten?"

"More to the point, *who did get eaten and why didn't you try to help them*?" added Hunter.

"I was too far away," moaned Dannard. "By the time I got close enough, they was already gone."

"Who was?" asked Stitch.

"Does it matter?" asked Dannard, angrily. "I'm telling you there's terrible dangers in them marshes and we should steer clear of 'em!"

Ballorn had had enough. He suddenly lunged forward and grabbed Dannard by the collar with both hands. Lifting him easily from the ground, he pulled him close, "I want to know who you are!" he growled. "You're no cooper, that's for sure. I've always been wary of you, runt, and those young chaps last night knew you from somewhere!" He glanced down at Dannard's dangling body. "But you didn't look like this, did you? They knew you as somebody else. Start talking, or I'll wring your scrawny little neck!"

Dannard smiled. He glanced around briefly to make sure that the four of them were not being watched. His head began to shrink, and his body began to grow. His tiny, tufty beard grew into a long black one and Ballorn suddenly found that he was holding the robes of a young man much taller than himself, "Barden Oldman," he whispered. "And I am here to help."

Ballorn released his grip.

"You rotten stinker!" exclaimed Stitch. "For years you've fooled me into thinking you were my friend!"

Barden tilted his head as he looked at the tailor, "No, Stitch, you were never being fooled," he said. "I am your friend... I just look a little different to what you are used to."

"Why?" asked Hunter from behind the wizard.

"Rules," replied Barden. "And you can put down the bow," he added turning to face the arrow that was aimed at his head. "I mean you no harm."

"What rules?" asked Ballorn, bluntly.

"We wizards are not allowed to interfere with the natural order of things, Ballorn. However, if I do not, you and everyone you know could soon be wiped from the face of this planet."

"Why take the risk helping us if it's forbidden?" asked Hunter, still holding his bow.

"Isn't it obvious?" laughed Barden. "I like you!"

"You've got a funny way of showing it!" exclaimed Stitch. "Lying to us, pretending to be somebody else... and not the most pleasant of somebody's either!"

"Why not simply come and offer to help? You didn't need the disguise," said Ballorn.

"Offer to help you?" laughed Barden. "Come now, Ballorn, you never would have accepted, you're far too proud for that."

"How would you know?" asked Ballorn, growing suspicious. "The only times we spoke to one another was when you were trying to diddle me out of getting paid!"

"Oh dear," laughed Barden. "Was I that convincing?"

"I wouldn't say *convincing*," said Ballorn. "More... *annoying.*"

"I played my part well then, it's exactly what I was aiming for. I needed to stay at arms-length, Ballorn. I wanted to offer my aid from the first time we met, but I knew that you would flatly refuse. I doubted that you would believe me at all."

"Believe you about what?"

"That there were dragons abroad, of course. You'd have thought me insane and I didn't want that! I chose irritating instead and it worked perfectly, even if I do say so myself."

"Oh yes," agreed Ballorn, "I'll second that. The irritating part was perfect!"

Stitch was livid that he had lost his friend, but the wheels in his head had been turning, "So, these... *woodles?*" he asked, "... they're just made up then?"

Barden shook his head and frowned, "Oh no, not at all. They're very real I'm afraid. They'll drag you down in the blink of an eye. Very dangerous creatures are woodles!"

Stitch gulped and tugged at his collar, "Oh dear," he said quietly.

"Woodles aren't the only things you should worry about either," continued Barden, "There are burgoons, goops, hobblers, gromties, bafflers and worst of all, gresps."

Stitch was now sweating a little and looking decidedly nervous, "And, erm, w-w-why are they the worst?" he stammered.

"Those teeth!" Barden shuddered, "Rows and rows of them. Tiny, razor-sharp teeth just big enough to get through your skin."

"So they eat people then!" gasped Stitch.

"Of course they don't, weren't you listening? They only eat your skin!"

"Right!" Stitch suddenly said loudly. "Count me out! I'm not having my skin nibbled off! Ballorn, you'll have to go on without me, I'm staying here. It's a big village and there's lots of people bigger than me, so the monsters will go after them first because they've got more skin than I have!"

Ballorn shook his head, "He's just winding you up, Stitch," he said, reassuringly. "Chances are we won't see any of those things. They're like all animals, hear a noise and run for it. That's what they all do."

"Bafflers don't," mumbled Hunter. "When they hear a noise they hide in the reeds, then as you're going past… GOTCHA! You're halfway down their gullet with your feet sticking out of their beak before you can blink!"

"Well we'll just have to keep clear of the reeds then, won't we!" exclaimed Ballorn, glaring at him.

Hunter realised what he had just said, "Oh, erm… nothing to worry about anyway," he said unconvincingly, "Bafflers haven't been seen within a hundred miles of here for years."

Barden raised an eyebrow, "There is something else to consider," he added.

"Which is?" asked Ballorn, frustrated that Hunter and Barden seemed determined to give Stitch every possible reason to stay behind.

"Dragon worshippers," whispered Barden. "Far more dangerous than any beast you'll find out in the wilderness."

"What?" asked Ballorn, scrunching up his nose. "Who'd want to worship a dragon?"

"They're a nasty bunch, Ballorn," Barden warned him. "Strange race they are… *shapeshifters*. They want to be dragons, so they look out for the real ones. They protect them in the hope of becoming one themselves."

"Why would they want that?" asked Stitch. "Nobody likes dragons, everyone's scared to death of 'em."

Barden wagged his finger, "That's exactly why they want to be dragons," he said, winking. "They aren't a large race, barely half the size of you nemilar. They're a cold, cruel bunch that's for sure. You can't trust a word they say, that's if you ever get to meet one in their true form of course."

"What are they called?" asked Stitch.

Barden leaned forward, "*The vikkery,*" he replied quietly.

CHAPTER 17

Fellis followed Gelbran as he marched confidently toward the cave. Everything he had said seemed quite logical, well... *mostly*.

"This is not one of your best ideas, Gelbran!" hissed Asdor from behind them. "If you're wrong that dragon'll be picking us out of his teeth tomorrow morning!"

Gelbran paused and glanced back, "Stay here then, nobody said you had to come along!" he sighed.

"Yes, you'd love that wouldn't you? The rest of the clan find out you went to challenge a dragon and I didn't lift a finger to help, then they hang me up by my toes and beat me with sticks for a week! But you won't be there to stop them, will you? Because you'll be in a dragon's belly when it happens, you pillock!"

Fellis smiled, "He makes a good argument."

"Hmph, that's always been his problem," grunted Gelbran. "He argues about everything!"

"Sorry for trying to keep you alive!" Asdor protested. "But if you insist on doing this, I'll be right here doing it with you. Honestly, *I'm a bigger idiot than you are*!"

"No denying that!" mumbled Gelbran. He slowed slightly as he neared the cave mouth and called gently,

"*Cordain.*" There was no sound of movement within the cave. "Cordain, you can come out, we know it's you. There's no need to feel ashamed or embarrassed. Come out and we'll see if we can fix this."

Flame erupted briefly but ferociously from the entrance, and a single word was snarled in rage, "LEAVE!"

"Cordain," said Fellis, softly. "It's me, Fellis. Come out, I'm sure we can help if you give us a chance."

Loud scrapings were heard as the dragon moved around, hidden in the darkness.

"Well, Cordain or not, it knows we're here now. I hope you've got a back-up plan in case you're wrong," whispered Asdor.

As he spoke, the dragon appeared in the cave entrance, "What do you want?" it growled.

Gelbran moved closer, "Cordain? I am right, it is you, isn't it?"

"NO, NOT ANY MORE!" the dragon bellowed. "DOES THIS LOOK IN ANY WAY FAMILIAR TO YOU?"

"Cordain, just tell us what happened and we'll find out how to turn you back. It's obviously a mistake. Let us help."

Cordain stared down at Gelbran, "YOU? HELP? IT'S BECAUSE OF YOU THAT I LOOK LIKE THIS!"

"I know, and I'm sorry, but I won't rest until I've put it right. You have to trust me."

"Trust you? Tell me, Gelbran, why should I trust you? Why should any of us have ever trusted you? You wait until we're asleep and start doing deals with wizards without consulting us! You turn us into freaks who would never be accepted by any other than our own kind. Even then you never thought to ask the wizard if there was a catch. Ask me something, Gelbran! Ask me how it feels to be trapped like this! Ask me how painful it was to have my skin seared off to allow this thing to grow from within me. Ask me how painful it was as every one of my bones snapped as I was transformed against my will! COME ON... *ASK ME*!"

Tears were streaming down Fellis's cheeks and she found herself walking toward Cordain, "Please," she pleaded, "let us try to help you."

Cordain snorted. Unfortunately, a small flame shot from his nostril and singed the top of Fellis's hair. Cordain immediately pushed away, "I'm so sorry, Fellis," he said in a complete change of tone. "It was an accident... I never, I'm really sorry. I'm sure it'll grow back alright!"

Fellis began to laugh, "Listen to you," she giggled. "You've been turned into a dragon, but you're more concerned about my hair getting a bit singed than you are about your own troubles."

Cordain took a deep breath, "I know, but what I did to you was an accident," he said. "However, I suspect that what has happened to me, *is deliberate*!"

"Oh no, you can't think that," she cried. "Gelbran would never do such a thing to any of us."

Cordain stared hard at Gelbran, "No," he said quietly. "But I think that stain of a wizard would."

"Does this mean you're not going to roast us all then?" Asdor shouted from behind a rock.

"Not today, no," replied Cordain. "But I'd tread lightly if I were you, Asdor. You're really annoying at times. You always cross the line."

Asdor popped his head over the top of the rock, "All part of my charm, dear boy."

"And you've already got one toe on it," Cordain warned him. To see a dragon raise one eyebrow, although they don't actually have any, was a sight to behold.

"Was it really that bad, my boy?" asked Gelbran, sincerely.

"What, you mean being set on fire?" Cordain asked sarcastically. "What do you think!?"

"Sorry, stupid question really," admitted Gelbran.

"If I'm honest, it wasn't that bad," Cordain confessed. "The pain was excruciating, I've never felt anything like it before, but it only lasted a few seconds. I must have passed out, or fallen asleep, I'm not sure which. But waking up and trying to rub your face and seeing…" he held up his claws, "… these! Well, that was the biggest shock of all. I was hoping it was just a terrible nightmare, then I woke up in that cave. That's where I've been ever since. Then you three turned up."

Asdor eyed him thoughtfully, "But you're not feeling like you should be out there in the wilds tearing things apart?"

"There's only one thing I want to tear apart." He flexed his claws, "That poxy wizard." He looked down at Gelbran,

"Then again," he added, "if you don't get this sorted out pretty soon, I could start a list!"

"Well you can't do that can you?" said Asdor, chuckling. "How would you hold the quill?"

Gelbran and Fellis glared at him.

***

"There's nothing else for it, pal of mine," sighed Yello. "We're going to have to spy on the slimy little toad!"

"Impossible," replied Emnor. "As much as we can't stand the git, you cannot deny his prowess as a wizard."

Yello curled his lip, "I can deny what I damned well like!" he laughed. "He's not that good a wizard. Either of us could out-perform him any day!"

"Oh, I never meant I thought he was more gifted than us, just that he's better at kissing the right backsides."

"Ooh, hang on!" Yello suddenly yelled as he released a huge ball of flame.

"Do you think this is really the right time to be having this conversation?" Emnor asked thoughtfully.

"It's as good a time as ever," replied Yello frowning.

"So, it doesn't matter to you that we're fending off an attack from a hoard of giants whilst we try to figure out what Barden's up to?"

"Not at all," said Yello. "It actually helps me think more clearly when I'm occupied. DUCK!"

A huge rock flew right above their heads, a rock hurled by one of the giants that would have undoubtedly crushed Emnor, but for Yello's warning. "That was a close one," Emnor smiled.

"I think that one's getting a bit tetchy," said Yello, pointing at the giant who had thrown the rock.

"I don't doubt it!" exclaimed Emnor. "Mind you, I think I'd probably be a bit tetchy if someone had just set fire to *my* bits!"

"Lucky shot," grinned Yello, as he let fly once more. "Anyway, we've got them on the run now. Look, they're scarpering toward the hills."

"Right, so what are we going to do about Barden?"

"What can we do, Emmy? We don't actually know that he's *up* to anything!"

"Oh, come on!" exclaimed Emnor. "He's always up to something! Why would he disguise himself as a nemilar for a start? And what was that crap he was spouting about the dragons being on the move? I've not heard so much as a whisper of any dragon sightings and neither have you. Surely, we would have heard any rumours that were going around. We've been travelling for…" Emnor thoughtfully started to count his fingers, "Good grief! We've been wandering around for over eight months!"

Yello grinned again, "I know," he said. "It's been great, hasn't it? Just you and me, loads of ale and wine, and the occasional punch up to keep it interesting."

Emnor peered at him through half-closed eyes, "Barden?" he asked, quietly.

"Look, if we try to follow him, he'll know we're there! He'll sense us if we get within half a mile of him!"

"We'll have to stay a bit further away then, won't we?"

"And do what?" protested Yello. "It's all well and good if he's out in the open, but once he heads into, I don't know, the woods or into the hills perhaps, we won't be able to see anything."

"Not if we're behind him," admitted Emnor, "But what if we were above him?"

"You can sod off!" Yello yelled, "I'm not falling for that one again. You nearly got us both killed last time!"

"It won't be like last time," Emnor reassured him. "I've made a lot of improvements since then, trust me, Yello… *it will fly.*"

"That's what you said last time! And me being the moron I am, I believed you!"

"Oh, come on, Yello, it wasn't that bad," chuckled Emnor.

"Wasn't that bad!" exclaimed Yello. "We ended up hanging from one of the highest towers in Reiggan! If they hadn't just delivered all that hay, we'd have ended up as two pools of goo in the courtyard."

"I thought you liked a bit of adventure! It's what you're always telling me," Emnor smiled.

"Adventure is one thing!" argued Yello. "Even when you mix in a bit of peril, it's still fun! But what you did was downright reckless stupidity. We're wizards for goodness sake. We aren't meant to fly!"

"I've changed the design completely!"

Yello shook his head as he stared at his friend, "You're not even listening to a word I say, are you?"

"The secret was thicker hide, and of course the seams which are now double-stitched. I was right about the warm air though. But I think you were right that the fire should have been set in some sort of metal container suspended above the floor of the basket."

"I told you that before the thing left the ground! I said it was going to go up in flames, and it did!"

"No it didn't, you're exaggerating again. It was just, well alright, it got a bit out of control, but we soon put it out."

"Correction, Emnor. *I* put it out! Which reminds me. You never did pay me back for that cask of wine I wasted."

"May I point out the flaw in your argument, Yello? Nobody told you to use it to put out the fire."

"Well it was either that or go up in flames a thousand feet in the air!" protested Yello. "What was I supposed to do?"

Emnor waved his hands, "We're getting a little off track," he said, shushing Yello, "This time, we'll be fine."

"Well I will be!" snorted Yello, "'Cause you're not getting me up in that infernal contraption again. Hot air balloon indeed!"

"Alright then, you figure out a way we can follow him without being spotted."

"Easy!" replied Yello, "We just need to pinch something that belongs to him."

"And then he discovers that something has been stolen, realises it was you or me, and comes looking for us? Brilliant! Absolutely brilliant. When he leaves, we'll just walk beside him to save time, shall we?"

"Sarcasm doesn't suit you, Emnor," Yello said slowly. "You should leave that to us professionals." Reaching inside his robes, he drew out a locket. "Say hello to the Tallarans Eye," he said. "No matter where he goes, we'll be able to find him with this."

"But that still won't allow us to watch what he's doing, will it?"

"Well, no, not really. But face it, Emmy, if he meets up with a dragon, we're bound to hear the screams if we're close enough."

"And do what?" asked Emnor.

"Well…" a fiendish grin spread widely across Yello's face, "… if we take our time getting to him, we can just sweep him up."

"Really?" asked Emnor with a blank look. "That's your plan? *Sweep him up.*" Yello nodded enthusiastically. "And what about the nemilar he's with? Do we sweep them up as well?"

"I never said it was a perfect plan," replied Yello, smirking. "But you have to admit, *the first part of it's a cracker.*"

CHAPTER 18

Barden, having managed to quell Ballorn's reservations of being accompanied by a wizard, walked alongside him. "I discovered some ancient scrolls that told of one who would rise up to protect against the tyranny of dragons," he said. "I had no idea who that person was, but I sensed that there was one in your village unlike the rest. To appear as one of your own seemed far better than raising suspicion and anguish, we wizards tend to unnerve folk we meet out here."

"Good word that... *suspicion,*" said Ballorn.

Barden smiled, "I know you don't like me," he said, "I also know that you don't trust me. But think about it, Ballorn. What purpose could I have here other than to help you?"

"Good question," said Hunter. They had not seen him and glanced up at the tree in which he sat. "After all, surely if you were needed, Keldenar would have somehow included you in his plans."

Barden nodded, "Good point," he admitted, "but how do you know that you can trust the word of a dragon?"

"Well, there's the fact that he has now given Ballorn ten times the strength that he himself possesses, oh, and he hasn't tried to kill us," replied Hunter.

"Admittedly I have not granted you the strength of ten dragons, but it seems that different rules are applied depending upon who you are. After all, I haven't tried to kill you either. Yet you condemn me all the same."

Ballorn snorted, "*You?*" he scoffed. "Do you seriously believe that you could kill us as easily as a dragon would?"

Barden held out his hand. Sparks arced between his fingers as he looked into Ballorn's eyes. "Very easily, Ballorn," he said, quietly. "Have you ever seen lightning strike water?" he asked. "At any time whilst you were tending your forge. The moment you drove any piece of metal into the trough to cool it, well, you see my point." He held up his other hand, flames licking around the palm, "What if your bellows had developed a fault?" The flame in his hand leapt higher. "A simple accident causing your entire forge to explode, and you along with it." He rubbed his hands together and the spells disappeared. "But, as I said, I was there to protect you, not to do you harm."

***

They were now approaching the marshes and Stitch was becoming nervous, "I think I'll ride in the cart for a while," he called to Ballorn. "My ankle is aching something terrible, might have twisted it a bit. Best rest it before we get too far out, I don't want to slow us down."

Not turning around, Ballorn smiled, "Yeah, you do that, Stitch," he replied. "Best not take any chances."

Mark of the Nibrilsiem

The ground was much softer now, and Hunter pointed out that the tracks from the cart were far deeper than they had been previously, "Three or four miles at most," he called, "Then I think we'll have to abandon it and just take the pony."

"W-what!" cried Stitch. "We're going to leave the cart! But that means we'll have to walk, and what with my twisted ankle..."

"You can ride the pony," interrupted Ballorn. "We'll offload the stuff into that bag thing you made me, and I'll carry it." He turned around and pointed at Stitch, *"Because I'm not carrying you,"* he sniggered.

Although the ground was soft, the track they were on was easy enough to follow and it was not long before Ballorn was sifting through their supplies and filling his backbag. "You've done a cracking job with this thing," he said, hoping that complimenting Stitch would help to distract the tailor and calm his nerves. Stitch said nothing.

"Don't put too much in that thing," warned Barden. "Put a foot wrong here and the bog will suck you in quicker than you can blink with all that added weight."

"I'll be fine, don't worry about me."

"I'm not worried about you!" exclaimed Barden. "I'm worried that you're carrying all the food on your back! If you go, it goes. If we're deep into the marshes and that happens, the rest of us could starve to death!"

"Well it's not going to happen, so stop fretting," said Hunter. "Anyway, Ballorn, why are we here? I mean here, specifically. Do you know something we don't?"

"No, not really," replied Ballorn, not taking much notice. But after a brief pause, he added, "But then again, yes."

"Go on then," urged Barden, "don't keep us in the dark. What is it?"

"I see things," Ballorn mumbled. "At first it happened when I was sleeping, but more recently, I see them when I'm wide awake. They're not visions, as such, it's more like I'm seeing through someone else's eyes. Or should I say… some… *thing*."

Stitch was pacing nervously, "What kind of something?" he asked.

Ballorn shrugged his shoulders and resumed his packing, "I'm not sure really," he said. "But in one of my, well I suppose you'd call them *visions*, there was a lot of steam in the air. To make steam you obviously need water. Now, where, other than an ocean would you find more water than here?"

"Oh, I don't know!" exclaimed Barden, "Let me think, HOW ABOUT ONE OF A THOUSAND RIVERS?"

Ballorn shook his head, "No, I thought about that, *Mr Shouty*. The water I saw was shallow." He turned and peered at the wizard, "*Really shallow*. More like surface water than a pool or lake. Trust me, we're headed in the right direction."

Stitch gulped, "The right direction for what?" he almost whispered.

Ballorn gave him a confused look, "To find the dragon, of course. Have you forgotten what it is we're supposed to be doing here?"

"So, you actually believe that you're seeing what the dragon's seeing?" asked Hunter.

"Absolutely!" replied Ballorn. "It must have something to do with the gifts that Keldenar gave us."

"So why aren't I getting these same visions?"

"Because, Hunter," replied Ballorn, "*you're not the Nibrilsiem.*"

Stitch suddenly seemed far happier, "Well, that's a good thing isn't it?" he asked, rhetorically. "If you can see what the dragon can see, it won't be able to sneak up on us!"

"Yes, because dragons do that all the time, don't they, sneak up on people," laughed Hunter.

"It could also be a very bad thing," warned Barden. "What if it works both ways and the dragon can get glimpses of what you see? Surely, that would take away any opportunity that we may have of sneaking up on *it*. It may be listening to our conversation at this very moment."

Ballorn leaned against the cart and stared at the ground. He clicked his tongue against the roof of his mouth a few times, a clear sign of his frustration. "Are you done?" he asked quietly as he looked at them in turn. "This is something I have, for whatever reason, been tasked with. The rest of you, however, are free to do whatever you want. The pony is there, the cart is there, and the road back to the village is right behind you. You owe me no loyalty nor allegiance, you're free to leave whenever you wish. But hear me now. Should you decide to join me in this quest, this pessimistic attitude ends now! No more guessing, no more whining, and no concerns over what may happen to me!" he growled. "I'm heading into that swamp in one hour and anyone who decides to follow me had better do so quietly." He glanced at the tailor, "And Stitch," he said winking at him, "I suggest you feed that pony before we leave. We don't want him getting stroppy and dumping you in the water."

***

They were now deep into the gloomy swamp, trying their best to pass through it as quietly as possible. Unfortunately, what with the sploshing of the water and the sound of the pony's hooves clopping on exposed rocks and pebbles occasionally, they weren't having much success. Hunter was finding it quite amusing, watching as the others stumbled and cursed the uneven ground. It was something he himself was not having to contend with, as he was travelling above them through the lower branches of the trees. Every now and then he would call out encouragement, or a warning if he saw anything that may block their path. He knew that the nemilar and the wizard would have no problems, but he would have hated to see the poor pony get hurt.

"Oh wow," Stitch suddenly cried, sliding down from the pony, "Isn't it absolutely adorable?"

At first, no-one could see what he was referring to. Hunter dashed as quickly as he could to get ahead of the tailor… but was not quick enough.

Stitch stooped down and reached out his hand, "Come on, little one," he cooed, "I'm not going to hurt you."

Right in front of him, sat on, what looked like a small lily pad, was a small, blue, fluffy animal with soft yellow eyes. It was no bigger than his hand and looked totally unafraid. "Would you like me to take you with me away from this nasty damp swamp?" Stitch continued, "Somewhere nice and warm, and dry." He never noticed the ripples from the edges of the pad as it moved closer toward him, until it was too late.

There was a sudden eruption of water as a giant toad-like creature emerged from beneath the surface. Its tongue shot out and stuck to Stitch's forehead as if it had been glued there and the beast immediately started to retreat into the water, dragging the shrieking tailor along with it. Hunter released two arrows that both pierced the monster's tongue, but it still did not release its prey.

Ballorn raised his hammer and was about to throw it full force, *but what if his aim was off and he hit Stitch*. He was sure that the tailor would never survive such an impact.

Barden too, was at a loss. The creature was already too low in the water for a fire spell to have any effect, and he couldn't risk a lightning spell as that would be as fatal to the prey as it would the predator.

Suddenly, there was a bellowing cry. A stranger came charging toward the chaotic scene, "Get off him you, slimy old toad," he roared, and threw a strange powder into the air above the beast. It immediately began to screech, and its skin started bubbling as if it were being boiled, but Stitch seemed unharmed by it as the toad released its grip and plunged back into the water. The stranger grabbed Stitch by the back of his collar and hoisted him to his feet. He rubbed his wet sleeve roughly across Stitch's face to remove the slime that had been left there by his attacker. "No harm done," he said, reassuring the tailor that he would be fine. "That stuff won't hurt you, just doesn't feel very nice, that's all." He panted a few times, he was not the youngest person they had ever met, "Damned woodles!" he exclaimed. "I wish the council would listen to me just this once and let me wipe the damn things out, nobody's safe from 'em. Slimy, sly little shi..."

"Porflax!" Barden suddenly exclaimed, "Is that you?"

Porflax stopped talking and peered at Barden, "Oldman!" he suddenly cried, "What are you doing out here? I was hoping I wouldn't see you again, you horrible little snot! And it's *Master* Porflax to you, boy."

Ballorn smiled at Barden, "Friend of yours?"

Barden gave him a scathing glance and muttered under his breath before turning his attention to Porflax again, "My apologies, Master Porflax," he said, insincerely, "but what reason could possibly bring you into the middle of Slymeer swamp?"

Porflax studied him for a moment as questions of his own began to form, "I could ask you the same thing, Barden," he said. "Especially as you seem to have acquired some new acquaintances." He looked from Ballorn to the others, "Nemilar, if I'm not mistaken."

Ballorn stepped forward, "No, you're not mistaken," he said. "Why, do you have something against our people?"

Porflax shook his head briefly, "None whatsoever," he said, his voice getting higher as he spoke. "What I do have something against though," he began, looking at Barden, "is wizards who interfere with things they should leave well alone."

"And how do you know that young Barden should stay out of our affairs if you have no idea why we're out here?" asked Hunter.

"Because of who he is," scoffed Porflax. "He's always up to no good, poking around in other people's business and causing problems."

Hunter smiled, "I'd put that down to his age," he said, "I got myself into a few scrapes when I was younger, but my intentions were always good."

"That's as may be," replied Porflax, wagging his finger, "but if you make a mistake you don't end up blowing half a building to smithereens."

"That was an accident!" protested Barden. "And, it was years ago!"

"You see, there's the proof!" exclaimed Porflax. "He doesn't even have the decency to take responsibility for his own actions!"

"I apologised! It took two days to put right, but I did it, didn't I?"

Porflax began to move toward Barden, but Ballorn moved between them, "Look, I don't really care what went on in the past," he sighed. "What I do care about is that this young lad might be of some use to me. So far, now that we know who he truly is of course, he has done nothing to arouse our suspicions and as long as that remains the case, we're..." Ballorn chose his next word carefully, "... erm, *satisfied*, that he'll aid us should the need arise."

Porflax raised his eyebrows, "Oh, dear," he breathed. "You don't know him at all then, do you?"

"If you're that worried about him," said Hunter, "why don't you tag along with us? That way, you can keep an eye on him."

Ballorn gave him a questioning look and received a wink as a response.

Porflax pondered over the offer before answering, "Well, I have no real destination," he said shrugging his shoulders. "I suppose my search can continue in whatever direction you're headed. But if the journey takes us toward an area I've already been, we'll part ways and you'll have to keep watch over this…" his voice tailed off as he gestured at Barden.

Stitch, a little wary of Porflax, at last found the courage to speak, "What is it that you're looking for?" he asked.

Porflax was surprised that it had taken them so long to ask the question and smiled at Stitch, "Not *what*," he said, "*Who*."

"Alright then, *who* are you looking for?" asked Stitch.

His name is Zendran. He's been missing for weeks and we have no idea where he's gone. It's not in his nature to wander off by himself, he's a very timid fellow you see, and we're getting quite worried about him."

"We?" asked Hunter.

"My fellow wizards at the council of Reiggan," replied Porflax. "But I am not allowed to discuss that, I'm afraid."

"But you're all friends?" suggested Stitch.

"Well, not friends exactly," replied Porflax, "but we do share the same views on most things, so we make decisions jointly, unlike stupid here." He nodded at Barden.

"Insult me all you want," sneered Barden. "It's about time things changed at Reiggan, why shouldn't I be the one who tries to change them?"

"You!" laughed Porflax. "You couldn't change your own socks without one of us giving you instructions, and even if you had some original ideas, nobody trusts you enough to try anything you would ever suggest. As for insulting you, I'll keep doing that whether I have your permission or not."

"Why don't you just sod off!" bellowed Barden. "You're not needed here so…"

"Keep a civil tongue in your head, boy," Ballorn warned him. "I'll say who is welcome here and who is not, so shut it!"

Porflax did not seem the least bit rattled by Barden's outburst as he addressed Ballorn, "May I ask what it is that has brought you to the marshes?" he asked. "I'm sure it was not simply to feed your friend to the woodles."

"No," smiled Ballorn, "And we owe you our thanks for coming to our aid," he added. "Tell me, what was that strange powder that you used to drive it away?"

"Oh that," said Porflax, chuckling. "You'll have some with you, I've no doubt of that. It's just been ground down into a powder." Ballorn gave him a blank look. "*Salt*, my dear fellow, nothing but salt, these things don't like it at all! Well, you saw the way it burns them. Always make sure you have some salt with you when you have no alternative but to enter the marshes."

Stitch immediately began to rifle through their supplies, "Blasted things won't try sucking me under the water again," he chuntered.

"Forgive me," said Porflax, "but you never answered my question."

Ballorn looked deep into his eyes. Somehow, as eccentric as the old wizard appeared, it seemed that he could trust him, "We're searching for a dragon," he sighed.

"Oh," said Porflax, jerking his head back slightly, "What sort?"

Ballorn gave him a quizzical, yet amused look, "Sorry?"

"Well I've come into contact with a few over the years and I thought I might be able to head you… well, *us*, in the right direction."

"You've come face-to-face with dragons?" asked Hunter, dubiously.

"Not face-to-face exactly, but I have seen them," Porflax replied enthusiastically. "Mind you, it's been some time since I last saw one. Centuries now I come to think of it. But you never know, they may still be around."

"And you've not seen or heard anything that might make you suspect that there could be one here in the swamp, or nearby?"

Porflax frowned as he stared at Hunter, "What would a dragon be doing in a swamp?" he asked. "They don't like water for a start and it's far too cramped for them in here."

He placed his hands on his hips, "You do realise how big they are don't you?"

Ballorn began to laugh, "Well I know how big the one that tried to get me was!"

Porflax's eyes widened, "You've survived a dragon attack?"

"Only through pure luck, the protection of a tree and a passing hunter who helped heal my broken leg," replied Ballorn.

"I have to disagree with you there, Ballorn," said Hunter. "I only gave you the pollum leaves to ease the pain. It was the dragon who fixed your broken leg."

Porflax was even more intrigued and, placing his arm around the Nibrilsiem's shoulder, whispered in his ear, "It seems you and I need to discuss a few things," he said, "And we mustn't forget to find Zendran whilst searching for your dragon, he may have some ideas if you're looking for a little vengeance."

Ballorn had no reason to distrust Porflax, after all they had only just met, and he had saved Stitch from a very grisly end. Despite this, something did not ring true with him. *Why would the old wizard be willing to help them so readily?* he thought. He shook his head slowly, "There was a time," he admitted, "when I was driven by revenge. But my views are somewhat different now. You see, I no longer want to kill the dragon, despite what it is guilty of." He paused, thinking over what Porflax had said a few moments before, "What made you think I was looking for revenge?" he asked, slowly.

"Would anyone be searching for a dragon for any other reason?" laughed Porflax. "I'm sure you're not searching for it to make friends. Then, there's the look in your eye. That dragon has caused you great pain, and I do not mean the physical kind alone."

"Can you two talk about this later?" pleaded Stitch. "Let's get out of here before any of those nasty woodles come back and try to eat me again!"

"He's right, you know. They aren't the most intelligent of beasts out here. Doubtless, they will return before long."

Porflax scowled. He was making no secret of his abhorrence of Barden.

"Let's get moving then," Hunter said quickly. "Stitch, make sure you're holding tight, we don't want that pony getting startled and throwing you back in the water."

Ballorn took the lead with Porflax at his side. Hunter followed, holding the reins of the pony to help Stitch feel a little safer with Barden trailing behind.

"You should be careful." Porflax paused, "Good grief, in all the excitement I didn't get your name!"

"Ballorn. That's Stitch on the pony and Hunter leading it. And, of course, you already know Barden."

"Yes, unfortunately, I do," replied Porflax. "He's the one who I need to warn you against, Ballorn. Do not trust him. Whatever he says or does, there will be an ulterior motive for him to have aligned himself with you and your friends."

"Such as?" Ballorn asked.

"I'm not sure," replied Porflax. "But I'll find out one way or another. Give me a little time and I'll let you know what I uncover."

"Oh, come on!" scoffed Ballorn. "He's not much more than a kid!"

"That's what he wants you to think," Porflax warned him. "But have you seen him perform any spells or use any magic whatsoever?"

Ballorn shook his head, "Well, not as such. He did this thing where he had flames licking around his fingers and a few sparks, but nothing more impressive than that. I think he was just showing off, you know, trying to scare me. It didn't work by the way."

"Oh, any five-year-old wizard can do that. Take my word for it, Ballorn. I know wizards, centuries old, who have never managed to perfect the skills that Barden is easily capable of. It's as if he's already lived one life and, after rebirth, still retains all of the powers he learned in it."

Ballorn smirked, "Really? You think that he's managed to die and be born again?"

"Of course not. I was simply trying to give you an idea of how powerful he is! I might look a bit odd, but I'm not a loony!"

Ballorn took a deep breath, "Well," he said, exhaling loudly, "we'll find that out soon enough, won't we!" he grinned.

Porflax chuckled, "Yes, I suppose you will."

"So, how long have you known him?" asked Ballorn.

"Too long," sighed Porflax. "Let's think now. The first time I saw him in Reiggan was about five years ago. Scrawny little wretch with pimples and bad breath, and those were his good points. He has a knack for annoying people by simply being in the same room. I don't remember him having a single friend in all the time he's been there."

"What's *Reiggan?*" asked Ballorn.

Porflax eyed him briefly, "You seem the sort of person who can be trusted," he said, "we're not supposed to mention it to outsiders, you see. They're very strict about that."

"Who are?" asked Ballorn, still none the wiser as to what Reiggan was.

"It's… well, it's kind of a retreat for wizards," said Porflax. "Although a few of them are starting to refer to it as a fortress. Makes it sound far too sinister if you ask me."

"And who are *they?*" Ballorn repeated.

"We thought it best to have a council to keep control of the comings and goings, it is quite a large place and they wanted to make sure that all wizards would obey any rules that were imposed. So, we chose a select few of the oldest and wisest wizards to make the rules and ensure that they were adhered to."

"Sounds like a right rigmarole. Can't you wizards keep yourselves in check? Do you need someone to make rules for you to stick by?"

"Absolutely!" Porflax replied adamantly. "There are certain wizards who would enslave anyone they came across simply because they could. They would use dark magic to rule over many lands on this world, Ballorn! But there is no need for concern, the rest of us will make sure that that never happens."

"Glad to hear it," chuckled Ballorn.

"Ballorn," called Hunter. "The light is failing. I think we should find somewhere to camp. I'll go on ahead and see if I can find somewhere dry."

Ballorn waved his hand.

"If we're sleeping in these swamps tonight," grumbled Stitch, "we're having two campfires! And I'm sleeping between 'em. Anything that comes near me in the night is going to get a flaming torch up its jacksey!"

Ballorn looked confused.

"Something wrong?" asked Porflax.

"I don't know," replied Ballorn. "This might sound strange, but I'm getting a real urge to do some cooking!"

Hunter returned a few minutes later, "We're in luck," he called down from above. "Just up ahead there's a raised area, nice and dry for us to spend the night."

Soon they were busy setting up camp. Stitch scampered around grabbing anything that would burn, he was determined to have his two fires. "It's not enough!" he grumbled, and promptly tried in vain to grab at the overhanging branches in his frenzied attempt to gather more fuel.

"Would you like some help with that?" Hunter asked, smiling at the tailor.

"We need more firewood!" Stitch replied, panting. "No matter how much I jump, I can't quite reach."

Hunter immediately leapt into the lower branches and, drawing his hunting knife, began to hack some of the smaller limbs and pass them carefully down to Stitch."

"Excellent!" Stitch cried with glee. "This should keep all the monsters away."

Ballorn smiled at him, "There are no monsters in the swamp, Stitch, only animals."

"I wouldn't be so sure of that," Porflax said gruffly as he stared at Barden.

"Enough!" Ballorn snapped. "You may not like him, Porflax, but you'll just have to accept that he's a part of this group. He's done nothing wrong." He thought for a moment, "Apart from passing himself off as a cooper for five years, but nothing that has endangered us in any way," he added. "Keep an eye on him if you must. Stay awake all night and watch his every move if it makes you feel better, I honestly don't care! But stop having a dig at him in front of us all the time!"

"Who's hungry?" Hunter asked, breaking the tension.

"Ah, funny you should ask that," Ballorn said enthusiastically. "I was wondering, did you pack any herbs amongst the provisions? Only I've had this idea…"

After a sumptuous meal which Ballorn had insisted on preparing, they all settled close to the fires. None of them was quite sure what kind of meat it was that Hunter had unpacked and felt that it would be impolite to ask. But once Ballorn had added a few select herbs and spices, they agreed that it was one of the most delicious dishes with which they had ever been presented.

"Has it always been a passion of yours?" Porflax asked, "Cooking, I mean?"

Ballorn shook his head, "No, not at all. I've always been able to throw a decent enough stew in the pot, but you couldn't call it a passion, and it never tasted as good as what I just made. After all, it was only for me, so it didn't really matter if it wasn't quite right."

Stitch wasn't paying much attention, too engrossed in tenaciously tending the two campfires. He was determined to not let the flames fall below a certain level. "Got to keep them out," he kept mumbling, glancing up occasionally at the mist that was beginning to form around them.

"You're quite safe, Stitch," Hunter said quietly. "Look, I have my bow right beside me should we need it."

Stitch did not look away from the fire, "Didn't work against that woodle though, did it?" he said grumpily. "If he hadn't come along, I wouldn't be here now. Just leave me be, I know how to protect myself against those horrible things now!" Reaching into his pocket, he took out a pinch of salt, "And my pockets are full just in case."

"It needs to be ground into a powder," Barden reminded him. "Would you like me to do it for you?"

Stitch glared at him, "That's it, you just make fun of old Stitch. Can't even grind up a bit of salt to stop himself being eaten by monsters!"

Barden smiled gently at him, "Stitch, I have always been your friend. I would never mock you."

"You're not my friend!" growled Stitch. "Dannard was my friend and you took him away from me!" He pointed at Barden, his hand shaking, "You just stay away from me, you hear?"

Porflax raised his eyebrows as he looked at Ballorn, "As I said, *he has a knack.*"

The rest of the evening was spent with Porflax regaling them with tales of his many adventures, as he had travelled extensively throughout his long life. Some of his tales were amusing, some exciting, some awe-inspiring and others, to be frank, a little far-fetched. However, it helped to pass the time and soon they were all settling down for a good night's rest, but not before Stitch had added a few more branches to the fires.

***

Ballorn opened his eyes, slightly startled by whatever was prodding his shoulder. Porflax placed his finger to his lips and pointed to the other side of the camp. Ballorn saw a shadowy silhouette disappear into the mist and gave Porflax a puzzled look.

"Barden," whispered the old wizard. "I told you he was up to something. Who would venture into the swamp at night alone, unless they had something to hide?"

"Maybe he needs to…" Ballorn jerked his head to one side, "… you know. He's hardly going to do that with all of us watching!"

"He wouldn't slink off like that just because he needs to pee, Ballorn. Would you? Of course you wouldn't, you'd want someone else to know where you'd gone in case you got into trouble."

"What are you going to do?" Ballorn asked, sleepily.

"I'll follow him of course. You go back to sleep and I'll let you know what happens in the morning, unless I don't come back," he sniggered. "Then you'll definitely know that Barden has bumped me off to cover his tracks."

The wizard moved away quietly and Ballorn laid his head back down, "Ruddy wizards," he mumbled, "wish I'd never met either of them."

CHAPTER 19

"Now you're absolutely certain there's one in there?"

"How many more times, Fellis? I saw it go in there just before dawn!" He thought for a moment, "Do you think they're afraid of the light?"

"They aren't afraid of anything, Asdor! Unfortunately, I don't think they're stupid either. Being the size that they are, it must be easier for them to use the darkness to their advantage."

"How are we going to do this?" asked Gelbran. "Do we lure it out like we did with the first one, or do we head into its lair and hope it's sleeping? I must admit that I'd be far happier to catch the thing off guard."

"I have a couple of ideas," said Asdor. "What if there was a way of bringing the roof of the cave down on it? That way, we'd be in no danger at all."

"Not a bad idea," replied Gelbran, considering his suggestion. "But, if we made any noise it would be on us in a flash, then there's the risk that we may also be squashed. But if it worked, and we did manage to get out, even if the dragon isn't crushed, at least there is the chance that it would be trapped."

Fellis laughed, "You've had a good idea, for a change. What was the second one?"

"I go in and scout around on my own whilst you wait by the entrance. I find out whether or not my first idea is a good one and if the dragon discovers me, I keep it occupied, allowing you to attack it from behind."

"What!" exclaimed Fellis, "You're saying that if it all goes wrong, you'll use yourself as live bait?"

"Exactly," replied Asdor. "What's the worst that could happen? I'll get roasted or frozen for a few seconds! Regardless of what sort it is, I'll be turned into a dragon! Imagine! It'll have you lot charging toward it but will never suspect that one of its own kind is about to attack from behind."

"Have you gone completely insane!" cried Gelbran, "Do you think I would risk leaving you to face a dragon alone?"

Fellis peered at Asdor, "No, Gelbran, he's not insane. He's a crafty swine, that's what he is! That's the whole idea, isn't it, Asdor? *You deliberately want to be turned into a dragon!*"

Gelbran was horrified, "Asdor, surely not!" he exclaimed.

Asdor shrugged his shoulders, "Can't you see?" he smiled. "It makes perfect sense. If we have to keep going after these things, what better way is there than to be one? Think about it. As a dragon, I'd be immune to dragon fire, so none of us would ever be in danger again."

"And what if you turn into a frost dragon, do you think you'd be immune to dragon fire then?"

Asdor wrinkled his nose, "To be honest, I hadn't really given it that much thought."

"You haven't given it any thought!" Fellis yelled, "You're a blockhead, Asdor. What made you think that either of us would ever agree to a stupid plan like that?"

"Because, if I can't convince you to let me do it today, I'll do it another time when you're not there to stop me," he sighed.

"And what of your future?" Gelbran bellowed. "You'll never have a wife, so there'll be no children to carry on your family name if we don't find a cure!"

Asdor pointed at his own face, "Have you had a good look at this lately?" he asked. "Seriously! What kind of girl would want to marry this?"

Neither Gelbran nor Fellis answered.

"Exactly!" exclaimed Asdor with a shudder. "*The ugly ones!* No thank you very much, I'd rather take my chances as a dragon than be married to someone as repulsive as I am! *Just think how hideous our kids would be!*"

Fellis threw her arms around him, "But you're our friend, you can't sacrifice yourself like this. What if the dragon decides to eat you instead of using fire or frost?"

"It'll be doing me a favour," he laughed. "After all, I've got two choices, a few seconds of being chomped on or a lifetime of pain being married to an ugly woman! I'll choose option one, thank you very much."

Gelbran sat on the floor, rested his elbows on his knees and held his head in his hands, "You do realise..." he began, "... that the transformation may be permanent?"

Asdor, still smiling, nodded.

"We have no idea whether you will remain as yourself once you become a dragon, Asdor. It may change you over time. You may become the very thing that we are defending against, and if that happens..."

"Then you'll have to kill me too," said Asdor, finishing his sentence. "I know that, Gelbran. But as we've seen with Cordain, I will remain as myself for at least a while. And I, Asdor, *your friend*, will be by your side to destroy as many dragons as possible until that decision has to be made."

They all turned to face the cave. Asdor patted Gelbran gently on the shoulder, "You just wait there a while." As he walked away, he called back to them, "I'll be back before you know it."

Fellis leaned on Gelbran's shoulder and whispered frantically, "We're not really going to let him do this are we? Tell me you have a plan to get him out of there."

Gelbran lowered his head, "You heard him as clearly as I did. If he doesn't do it now, he'll try it later when he's alone. We may at least be able to offer him some support if this goes badly. If he does it alone, who knows what the outcome could be?"

"I do!" exclaimed Fellis, "He either turns into a dragon or he dies trying to become one! This is madness, Gelbran. We have to stop him!"

Gelbran glanced up but could no longer see his friend. However, it took only a few seconds before he saw, emerging swiftly from a dense patch of long grass, a large grey wolf. It seemed that Asdor had thought this out thoroughly before suggesting it to Gelbran. Cordain had taken the same form when he had faced the dragon responsible for his change. Perhaps Asdor believed that by mimicking Cordain's actions *he would have a better chance of success*? The wolf paused, glanced back... then disappeared into the gloom of the cave.

A few minutes passed. Fellis gripped Gelbran's arm tightly, "Do you think he's alright?" she asked nervously. "Perhaps we should follow him!"

"No," replied Gelbran, solemnly, "I'm afraid we will have to let this one play out, my dear. If we go in there now, we could do more harm than good."

"But, what if he's already...?"

Gelbran patted her hand, "Don't go thinking like that, little one," he said reassuringly, "I've known Asdor all my life. Trust me. Somehow, he'll make this work."

Their blood ran cold as they heard the roar. With eyes fixed on the cave, both of their hearts skipped a beat as they saw the eruption of flame billowing from its mouth. *Would Asdor emerge as a dragon, or was the real dragon simply roaring in triumph having dispatched the intruder to its lair?*

"We should have gone back and fetched the others," sobbed Fellis. "How did we let him talk us into this? If only..."

The roaring began again, but it was clear to them both that there was now more than one dragon hidden in the darkness. There were crashing noises as something heavy was driven into cold stone walls. Flame erupted frequently, but it was too deep within the cave and revealed nothing of what was happening. They edged closer, hoping to get at least a glimpse of what was unfolding. Although still some distance away, they reeled back as the two dragons crashed through the rocks at the side of the cave mouth, raking and gnashing at one another, both engulfed in flame.

"We must help him!" screeched Fellis.

"I know," Gelbran replied angrily, "but which one is Asdor?"

The dragons rolled around, each attempting to outdo the other. Suddenly one of them managed to pin the other by the wing and hold it securely before tearing a huge chunk of flesh from the other's throat. It then grasped the wing, sinking its claws in and tearing it clean from its opponent's body before glancing at the stunned vikkery, "The ugly one, of course!" it roared. "Fancy giving a dragon a hand?"

***

"Ballorn, can you hear me?"

"Of course I can hear you, I've only just closed my eyes."

"I suggest that you open them again, my friend. We have much to discuss."

"Can't this wait until the morning? I'm trying to get some sleep! First that barmy old wizard and now..." With his eyes still closed, Ballorn realised that he recognised the voice. *Great*, he thought, *now I'm dreaming about dragons*!

"Dream or not, Ballorn, you still need to open your eyes."

Frustrated that he was not to be left in peace, Ballorn sat up quickly and opened his eyes. He scowled at Keldenar, who was a few yards away, "How did you get here, dragon? I've heard that your lot don't like water, so what's so important that it would bring you into a swamp?"

Keldenar tilted his head, "But we're not in a swamp, Ballorn."

Ballorn glanced around. The dragon was right. An inky blackness surrounded them both, so much so that Ballorn could not even see the dragon's body, only his head. "What is this place? Oh, hang on a minute, *I am dreaming*!"

"This is no dream, fool!" came an angry voice from behind him.

Ballorn turned and was immediately alarmed by what he saw. He jumped back, his eyes darting from place to place as he sought his silver hammer.

"It's not here," growled the second dragon. "But even if it were, it would do you no good in this place."

"It doesn't matter!" roared Ballorn. "I don't need it to defeat you!" He ran at the crystal dragon, swinging a punch strong enough to fell a tree, a pointless act, as he would soon realise. His fist connected with nothing and passed straight through the face of his nemesis.

"Ballorn, would you please calm down and listen?" pleaded Keldenar. "This is not a dream, but neither is it true reality. I have brought you here so that you may fully understand what it is that you must do."

"I know what I have to do!" growled Ballorn, taking another futile swing at his foe.

The look on the crystal dragon's face changed. He seemed confused, full of anguish and in pain. "You must destroy me, Nibrilsiem. Take my life and bring the suffering of innocents to an end."

"What?" exclaimed Ballorn, "You want me to kill you!"

The crystal dragon shook its head violently, as if to cast off an annoying insect. "I will crush your puny body, before tearing you into a dozen pieces, mortal. You have no hope of defeating me," it sneered.

"But you just said…"

"Now you see the true predicament that we face, Ballorn," sighed Keldenar. "You look into the eyes of one, but behind them two souls are trapped in an endless struggle for control. One is pure and peaceful, the dragon itself. The other, a parasite that tarnishes it. The ceaseless battle rages within, sometimes good prevails, but as time goes on it is becoming weaker and the evil will of the parasite will eventually win the war if we do not find a way to tip the balance."

"That's why you told me not to kill it! You know that if I slay the body, both souls will be lost."

The crystal dragon glared and snarled at them both.

"He has been my closest friend for nigh on a thousand years, Ballorn. I would happily give my own life to save his. Alas, that is not an option. Study the crystal in his brow, that is the source of the evil that controls him. When it grows near to any of our kind it affects them also, we have no resistance against its power."

Ballorn looked from one dragon to the other, "So, you could become as bad as he is then?"

Keldenar shook his head, "Not quite… and not permanently," he replied. "We are only affected when the crystal is near to us. When it moves away, we become ourselves once more."

"So, if I can get close enough to knock that thing out of him, your friend will be alright. Is that what you're saying?"

"Unfortunately, no," Keldenar replied solemnly. "He has been possessed far too long to be able to survive. Even if the crystal is successfully removed, his body will surely die."

"Then there must be some other way!" exclaimed Ballorn. "We cannot allow your friend to die after all the suffering he has endured!"

"I said that his body will die, Ballorn. He, however, will not be lost entirely. I have friends who have already crafted something that will allow his essence to survive."

Ballorn looked hard at the crystal dragon, then turned to face Keldenar, "Don't suppose they could do the same for me, could they?"

"You should not doubt yourself, Nibrilsiem," Keldenar replied confidently. "I have bestowed upon you the strength of ten of our kind. As apprehensive as you are, you must trust me, *you will not fail.*"

CHAPTER 20

Ballorn opened his eyes, the lids feeling heavier than they had ever felt before. *Had it all been a dream? Had the conversation with Keldenar actually taken place?* He had no time to ponder his own questions as his blurred vision cleared and he saw Stitch. The tailor had pulled a log over to where he was sleeping and now sat silently staring at him.

"Something I can do for you, Stitch?" he asked, yawning.

"You can stop putting me in danger for a start," Stitch immediately replied.

"Oh," said Ballorn. "That wasn't actually my fault. If you hadn't jumped down from that pony…"

"I'm not talking about that!" Stitch whispered. "I'm talking about you leaving me alone with those two," he said, pointing at the wizards. "We know one's a liar and the other one's a stranger, yet you don't seem bothered by it. You were in such a deep sleep they could have murdered me and killed you where you lay, and you wouldn't even have known it had happened!"

Ballorn pushed himself up on his elbows, "You weren't alone, Stitch, Hunter was here the whole time. Besides, do you honestly think that the wizard who saved you from being eaten alive, now wants to murder you? Do you realise how stupid that sounds?"

"I don't care how stupid it sounds *I don't trust either of them!*"

Ballorn, now fully awake, ran his fingers through his hair, "I can understand your reservations about Barden," he began, "but I'm certain you can trust Porflax. We saw Barden sneaking off into the forest alone last night and Porflax went after him. He said he'd tell me what happened this morning, so give me a while and I'll find out what he got up to. If there is anything to be concerned about, I'll talk to you about it later, okay?"

Stitch glared at him, "You'd better not keep any secrets from me, Ballorn, or I swear I'll... I'll... well I'm not sure what I'll do, but you won't like it!"

Ballorn smiled, "No secrets, Stitch, I promise." He rose and looked around.

"Up here," called Hunter from the trees above. "Just keeping an eye on things, not that there's anything to see."

"Sounds good to me," groaned Ballorn as he stretched himself. "Nothing better than a report with nothing in it. What about the wizards, what have they been keeping themselves busy with?"

"Oh, they're an absolute joy to be with," Hunter sighed. "If Barden's head were any lower it would be dragging on the ground. Mind you, I'm not surprised, Porflax hasn't given him a minute's peace all morning."

"Is it that late already?" asked Ballorn, concerned that he had slept far longer than he had intended.

"No, no, it's still early," replied Hunter, "but those two were up before dawn."

Ballorn called over to Porflax, "Good morning."

"Good morning," replied the wizard, pleasantly. "I trust you slept well?"

Ballorn nodded as he approached, "Anything you need to tell me?"

Porflax looked a little embarrassed, "Ah, no," he said, lowering his head. "Things didn't go exactly as I would have hoped. I lost him I'm afraid. It was so dark, I could barely see my hand in front of me and if I'd have lit a torch, it would have alerted him of my presence. I'm terribly sorry, Ballorn."

Ballorn held up his hand, "No need for apologies," he assured the wizard. "However, was he gone for long?"

"I... fell asleep," Porflax sighed. "This old age thing is so infuriating! There was a time when I could go without sleep for days and still feel..."

"Never mind," smiled Ballorn. "At least he didn't murder us all in our sleep."

"Well he'd have struggled with that one," Hunter said quietly. "Not all of us *were* asleep."

"Well you never sleep, at least, I've never seen you," laughed Ballorn.

Hunter sucked in his bottom lip for a moment, then looked across the camp at Stitch. "True," he replied. "But I wasn't referring to me." Ballorn and Porflax glanced over at the tailor, who was unaware that he was now the topic of their conversation. "He followed you both, but he came back after just a few minutes. He probably lost his nerve in the dark and scampered back to camp as quickly as he could."

Porflax suddenly seemed slightly angry, "The little sneak," he growled.

"Problem?" asked Hunter staring hard at him.

"Yes!" exclaimed Porflax. "He could have waited for me. Ten minutes trying to find Barden, but a blasted hour to find my way back. He could have shown me the way and saved me from getting wet feet," he laughed.

Despite his mood, Stitch had started to prepare breakfast. Ballorn soon took over. Within the hour, they were all fed, packed up and on the move. Stitch's mood did not change and he glared at the wizards who were now leading them through the swamp.

Porflax bombarded Barden with questions with each step they took and would suddenly bellow at him if he didn't get the answers he was looking for, "Are you some kind of retard, boy?" he roared. "You'd kill everyone in the room if you did that! Have you learned nothing during your time in Reiggan?"

Barden sighed. For him, this was going to be a very long day.

For many hours the water stayed at a constant depth and the cold began to tell on the travellers. Other than Hunter who was still clambering through the trees, they were oblivious as to how much their pace had slowed. Needless to say, it came as a great relief when the swamp became shallower and they were eventually able to walk on dry land.

"We should set a camp here," suggested Hunter.

"But it's only mid-afternoon," protested Ballorn. "There's hours of daylight left."

"And there'll be hours of blisters and chafing which will slow us even more if you don't dry your boots," said Hunter. "We don't have dragon-given powers like you, Ballorn. We need to dry our things and rest. You'll find that we'll make far better progress tomorrow if we recuperate for a few hours extra today."

Ballorn sighed, "Well, seems like a shame to me, but I suppose you're right. I keep forgetting that I've got more energy than I used to have."

"Hmph," snorted Stitch. "Is that why you sleep like the dead every night? I put my finger under your nose three times last night to make sure you were still breathing!"

"Ah, how sweet," laughed Ballorn. "You do care after all."

"It won't stop me running away when that dragon bites your head off!" snapped Stitch, sticking his tongue out.

"I, erm… I'm going to scout ahead a little," Barden called, "see if I can get an idea what we'll be facing tomorrow."

"You're going nowhere!" growled Porflax. "You'll stay right here with the rest of us!" He gave Barden an insipid smile, "Where we know you're safe and sound."

Barden went into a rage, "I've had enough of you, old man. You don't own me, and I don't take orders from you. I'll do what I damn well please and there's nothing that any of you can say or do to stop me! You need my help more than you realise!"

"Is that a fact?" asked Ballorn, quietly. "Why are you so sure that we need you, Barden, is there something you're not telling us?"

"I've withheld nothing from you, but you'd rather take the side of this unruly, undisciplined risk-taker than trust me! You have no idea who he is, what he has done in the past or what he is capable of. He's one step from being banished from Reiggan for good. I'll bet he hasn't mentioned that to you has he?"

Porflax began to glow as he pointed a shaking finger at Barden, "You'll hold your tongue, youngster, if you know what's good for you! Wizards like you are all that is wrong with Reiggan! It was founded by fools with self-righteous morals and ideals. The power of magic makes us superior beings, but there are consequences that come with its use, boy, and only the strongest amongst us are able to live with them!"

"You know what?" Ballorn asked, loudly, "I'm starting to think that it'd be better if neither of you were to stay with us! I mean, look at you, you can't even trust each other. So why should we trust either of you?"

Porflax lowered his hand, "You're right, of course," he said, not taking his eyes off Barden. "Forgive me, Ballorn, it seems that my patience is not what it once was. These young wizards are impetuous and impatient. I was just like them once, but at least I knew right from wrong."

"And without an ounce of proof of any wrong-doing, you accuse me yet again, Porflax," said Barden through gritted teeth.

"Now why would I do that?" Porflax asked, folding his arms. "The fact that your behaviour is so suspicious perhaps? I mean, from what I could see, you didn't seem to be trying very hard to save poor Stitch from being eaten. Or is it that we all watched you sneak from camp in the dead of night without telling anyone? Would that be deemed normal, or would it seem that that person had something to hide?"

"You could have just asked!" shouted Barden. "I don't know anything about the creatures that attacked Stitch, so I didn't know how to fend them off! As for last night, I was out looking for your precious friend! I couldn't sleep! Seriously, have you heard him snore?" he raged, pointing at Ballorn. "Powers of a dragon? The roar of a dragon more like! So, I went out looking for Zendran!"

"Why would you do that?" Porflax asked, suspiciously. "You don't even know what he looks like?"

"How many people do you think there are wandering around a swamp at night? If I found anyone, chances are it would be him! Look, believe what you like or don't, I don't care anymore. But I will not be treated like a prisoner, so if you want to take this further, let's get it over with!"

Porflax looked at Ballorn and shrugged his shoulders, "Sounds like a challenge to me," he sniggered, turning his back on Barden.

Stitch folded his arms and looked totally disappointed, "So you're not going to kill each other then?"

Porflax grinned at him, "No, Stitch, we're not going to kill each other." He looked back at Barden, "Well, not today anyway."

CHAPTER 21

The vikkery were horrified. Learning that Asdor had actually chosen to become a dragon in order to help them find others, did not sit well with them. Gelbran and Fellis avoided the multitude of questions that erupted from the crowd, before finally facing them. "We've decided that it would be best if you were to all come and see him," Fellis announced, a suggestion that brought even more questions and some concerns.

"What if he turns nasty?" called one of them.

"We didn't really see eye-to-eye," called another. "What if he decides to eat me?"

"For goodness sake!" yelled Gelbran. "Do you think I'd suggest you visit him if I thought you'd be in the slightest danger? And somehow, I don't reckon he'll want to eat you however much he dislikes you, Lappet. When was the last time you took a bath?"

"Hang about, if we go up there and it's a *different* dragon, we'll all be killed!"

"Yeah, they all look the same, don't they?"

"No, they do not!" shrieked Fellis. "They're different colours for a start!"

There were mutterings amongst the crowd. "Well I'm up for it," called one of them, "I always liked old Asdor, it'll be fun to have a chat with him now he looks like a real dragon."

"He *is* a real dragon!" exclaimed Gelbran. "What part of this can't you get into your thick heads?"

Lappet stepped forward, "Alright, Gelbran," he said confidently, "you've taken care of us all until now and I trust what you say. Lead on, we'll follow."

The muttering began again.

"I said, WE'LL FOLLOW!" bellowed Lappet. "I'm the one he doesn't like, remember? If he comes after me, at least you lot will be able to scram before he's finished."

With a brief smile Gelbran turned away, and the rest of the vikkery followed him.

Some time later, they approached the cave. A few of the vikkery recoiled and there were many curled lips at the sight of the dragon they had slain earlier that day. The sight of it was not, however, why they were so disgusted. *It was the smell!*

"Oh, my days!" exclaimed one of them before retching, "It stinks worse than your feet, Lappet."

Lappet blushed, "No need for that!" he chuntered.

Suddenly, flames erupted from the cave mouth. The dragon crashed against the side of the entrance as it appeared from the gloom, its jaws snapping and spouting more fire. It immediately saw the vikkery and its eyes flashed red as it glared at them. The vikkery froze in their tracks, it would have been pointless to run from the dragon who was now charging toward them. As it reached them, it raised its huge claws into the air.

"WILL YOU PACK IT IN, ASDOR?" bellowed Gelbran. "You're not funny you know!"

Asdor lowered his claws, "Oh, come on, it was a bit funny," he laughed.

"I've brought everyone here to show them there's nothing to be afraid of, and you pull a stunt like that!"

"Calm down, Gelbran," laughed Asdor. "It was just a joke, that's all."

"You're lucky they didn't all take you for a real dragon and attack you!"

"I thought you said he *was* a real dragon," said Lappet looking slightly confused.

"He *is* a real dragon," Gelbran replied. "But he's not a dangerous dragon."

"He looked flippin' dangerous enough to me, what with all the fire and teeth and claws!" snorted Lappet.

"Well, of course he's dangerous, he's a dragon!" exclaimed Gelbran. "But he's no threat to us. He's our friend."

"He was no friend of mine before, why would he be one now?" Lappet argued.

Gelbran took a deep breath, "Because you are a vikkery and he cares more for us than he does for dragons!" he sighed.

"Mind you," said Asdor, "I could be persuaded to make an exception in your case and bite your head off, you smelly little sh…"

"I think we're getting a little side-tracked!" Fellis suddenly called out. "Asdor, just talk to the rest of our people and prove to them that you are the person they have always known and respected." She shuffled forward quickly and beckoned him to lower his head, "And there'll be no more talk of biting people's heads off!" she hissed.

Asdor lay down and lowered his head, "Look," he said, "I'm as gentle as a spring lamb. Come on, I won't bite, I promise." His nostrils flared, "Not you, Lappet."

***

Ballorn felt an unusual sense of unease. The light in the swamp was beginning to fail and the familiar mist was starting to form on the surface of the water. But somehow, it looked different. The normal pale grey was now tinged with green, and it swirled as the water bubbled gently beneath it.

"Why's it changed colour?" Stitch asked nervously.

Apparently Ballorn was not the only one who had noticed the change.

"Probably just a build-up of algae in the water," said Hunter. "I'm sure it's nothing to worry about, Stitch."

Stitch stared hard at him, "Don't you lie to me," he said slowly as he pointed at the mist, "There's nothing normal about that!"

"Well at least there'll be nothing hiding in the water," Ballorn assured him. "It's not even deep enough to hide a woodle."

"Maybe not, but it might be deep enough to hide something else," suggested Stitch, "Something we haven't seen yet, or giant snakes and things!"

"Look, you've got Hunter right above you, me right beside you and two wizards to protect you! How safe do you need to feel?"

"Back in my own village, in my own bed with all the doors and windows bolted. That's when I'll feel safe, Ballorn!"

"Well that's not going to be for quite a while yet! So why don't you just have a lie down and I'll call you later when supper's ready?"

As Stitch snuggled down between the two campfires, Hunter dropped his cloak to him from above, "Put that over you," he called. "It'll keep the damp chill out." Moving along the branches, he dropped down silently next to Ballorn.

"I fear he has good reason to worry," whispered the Nibrilsiem. "There's definitely something wrong here."

"I wish I could be of more help, Ballorn, but I've never seen a mist this colour before. We should be on our guard."

"It reeks of magic to me, Hunter. Perhaps our wizard friends might have a little more knowledge of such things. Do you think we should consult them?"

Hunter shook his head, "I'm not entirely sure that they are not to blame for this. And listen, have you heard the swamp this quiet in all the time we have travelled through it?"

Trying to look as inconspicuous as possible, Ballorn reached down and picked up his hammer. "Keep your bow close to you, Hunter," he advised, "I think it's only a matter of time before the fun begins."

***

Darkness fell, making the mist more eerie than ever as it reflected the light from the campfires. Ballorn had cooked their supper and Stitch chewed slowly, mesmerised as he stared at the mist. He had surprised them all before they had settled, fervently searching the ground before reaching down and grasping a sturdy branch that lay there. At first, they thought he was simply going to place it on the fire, but as he sat down, he placed it beside him, patting it as if it were a faithful pet. It seemed that, he too, was preparing himself for the worst.

"You'll have to decide what you're going to do after all this dragon business is done with, Ballorn," chuckled Porflax. "You could resume your trade as a blacksmith if you wanted, but I'm sure you could make a damned fine living as a cook."

"I'm a blacksmith, Porflax. Always have been, always will be. But you're forgetting something."

Porflax smiled at him, "Which is?"

"I might not have to make the choice if I don't live through this," replied Ballorn.

"Oh, don't be so pessimistic, Ballorn. One day you'll look back…"

"Please! Please help us," came the weak voice from the mist, "We've been lost in the swamp for days without food. Melly can barely walk. Please help us!"

They all grabbed their weapons as three slender figures emerged slowly from the mist. They appeared to be nemilar girls. Their clothing had seen better days. Long elegant dresses that had been lovingly tailored, were now soiled and ragged and their faces were smeared with mud.

Hunter raised his bow, "Keep your distance!" he warned.

"What are you doing!" screeched Stitch. "Look at the poor things, we need to help them!" He rushed forward, only to be stopped abruptly as Porflax grabbed him by the scruff of the neck.

"I wouldn't do that if I were you," the old wizard suggested. "Not if you value your life, that is."

"They're just three harmless girls!" protested Stitch. "Are you telling me you're not willing to help them?"

"That's exactly what I'm telling you," sighed Porflax.

"You should be ashamed. What if it was someone you cared about and they needed help?"

"Tell me, Stitch, what do you see?"

"It's obvious what I can see, the same as you do! Three nemilar girls who need our aid, and I'm going to give it to them!"

"Now, there's the problem," Porflax said quietly. "*The girls I am looking at are not nemilar!*"

"Don't be stupid!" exclaimed Stitch. "How could you be seeing something different to me?"

"Simple, my dear Stitch," replied Porflax. "We're seeing what they want us to see."

The three figures inched closer.

"Take another step and I let this arrow fly," growled Hunter.

Barden backed away slightly, "Are they what I think they are?" he asked.

Porflax nodded his head slowly, "*Grezzlers,*" he replied, curling his lip. "Filthy, lying, devious grezzlers."

"No, we're not what you think," said one of the girls, sweetly. But its voice changed as it continued, "We need your 'elp," it rasped. "Ain't you gonna be nice and 'elp us?"

Ballorn marched forward and stood next to Porflax, "This won't go well for you, whatever you are. Go back where you came from and you can live through this."

"Aw, that's nice innit?" hissed the grezzler. "We comes for 'elp and you freaten us! We're just 'elpless little girls is all!"

"You're the slime that chokes the life out of places like this," growled Porflax. "Now begone whilst you still have the chance."

The grezzler sneered at him and began to quiver. Its anger was getting the better of it and it was finding it hard to keep the illusion of being something other than what it was. The smooth skin on its cheeks began to wrinkle and its slender nose became bulbous and covered in warts. It shrivelled and its fingers grew longer, sprouting razor-sharp claws from the tips. The cracking of bones could be heard as its spine became crooked and the pale blue eyes that had looked so soft moments before, were now as black as pitch. "'elp us, 'elp us," it screeched. "Let us come and sit wiv ya. We won't do ya no 'arm!" All three suddenly charged forward.

Hunter released his arrow and it struck one of them between the eyes, killing it instantly. Ballorn swung his hammer, splattering another as if it were made of jelly. Porflax raised his hand but was far slower than Barden, who blasted the talkative one to the other side of the camp. It was badly wounded and writhed on the ground, cursing them.

Porflax glared at Barden, he seemed enraged that the younger wizard had reacted more quickly than he, "I'll finish this one!" he bellowed, raising his hand.

"Wait!" cried Ballorn, stepping in front of him, "I want to know what this was all about and that thing may have some answers."

"It's not *about* anything, Ballorn! It's their nature to lie their way into any unsuspecting camp, murder its occupants, eat them and steal their belongings. It's what they are!"

Ballorn shook his head, "No, you're wrong," he snorted. "Three of them against the five of us? They could see how well armed we were, they wouldn't be so rash if they're as devious as you say."

"Even if you're right, it won't tell you anything. It'll just spout more lies, it doesn't know how to do anything else!"

"Well, let's hurry, if we wait much longer it won't be able to say anything, true or otherwise."

Walking across, Ballorn flipped the grezzler onto its back with the toe of his boot. "Why did you attack us?" he asked, demandingly.

"'elp me first an' I'll tell ya. Look, I's bleedin'."

"Answer the question and then we'll care for your wounds!"

The grezzler sneered at him, "'e told us we 'ad to. Said we could 'ave the swamp back for ourselves, like it used to be afore the likes o' you came about."

"He?" asked Barden "Who is, *he*?"

"The dragon," wheezed the grezzler. "The one wiv the sparkles and the shiny face."

Ballorn glanced at Hunter, "Where is it now, the dragon, is it still here in the swamp?"

"No, it went. We was supposed to go to it when you was dead."

"Go where? Do you know?" asked Barden.

Mark of the Nibrilsiem

"It's 'iding," coughed the grezzler, blood spilling from its mouth. "'iding in the ice in ellan…"

The fiery blast shocked them all and they turned to face Porflax as the flames subsided from his palm. *He had destroyed the grezzler.*

"What are you doing?" Ballorn bellowed. "It wasn't finished! We could have found out exactly where to find it!"

Porflax scowled, "It was lying, Ballorn, wasn't that obvious! Dragons hate the cold, even frost dragons hate the cold! There's no way any one of them would be able to survive anywhere where there's ice!"

"At least we'd have had some idea of where to go! It would have been better than paddling around in this blasted swamp for days on end!"

"You should both calm down," suggested Hunter. "What's done is done, there's no point arguing over it. Let's be honest, we weren't going to allow it to live anyway!"

Ballorn stared at him and Hunter's reply was simply to raise his eyebrows.

They sat together by the fire and watched as Porflax wandered away.

"Ellan-Ouine," said Hunter, quietly.

"What?"

"That's what the grezzler was about to say, Ellan-Ouine, it actually means land of ice, or something similar."

"So, you think it was telling the truth, you've heard of this place?"

"To be honest, that's all I know, what it's called and why, oh… and where it is."

"You know where it is?" Ballorn asked, excitedly. "How long would it take us to reach it?"

"That depends," sniggered Hunter. "How good are your climbing skills?"

Ballorn sighed and lowered his head, "Why?" he asked, forlornly.

"Because it's weeks away and, it's on the other side of the Muurkain Mountains."

Ballorn frowned, "Why does that name sound familiar?"

Hunter pointed at the wizards, "Because it's where that lot have started building their new… fortress, I think they call it."

"Oh joy!" groaned Ballorn, "We've got our hands full with just the two of them and we might have to deal with even more?"

"We don't have to go there!" laughed Hunter. "But if we get close to it, they might come to us. Then there's the chance that Porflax and Barden might want to pop in and say hello and want us to go with them. How would we tell them we don't want any more wizards involved?"

"We don't even want the ones we already have! I was just about to get some information out of that grezzler and one of them decides to turn it into a third campfire. Could we go around the mountain, by any chance?"

"It stretches for hundreds of miles, Ballorn. All the way to the Sebland Ocean in fact."

Ballorn rolled his eyes, "Oh well," he sighed, "let's worry about it tomorrow. We'll clear the swamp by late afternoon and see if we can find a village. I could do with sleeping somewhere dry for a change. I feel like this armour's been glued to me, although, surprisingly enough, it's still very comfortable."

Stitch had listened to their every word, "You're welcome," he mumbled, grumpily, "Goodnight."

***

"Don't you think it's about time we went and checked on Cordain?"

Gelbran looked at him inquisitively, "Why do you suddenly want to go and see Cordain?"

"Well, it's been a couple of days and I just want to make sure that he's safe," replied Asdor.

"He's a forty-foot dragon, what do you think could possible harm him?"

"Erm... *himself*!"

"Do you think he's going to go mad and start biting his own legs off or something?" Fellis asked, nervously.

"Of course not!" exclaimed Asdor, "But he might feel abandoned being left all by himself after the accident."

Gelbran shrugged his shoulders, "Alright then, let's go and visit him."

Asdor leaned down, a gleam in his eye. "Would you like a ride? You can jump on my back if you like, save your legs. You too, of course, Fellis."

Gelbran pulled his head back, "No thanks, I'm fine," he said with an uncomfortable smile. "The exercise will do me good."

"What about you, Fellis? Fancy a ride on a dragon's back?"

"Erm, not really," she replied. "You know I'm not good with heights."

"Oh, speaking of heights," said Asdor, nonchalantly, "who do you think is bigger, me, or Cordain?"

"Oh, my days!" screeched Fellis, "That's why you really want to go and see Cordain! You want to show off because you're a bigger dragon than he is!"

"What!" exclaimed Asdor, unconvincingly. "How could you say such a thing? I would never…"

"You're horrible, Asdor," Fellis yelled at him. "If you dare say one word to upset Cordain, I swear I'll pull your scales off one by one!"

They reached the cave where Cordain was hiding. Asdor had begged to be the first to speak and they had reluctantly agreed. "It'll be a nice surprise for him to find out he's not the only one," he said.

"Cordain," he shouted. "Come out and say hello."

"Sod off!" came the answer from within.

"Come on, I have a surprise for you," Asdor continued.

"Leave!" roared Cordain, flame erupting from the cave mouth.

"It's no use getting hot under the collar," laughed Asdor.

Gelbran and Fellis glared at him.

"Just a little joke," he whispered. "Cordain, please come outside, you'll be glad you did, I promise."

"If I come out there I might be tempted to bite you in half, you annoying swine!"

"I'd like to see you try!" laughed Asdor. "When you're big enough, I'll be too old."

Cordain charged from the cave and found himself face-to-face with another dragon lying directly in front of him. He drew himself to his full height and extended his wings to make himself seem more impressive, as if that were possible. The dragon before him never moved.

"Morning, Cordain," said Asdor, cheerily.

Cordain tilted his head to one side, "Asdor?" he said quietly.

"One and the same," replied Asdor, smiling.

"But I was the only one who was caught in the blast. How did…?"

"Take your time," sighed Asdor. "You'll work it out eventually."

"Another dragon?"

"There you go, I knew you'd get there in the end."

"When?"

"Couple of days ago. Anyway, enough of that, how are you?"

Cordain looked down at himself, "Oh, you know, no change."

"I bet you're starving aren't you, Cordain?" Fellis looked a little nervous, "Or did you manage to… do something about it?"

"No, I'm fine," Cordain assured her. "A couple of villagers wandered past yesterday, should keep me going for a while."

Fellis was horrified, "Oh, Cordain, YOU NEVER?"

"Of course I didn't," laughed Cordain. "What do you take me for? To tell the truth, I'm not hungry in the slightest."

"Strangely enough, neither am I," said Asdor.

"I'd have thought you'd need to eat tons of stuff considering your size!"

Gelbran closed his eyes as his head dropped. *Here we go*, he thought. *Nice one, Fellis.*

Asdor jumped at the opportunity, "I suppose we are quite large," he said slowly. "I'd probably have to eat more than you though, Cordain, what with me being bigger."

Cordain looked him up and down, "No, you're not!"

"Oh, I think you'll find that I am. Let's stand side by side and Gelbran can tell you by how much."

"It doesn't matter who's bigger!" yelled Gelbran.

"You never change do you, Asdor? Everything's a competition!"

Asdor, even as a dragon, looked a little sheepish, "Well, it just makes things a bit more... interesting."

"We're dragons you half-wit! We couldn't be any more interesting!"

"No, I suppose not," mumbled Asdor, "Sorry."

"So you should be," replied Cordain, lowering his voice. "It's bad enough having been turned into this," he said looking down, "but with all these new senses kicking in as well, it's even more confusing."

Gelbran frowned, "What new senses?"

"Yeah," echoed Asdor, "What new senses?"

Cordain looked wide-eyed at his friend, "Oh, you'll see, or should I say smell... or hear... or sense."

"I don't like the sound of that."

"It's not bad, Asdor. It only takes a while to get used to. Your eyesight will allow you to see for miles, although, everything seems to have an orange tinge to it. I can hear birds that I know are miles away," he paused, "and I can feel the presence of other dragons who are nearby."

"How come you didn't know I was a dragon before you came out of the cave then?" Asdor asked haughtily.

"I'm not sure. Perhaps because you haven't been a dragon for very long?"

"Fellis nodded, "Makes sense to me."

"So are there other dragons nearby?" asked Gelbran, with a slight growl in his voice.

"What? Oh yes, quite a few actually," replied Cordain. "The closest is only about twenty miles away."

"You said they were close!" giggled Fellis.

Cordain looked down at her, "That is extremely close for a dragon," he warned. "It could be here within the hour if it wanted. Or are you forgetting we can fly?"

"Ooh, yes I had for a while!" Fellis squeaked, excitedly. "How does it feel, you know, to soar through the air as a mighty dragon?"

"Ah, well," Cordain suddenly began examining his claws, "It's… erm…"

"You haven't tried yet, have you?" laughed Asdor. "The big strong dragon is afraid to fly."

"I am not afraid to fly!" argued Cordain. "But seriously," he said opening his wings, "look at these things. I've tried a couple of times, but I can't seem to get the hang of it! I flap them as hard as I can, but once I get a couple of feet off the ground, one side of me dips and I just fall over!"

"Balance was never your strong suit was it though?" laughed Fellis. "Every time we went out on the river you fell out of the boat."

"I did not! Well, not every time!"

"Most of the time then," added Gelbran.

"It's hardly the same thing is it?" said Cordain. "We're talking about flying, not sailing!"

"It'd be the same if you were trying to fly over water. SPLASH!"

Cordain's eyes narrowed, "You're starting to get on my nerves," he growled.

"Alright, alright," laughed Asdor, "I'm only pulling your leg," he held up his own claws, "or whatever it is these things are called. Why don't we both give it a try, you know, at the same time? We can watch each other and see what it is we get right, and what we get wrong. We'll have it sorted in no time."

"Later perhaps," said Cordain. "For now, however, I have important news."

"Oh, no," groaned Gelbran, "I don't like the sound of that."

"*I know which way the crystal dragon went.*"

Fellis gasped, "That means we can go after it!"

"Where has it gone?" growled Gelbran.

"I never said I knew where it had gone, Gelbran, only that I knew in which direction."

"That's good enough!" Gelbran replied angrily. "As Fellis said, we can go after it!"

"There's only one way we could do that, Gelbran," sighed Cordain. "If Asdor and I can perfect our flying skills, you would have to let us carry you. You see, *the dragon was heading for the Muurkain Mountains.* As resourceful as we are, our people could never hope to make that journey safely."

"Some are capable of transforming into birds, others could choose a beast that is suited to rocky terrain and whoever is left could be carried by the others!"

"The blizzards are too harsh, Gelbran. Ice would form in the feathers of birds and the extreme cold would eventually penetrate to the bones of the rest. The only way we would survive, should we need to cross the mountain, is to be as swift as possible. I am sure that none could travel at the speeds of which a dragon is capable."

Asdor shook his head, "I have a better idea," he said, quietly. "We must master the power of flight, Cordain. Once we are proficient, *you and I shall go on alone.*"

"But you can't go by yourselves!" exclaimed Fellis. "Not just the two of you! It's far too dangerous!"

Asdor raised himself to his full height, spread his wings and roared. "Look at us, Fellis. Are we not magnificent? What chance would one dragon have against the two of us?"

CHAPTER 22

Stitch ambled along behind the others. At last, his feet were dry, and he enjoyed the feel of the grass as it tickled his toes. His sodden boots with laces tied together, were hung on his shoulder and he winced occasionally as he caught a whiff of them. "They're ruined," he groaned. "They were my best ones as well. It took hours to get the stitching absolutely perfect, and now look at them. They look like a farmer's work boots."

Ballorn rolled his eyes, "You can have mine if you like," he called.

Stitch wrinkled his nose, "No thank you!" he replied, gagging. "I could never wear a pair of boots that have been on somebody else's feet."

"Alright, I'll buy you a new pair when we get to the village, it shouldn't be far now."

"They won't be the same," sighed Stitch. "Perhaps there's a good cobbler or a tailor who would let me use his workshop, then I could make my own."

"We won't have enough time for you to make your own boots, Stitch! We'll be there overnight at best!"

"That'll be enough time for me, Ballorn. Oh, hang on though. What if they don't have the right kind of leather?"

Stitch mumbled to himself for the next few miles, but the sight of the village outskirts in the distance immediately silenced him as a beaming smile swept across his face. He tore past the others and ran ahead, accosting the first villager he saw. It did not seem that he was happy with what he had just heard, as he flopped to the ground, nursed his head in hands and began rocking back and forth.

"What's wrong?" asked Hunter.

"They don't have a tailor or a cobbler in the village," Stitch moaned, "I'm doomed to wearing the stinking remains of my beautiful boots!"

"Perhaps I might be able to do something with them," suggested Hunter. "I've had far worse to work with out in the wilds."

Stitch glared at him, "You?" he shrieked. "Look at the mud-stompers you're wearing! Do you think I'd ever allow myself to be seen in something like those? You keep your hands off my things!"

Hunter held up his hands, "Only trying to help," he said calmly.

Stitch jumped to his feet, "I'm going to the tavern!" he yelled.

"Ah, are you sure that's a good idea?" asked Barden. "You remember what happened last time don't you?"

Stitch's face was beetroot red, "No I don't, that's why I'm going to the tavern, SO I CAN FORGET ABOUT ALL THIS NONSENSE FOR A WHILE!"

"But last time you drank too much wine, Stitch, you decided it was a good idea to sleep in a water trough."

"It was a warm night, I just wanted to cool down!"

"Cooling down is one thing, Stitch. Lying *face down*, is another thing entirely! If I hadn't been there to pull you out, you'd have drowned."

"You didn't pull me out, Dannard did! Dannard, my friend who you took away, pulled me out. The way I feel now, I WISH HE HADN'T BOTHERED!" With that, he stormed away.

Ballorn turned to Hunter, "You couldn't do me a favour could you?" he asked.

Hunter smiled, "I'll scout around and see what I can find," he replied. "They may not be as nice as his own were, but I'm sure I can find something."

"We'll meet you at the tavern. I'll see if I can rent us some rooms for the night," said Ballorn.

"I could sort out the problem with the boots if you want," Barden whispered.

Ballorn and Hunter turned to the young wizard and saw his hand sparking and steaming.

"They'd be as good as new in a few seconds."

Ballorn glanced at Hunter, "Better not, I think," said Ballorn, "if Stitch suspects you had anything to do with repairing his boots it'll only make him worse."

Barden shrugged, "Just trying to help," he sighed.

"Perhaps you should wait until you're asked," snorted Porflax. "You might get a reputation for sticking your nose in where it's not wanted."

"If I'd have waited for him to ask for help the last time he needed it, Stitch would be dead. Or would you have allowed that to happen?"

"I didn't let him get eaten by the woodles, did I? I don't remember him asking for help then."

Barden gave him a filthy look and then, he too, took his leave.

Ballorn and Porflax stood at the bar in the inn. Stitch had watched them enter and took a huge gulp of wine as he scowled at them but said nothing. The innkeeper was pleasant and handed the keys to three rooms to Ballorn with a nod. Although the travellers were weary it was a little too early for them to retire and Ballorn ordered a selection of dishes so that they might enjoy a meal indoors for a change. Hunter returned after a while clutching a sack which he candidly slid along the bench to Ballorn as he sat down. Stitch did not join them and chose to sit in the corner of the room, not hiding the fact that for now, he preferred his own company.

"Strange," muttered Porflax, "I can still taste the mist from the swamp." He raised his tankard of ale, "A few of these should rid me of it though," he laughed.

"Any idea where Barden went?" asked Ballorn.

"Not a clue," muttered Porflax. "Youngsters!" he scoffed, "They think they know everything and when you try to give them a bit of sensible advice, they throw it back in your face!"

Ballorn sniffed, "He might be young but you were right, Barden's nobody's fool."

"Far from it," agreed Porflax. "A little too clever for his own good at times though."

"What makes you say that?" asked Hunter.

"He argues with everyone in Reiggan. Always thinks he knows an easier way, or a better way of doing things that the senior wizards perfected centuries ago." He leaned forward, "And he doesn't care how dangerous his practises are either!"

Hunter decided to press the issue a little further, "What did he do that was so bad?"

Porflax glanced around the room, "Well, I can't tell you the exact details, as I'm sure you'll understand, but he took it upon himself to modify a spell that had been performed successfully for many years. He never consulted anyone beforehand and ended up destroying an entire wing of Reiggan. Luckily it wasn't occupied, and nobody was hurt, but if it had been, many people could have lost their lives in the blast."

"So, you're saying he's reckless?" suggested Hunter.

"Reckless?" laughed Porflax, "Downright bloody dangerous is more like it! If it were up to me, I'd have him supervised every minute of the day."

"Who is it up to then?" asked Hunter.

"It's not up to anyone, that's the problem. There is a council who can offer advice, but they are not lawgivers. Only if a wizard does something truly horrendous would they consider our intervention."

"Our? So, you are a member of the council?"

"Me?" replied Porflax, choking on his ale. "Good grief no, they'd never allow me at the table. No, when I say we, I mean the wizards who are tasked with apprehending or disposing of any who overstep the mark."

Hunter raised his eyebrows, "Disposing?"

"Oh yes. They don't all see the error of their ways and surrender peacefully. Some fight to the death!"

Ballorn leaned forward and placed his elbows on the table, "What would they have to have done for it to incur a death penalty?" he asked.

Porflax frowned, "We never impose a death penalty, Ballorn!" he said sternly. "Any who stray are given the opportunity to return to Reiggan and face judgement."

"But if you incarcerate them, there's always the possibility that they might escape," suggested Hunter.

"No wizard would ever be held under lock and key by one of his fellows," Porflax replied quietly. "No, they would face a much harsher sentence than that."

"Which is?"

Porflax stared at the table and shuffled his drink around, obviously ill at ease with the question. Nevertheless, he answered, "It is something from which we derive no pleasure..." he began, "... but, they would be drawn."

"And what is..."

"It means that the source of their magic is drained from them, Hunter," Porflax replied, anticipating his next question.

"Well that doesn't sound so bad," said Ballorn.

Porflax's eyes flashed as he glared at Ballorn, "No?" he snapped. "How would you feel if someone came along and cleaved your arms from your body, Ballorn? Would you get used to not having them? Would you be content watching others around you as they went about their daily business, or would you be bitter and jealous of those who tried to offer you aid out of a sense of pity?"

"I didn't mean to offend…"

Porflax cut him short, "No. No, it is I who should apologise," he said with a weak smile. "For a wizard to be drawn proves that our kind are not immune to feelings of pride and superiority. When it happens, which is a very rare occurrence I'm glad to say, it shames us all." He glanced up at Ballorn, the familiar twinkle having returned to his eye, "I'm just a tired old frump," he chuckled. "I always get a bit grouchy when I've had a hard day. I bid you goodnight, gentlemen." He rose from the table and headed toward his room.

"You definitely hit a raw nerve there."

Ballorn rolled his eyes, "Poxy wizards," he mumbled, "I've half a mind to leave whilst those two are asleep. I can throw Stitch over my shoulder and we'll leave those buggers behind!"

Hunter smiled, "Whatever you say, Ballorn," he laughed. "You know I'll follow your lead."

Ballorn sighed, "No, it'd be pointless. We'd be out all night trying to get ahead of them, but something tells me that somehow they'd catch up with us by dawn."

Hunter pointed, "Speaking of Stitch, I think we should go over and check on him. He's looking a little worse for wear."

The tailor was slumped forward, his head bobbing and his eyes half closed as they walked over. "Alright Stitch?" asked Hunter.

"Bugger off and leave me alone," slurred Stitch. "It's not as if you really care. None of you do." He wagged his finger as he tried to focus on them. "You never ask me what I think, and you don't listen to anything I say!"

Ballorn sat facing him, "I'm listening now."

Stitch tried to sit up and raised his goblet, getting more wine down his front than in his mouth. "Hah! You won't care anyway, with your bulging muscles and that big… erm… hammer! Yeah, that hammer. As for you…" he said, turning his attention to Hunter, "… you're just as bad with your owing barrows!" He paused, frowning, "Bow and arrows!"

Hunter sniggered, "Come on, Stitch, I think you should get some sleep."

Stitch shook his head, "What! And lie there so those nasty, stinky wizards can kill me in my sleep? I don't think so matey! When they come for me, I'll be ready for 'em!"

"You've got it wrong, Stitch," Ballorn said, trying to calm him. "The wizards are on our side. They're trying to help us."

"See!" Stitch exclaimed loudly. "You don't know nothin'… anything. You don't know anything."

"They don't even get on with each other, Stitch," said Hunter. "Even if one of them is up to no good, the other will side with us should he need to."

Stitch shook his head more vigorously, almost toppling off the chair as he did so. "See, I'm right, you know nothing." He leaned forward, "*They're working together!*" he whispered. Well, he thought he was whispering. "What's more, *I know what they're looking for!*"

Although they knew that Stitch had had far too much to drink, Ballorn and Hunter were now intrigued, "Go on," Ballorn urged him.

Stitch looked around the room and winked, "They're looking, hic, *for a hat!*"

Ballorn rubbed his face, "Right," he sighed.

"That's it!" snapped Stitch, "Doubt me again if you want, but you didn't follow 'em into the woods, did you?"

"And you think they're looking for a hat?" asked Hunter, dubiously.

"Well not just any old hat! It's a party hat, a very old party hat!"

Ballorn was trying his best, but his patience was wearing thin, "A very old party hat? What makes you think it's old?"

"'cause they said it was, when they were talking. Only they never said 'very old', they used another word, but I can't remember what it was."

"Aged?" suggested Hunter.

Stitch shook his head and pouted, "No."

"Antique?" suggested Ballorn.

"Nope!" replied Stitch, trying to rest his elbows on the table, only to miss and bang his chin instead.

"Ancient?"

Stitch sat up and pointed at Hunter, "That was it… *an ancient party hat!*"

Ballorn thought for a moment, "Stitch…" he asked slowly, "Could they have actually said they were looking for an ancient *artefact*?"

Stitch held up his hands, looking like a scarecrow blowing in the breeze, "Might have," he said, fighting to keep his eyes open. "They were quite a way away, I didn't want to get…" He yawned, his head dropped to the table, and he began to snore loudly.

"Are you thinking what I'm thinking?" Ballorn asked Hunter.

"That they're after the same thing that we are?"

"Precisely," replied Ballorn, slowly. "Why would they become our allies if they are looking to gain possession of the crystal for themselves?"

"Safety in numbers, Ballorn. Perhaps they're looking to use us as bait."

"But Keldenar said that I was the one who was destined to take it. How would that benefit them?"

"Simple," replied Hunter. "You take it from the dragon… then they take it from you."

Ballorn glanced at him, his brow furrowed, "They can try," he growled.

"Hang on though," said Hunter, "we keep referring to 'them', but I haven't seen Barden since we entered the village. I wonder where he went."

"And, what he's up to," added Ballorn.

"Well I'm not about to start searching for him," replied Hunter, standing. "I'm going to get this one to bed. Look at him. Sleeping like the dead!"

Ballorn cleared his throat, "I'll take him," he said, hoisting Stitch into the air with one hand. "I've seen ragdolls stiffer than that," he added, gently swaying the tailor from side to side.

"He's going to regret this when he wakes up in the morning," laughed Hunter.

"At least he *will* wake up in the morning. They tend not to put water troughs in tavern rooms."

CHAPTER 23

Porflax pushed the door open gently and peeped inside. He was not surprised to find the room vacant and headed down the narrow, beamed hallway to his own lodgings. Once inside, he bolted the door. He glanced around and saw the water jug that had been placed there for guests to wash themselves. P*erfect*, he thought. Snatching a tankard and the jug, he walked to the window and stared out. In the gloom he could just make out the treeline of the nearby woods in the pale moonlight. He sloshed the water into the tankard and gulped it down, immediately re-filling the tankard. He repeated the process four times before casting both the tankard and the jug aside. *That should be enough*, he thought. Pressing his hands against the glass, he studied the vista outside then, closing his eyes, he began to chant. A split second later... *he vanished.*

The night air was far cooler than Porflax had expected and he drew his robes tightly around him. Glancing briefly back at the village, he headed into the trees. With a wave of his hand an orb of light appeared before him and illuminated his path. Peering at the ground, he began chanting once more. *Ah, there you are*, he thought. A set of footprints glowed gently on the frozen ground, and he eagerly followed them, "There's no hiding from me, Barden," he said quietly, curling his lip.

He followed the tracks for miles hoping, with each rise of the terrain, to discover the young wizard on the other side. But his frustration grew as each time he only saw more of the same footprints leading into the distance. His temper rising, he began to talk to himself, "When I was younger, I could have run all the way! Now look at me, reduced to shuffling along at a snail's pace. These youngsters don't know how lucky they are. If I'd have known half as much as Barden when I was his age, the whole world would have been bowing before me long before now. Things will change once I have that crystal though. I'll regain my youth and have the power to sustain it. Everyone will fear me. Even dragons will tremble in my presence!"

He stopped suddenly and waved his hand. The orb disappeared and he was plunged into total darkness. He waited, staring at the firelight in the distance. He had found his quarry, it seemed. Inching forward, he grew closer to the clearing. He could hear the logs in the fire as they crackled and hissed, but he could see neither Barden nor anyone else.

"If you'd told me you wanted to come along, Porflax, I would have waited for you."

The sudden voice gave Porflax a start. How did Barden manage to detect him? *The light… it must have been the light.* He had not extinguished it soon enough.

"Do you realise how pathetic you looked as you stumbled around in the dark, old man?"

Porflax was angry, "I've warned you before, boy! Mind your manners when you're addressing me! I see you are not sure enough of yourself to come into the light and face me, you'd rather stay hidden, coward that you are!"

"Coward?" laughed Barden, "Oh, no, Porflax, I'm no coward. I sensed you from a mile away and I know why you're here. You planned to murder me whilst hiding in the darkness. So tell me, *who's the coward?*"

"Why would I want you dead, boy? All I wanted was to speak with you. There are too many prying eyes in the village."

"Then step into my camp and be seated by the fire. Surely the cold cannot be kind to bones as old as yours?"

"I am to trust you, when you mock me at every opportunity?"

"Ah, you need a sign of good faith, do you? Very well, allow me to be the bigger man."

Porflax watched as Barden emerged from the gloom and sat by the fire but was surprised when the young wizard looked up and stared him in the eye, "Come on then old man, make your move. Or are you courageous enough to sit and listen to what I have to say."

Porflax shuffled into the camp and sat opposite Barden. He would never let it show but Barden was right. The heat from the fire was most welcome. "Let's hear it then," he growled.

Barden smiled, "It's obvious that we both want the same thing, Porflax. I seek the crystal that controls the dragons, as do you. I have my own reasons, but yours are a mystery to me, I will admit. However, I must warn you that you are not the one who is destined to wield its power."

"And I suppose you are?" snapped Porflax.

"Me?" laughed Barden. "Oh, no. The one it is meant for is not even born yet. It will be many centuries before he enters our world."

"If that is the case, why should someone else not have the use of it until those centuries have passed?"

"Come now, Porflax, be honest. If you or anyone else were to have possession of such power, would you or they relinquish it freely when the time comes? It would grant the bearer unnaturally long life, a powerful motivation for clinging to something that is not rightfully theirs."

"And you would not be tempted to keep it for yourself, were you to obtain it?"

"Not at all. It will be the downfall of any who hold it, whether their intention be good or evil."

"And you know this, how?"

Barden leaned forward, "There is a race known as 'The Thedarians'. They live far from here and are a very wise people. They have scrolls and parchments that pre-date anything we have ever seen before. I have spent many hours studying their tomes and only the one whose destiny it is must be allowed to wield the power of the crystal."

"Can these people be trusted? Once they are given the most powerful artefact in the world, you expect them to just hand it over when the time comes?"

"The Thedarians will be entrusted with its safe keeping but are unaware of its true destiny. Very few live long enough to complete such a task."

"We do," argued Porflax. "Can you not see? *We* could use the artefact, share its power and rule the world, Barden."

Barden shook his head, "We would be destroyed, Porflax. Somehow it would know that we were not the chosen ones and bring about our downfall."

"You speak as if it's alive!"

"It is," replied Barden, adamantly. "In fact, it was the first life."

"I thought that the crystal dragon was the first thing to live in our world."

"No, it came much later. The artefact simply attached itself to the dragon."

"So, all the death and destruction is being done by the artefact, it's using the dragon as a weapon?"

"It seeks neither death nor destruction, Porflax. It is looking to restore the peace that once existed here."

"So once the crystal is handed to the Thedarians, the meaningless deaths will cease?"

Barden grinned, "Not exactly," he said slowly. "Let's just say… *postponed.*"

"Where does the Nibrilsiem fit in with all this?"

"Ah, I will admit that he is a complication. A complication of which I had no knowledge. Yet it may be one that could eventually prove to be of benefit, if we use it wisely."

"We?" asked Porflax, somewhat shocked that Barden had used the term.

"Are you telling me that you don't want to be a part of this, Porflax? The most exciting adventure since the beginning of time and you'd rather be nought but a spectator?"

"Well, now you put it like that," began Porflax, "it would be interesting to watch as this all unfolds. This Nibrilsiem could be a useful distraction."

"Precisely my thoughts, Porflax. All we have to do is stand back and wait for him to obtain the artefact for us. Then we shall relieve him of his burden."

"What about the other two?"

"We cannot leave any witnesses. I'm afraid they'll have to go. Shame really, I've become quite attached to old Stitch. I'll miss his stupidity more than anything."

***

An hour had passed since Ballorn had closed his eyes, but sleep eluded him. Recent events filled his thoughts, but he was unsure of what his next steps should be. Stitch was snoring gently. Hunter sat in a chair, his hand still clutching his bow. He too had managed to drift off.

"Ah, good, you're awake."

Ballorn opened his eyes.

"No, I'm not in the room with you, Nibrilsiem. I do believe that a dragon entering the village may be a little alarming to the fair folk who dwell there."

"Keldenar?"

"Were you expecting someone else?"

"I wasn't even expecting you," Ballorn replied, yawning.

"Wondering what to do next are you?"

"Yes… and, no," said Ballorn. "Hunter seems to think that we must cross the Muurkain Mountains if we are to find that blasted…"

"Go on, you can say it. *That blasted dragon.*"

"Well, I didn't want to offend you. How are we supposed to keep up with it, Keldenar? We can't fly."

"Easy! Find something else that is willing to help. Something that *can* fly."

"Do you know of such a beast? Perhaps something we have not seen, or a giant bird perhaps?"

Keldenar sighed, "You do make things difficult at times, you do know that don't you?"

"I make things difficult? You're the one speaking in riddles!"

"I'm talking about me, you fool! Or did you forget that I, too, am a dragon?"

"You'd be willing to do that? To have us ride on your back as if you were a mere horse or pony?"

"When was the last time you heard of a flying horse, Ballorn? And you said you didn't want to offend me!"

"It just seems... I don't know... beneath you!"

"You are the Nibrilsiem, Ballorn! Any dragon would deem carrying you upon their back to be a privilege! No, more than that... *an honour!*"

Ballorn frowned, "You're taking this Nibrilsiem thing a bit far, Keldenar," he grumbled, "I'm just a blacksmith!"

"You were just a blacksmith, Ballorn, but you are far more than that now."

"Alright, I get it! I'm the Nibrilsiem and you're going to carry me to the other side of the mountains!"

"Mmm," said Keldenar, slowly. "Not exactly."

"But you just said..."

"I can take you most of the way," Keldenar said, cutting him off. "Maybe halfway up this side of the mountains. But I cannot cross to the other side."

"What's the difference?" exclaimed Ballorn. "If you're going to take us halfway, you may as well get us to the other side!"

"It would be far too dangerous, Ballorn. If, as you say, he is on the other side, he would take control of me and turn me against you."

"He can do that?"

"Quite easily, I'm afraid. And should I try to resist..."

"Go on," Ballorn urged him, "If you should resist?"

"Do you remember the first time we met? Face-to-face, I mean."

"By Lonny's farm? Yes, of course I do," replied Ballorn, impatiently.

"Think back, picture our first meeting. What do you see?"

Ballorn thought hard. "Blood! Lots of blood... on the rock!"

"Yes, Ballorn, blood! My blood, to be precise."

"But how, what could do that to you?"

"*He* did. I was foolish enough to question him, and that was my punishment."

"He would do such a thing to one of his own?"

"No living being is safe from his wrath. Were I to carry you to the other side of the mountain, my punishment would be far more severe. I am not strong enough to resist his will, Ballorn. He would see my siding with you as the ultimate treachery and would undoubtedly destroy me once he had used me against you."

"Well, halfway is better than nothing I suppose," sighed Ballorn. "I'm presuming you have a meeting place in mind?"

"I do," replied Keldenar. "You must leave here at first light tomorrow, that way we shall meet around noon. Follow the route you had already planned for fifteen miles or so and you will come to a tree whose trunk has split in two. They call it the lightning tree."

"Why do they call it that?"

"Because it was split by lightning of course!" sighed Keldenar. "Now get some sleep, you'll need it."

"One more thing, before you go," Ballorn whispered. "Can I trust the wizards? They act as if they're here to help us, but I have my doubts."

"Their motives are unclear to me, Ballorn. Take them at face value for now, that's all you can do to be honest. We dragons are magical beings, as are the wizards, and it makes it impossible for us to see into their hearts. Be watchful, be wary, it is all the advice I have to give."

Ballorn nodded knowingly then glanced at his friends, "I'm surprised we didn't disturb them!" he laughed. "They must be exhausted."

"Oh, them!" Keldenar said loudly. "Don't worry about them, they can't hear us. After all, *I'm not even here!*"

CHAPTER 24

"Not a chance!" exclaimed Gelbran.

"Oh come on, it's not that bad."

"Not that bad?" laughed Fellis. "Look at it, Asdor! It's ten foot deep, twice that in width and a hundred feet long!"

"Well, I'll admit my landing did lack a little finesse, but it's better than Cordain's attempt. He virtually flew straight into the ground."

"And why's that, Asdor? Oh yes, because you crashed into me as we came in to land!"

"There's no need to get upset, Cordain. Just because I'm getting the hang of this flying lark before you, doesn't mean you won't…"

"How do you work that out?" screeched Cordain. "You caused every accident I've had so far!"

"I DON'T CARE WHO CAUSED IT!" bellowed Gelbran. "You're just not safe, either of you! Riding on your backs is one thing, but what use is it if we're all killed the moment you try to land?"

"Don't you think you're exaggerating a bit? I mean look at it! Alright, I may have landed a bit heavy, but look how straight a line I kept."

"Asdor, we were nearly buried alive by the wave of dirt and mud you ploughed up!"

Asdor lowered his head as he looked sideways at Fellis, "Yes, I know... sorry about that," he said quietly. "But you have to admit, I am getting a lot better."

"Say what you like, Asdor, I'm not interested. If we *must* cross the mountains, we're going on foot. I'd rather brave the snow and ice than be splattered into the ground on a dragon's back!"

Cordain raised a claw, "I have an idea," he said enthusiastically. "What if you ride on our backs, but we don't fly? You have to admit that we'll be able to walk a lot faster than any of you."

Gelbran pondered over his suggestion for a moment, then shook his head, "No," he said slowly. "Still too risky. The moment we reach a spot that is difficult to pass you'll suggest that we 'just fly over that bit' to save time!"

"I'm hurt, Gelbran," sighed Asdor. "You mean you can't take us at our word?"

Gelbran laughed, "You? Too damned right I won't take you at your word, Asdor! I've known you all my life and you've always been one to cut corners. I've lost count of how many delays you've caused with your brilliant schemes to save time!"

"That's not true!" exclaimed Asdor. "Name one single time that one of my ideas didn't work!"

"Well, there was the time we had gathered a load of supplies from upriver, and you suggested floating them back on a raft. You said it would be quicker and save us having to carry them. What about that time?"

"Ah, now, I was not entirely to blame for that."

"Yes you were!" laughed Gelbran.

"You could have stopped me!"

"How could I have stopped you? I was in the forest hunting! You built the raft and pushed it into the river before I returned, and what happened?"

"The supplies went over a waterfall," mumbled Asdor.

"Exactly, the supplies went over a waterfall. You didn't think to tie a rope to the raft so that we could simply follow it!"

"It was a mistake anyone could have made, I just thought…"

"You just thought it would be quicker!" Gelbran said finishing his sentence.

"It'll take us weeks to cross the mountains."

"Yes, Cordain it will, but at least we'll get over them in one piece," replied Gelbran.

Fellis kicked the loose dirt with her toe, "I don't want to sound horrible or anything," she said nervously, "but I don't think you two should come with us." Her remark stunned them all. "There will be a lot of loose snow and ice up there and, well, you're not exactly light on your feet are you? You two stomping about could bring the lot down on us."

"But, you can't go alone! There could be all sorts of monsters and nasties up there just waiting to pounce on an unsuspecting passer-by."

Fellis transformed into a bear, "They'll have their work cut out for them if they think they can beat this!" she snarled.

"And what if it's something bigger than a bear?"

"More than one of us can turn into a bear or something more ferocious, Cordain. Nothing up there could possibly cope with that!"

"He's right you know, Fellis, but how about this for an idea? You two can be our scouts."

"Ooh, I like the sound of that. We could go on ahead and make sure it's safe for you to follow."

"However, Asdor, it does mean that you may have to wait some time before we manage to catch up. And dragons do not fare well in the cold."

"We'll find a cave and light a fire!" said Cordain, gleefully.

Asdor gazed at him, eyes half closed, "What, you think there'll be plenty of firewood up there do you?"

"Of course not!" sighed Cordain. "Are you forgetting something? Dragonfire will turn solid rock into glowing coals. How much more heat could we need?"

"Are you sure this is a good idea, Gelbran?" asked Fellis.

"It's no longer an idea, Fellis. *It's a plan!*"

"But it doesn't resolve the issue that there'll be two dragons crashing about whilst we're on the side of the mountain! We may as well jump on their backs now and get being crushed over and done with!"

"When you reach us, you enter the cave, where you'll be safe. Then we move on further up the mountain," suggested Asdor. "Then, after a while, you follow us again."

Fellis thought about it for a moment, "I suppose that could work, providing you can find a cave that's big enough to hold two dragons of course."

"Shall we go now then?" asked Cordain.

"Of course not, you lump. It's going to take a few days to get everyone ready for the climb. We'll come back once we're ready. In the meantime," said Gelbran, gazing into the trench, "... I suggest you keep on practising!"

***

Ballorn held up his hands, "This is the place," he said. "It has to be! Look, there's the lightning tree. There can't be two like it, surely."

"Doubtful," replied Hunter. "So, where's Keldenar?"

"Maybe he's hiding behind it," suggested Stitch.

Ballorn stared at him in disbelief, "Hiding behind it? Keldenar? He's fifty feet tall, you bonehead! How could he hide behind a single tree?"

"He's magic, isn't he!" Stitch said quickly, frowning at Ballorn. "He could make himself smaller or something!"

"They are *magical* beings," Hunter agreed.

"That's as the case may be," said Porflax, "but he's not entirely correct. Dragons are indeed magical creatures, but they cannot perform spells as a wizard or sorcerer would.

"What's a saucer?" asked Stitch, innocently.

Porflax smiled at him, "A *sorcerer*, Stitch…" he replied, correcting him, "… is someone who would use only the darkest of magic. Magic that would do harm to others. Fortunately, we have ways of detecting them before they go too far."

"And how far is *too* far?" asked Hunter.

"And how do you manage to detect them?" asked Ballorn.

Porflax shook his head, "I'm afraid I can't tell you that," he replied. "Trade secrets, you know. The seniors would roast my behind if I were to start telling outsiders how things are managed in Reiggan."

"And you wonder why people are wary of you," Ballorn grunted.

"I'd rather them be wary than terrified," Porflax mumbled. "If they only knew what a rogue sorcerer was capable of, they'd never leave their houses again!"

"I think you've said enough!" growled Barden. "In fact, I think you've said too much already!"

Porflax glared at him, "I'll be the judge of that, boy!" he snapped. "There's nothing wrong with offering a friend a word of warning. Chances are they'll never meet with any of our kind who would wish to do them harm... *but one cannot be too careful.*"

Hunter glanced at Ballorn. *Was this his way of telling them to be watchful of the young wizard*? he thought.

"If you have all finished bickering, perhaps we should make a move?"

They all looked around. They could hear Keldenar, but could not see him.

"You'll have to tell me how you do that," laughed Hunter. "It would come in handy if I get into a scrape."

The ground began to tremble, and the earth began to heave. A huge crack opened before them, a red glow shining through as it widened. Keldenar's huge head appeared as he pushed his way from beneath the ground, soil and dust erupting as his shoulders followed. "Sorry about that," he said, yawning. "I must have overslept. Good thing you lot were making so much noise."

Stitch moved closer and peered into the pit in which Keldenar was still partially nestled. "Is that how you sleep?" he asked. "You actually bury yourself?"

"I had to!" replied Keldenar with surprise. "There are no caves for miles, and I knew we had an early start! I didn't want to be late! Well, not really late anyway."

"But, how do you breathe?"

"Could you save your questions for later, Stitch?" sighed Ballorn. "We really must get going."

Keldenar climbed out of his resting place and studied it for a moment. "Oh dear," he said, quietly, "I have made a mess." Leaning down, he released a gentle breath over the pit. The ground began to move, sliding back to fill the hole and becoming even. The black soil shimmered as tiny shoots of grass appeared and, within seconds, it was as if the hole had never been there.

Stitch was fascinated, "Wow!" he exclaimed. "I wish I'd have had you around to help me with my garden at home in Krevick.

Keldenar turned and looked at the tailor, "You will have another garden, Felidan Portwitch. But we must attend to other things first. Perhaps I could come and visit you? However, I do think that it would be best that I come at night, we don't want to alarm your neighbours."

Stitch smiled at him and nodded. "I'd like that," he said.

Keldenar lay down and extended a wing. "Climb on," he instructed. "The mountains are much farther than they appear. Oh, if you have any extra clothing, I suggest you put it on now. It can get a bit chilly up there. Not you, Ballorn, you'll be fine as you are."

"So, it's alright for me to freeze then?"

"You are the Nibrilsiem, Ballorn, you won't even feel the cold."

Ballorn reached into his backbag and withdrew two large hooded fur coats for Hunter and Stitch.

"Where did you get these?" asked Hunter. "I've been with you the whole time we've been travelling, and I don't remember you doing any shopping!"

"I don't care where he got them from!" said Stitch, happily thrusting his arms into the sleeves. "I just know this is going to keep me nice and toasty."

Ballorn delved into his backbag again. This time he pulled out two thick robes and cowls for the wizards. "Don't say I never do anything for you," he grunted as he threw them across. "Make sure the cords are nice and tight around your waist to stop the wind getting through."

Hunter looked puzzled, "How did you know?"

Ballorn glanced up at Keldenar and winked, "Let's just say a little bird told me," he said quietly. "Well, a big one actually," he mumbled under his breath.

Now wrapped warmly, they clambered onto Keldenar's back.

"Hold tight," instructed the dragon. "You might feel a bit of a jolt when we first take flight, but it'll be much smoother once I'm cleaving the air."

"Not just yet," muttered Ballorn. "We're still one short."

Keldenar glanced down and saw that Stitch had not followed the others, "Something wrong?" he asked.

Stitch stared back at him, a look of dread on his face, "I was… erm, I was just thinking," he squeaked. "Perhaps you should go on without me. I mean, you'll already be carrying four people on your back so you could do without a fifth. The extra weight might slow you down or send you off balance, and you wouldn't want that would you?"

Keldenar lowered his head to Stitch, "You needn't worry, you'll be quite safe. I could carry fifty nemilar the size of Ballorn on my back and barely notice they were there."

"Err, all the same, best not risk it, eh?"

"Stitch, will you stop messing about and get up here," yelled Ballorn.

"I'm only thinking of you!" Stitch shrieked loudly, "I'll probably get in the way or do something daft, you know how clumsy I can be at times!"

Ballorn glared at him, "Get up here, or I'll come down and carry you up!" he said, menacingly.

"Now, now, Ballorn," Porflax said, soothingly. "You can't force the poor fellow to do something he doesn't want to."

"No," began Stitch. "It's not that I don't want to. I mean, there's nothing I'd like more than to…"

"If he wants to be afraid of every new experience that presents itself, who are we to judge him?" Porflax continued, "I mean, look at him. I can see his legs shaking from here, it's a wonder we can't hear his knees knocking together he's so scared."

"I am not scared!" Stitch protested, "And my legs aren't shaking either!"

"You're right, of course," sighed Ballorn. "We can't order him to do anything, but I will feel a little guilty leaving him here by himself."

"Eh!" exclaimed Stitch. "You'd leave me here alone?"

"I don't want to leave you behind, Stitch, but we are pressed for time. Just keep your eyes on Keldenar and you can follow on foot if you like."

"Follow on foot!" yelled Stitch. "How could I possibly keep up with a dragon?"

Hunter laughed, "Don't be absurd, Stitch. We know you can't *keep* up. But if you put in enough effort, you may be able to *catch* up."

"And with a good brisk pace and that fur coat, you should stay warm enough when you get onto the high mountain paths," added Barden.

"Alright!" Stitch yelped. "I'll get on the dragon, I mean *Keldenar's* back. Just give me a minute to work myself up to it!"

The wizards and nemilar smiled at one another as they watched poor Stitch pacing back and forth mumbling to himself, "Come on now, Felidan, you can do this. It'll be just like riding that pony, only higher." He gulped, "Much higher! Oh dear, I'm not sure I can!" He shook himself, "Yes, you can! That lot are laughing at you, thinking you're a scaredy cat, you've got to show them you're as brave as they are!" He glanced up at them, "One more minute," he announced.

"Don't you think we're being a bit mean to him?" whispered Hunter.

"Not at all," replied Porflax. "It'll do him good to realise that he can achieve anything he sets his mind to."

Stitch sidled up to Keldenar's wing and stared down at his new boots. *They're not the best,* he thought, *but at least I managed to get a shine on them this morning. Now they'll get all scratched when I climb up on his scales.* He was struggling to even look at Keldenar and edged sideways with his arm outstretched. *They're going to be as rough as tree bark, I know they are.* His hand met with the scales and a look of surprise appeared on his face, "They're as smooth and soft as leather!" he said aloud as he looked up at Keldenar.

"Thank you," said the dragon. "I do try to take care of them so be careful where you put your feet, there's a good chap."

Stitch smiled at him and started to climb slowly toward Ballorn and the others. "Aren't his scales lovely and soft," he sighed as Ballorn reached down to help him. However, once he was seated next to him, the expression on the tailor's face changed once more as he looked down, "Oh my days, what was I thinking? I don't feel well! As a matter of fact, I think I'm going to…"

"I promise you, Stitch, if you do, you won't be happy with what happens next," warned Keldenar.

"Just take a few deep breaths," suggested Porflax. "Look straight ahead instead of down and you'll be fine."

Stitch nodded, which was difficult for him because he now had a death grip on one of Keldenar's scales and was rigid with fear.

Barden, having known Stitch for so long, began to pity him. Without warning, he held out his hand. A pale mist formed in his palm and he leaned forward and blew it toward the terrified tailor. Porflax glared at him once he realised what he had done, but Barden didn't care and stuck his tongue out at the old wizard. Stitch quickly relaxed and a dreamy smile appeared on his face, "It's quite nice up here once you get used to it," he sighed.

"What did you do?" demanded Ballorn. "If you've hurt him, I'll…"

"Are you forgetting that he was my closest friend for five years, Ballorn?" snapped Barden. "It's a simple charm to relax him, that's all. Or would you rather he sit there petrified for the whole journey?"

"Yes, Ballorn. Let the young wizard use as many charms as he wants!" said Keldenar, sternly. "Better that than Stitch vomiting all over my nice clean scales!"

The dragon launched himself into the air. Ballorn found the sudden rush of wind exhilarating and could not keep his feelings hidden. "YES!" he roared, "Now this is more like it!"

The wizards looked slightly nervous, Stitch was oblivious and Hunter, well it was always difficult to tell how Hunter was feeling as he always seemed to take everything in his stride.

Ballorn had never felt so alive. To him, it was as if he were a part of the dragon. He could feel its chest expanding as it took each breath, feel the muscles contract as they beat the huge wings either side of him and see through its eyes as it scanned the scenery below them. For the first time, he realised that he *was*… The Nibrilsiem.

"Where are you taking us, Keldenar?" called Porflax.

"I'm taking you home," replied Keldenar. "I'm taking you to the wizard fortress you've become so fond of."

"Why?" shouted Barden.

"Because it's as far as I dare go. And you don't have to raise your voice, I can hear you quite clearly."

"I don't understand," said Barden, "Dare?"

"If I get too close, *he* will sense my presence and undoubtedly take control of my mind. Neither of us would want that, my young friend."

"So, you'll wait for us there whilst we continue our journey?" asked Ballorn.

"Oh no," laughed Keldenar, "I'll come back this way and wait for you. I doubt very much that the elders of Reiggan would be comfortable knowing that a dragon was sitting on their doorstep."

"But that makes no sense," replied Ballorn. "We have two of their own aiding us, why would the others not feel the same?"

"Because they're miserable old sods who are stuck in their ways, Ballorn. They'd never listen to any advice from me and as for Porflax, well, they think he's cracked in the head."

"Eccentric, if you don't mind, boy!" exclaimed Porflax. "The word they used was eccentric!"

"Same thing!" sniffed Barden.

"How long will it take to get there?" asked Hunter.

"Not long," replied Keldenar. "A couple of hours, maybe a bit longer. Wait a minute, what's that down there?"

Ballorn scrunched up his eyelids and could immediately see through Keldenar's eyes. "People," he whispered, "Tiny people, loads of them."

"What are they doing?" asked Hunter.

"Climbing, they're climbing the mountain for some reason. Oh dear, I hope I can get back in time or they're going to be in a lot of trouble!"

"Why, what's wrong?"

"Let's just say, there's something waiting for them that they won't be able to cope with. They're some distance away yet though, they'll be safe enough until I return."

Ballorn could hear Keldenar's thoughts. *You must not tell them what you have seen, Nibrilsiem, they would not understand.*

Are they being controlled?

I do not believe so, but there is something strange about them. I will tell you once I know more.

CHAPTER 25

It was not long before, with the grace of an eagle, Keldenar landed and allowed his passengers to slide from his wing.

"How far are we from Reiggan?" asked Hunter.

"It's just up ahead," replied Porflax. "See those niches that have been carved into the rock?"

Ballorn curled his lip, "Are they supposed to signify something?"

"Yes," replied Porflax, proudly. "Well, they will when they're finished."

"Why, are you going to make them bigger?" sniggered Stitch.

They turned in surprise at the sound of the tailor's voice. He looked refreshed and very... smiley.

Ballorn peered at him thoughtfully, "Stitch... are you alright?"

Stitch smiled at him, "Yes, fine thank you," he replied. "I must have dozed off or something, but I feel all the better for it. Just out of interest though," he stared around him, *"How did we get here?"*

"Oh, a bit of jiggery pokery," laughed Porflax.

"More like trickery and sorcery," mumbled Ballorn.

Porflax stared hard at him, "Keep your voice down," he whispered, "And we do not use sorcery!"

Ballorn shrugged his shoulders, "Whatever," he grunted.

"We were brought here by Keldenar," Hunter informed the tailor truthfully, but then added, "You were so looking forward to it as well, shame you slept through the whole thing. You must have been exhausted!"

Stitch eyed the dragon with a puzzled look, "Was I?" he asked. "I must say, I surprise myself at times. I would have thought the idea of riding on a dragon's back would have terrified me. Being with you lot really must be toughening me up."

Ballorn could hardly keep a straight face, "Perhaps a bit of the Nibrilsiem magic spilled over onto you, Stitch. You'll be wanting armour and a hammer of your own before long."

"Oh, I don't think so," Stitch said, smiling. Suddenly a thought popped into his head, "Ooh, but a pair of boots with some lovely silver toecaps might be an idea!"

"Nibrilsiem, I must leave you now," announced Keldenar. "Be watchful, these are uncertain times." He peered into Ballorn's eyes, his thoughts as one with him. *Be wary of the words of wizards, my friend. Believe only in those who are closest to you.* He bowed his head in respect and with a surge of strength, launched himself skyward once more.

"He certainly knows how to make an exit, doesn't he?" laughed Hunter. "Mind you, you'd find it difficult not to really, if you were his size."

Barden was neither impressed nor amused. "We should proceed," he said sternly. "You can stay in Reiggan tonight and we'll resume our search tomorrow." He marched off, not waiting for them to follow.

"What's up with him?"

"Take no notice of him, Stitch," replied Porflax. "He's like a spoilt child some days, and he hates the thought of anyone but a wizard entering the gates of Reiggan. Doesn't like sharing his toys, that's his problem!"

They reached the gates of Reiggan and Porflax raised his hands high in the air. He chanted a few words that were inaudible to the nemilar and the gates began to part.

Stitch was amazed, "Now that's impressive!" he said excitedly. "Look at the size of those gates, Ballorn, they're not even making a noise! You'd expect to at least hear them scraping on the ground or something."

They followed Porflax into the courtyard, where Stitch now stood open-mouthed in awe. They were greeted by three more wizards who looked decidedly older than Porflax.

Porflax bowed slightly and gestured toward Ballorn, "I present to you, Ballorn, the Nibrilsiem," he said solemnly.

One of the elders approached Ballorn, his wrinkled face showing no sign of expression. He circled the nemilar and, now facing him, pointed at his breastplate. "I see you bear the mark," he said, "but only your heart will prove whether you are worthy of wearing it. Tell me, *do you think you are worthy?"*

Ballorn pursed his lips, "Not for me to decide, is it?" he replied. "There is one who knows its significance far more than I, and he feels that I should be the one to bear the mark. As for me being worthy, well, time will tell I suppose. There are only two things of which I am sure. Firstly, I'll be damned if I'm going to walk away from the trust placed in me. Secondly, and more importantly, *it's none of your bloody business!"*

Porflax cleared his throat nervously, "I, erm... I think what he..."

The ancient wizard held up his hand and smiled, "I do believe that the Nibrilsiem has stated his case quite eloquently," he smiled. "My name is Zolban, I am the head of Reiggan," he announced. "And, I must add, it is a great pleasure to meet you, Ballorn."

Ballorn nodded, "Well, same here, I suppose," he mumbled.

Zolban beckoned two young wizards from the other side of the courtyard. "Emnor, Yellodius, take care of our guests and see to their needs," he instructed. He faced the nemilar, "You must be hungry. Get a little rest and we can talk later." He turned his attention to Porflax and Barden. "Gentlemen, follow me, you must have plenty of news you wish to share regarding your other adventures."

"Oh, and you can stop fretting about old wotsisface, we found him for you," laughed Yello. "Silly old goat."

Porflax turned sharply to chastise the young wizard but Zolban placed an arm around his shoulder, "A standing joke I'm afraid, Porflax." He stared wistfully at Yello, "And one in poor taste in my mind," he added. "Come with me, I'll explain."

Emnor nudged his friend, "You always have to push it too far don't you? Can't you just keep your mouth shut for a change?"

Yello twitched his eyebrows mischievously, "Where's the fun in that?"

"Go on then," called Barden, "Off you go and be the good little slaves that you are. Food and drink for our guests, chop chop!" he sneered, as he walked away.

"I'd like to push him too far!" Yello mumbled, "Straight off a bloody cliff!"

"Not one of your closest friends I take it?" asked Hunter.

"Not exactly," replied Emnor. "More like, the farthest you can be from being a friend. Perhaps we gave you the wrong impression when we met in Gendrim."

"So, neither of you like him?" asked Ballorn.

"We absolutely loathe the little slimebag, most of the wizards here do. The only reason they let him stick around is so they can keep an eye on him," replied Yello.

"Yet he's allowed to wander freely without supervision. They can't believe him to be that much of a threat?"

Yello smiled at Ballorn, "So, you think that Porflax turning up was just a coincidence, do you?"

Ballorn hesitated as he looked into Yello's bright eyes, "Not now I don't, no."

"Don't you worry, they've always got someone watching over him," said Emnor.

"How do you know?" asked Hunter.

Yello grinned at Emnor, "Because it's usually us two," he whispered.

Their conversation was interrupted by a very embarrassed Stitch, whose stomach began rumbling loudly. Emnor placed a hand on his shoulder and steered him toward the double doors to their left, "We'd better get this one fed before he wastes away," he laughed.

Ballorn and Hunter followed, both gripping their weapons tightly. Hunter was only following Ballorn's lead, but Ballorn could still hear the words that the dragon had spoken only a short while before. *Be wary of the words of wizards.*

Despite his excitement, Stitch was managing to wolf down copious amounts of food. With a simple wave of a hand, the wizards had produced mutton, beef and a selection of fruits and vegetables worthy of a king's table. The tailor was delighted every time one of them waved his hand and wracked his brains to think of exotic dishes he had heard of, but never tasted, before asking for them.

Yello frowned at him, "We can't produce things out of thin air, Stitch."

"But you just have!" argued the tailor, "I watched you do it!"

"No," Emnor said, correcting him. "It all came from the kitchen. All we did was get it from there!"

Stitch pouted, "So it's not really magic then?" he sighed with disappointment.

"No, not at all!" exclaimed Yello. "We only managed to get it from there to here, through stone walls from a hundred and fifty yards away without carrying it! How could it possibly be magic?"

Stitch tried back-peddling, "Ooh, no, when I said not magic, I didn't mean… it's obviously magic, but…"

"Oh, do be quiet, Stitch!" groaned Ballorn. "You're being gormless again! Just say sorry and we can all forget about it!"

"Sorry," mouthed the tailor. "Won't happen again."

Yello sniggered, "It's okay, only pulling your leg."

"So, what does a Nibrilsiem do then?" asked Emnor, blatantly.

Ballorn glanced at Hunter, "This and that."

"You didn't have to go into so much detail!" Yello said, "After all, you don't want to give away all your secrets."

"Leave him alone, Yello, can't you see he doesn't trust us."

Yello tipped his head back and peered at Ballorn, "Can't say as I blame him, Emmy. After all, he only has Barden and Porflax to set his standards by, so we shouldn't be surprised."

"Perhaps we'd have more faith in wizards if you didn't run each other down at every opportunity."

Yello and Emnor were slightly taken aback by Hunter's comment.

Ballorn leaned forward and placed his elbows on the table, "You keep saying how terrible Barden is but, as we told Porflax, he's posed us no problem."

Yello sniffed, "That's because he still needs you. Trust me, when the time comes, you'll feel the knife in your back."

"Or is it mere jealousy because he is involved in something that you are not?" asked Hunter.

Emnor sat back and drummed his fingers on the table, "Why would you think we're not involved?" he asked.

"Well if you are," began Stitch, "how do we know it's not you who's up to no good? You've already told us you've been spying on him. Have you been spying on us as well?"

Ballorn was pleasantly surprised by the tailor's question and looked at him admiringly, "It's a valid point," he said. "Are you going to answer him?"

Emnor smiled, "Observing," he replied. "A spy has an objective, we do not. The elders know that what you seek is an end to the chaos that is being created by the rogue dragon. We shall not interfere with you, but neither shall we allow any other to do so."

Stitch wagged his finger at the young wizard, "Ah, so you admit it! You have been spying on us!"

Emnor frowned, "I thought I'd just explained that."

Stitch was outraged. Turning to Ballorn, he started banging the table with his fist. "We can't trust these, these... *wizards*," he blurted out. "They want it for themselves! They're making out that Barden will turn on us, when it's them we should be careful of!"

Yello sat forward, a look of astonishment on his face, "Excitable little fellow isn't he, your friend!"

"Doesn't mean he's wrong though," Ballorn said calmly. "Stitch, calm down, you'll do yourself a mischief."

"But, but, Ballorn... he just said..."

"There's nothing wrong with my hearing, I heard what he said."

"So, what *do* you want?" asked Hunter.

"The same as you," replied Emnor. "An end to all the death and destruction that the dragon leaves in its wake."

"And what prize would you expect, should you be needed to intervene?" asked Ballorn.

"None," both wizards replied simultaneously.

Ballorn held up his hand for his companions to be patient, "Come on now," he scoffed. "You know more than you're letting on, and there must be something you're expecting to get out of sticking your noses into our business."

"I suspect that you are referring to the crystal," Emnor said quietly.

Ballorn folded his arms as he sat back, "You know about that then?" he asked, slowly.

"Yes, we do, of course we do!" snapped Yello. "And we couldn't give a toss about it! We simply want to make sure that it doesn't fall into the wrong hands!"

"And whose hands would they be?" asked Hunter.

"That snotty little pipsqueak you've got tagging along with you!" exclaimed Yello. "*Stamp my staff!* Isn't it obvious who we've been talking about all this time?"

"But you can't prove that!" Stitch shouted, banging the table again. "It's your word against his!"

"Pah, we're wasting our breath," snapped Yello, "It's like talking to a bunch of kids!"

Emnor took a deep breath, "Cast your mind back, Stitch. How did you first meet him?"

"When he first came to the village," replied Stitch. "About five and a half years ago."

Emnor leaned forward, "Yes, but it wasn't actually him, was it?"

"Well, no, not exactly. It was Dannard."

"Exactly my point," Said Emnor. "If he had nothing to hide, why didn't he enter the village as himself?"

"He said he didn't want to scare anyone. Wizards don't have the best reputation where we're from. The only ones you hear about are the ones that go about hurting innocent folk."

"So why did he not announce himself properly and disprove the tales that all wizards are evil?"

The question flustered Stitch a little, "I don't know! Why don't you ask him?"

"We already did," replied Yello. "And he came out with the same crap that he told you."

"Do you honestly believe he's that much of a threat?" asked Hunter.

The two wizards cast a knowing glance at one another. Emnor decided it was best that he speak for them both, "He is a dangerous individual, make no bones about it. We see far more in his eyes than you do, my friends. He is capable of things that would haunt your dreams for the rest of your lives. You will be allowed to continue with your quest, but we shall not accompany you. However, we shall never be far away, should you have need of our aid."

Ballorn breathed out loudly and slow, "Alright, I believe you, but it begs the question. If we are successful, and we somehow manage to seize the crystal from the dragon, *what do we do with it?*"

"Hasn't your friend offered any suggestions?" Ballorn glanced at Yello. "You know, *the dragon who brought you here.*"

Ballorn squirmed in his seat, "Ah, you know about him then?"

"Here we go again!" sighed Yello. "*Yes!* We know about him!"

"The subject never came up," Ballorn replied sheepishly.

Yello arched backwards over his chair and placed his hands over his face. "Oh, this just keeps getting better! A dragon gives him the strength to pull trees from the ground with his bare hands but doesn't realise he still only has a brain the size of a pea!"

Ballorn scowled, "Any more insults like that, *wizard,* and you won't have a head to keep your *own* brain in."

"And he reckons Stitch is a bit excitable," laughed Hunter. "Saying that, it was quite a good one, as insults go."

"I suggest we all take a deep breath before this goes too far," Emnor said hurriedly. "Yello, you should apologise."

Yello curled his lip as he stared at Emnor, "Get stuffed," he said gruffly. "When have you ever known me to apologise for anything?"

"He can shove his apology!" Ballorn grumbled, "I don't want it!"

"Good thing!" yelled Yello, "'Cause you're not bloody getting it!"

Hunter smiled as he looked from Ballorn to Yello, "I do believe a beautiful friendship has been born," he sniggered. "You two could be twins!"

***

"It wasn't my fault!"

"Of course it was your fault! If you hadn't crashed so heavily, the avalanche would never have happened."

"It's not as if I did it deliberately, Asdor. At least allow me that defence!"

"I know it wasn't, Cordain. But it doesn't change the fact that we now have a ton of snow to clear before the others get here!"

"Shame really," sighed Cordain, "that cave looked ideal, we can all fit in there. If we're quick enough, we'll still have plenty of time to get it lovely and warm for when they arrive."

"Yeah, once we've covered half a mile to get to where you brought half the flippin' mountain down on the trail they've got to follow."

"Alright, I've said I'm sorry. There's no need to keep going on about it!"

"What do you suggest then? Do we sweep the snow off with our tails, or try to melt it?"

"How should I know!" shrieked Cordain. "What am I, the snow-clearing dragon expert?"

They bickered all the way to where the snow had blocked the trail. Following the natural curve, they froze at the sight of what now faced them. A fearsome looking dragon, even larger than they, lay blocking their path. It stared at them but showed no sign of aggression. It seemed more confused than agitated as it tilted its head and studied them both.

"What are you?" it asked.

They were unprepared for the question, and more than a little nervous.

"Do you have a problem with your eyes?" Asdor began, "We are the same as…"

"You," said the dragon, "are not the same as I."

"Look at us," said Cordain, his voice shaking slightly, "We are dragons."

"You may look similar," yawned the dragon. "But you are not dragons. So, I ask you again, *what are you?*"

"What do you think we are?" asked Asdor, trying to think of an answer that would not infuriate the dragon.

"I'm not sure, your scent is completely unfamiliar to me. Are you wizards, or sorcerers perhaps, looking to cause mischief?"

"Neither, and, no," replied Asdor. "We are merely crossing to the other side of Muurkain."

The dragon shook his head, "I cannot permit that," he said. "And, if it is as you claim, why are you lying in wait for the little people to arrive. Is it your plan to devour them, or simply murder them?"

Asdor and Cordain glanced at one another, "Little people," mouthed Asdor.

"Oh no," Cordain suddenly replied, "No, we don't want to harm them. Just the opposite, in fact. We're making sure the path is clear for them so that they can pass unhindered."

"What if that was his plan?" muttered Asdor. "Well done, genius."

"My name is Keldenar," announced the dragon. "And it was not my plan to harm your friends either," he added, peering at them both. "Keldenar is my given name you understand, you would not be able to pronounce my real name, *as you are not dragon kind.*"

"Okay I'll admit we're not real dragons," said Asdor. "Well, we are, but we weren't born as dragons."

"Fascinating," replied Keldenar, yawning again and lowering his head to the ground, "Tell me more."

"We're vikkery," said Cordain.

"Oh dear, are you really?" replied Keldenar with a slight semblance of interest. "I'm sorry to hear that, anything I can do to help?"

"He means our race," said Asdor. "We are called the vikkery. Those are our people following us."

"You don't look very much like them though. Did you have some sort of accident?"

"Well, I suppose in a way we did," replied Asdor. "Mind you, everything would have been fine but for that blasted wizard."

Keldenar raised his head, "Wizard?" he asked, "What wizard?"

"We never actually saw him," replied Cordain. "He sneaked into our camp and met with our, well I suppose you'd call him our leader. He said he could offer us a gift so that we could get revenge on…"

"On one of our enemies," Asdor interrupted quickly.

"Go on," Keldenar urged.

"Well it turned out to be a curse, not a gift."

"In what way?" asked Keldenar. He waited, but neither Asdor nor Cordain could think of an answer that would not include 'dragonslaying'. "Ah, now I understand," said

Keldenar, nodding. "If the dragon you were hunting struck first with its breath, you would become the very thing that you sought to destroy? Am I correct?"

"We don't have a problem with dragons…" Asdor began nervously.

"Do you not?" Keldenar asked, wearily. "I do. They can be the most obstinate of creatures at times, and that's the nice ones. Some of them are downright obnoxious, stepping on anything that gets in their way just because they can, or setting everything alight simply because they don't get their own way. It's just so undignified!"

"Are you alright?" asked Asdor, sincerely.

Keldenar opened his eyes wide, "Me? Good heavens no, *I'm exhausted.* Have you ever had to listen to the Nibrilsiem screaming down your ear simply because he's riding through the clouds for the first time, or had a tailor threaten to vomit all over your freshly preened scales? Honestly, I don't think I'll ever recover!"

"Sounds to me like you deserve a lie down and a nice rest, friend. We'll go about our business and leave you in peace," said Asdor, winking at Cordain.

"Yes, that sounds lovely," sighed Keldenar, his eyelids flickering a few times before they closed. "But I'm afraid the answer is still no. You must turn back, and take the rest of the bokkery with you."

"Vikkery," said Asdor, correcting him.

"Yes, if they're here you must take them as well, you wouldn't want to leave them stranded up here would you?"

Cordain leaned close to Asdor and whispered, "We'll just go back along the trail where he can't see us. Look at him, he'll be sound asleep before you know it, then we can easily sneak past."

"Not as easily as you might think," yawned Keldenar.

Cordain was astounded that the dragon had heard his whisper.

"Fatigue has no effect on one's hearing you know," continued Keldenar, his eyes still tightly shut. "I'm not trying to be difficult, but you have no idea what awaits you should you continue on your foolish quest."

Asdor tried reasoning with Keldenar, "We understand that you have our best interests at heart, my dear dragon, however, I do not believe that our leader will be so easily dissuaded. Will you not allow him to decide the fate of his own people?"

Keldenar opened his eyes slightly, "Do you mean that he would readily put you all in danger?"

"Of course not, but he is headstrong and would probably challenge you to battle if it were the only way to pass," said Cordain, with a certain amount of admiration.

"Ah, so he is as stupid as he is brave?" snorted Keldenar.

"He's far from stupid!" snapped Cordain. "If it wasn't for him, many more of us would have died instead of…"

Keldenar stared at him, "Instead of… who?" he asked.

"Instead of a couple of dragons!" replied Asdor, loudly. "Happy now? We hunt dragons! Your kind have hunted us for far too long… now we've turned the tables and it's our turn to be the hunters!"

"Mmm, interesting," Keldenar said, quietly. "Do you think you could prevail against the one whom you seek most? He is far larger and stronger than any you would have seen so far. He controls any dragon who ventures near and, although you are not true dragons, he would control you in the same way. Not only would you not harm him, you would willingly destroy any whose intention was to cause him harm."

Cordain peered at him, "But how do we know you're telling the truth?"

Keldenar pushed himself up to a sitting position, "You have only my word," he replied. "I have had to abandon my friends to their fate, for I too, would turn against them if I were commanded to by *him*."

"What friends?" asked Asdor.

"Friends who have a better chance of success than others who would foolishly face such a colossal enemy," replied Keldenar. "There is one amongst them whose destiny it is to defeat him and put an end to his tyranny."

"One?" laughed Cordain. "As if one person could win against a dragon!"

"He would have a better chance than two *imitation* dragons would against a *real* one."

"I don't like being threatened!" growled Asdor.

"Not a threat," sighed Keldenar, "a fact. Face facts, dear boy, you can't even land properly. Look at the mess you made!"

"Flying and landing aren't the same as fighting!" snarled Asdor. "Now I suggest you get out of our way before our tempers start to fray!"

Keldenar laughed as he spread his wings. With one hefty surge, he pulled them forward. Asdor and Cordain were taken completely off guard and were blown off their feet. Scrambling to face Keldenar, they glared at him.

"You see," said Keldenar, calmly. "I could crush you both within seconds... *how long would you expect to last against one I would dare not face?*"

"We'll see!" yelled Cordain. "You won't find it so easy when the rest of our people arrive!"

"I'm trying to help you!" exclaimed Keldenar. "Can you not see that? You have blocked the trail with a bit of snow, I'll bring down half the mountain to prevent you from putting yourselves in danger. Turn back, turn back now!" he pleaded. "There is no need for you and yours to put yourself in harm's way, *the crystal one will be defeated!*"

Realising that they would never be allowed to pass, the vikkery turned away. "You'd better be telling the truth, *dragon*," Asdor called back. "Because if you're lying, I'll come looking for you."

"What do we tell Gelbran?" asked Cordain.

"We tell him the truth."

"Seriously?"

"Absolutely, Cordain!" Asdor replied emphatically, "We tell him the trail is blocked because you crashed and caused a landslide that's impassable!"

"What about the dragon, do we tell him about that?"

"I can't see how telling him every detail would help," replied Asdor, timidly. "Best leave that bit out, just knowing that there's no way through is enough."

"And what if he goes and has a look for himself?"

"You always have to look on the bleak side, don't you!" exclaimed Asdor. "Gelbran is my closest friend, he'll believe whatever I tell him!" He gulped, "I hope."

CHAPTER 26

Ballorn lifted his backbag. Glancing across, he noticed the coats he had left at the foot of the bed the night before. "Well we won't be needing those any more," he muttered, "Might as well leave them here."

Focussed on his packing, he had not noticed Zolban, who now stood in the doorway. "You may not need yours," smiled the old wizard, "but your friends will be glad of theirs. Take them with you, it gets more than a little chilly out on the ice flats."

Ballorn looked at him inquisitively, "You've been there before then?"

"Oh yes," replied Zolban, "many times. But not for a great number of years. These old bones of mine don't like the cold."

"It's a frozen wasteland. What could there possibly be out there that would be of interest to a wizard?"

"Put a wizard anywhere in the world, Ballorn, and he'll find something fascinating there," chuckled Zolban.

"What, wizards are fascinated by snow and ice?" giggled Stitch.

"Of course, and what can be found beneath it," replied Zolban.

Stitch frowned, "Like what?"

"Oh, well, plants, fungi, algae and other such things that have strange properties for healing. Although we do discover more that are poisonous than those of a restorative nature. There are hidden caves that house strange beasts and lifeforms that would make your hair stand on end! All sorts of wonders can be found out there if one knows where to look!"

"Beasts?" groaned Stitch. "You mean monsters, don't you? Why can't we go somewhere nice for a change where all the animals are fluffy and nice and only eat leaves?"

"Because," replied Hunter, slapping him on the shoulder, "this is the real world, and nothing is ever that easy. Where there are fluffy animals that eat leaves, there are also beasts that eat fluffy animals."

"And people who like fluffy animals!" sniggered Ballorn.

"You'll be quite safe, Stitch," Zolban assured him. "You'd have to venture into the deepest caverns to find anything that could do you any real harm."

"Ah, good," sighed Stitch. "So where are we going then?"

"We're going to the ice fields, Stitch," Hunter told him.

"Sounds cold," said the tailor. "But, at least we'll be above ground," he added happily.

"Eventually," said Ballorn, "Once we've travelled through the caverns to reach them."

Stitch's face dropped, "I knew it, I flamin' well knew it," he moaned.

Barden, Porflax, Yello and Emnor entered the room.

"What's wrong with him?" asked Emnor, pointing at Stitch. "He looks a bit peaky."

"Ballorn smiled, "He's just had a bit of bad news. Don't worry, he'll be fine. He's a lot tougher than you'd think is old Stitch."

"I don't feel well," grumbled Stitch.

"Yeah," chuckled Yello, "tough as old boots that one."

The procession entered the courtyard and approached the gates. Barden was ahead of them and seemed agitated.

Hunter nudged Ballorn, "He's in a bit of a mood, isn't he?"

"It's because he's had a bit of bad news of his own," whispered Emnor.

"Oh yeah, what's that then?"

"We're coming with you," replied Yello.

"Why?" asked Hunter.

"Safety in numbers," Zolban replied.

Yello couldn't hold his tongue, "And the fact that we don't trust the little git!"

"Yellodius!" snapped Zolban, sternly.

Yello immediately regretted having opened his mouth, "Sorry, Master Zolban," he said hurriedly. "My apologies."

Zolban spoke softly to Ballorn, "Don't worry about Barden," he said. "He has the best intentions but can be a little… *impetuous*."

"The boy's an arse!" exclaimed Porflax. "I still say we'd be best to leave him here!"

"But I am the head of Reiggan and I say he's going with you!" replied Zolban, firmly.

"Alright, I know!" continued Porflax, "You're in charge, so we'll do as you say. If we're lucky, he'll get eaten along the way!"

Stitch grabbed his sleeve. "Eaten!" he shrieked. "Are there things in the caverns that will try to eat us then? Can you throw salt on them like you did with the woodles?"

Porflax patted his hand, "There's nothing in the caverns, Stitch, don't fret. I'm just saying that, if he's not careful, a dragon might just get a surprise breakfast."

"Oh," sighed Stitch, "That's a relief… Oh, no," he groaned, "I'd forgotten about the dragons."

The gates slid open silently and they ventured outside. Headed back to where they had parted from Keldenar, they noticed the entrance to the caverns.

"How didn't we see that before?" asked a bemused Stitch. "Was it there all along or have the wizards used magic to open it up?"

"We're good, Stitch, but we're not powerful enough to open and close passageways in mountains," Yello told him. "It was always there, you were probably tired and focussed on reaching the gates, that's why you didn't see it."

Mark of the Nibrilsiem

"Oh, can I walk between you and your friend though? You seem to know this place and I'd feel a lot safer with you two either side of me."

Yello turned and watched as the gates closed, Zolban waving them a last goodbye as they thudded together. He breathed a sigh of relief, "Oh it's so good to get out of that place. Emnor, do me a favour and walk in front of Stitch will you? I'll stay behind him. Don't worry, my needle-pulling friend, we'll take good care of you."

The gloom soon enveloped them as they entered the cavern. The four wizards produced torches from thin air, illuminating the walls as they sparked into life.

"What am I doing?" mumbled Porflax. "I haven't used one of these for ages!" Handing the torch to Hunter, he held out his hand. The familiar ball of light he had used previously appeared and hovered before him, moving forward with each step he took.

Stitch was impressed, "Can you do that?" he asked Yello, excitedly. "It would save you having to carry that torch."

Yello sneered, "No... that's one of his own spells," he mumbled. "He won't share it. The old ones prefer us to learn our own spells."

"But it's only a light!" exclaimed Stitch.

Barden turned and offered Ballorn his torch as he duplicated Porflax's orb spell. "Here you go, you have this," he said, sniggering.

Yello glared at the back of Barden's head, "As for that one, if he had a piece of mouldy bread he wouldn't hand it to a starving man. All he cares about is himself."

As they went deeper into the caverns, Stitch was fascinated by the glowing algae that had formed on the walls.

As he stretched out his hand, Yello grabbed his wrist, "Don't touch that!" he warned. "It stinks! You won't get rid of the smell for days if it touches your skin."

The corners of Stitch's mouth curled down, "Thanks," he muttered, "That could've been nasty."

"And watch your footing," called Barden. "We don't need you breaking your leg down here."

"Don't worry, Stitch. A broken leg doesn't hurt as much as you'd think," said Ballorn, smugly. "After all, I should know."

"Thanks to yours truly," said Hunter. "You'd have been in agony after a while if I hadn't been there. Come to think of it, you probably wouldn't have been around at all. You'd have been beastie food."

"I'd have managed somehow!" snorted Ballorn.

The light ahead of Barden cast an eerie shadow across his face and Stitch scowled as he caught a glimpse of him in the darkness. "Was he real?" he called.

"He's talking to you, dung head," said Emnor, nudging Barden in the back.

"Was who real?" said Barden, ignoring the insult.

"Dannard. Was he a real person or someone you made up?"

"Oh, he was real, alright," replied Barden. "But you wouldn't have liked him, Stitch. He was a most surly and abrasive character."

"So all you had to do was change your appearance then," laughed Yello. "You already had the same personality."

"Be quiet," said Barden.

"Oh, come on, Barden," said Yello, still laughing. "Where's your sense of humour?"

"No," whispered Barden, sternly, "I mean, *be quiet*. There's something lurking ahead of us."

They all listened carefully. They could hear something shuffling around in the gloom and, for a split second, saw something move, revealed by the glow from the strange algae. Then, *it began to growl*.

"Oh, dear," whimpered Stitch, "What is it?"

"Oh, get out of the way!" raged Yello. "It's probably a zingaard. Make a bit of noise and flash a bit of fire and it'll soon scarper!" He held up his hands and flames erupted, lighting up the entire cavern and revealing the beast that had been hidden in the darkness. Whatever it was, it was huge! Startled, it turned to face them, the matted fur hiding its features but revealing large canine teeth that glinted as the light caught them. It stood at full height and roared, the razor-sharp claws on its hands clearly visible.

"We're gonna die, we're gonna die, we're gonna die," whined Stitch. "Why didn't I stay with the other wizards? At least they had walls to keep the nasties out!"

However, Yello was correct. The creature suddenly turned and began to scale the wall behind it in a bid to escape the fire-wielding interlopers who had invaded its home. Pausing briefly, it turned and roared again, before fleeing back into the safety of the darkness.

The flames disappeared from Yello's palms and he wiped them on his robes, "See," he said, smugly. "Only a zingaard. Easy enough to deal with if you know how."

Emnor looked at him inquisitively, "And just when have you had to deal with those things before, exactly?" he asked.

Yello smiled at him and tapped the side of his nose, "We're not always together, my friend," he replied. "I may have had a bit of a mooch around down here by myself in the past, for my own reasons, of course."

"What reason would anyone have to crawl around in the darkness when they know there are probably monsters waiting for them?" squeaked Stitch.

Yello frowned at him, "Well I never knew that those things were down here the first time I visited, obviously," he sighed, "I just... *hoped*."

Emnor shook his head, "Yellodius, you may be my dearest friend," he said quietly, "*but you're mental!*"

"I know," replied Yello with a grin, "*Fun isn't it?*"

"You came down here," exclaimed the exasperated Stitch, "and you were hoping to find monsters?"

Yello folded his arms, "Absolutely!" he replied. "It'd be boring otherwise."

"Have you finished?" growled Barden. "Can we continue, or did you want to hang around and have some more... *fun?*"

Yello raised his eyebrows, "See what I mean? No sense of humour, that one."

***

"Are you sure?"

"We've just told you! There's no way we can get past. The trail is completely blocked. We could probably clear it eventually, but it would take weeks."

Gelbran stared at them, "We'll have to find another way," he chuntered. "You'll have to keep searching until you find a safe passage we can take."

"There is no other route, Gelbran! We've been flying around for hours, knowing what you'd ask us to do, but there's nothing!"

Gelbran pointed up at Asdor, "You got us into this mess, it's up to you to get us out of it!" he bellowed.

"The only way is if you're prepared for us to carry you on our backs," mumbled Cordain. Asdor gritted his teeth and glared at him. "Erm, but you know that's not safe, so I don't know why I even suggested it!"

Asdor looked sideways at him, "That'll be because you're a pillock."

Gelbran held up his hand, "It might be the only way though," he mumbled. "Have you managed to learn how to land a bit better now?"

"Oh, no, not in the slightest!" Cordain said quickly. "I mean, look at the state I made of the trail. No, Gelbran. You'd have to be mental to want to ride on my back! None of our people would have a chance of surviving one of my bungled descents."

"And you?" Gelbran asked, peering up at Asdor.

"Afraid not," he sighed, casting another sideways glance at Cordain, "I'm almost as bad as him. Admittedly, I didn't bring down half a mountain, but, no I couldn't guarantee anyone's safety."

"This is so frustrating!" bawled Gelbran. "How can there be only one way to get over a mountain? There must be another trail somewhere, buried beneath the snow perhaps?"

"We melted the snow anywhere that we thought there might be a path," lied Asdor. "There is no other route."

"It'll have to be just the three of us then!" Gelbran suddenly announced. "The others can make their way back down, but there's no reason for us to quit."

"What!" exclaimed Asdor. "You want to keep going?"

"Well I'm not giving up if that's what you mean," Gelbran huffed.

"Weren't you listening?" Cordain asked. "You won't be able to do anything whilst we're in the air, and you'll probably be squashed by one of us two when we try to land!"

"It's my life, it's up to me what I do with it!" snapped Gelbran.

"That's as the case may be!" argued Asdor. "But how could either of us carry on knowing that we were responsible for your death, you pig-headed fool? Well I'll tell you something right now. Leader or not... *I won't take you!*"

"Neither will I," said Cordain, "If you want to cross this mountain so bad, you'd better start climbing!"

"We tried our best, but now it's time to turn back, Gelbran." Gelbran, Asdor and Cordain turned to see Fellis watching them. "You can't ask your friends to put your life in danger like that, it's not fair."

Gelbran sank to his knees, "But... we're so close," he whispered in a pleading tone. "We almost had him. He's just the other side of the mountain. We could end all the killing."

Fellis knelt beside him and placed her arm around his shoulders, "We'll have our chance, Gelbran. We'll watch and we'll listen, and when the time comes, we'll get him. At least your little Grubb will get his daddy back this time. Think about that, eh?"

"He's one lucky kid, Gelbran," said Asdor. "He'll grow up with a mom and dad who love him, and he'll be the envy of the whole village. I mean, none of the other kids will have two pet dragons, will they?"

"Aren't you forgetting something?" mumbled Gelbran, "We no longer have a village, Asdor. That thing destroyed it."

"We'll just have to build a new village then, won't we? We can go anywhere we want and make a new life for ourselves and your little Grubb," Fellis said with a smile.

"And if that thing decides to come back, he'll have two dragons and a giant to contend with. He won't survive that, will he?"

Gelbran glanced up at Asdor, "No," he replied quietly. "No, I don't suppose he will."

They walked slowly back to the cave. Gelbran's mind was in a whirl. To have come this far only to tell his people that their efforts had all been in vain was almost too much for him bear. Entering the cave, he looked at the expectant expressions on the faces of his kin and lowered his head, "It gives me no pleasure to tell you this," he said solemnly, "but we must turn back."

There were murmurs amongst the crowd and Gelbran glanced at them. Their expressions had changed. He could tell that some were confused by what he had just announced, others were angry and more than a few, relieved.

"Our way is barred," he continued. "A landslide has destroyed the only route we could take to cross the mountain. Asdor and I contemplated clearing the path, but it would take all our efforts to accomplish and the danger of causing more rockfall is very real. I will not endanger a single life purely for revenge. We will leave this place and find a new home. We will rebuild our lives far from this accursed place and we will become strong and proud once more. I am sorry for all of the hardships you have had to endure, but I will make it my life's work to see you all happy and safe again. For we are... *the vikkery!*"

Fellis took his hand as he turned away, "Everyone knows you did the best you could, you know," she said soothingly. "They trust you, Gelbran. They always have and they always will."

"Oh they trust me alright," Gelbran scoffed. "I've marched them hundreds of miles and halfway up a mountain so that they can get even with a marauding dragon which would probably have killed them anyway, only to tell them that we can't go any farther because of a few poxy rocks being in the way! Yeah, some leader I am!"

"Do you hear any of them complaining?" Fellis asked him, leaning down to look him in the eye. "They never wanted to come after the dragon, but they knew that you wanted to. That's why they're here, Gelbran! They're here for you!"

"You mean, none of them wanted revenge on that thing?"

"Of course they wanted it dead, but none of them felt that they would be the one to kill it!" she paused, "Well maybe Asdor did, but he's an idiot."

"I heard that," came a voice from outside the cave.

Gelbran sat on a rock with a weary grunt. Fellis knelt in front of him, "Where shall we go then?" she asked, excitedly.

Gelbran shrugged his shoulders, "Haven't had time to think about it to be honest. Any ideas?"

"Somewhere nice and warm," Fellis replied, dreamily. "Somewhere by a river so we can build some boats and go fishing. Somewhere with lots of trees the children can climb. Somewhere with long grass so that we can lie in the sunshine. Somewhere… *magical!*"

A slight smile raised the corners of Gelbran's mouth, "Haven't you had enough of magic? Look what we've become since we met that wizard. We're nothing but a bunch of freaks now."

"But look at what we'll be able to achieve now that we're freaks, Gelbran. Once we find the right place, we'll be safer than we've ever been. We'll have sentries soaring in the clouds, we'll have wolves and bears guarding our borders. And in the middle of the village, we'll have a giant who could crush any who would dare threaten us!"

"Tell me, young lady. How long have you been planning this new life for us all?" asked Gelbran, now smiling fully.

Fellis smiled back at him, "Ooh, let's work it out," she replied thoughtfully, "*Always!*"

"What does that mean?" Gelbran laughed.

"I've always thought the village should have been somewhere else, even before the attacks began. Whoever chose that place to build a village needs his head looking at!" She grimaced as she looked at Gelbran, "It was you, wasn't it?" she asked nervously.

Gelbran nodded, "Seemed perfectly fine at the time," he chuckled.

CHAPTER 27

Stitch breathed a sigh of relief as he saw the daylight peeping through a crack in the rock ahead of them. "At last!" he gasped, "Fresh air!"

"You won't say that once we're out of this cave," grunted Barden. "It's absolutely freezing out there!"

"Ooh, do you think that's why they call them the ice fields?" asked Yello, sarcastically.

"Why don't you just shut it, Tarrock," snapped Barden.

"Why don't you make me, you little oik?"

"Why don't you both shut up and get a move on?" Porflax asked, loudly. "Damned kids! Grow up, the pair of you!"

"Oh go on, let 'em fight," chuckled Ballorn. "We could have a little wager on who might win."

"The one thing you wouldn't want to see, Ballorn, is two wizards duelling. It always gets out of hand and one of them inevitably ends up dead!"

"Might as well make the wager a big one then," laughed Ballorn. "There won't be any chance of a re-match."

Hunter nudged him, "Probably not a good idea to goad him too much, Ballorn. He seems quite serious."

"Why wouldn't I be?" bellowed Porflax. "I've seen what these youngsters are capable of when tempers are frayed. They give no thought to innocent bystanders once the spells start flying!"

"We'll hide behind the rocks then," continued Ballorn, who was having far too much fun to stop now.

"You could hide behind what you like!" exclaimed Porflax. "You still wouldn't be safe! You'd just blown up along with whatever it was! They have no self-control I tell you!"

"Erm, sorry to interrupt," Emnor said quietly, "but Barden's already gone, and Stitch followed right behind him."

"That blasted tailor!" chuntered Ballorn. "I told him to stay where I could keep an eye on him!"

"You can't blame him, Ballorn. He couldn't wait to get out of here, and you knew that."

Ballorn glared at Yello, "Oh, just, just… shove it, Yello," he growled.

Charging forward, he headed toward the light. Bursting into the cold daylight took his breath away, not only the freezing air, but the clean, crisp beauty of the landscape that sprawled before him. "Wow, would you look at that!" he sighed, feeling a tug at his sleeve.

"N n n never mind that," said Stitch, shivering, "G g g give me one of those coats before I f f freeze to death!"

Ballorn hurriedly rammed his hand into his backbag, grabbing the fur coat and quickly wrapping it around Stitch. "You can't be that cold, surely? You've only been out here for a minute, at most!"

"F f far too long without a c c coat, Ballorn. We…" he shuddered, "we aren't all lucky enough to b be the n n…"

"Alright, Stitch. I get it," Ballorn said, rubbing the tailor's back to warm him. "Hunter, you'd best put the other one on." Then, something dawned on him. "I never packed those heavy robes," he said, looking horrified at his omission.

"We know," said Yello. "But don't worry. We know what it's like out here so we're already wearing them. That's the thing with our robes, they all look the same."

"Thank goodness for that," said Hunter, "Otherwise we'd be sliding four icicles along the ground to get you home."

Yello sniffed, "Well… three, anyway," he said as he glanced at Barden.

"Enough," Emnor warned him. "We need to move on."

"What?" cried Stitch, "Not yet! You can't expect us to go already? I can't walk, I can't even feel my legs they're that cold!"

Ballorn eyed Stitch for a moment, then opened his backbag, "I've got an idea," he said. "Stitch… climb in."

"You can't carry him!" laughed Hunter.

"I'm not going to," replied Ballorn. "This is snow, right? Snow is slippery, so he gets in the pack, I hold the strap and

I'll slide him along behind me. He'll be nice and warm and, more importantly, he won't slow us down."

Stitch had a huge smile on his face, "That sounds like a wonderful idea to me!" he said happily. "It'll help me save my strength for when it's needed most as well. I can leap out at any time and…"

"Just get in the bag!" bellowed Ballorn.

Doing as he was told, Stitch climbed in and shuffled as deep as he could. Wrapping his coat tightly around him, he smiled. "It's quite cosy in here you know. We should have one of these each."

"That's not a bad idea, Stitch, apart from one thing," said Ballorn.

"What's that?" asked Stitch, innocently.

"Who'd pull us along!"

"Ah, good point," replied Stitch. "Maybe we could get some ponies to pull us along, that'd work."

"Brilliant!" Ballorn said with fake glee. "You pop off and get us a few ponies then and we'll wait here 'til you get back."

"There's no need to be nasty! You know there aren't any ponies here, I meant for in the future. You know, if we ever have to travel in the snow when we get back home."

"If indeed, we do get back home," mumbled Hunter.

Ballorn gave him a surprised look. Hunter had never taken a defeatist attitude and it took him aback slightly. "Now, now, we'll have none of that," he said reassuringly.

"We're all going home when this is done, but seriously, Stitch, when can you remembering it ever snowing in Krevick?"

"There's a first time for everything, Ballorn." He clapped his hands together. "We should give your new idea a name! What about... a *slider?*"

"It's already got a name, Stitch. It's called, a *bag.*"

"Not when you use it like this it's not!" argued Stitch. "We could make some out of old bits of wood, they'd last much longer if they were made out of wood, wouldn't they?"

"I wish you were made of wood," groaned Ballorn, "then you wouldn't be able to talk so much."

"Ha, see! You know it's a good idea and you're grumpy because you never thought of it first."

Ballorn turned his back and carried on walking, towing the tailor behind him. "I've got enough to think about without coming up with stupid ideas on how to use old bits of wood to drag people around in the snow. Now do be quiet, there's a good chap. Pull your coat up over your mouth for a while. It won't stop you talking, but at least it'll muffle the sound enough for me not to be able to hear you!"

Hunter walked beside him, "What are we looking for out here, Ballorn?" he asked.

"Not sure. We're in the hands of young Barden now. He said he had friends who could help us, but I have no knowledge of anyone living in such a harsh place as this."

"Help us in what way?"

"Well, to defeat the dragon I suppose."

"Keldenar said that you must be the one to defeat it. Aren't you concerned that whoever these friends are might want to kill it, not just stop it?"

Ballorn leaned closer, "If it comes to it, I'll kill the thing myself!" he hissed. "It sounds harsh I know, but one way or another... *the dragon will be stopped!*"

Throughout the day, they trudged on, battling against the relentless blizzards of Ellan-Ouine. They could see no more than a few yards ahead of them as they followed Barden, who seemed to know exactly where he was going. A few times, Stitch climbed out of his new *slider* and walked beside them. He felt slightly guilty and insisted that, although the Nibrilsiem had immense strength, he should conserve as much of it as possible. "We could come face-to-face with that thing at any moment and you'll need all the energy you can muster to tackle it, Ballorn."

Unfortunately, his good intentions lasted but a few minutes before his pace started to slow and he had to clamber back into the backbag. "I'm so sorry, Ballorn," he would say apologetically, "I'm simply not built to deal with the cold."

At last, they had a reprieve. The wind died down and the driving snow calmed to an occasional flurry. The scene ahead became clear, but their hearts sank as they stared in bewilderment. They had surely travelled many miles, but none were certain how the terrain would appear once they had cleared the blizzard. But they were not expecting this. It was identical to what they had seen when they had first left the caverns. Mile after mile of open, frozen wasteland lay before them. There were no hills, mountains, nothing higher than an occasional bump or hillock of snow that had perhaps buried a hardy plant or fern.

Looking back, Ballorn could see the faint shadow of the Muurkain Mountains on the horizon. "They look so small!" he gasped, "Another hour and we won't be able to see them at all!"

"Which means we aren't even halfway to wherever Barden is leading us," whispered Hunter.

"But... but we can't survive this!" whimpered Stitch. "We can't stay out here at night! Once the sun goes down, it'll get even colder and," he gulped, "we'll be nothing but blocks of ice by morning!"

Porflax tutted, "As if we'd expect you to be out here at night," he snorted.

"Thank goodness!" Stitch said with a sigh of relief, "So there's a secret place you're taking us to where we'll be warm and safe then?"

Porflax frowned, "What, you think I have a log cabin stored in my robes? I simply meant that it never gets dark when you're this far into Ellan-Ouine! So stop fretting, Stitch, it won't get any colder. But tell me, have you ever been lucky enough to spend the night in a proper wizard's camp?"

Stitch pulled his coat up around his face and they could hear his muted ramblings, *"Won't get any colder... never gets dark... proper wizard's camp? Why didn't he tell us about that when we were stuck in Slymeer swamp?"*

"Barden!" called Porflax, "We should set up camp for the night."

Barden looked up at the sky, "We need to press on whilst the calm weather holds," he replied, frustrated by the suggestion. "We'll make better progress now!"

"The nemilar need to rest, Barden," Porflax replied adamantly. "We'll set camp now!"

Barden stormed back toward them, "We need to be there first thing tomorrow or…"

"Need to be where?" Ballorn asked, slowly.

Barden glared at him, "You'll find out when we get there," he replied angrily. "If we ever get there. Four hours, that's all the time we can spare," he added, "less if the storm returns." He leaned down and looked into Ballorn's eyes, "*Make the most of it!*"

Ballorn twitched and Hunter grabbed his arm. Ballorn glanced sideways at him and nodded knowingly, "Four hours it is," he said, looking back at Barden.

"Right," cried Porflax, loudly. "*Watch this!*"

He raised his arms and began to chant. A shower of sparks rained down and they were surprised that, when a few strays landed on their skin, they were not burned by them. All around, the snow started to bubble and bulge with small cracks appearing as slender sticks poked up through it. The bubbling became heaving and suddenly they were covered with snow as large tents erupted from beneath the crisp white blanket that had lain before them a split second before. Flames erupted, but the sudden inferno shrank to become a large campfire, complete with a kettle hanging over it.

Porflax lowered his arms and folded them, "There we go," he said contentedly. "That should make things a little more comfortable for a while. Tea anybody?"

The nemilar didn't care how Porflax had done it, all they cared about was the roaring campfire to warm themselves by and tents that, when inspected, had not only cots, but large cushions on which they readily made themselves comfortable. It was not long before they, as well as Yello and Emnor, were settling themselves in for a few hours well deserved rest.

Ballorn pushed himself up on one elbow as he surveyed the two young wizards, "How come you never say anything?" he asked. "Why don't you get involved? Those two clearly don't get on but you don't say a word."

"Not our place," replied Yello, shrugging his shoulders.

"We're here to observe, not interfere," muttered Emnor.

"You must realise there's something going on between them though?"

Emnor raised his eyebrows as he looked across at Hunter, "Well, we... *suspect*. That's all we can say, I'm afraid."

"They're as dodgy as the day's long if you ask me." They were all surprised by Stitch's sudden comment, because they believed he was already asleep, "Barden seems to be running the show and Porflax is just waiting for his orders. We'll have more than just a dragon to contend with when it all kicks off, we'll have to keep an eye on that pair as well. You mark my words."

"Well, well, well," chuckled Ballorn, "They say it's the quiet ones you have to watch. You've got this all figured out by the sounds of things, Stitch."

"Yes, I have. Only one thing is bothering me though."

"Which is?" They all sat up, eyes transfixed on the tailor, who hadn't even bothered to open his.

"Well I'm convinced it's not the dragon, but when we get to wherever it is we're headed, I think there's going to be someone there waiting for us. I also think it's about time we started pressing our two travelling companions for a little more information on who that person is."

"You've been doing a lot of *thinking* then," Hunter said, inquisitively.

"Not much else to do when you're stuck in a bag by yourself for a whole day," replied Stitch, yawning. "The only thing we can hope for is that the mystery person, or persons, are on the right side. By that, I mean *our side*."

"Whatever plans they had laid hadn't included a couple of things," sighed Emnor.

"You and him?" said Hunter, pointing at Yello.

"Precisely," replied Emnor, with a smile.

"I'm not sure about that either," muttered Stitch. "Because you two are up to something as well. I'm not sure what, but you're up to something."

"Charming!" snorted Yello. "He doesn't even trust us after all we've done for them!"

Stitch held up his hands, his eyes still closed. "You haven't done anything for us though, have you. Alright, you stopped me putting my hand in that stinky stuff, but nothing else comes to mind."

"Well, really!" exclaimed Yello.

"Oh, don't come with the fake feelings of insult, Yellodius. If you trusted us, and you yourselves were trustworthy, you'd tell us why you're really here."

"We may be young compared to Porflax, but I can assure you that we are men of the highest integrity, Stitch. If we, in any way..." he paused, "Stitch? Stitch, are you... well I never!"

Emnor's protest had been interrupted by Stitch, who was now... snoring.

CHAPTER 28

Neither Ballorn nor Hunter had slept. Emnor and Yello had snoozed occasionally but were easily awoken as the slightest breeze ruffled the sides of the tent. However, the brief respite had done them no harm and they had been glad of it.

Then, of course, there was Stitch. He lay, fast asleep, clutching one of the larger cushions as if he were holding on to a piece of driftwood while stranded at sea. Ballorn stared in disbelief at how serene he looked.

"Stitch, time to move," Hunter said softly.

Stitch never stirred.

Hunter raised his voice, "Come on, Stitch. Time to get up."

But still the tailor never moved.

"Get up, you lazy git!" bellowed Ballorn. "We've got to go!"

Stitch stretched out his arms and opened one eye, "Just five more minutes," he whispered, and promptly wrapped his arms back around the cushion and began snoring.

"I said... *get up!*" bawled Ballorn, grabbing the cushion and wrenching it from Stitch's grip.

Stitch sat up slowly and rubbed his eyes, then scowled at Ballorn, "You didn't have to be so rough!" he complained. "All you had to do was call me!"

"We did call you... *twice*, and you weren't moving. Now come on, on your feet."

"Oh dear, I'm shattered," yawned Stitch as he rose from the cot. "I thought we had a few hours before we had to move. It could only have been about ten minutes since I closed my eyes."

"It has been hours, Stitch, almost four," Hunter informed him. "Now get outside, Porflax needs to dismantle the camp."

Poor Stitch shuffled through the tent flap and immediately shivered as the cold breeze hit him, "It's such a shame," he groaned, "It wasn't exactly warm in there but at least we were sheltered from this horrible wind. Wish I had a hat," he whined, "or a scarf I could wrap around my head to keep my ears warm."

Yello walked up behind him, "Here you go," he said, dumping a huge fur hat on Stitch's head, "Will that do?"

"Excellent!" cried Stitch. "Where did you get it from?"

"Does it matter where it came from?" sighed Ballorn. "You wanted a hat, and you've got a hat. Now get in the bag!"

"No, I'm alright," Stitch assured him, "I can walk for a bit."

Ballorn glared at him.

"On second thoughts," said Stitch, nervously, "Maybe I'll get in the bag."

With the tailor secured in his transport, they made good time. They had to endure no more than an infrequent flurry of snow and the ground was level and smooth. However, there seemed no end to the vast expanse of Ellan-Ouine.

"How much farther is it?" Ballorn called to Barden.

"How much farther is what?"

"Wherever it is you're taking us."

"Well, on foot it's about three days," replied Barden.

"Three days!" screeched Stitch. "You mean we're going to be out here for another three days?"

Barden paused and looked back at him, "I never said that."

"Yes you did!"

"No, I said, *if on foot*, it's three days," said Barden as he rolled his eyes.

"Well how else are we going to get across this ice?" complained Stitch. "None of us have wings, or had that escaped your notice."

"Just be patient!" replied Barden, angrily. "You'll have all the answers in a few hours!"

"Did you hear that, Ballorn?" whispered Stitch. "*A few hours!* You'd better keep a tight hold on that hammer of yours, 'cause it sounds like we're going to be ambushed!"

Mark of the Nibrilsiem

Ballorn chuckled, "How could anyone be ambushed out here, Stitch? There's nowhere to hide for a start, unless some bandits decide to bury themselves in the snow."

Stitch felt a tap on his shoulder. Looking around, he saw the curve of Hunter's bow. "There'll be three of them dead in the first second, my friend. I doubt any of them will hang around after witnessing that. That is, of course, presuming that there are bandits lying in wait for us."

"I never said anything about bandits!" hissed Stitch. "But what if Barden's in league with the dragon and *it's* waiting for us?"

"I hope it is," replied Ballorn, gruffly. "It's about time it stopped running and faced me."

He heard Keldenar's voice in his mind, '*Not yet, Nibrilsiem… not yet.*'

"What's that?" Emnor suddenly asked, pointing to the horizon.

Yello squinted, "No!" he said with amazement. "It can't be!"

Emnor smiled at him, "I think you'll find it is."

Yello looked a little uncomfortable, "But he's never forgiven me for, erm… well, you know?"

"It was a long time ago, Yello. I'm sure he's forgotten about it by now," laughed Emnor.

Yello shook his head, "Not him," he said slowly. "He never forgets anything!"

"What are you two on about?" asked a very curious Ballorn. "I can't see anyone."

"You will soon enough," groaned Yello, "And just in case it goes wrong, it was a pleasure meeting you."

"You sound as if you're about to die!" laughed Hunter.

Yello looked at him with concern, "That's probably because there's a distinct possibility that I might."

"Oh, stop it!" chuckled Emnor, turning to Hunter. "You see, there was this girl…"

"They don't need to know anything about that…" began Yello.

Hunter held up his hand, "It's alright," he said, trying to save Yello the indignity of his misdemeanours being aired in public, "we get the idea."

"I still can't see anything," said Ballorn. "Wait a minute, there it is. There are lights up ahead."

"Here we go," groaned Yello.

The stranger never moved nor spoke as they approached him. He looked them up and down in turn and seemed completely baffled as to why Stitch was being dragged along in a bag. He nodded at Barden, they were obviously acquainted, but the look he gave Yello was one of complete disdain. He eventually stepped forward, circling Ballorn and studying him intently.

"You are the Nibrilsiem?" he asked, with an air of disbelief.

"That's what I'm told," replied Ballorn, bluntly. "And who are you?"

The stranger's brow furrowed as he looked to Barden, "You have not told him?"

"I thought it might be better coming from you."

"Mmm… perhaps," replied the stranger thoughtfully. "But not here," he continued. "You must all come with me. Climb aboard my sleigh and we shall depart for my home."

"We're not going anywhere with you until you tell us what's going on," Ballorn said adamantly. "Surely, having only just met, you can't blame us for being wary of you."

'You must accompany him, Ballorn. You are quite safe,' said Keldenar's voice.

The stranger tilted his head to one side as he looked into Ballorn's eyes, "Good enough?" he asked.

"You heard that?"

"Yes, but only because he wanted me to," replied the stranger, smiling.

Stitch was not happy. He glared at the sleigh. *I knew it was a good idea*, he thought, *and now I find out somebody else thought of it first! It's not fair… it's just not fair!* The sleigh was huge, but what stood before it was even more impressive. Four beasts were secured by soft leather harnesses in order to pull it. They were as big as horses but had no tails and were covered with thick white fur. Stitch was ecstatic. He marvelled at the way their horns splayed out like the branches of a tree, their wide faces sporting huge tusks that any dragon would be proud of and their thick legs ended in wide, clawed hooves that allowed them to grip the ice. Stitch's eyes twinkled as he gazed at them. *I've never seen anything as strange as these things*, he thought as he climbed into the sleigh. "Where are you taking us?" he asked quietly.

The stranger glanced at him briefly, "To my home, little one," he replied, "*I'm taking you to Thedar.*"

Stitch studied his every move as the sleigh lurched into motion. The strange beasts may have looked cumbersome, but Stitch couldn't believe how swiftly they were moving within seconds. No horse or pony he had ever seen would have been able to reach the speed they were travelling at, even at full gallop. Stitch spoke loudly so that he could be heard over the sound of the wind and whooshing of the sleigh.

"What are they called?" he yelled, pointing at the beasts.

"That's Dolly, then there's Nobby, Sally, and that one's Gin." He leaned over and whispered, "Gin's my favourite, but keep it quiet, I don't want to upset the others."

Stitch shook his head, "No, I never meant their names!" he giggled. "I meant… what *are* they? What sort of animal?"

"Oh, my mistake!" laughed the stranger. "They're *terralopes*." He looked at Stitch with surprise, "Don't tell me you've never seen a terralope before?"

"No, never," replied Stitch. "Do you only get them where there's snow?"

"I believe so. Mind you, I very rarely leave my home so I couldn't say for sure."

Mark of the Nibrilsiem

Feeling more relaxed, Stitch shuffled a little closer to the stranger, "I'm very sorry," he said, "but I didn't catch your name." He hadn't really looked at him before, but Stitch began to realise that this was no mere nomad who wandered the wintery expanse of Ellan-Ouine. He had a regal air about him. The way he sat bolt upright, the way his white skin glistened, almost sparkled in the light, and the creases around his eyes that revealed an age-old wisdom that was tinted with kindness.

"That's because I never said it," replied the stranger as he nudged him. "But there'll be plenty of time for introductions later. For now, just know that you are safe and will soon be comfortable and warm."

A dreamy look appeared on Stitch's face as he dwelled on the stranger's final word. "Oh... *warm*. I haven't been warm for days, even with this huge coat on!" he sighed. "How long before we reach your home?"

"A few hours to reach the edge of the ice and then one more after, I'm afraid you'll have to walk for a while. Stitch, is it?"

"Well, that's what this lot call me, because I'm a tailor. But my real name is Felidan Portwitch."

"How delightful!" chuckled the stranger, "I like it! A name like that holds a certain... nobility."

Stitch was liking the stranger more and more. A *nobility*, he thought. *Nobody's ever said anything as nice as that about me before!*

Ballorn shoved him in the back with his foot, "Enough questions, Stitch," he suggested. "Let the fellow concentrate. We don't want this thing crashing do we!"

Stitch stood up and briefly glanced in all directions, "Into what!" he exclaimed. "There's nothing out here to crash into!"

Hunter grabbed him and pulled him back onto the bench beside him, "He means... stop being nosey. Now be quiet and get some rest!"

Stitch folded his arms in a huff, "I was only being friendly!" he chuntered.

The stranger looked back at them and smiled, "But there is still an element of doubt in their minds, Felidan. They're not sure if I am a friend."

"A bit of caution never went amiss," replied Ballorn, looking deep into the stranger's eyes. "Let's see what happens when we get to your... *Thedar*. We'll decide then whether you're friend or foe."

"Ballorn, shut your mouth!" protested Barden, "You have no idea to whom you are speaking!"

"Perhaps we should all reserve judgement?" advised the stranger. "We've only just met and already the seeds of doubt are beginning to spread their roots. My only surprise is that Yellodius hasn't graced us with a few choice phrases." He turned and stared at Yello, "Oh, don't worry, young wizard. I've not forgotten about you," he added menacingly.

The hours passed slowly for some, but far more quickly for others. The stranger was the first to climb down from the sleigh and he immediately began to detach the harnesses from the terralopes. "Time for us to take a little stroll," he announced.

Stitch ran ahead, crossing the last smatterings of snow and falling backwards onto the lush green grass, "Oh, it's dry!" he cried. "There's not so much as a drop of dew on it. Thank you, erm, whatever your name is. I've never been so happy to see so much greenery!"

"Indeed!" replied the stranger. "I expect you'll be overjoyed when we reach the forest."

The comment peaked Hunter's interest, "Is it large?" he asked.

"Far larger than you've seen before, I'd wager," replied the stranger. "Just be wary of the nymphs, they can be little monsters when they're disturbed."

"*Monsters?*" moaned Stitch. "*Here we go again!*"

"You'll be safe enough, Felidan. Leave them be and they'll stay away from you."

"But what if we meet up with them accidentally? I suppose they'll try to eat us like all the other monsters do?"

"Nymphs do not eat people, Felidan! They are magical beings. The worst they'll do if agitated is, well... make sticks sprout from your fingers... or other places. I heard about that once, but it was only a rumour, I'm sure."

"You'll warn us then, won't you? I mean, if you see any?" Stitch grabbed the stranger's hand, "I don't want sticks growing out of my other places!"

"Am I allowed to climb the trees?"

"By all means," replied the stranger, glancing at Hunter. "But don't you hurt them. That would be the quickest way to raise the ire of the nymphs! Mind you, I wouldn't be too happy about it either."

Hunter frowned, "I have lived with nature my entire life, friend, and it has always been good to me," Hunter stated adamantly, "I would be the last person to bring it any harm!"

"Ooh, a breakthrough," grinned the stranger. "You called me *friend!*"

"Figure of speech," grunted Ballorn as he walked away.

***

As they reached the edge of the forest, the stranger ordered them to halt.

"What's wrong?" asked Stitch nervously, worried that some horror was lurking just beyond the treeline. "Are there nymphs waiting for us in there?"

"No, Felidan, not nymphs, something far more dangerous. Well, they would be if I were not accompanying you." He placed his fingers against his lips and whistled. Figures began to appear from everywhere. Their glistening skin was very similar to the stranger's but seemed to have a green hue. One of them stepped forward. Grasping the hilt of a beautiful curved, silver sword, he dropped to one knee and bowed before the stranger.

"Your majesty," he said with a serene tone. "It is good that you have returned safe and well."

"Ooh, Ballorn!" whispered Stitch "He's a king! You could be in trouble now for the way you spoke to him," he sniggered.

"I'm shaking in my boots, Stitch," replied Ballorn, pretending to be scared.

"Well I'm not," said Stitch, excitedly. "Look at 'em! They're beautiful!" He straightened his jacket and tried to look as presentable as possible. "I'm going to say hello." With that he promptly marched forward.

Ballorn and the others watched him as he made a beeline for the man who had knelt before the stranger. "Hello," he chirped, holding out his hand, "my name's Felidan. Pleased to meet you."

"Say hello, Selinar," his king commanded, quietly.

Selinar stared down at Stitch, "There's nothing in it," he said dryly.

Stitch was now as confused as Selinar. "There's nothing in what?" he asked with a nervous laugh.

"In your hand," sighed Selinar. "Did you mean to present me with something and forget to pick it up?"

"It's the way we greet one another where I'm from," Stitch replied, gently raising Selinar's hand and grasping it firmly.

Selinar frowned, pulling his hand free and wiping it on his tunic, "How strange."

The king smiled and waved him away. Turning to face Stitch, he addressed both him and the others. "I am King

Volknar Fellentheen," he announced. "Welcome to Thedar."

Ballorn stepped forward, "My name…"

Volknar waved his hand. "I know," he said. "You're Ballorn, he's Hunter." He pointed at them in turn, "Porflax, Emnor and Barden, with whom I am already acquainted and my new friend Felidan." He paused and stared at Yello, "Oh yes, and him."

"You've got it all wrong, your majesty!"

"Silence!" bellowed Volknar. "She is my daughter, Yellodius! She was betrothed to another… and then you came along and ruined it!"

"But I never did anything," Yello protested. "I can't help it if she never cared for him enough to go through with the wedding!"

Volknar stared at him thoughtfully, "Perhaps not, but you were the one with whom she was infatuated!"

"Well," began Yello, pompously, "It wasn't my fault, it was that blasted simbor! And after all, I can't help being so handsome. Girls always…"

Emnor stepped in, "Forgive me, Majesty. As you can plainly see, *he's not quite right in the head.* He neither realised that he was doing any wrong nor that she was your daughter."

"I say, steady on, Emmy old chap…"

"See what I mean!" exclaimed Emnor, slyly kicking Yello from behind. "Only a fool would object to valid points being raised in their defence!"

Yello's mouth fell open, his contorted expression a testament to the excruciating pain now shooting through his leg.

Volknar folded his arms, his fingers drumming his bicep as he considered what Emnor had said, "Alright," he finally said, "but you stay away from my daughter whilst you're here, Yellodius." He paused, "On second thought, stay away from all females whilst you're here, *do you understand?*"

Yello forced a weak smile, "By your command," he whispered.

Volknar turned his attention to Ballorn, "Come with me, Nibrilsiem," he said, gesturing for Ballorn to follow him. "We have much to discuss." Glancing down, he smiled at Stitch, "I think you should join us Felidan, it seems to me that you have been omitted far too much during your adventures. What say we change that?"

Stitch nodded enthusiastically, "I'd like that."

As the three walked ahead, Volknar called back to the others, "The rest of you follow my warriors, they will see that you are fed and made comfortable. You must be well rested. Tomorrow will be a big day."

Hunter would not be dismissed so easily and hurried to speak to Ballorn, "We started this together, Ballorn! I will not leave your side now! I should be included in your talks."

"And you will be, but later," said Volknar, reassuringly. "You will be told everything you need to know."

"Yes, and I need to know he's safe! That's why I'm staying by his side!"

Volknar lowered his head, "Hunter, look around you. Two hundred of my finest Thedarian warriors surround you, yet you feel that your friend may still be in danger?"

"I know how many surround us," said Hunter, stepping close to Volknar. "They're the reason why I feel he may be in danger!"

"I'd step away if I were you," said Volknar, smiling. "It is not recommended to show aggression towards one who is merely trying to help. Oh, and there are at least ten arrows aimed at your head, you may also want to consider that."

Ballorn placed his arm across Hunter's chest, "Come on, friend," he advised, "You'll be no help to me tomorrow if you're riddled with arrows."

"You call yourselves Thedarians then?" Stitch suddenly asked.

Volknar nodded, "Because our homeland is called Thedar," he replied.

"It's very grand, isn't it," said Stitch, puffing out his chest, *Thedarians.*"

"I'd never really considered it," chuckled Volknar.

"Could I be a Thedarian? If I came and lived here of course?"

"I am afraid that would not be possible, Felidan," replied Volknar. "You see, my people are mistrustful of strangers and would never make you welcome here."

"So you're allowed to mistrust us, yet you ask us to trust you?" snorted Hunter.

"We are always respectful of visitors and guests in our lands, Hunter, but we do not allow any to reside here. There is a huge difference between one who wishes to merely gaze upon our beautiful lands whilst passing through and one who would choose to change them by settling here. Surely, as one who has been at one with nature for so long, you can see that difference?"

"I suppose so," sighed Hunter. "The first thing settlers do is start felling trees and churning up meadows to make way for even more of their kind to follow."

"And that is the very reason why we will not allow any to settle in Thedar."

"My apologies, Volknar," Hunter said quietly. "Ballorn, come and find me when you're ready, I'll be waiting."

Volknar watched him with interest as he walked away and turned to Ballorn, "He is a very loyal friend."

Ballorn nodded, "One of the best," he agreed.

"We all are," Stitch said quickly. "Loyal, I mean."

"Oh, of that there is no doubt," chuckled Volknar. "You would not be with him if you were not." He had an unexpectedly grave expression on his face, "But your loyalty is about to be tested to its limit, Felidan. The Nibrilsiem needs the strength of all those who accompany him as he faces his worst fear."

"I'm not scared of the dragon," Ballorn said quietly. "In a way, I pity it."

"You are lying to yourself, Ballorn. A show of bravado is all well and good in front of your friends but if you choose to deny your fear and take your enemy lightly, it could be your undoing."

Ballorn stared at him, a myriad of questions racing through his mind, "How is it that you are involved in all this, Volknar? It seems the dragon has not troubled you in any way, *so why are you so eager to help?*"

The King, for the first time since they had met, seemed unsettled. "Ahem, ah, well," he mumbled, "I'm afraid that we are, in a way, responsible for what he has become."

"Ooooh," said Stitch, his eyes wide. "Was it you that upset him then?"

"No, nothing as simple as that, I'm afraid," replied Volknar, shaking his head. "We accidentally allowed him to be possessed by the crystal."

"What!" exclaimed Stitch, "Why would you go and do a thing like that?"

"It wasn't deliberate, Felidan," Volknar replied defensively. "We had never conceived that a dragon would delve so deeply underground. Obviously, we were wrong."

"Nope," said Stitch, shaking his head. "You've completely lost me now!"

Volknar sighed. *How to explain*, he thought. "We became complacent, I'm ashamed to say," he said solemnly. "We had kept the crystal hidden for thousands of years and thought that we had found the perfect hiding place…"

"But the dragon found it," Ballorn added.

"Not exactly," said Volknar. "He simply wanted somewhere quiet and secluded to rest undisturbed and discovered the caverns in which we had hidden the crystal. Over many years it bound itself to him and corrupted his soul. The purist of hearts had been blackened and even his own name was forgotten." A shadow seemed to appear across Volknar's features, "What eventually emerged from the depths was far different to what had entered, something that was bent on death and destruction. He is a force far greater than any other to bring terror to our world of Pordan. *He is Grimbarr!*"

Ballorn stared at the grim expression on Volknar's face, "Don't you think it's about time you told us where these caverns are?" he asked.

Volknar forced a brief smile, "All in good time, Nibrilsiem," he said softly. "All in good time."

"So the dragon himself is not actually evil then?" asked Stitch.

"Oh, not at all!" exclaimed Volknar. "Quite the opposite in fact. He was a delightful conversationalist, we spent many evenings together discussing a range of obscure subjects."

Stitch looked puzzled, "You mean, you spoke to him?"

"Indeed," replied Volknar. "And he spoke to me. That is why we must save him! He was always one of my closest friends."

"But we were told that once the crystal is removed, he cannot possibly survive."

Volknar lowered his head, "True, his body has little chance of survival," he said softly, "but we can save his essence if the timing is right. I will still be able to communicate with him even after his flesh has perished."

"You can do that?" asked Stitch.

"Absolutely, Felidan!" replied Volknar, confidently. "However, I must ask for your help."

"Me!" breathed Stitch. "I don't know anything about souls or dragons. What use could I be?"

Volknar reached inside his cloak. You must place this beside him at precisely the moment of his passing," he said, revealing what, until now, he had kept secreted within the numerous folds of fabric. "It will absorb his soul and allow him to live on."

Stitch stared at the object. "Is that a crown?" he asked, pulling a face. "Because if it is, it's got to be the ugliest one I've ever seen!"

Volknar frowned, "It was not forged to be aesthetically pleasing, Felidan. It was created to save my friend."

Ballorn snorted, "That thing's never seen a forge!" he scoffed. "I'd say it's never felt any more heat than the palm of your hand." He tilted his head as he gazed at Volknar. "Or am I mistaken?"

"It was forged in flame," Volknar assured him. "Okay, it was a green wizard-flame, but a flame nonetheless!"

"I should've known!" laughed Ballorn, "It was Barden, wasn't it? You do realise that the other wizards don't trust him, don't you?"

"There was a time when wizards were not welcomed by we Thedarians for, many years ago, they wronged us greatly. But they are no longer as they once were. I understand that Barden's association with those in Reiggan has been a little fraught in the past, he is young and headstrong, something that is frowned upon by his seniors. Barden has become a close friend of mine and proven his loyalty on many occasions. Trust me when I say he only wishes to help. After all, the crown was his idea."

"Well I think it's a stupid idea," sighed Stitch. "That thing will never fit the dragon, it's far too small."

"It's not supposed…!" Volknar paused and took a deep breath. "It has been crafted to fit *me*, Felidan," he said calmly.

"Good job really," laughed Stitch, "'cause you'd need a ton of gold to make a crown big enough to fit a dragon."

CHAPTER 29

Volknar had insisted that they rest overnight and as dawn broke there was a palpable tension in the air. Other than a few morning greetings, very few words passed between them as they prepared for their confrontation with Grimbarr.

They followed the king, who was now flanked by a number of Thedarian warriors. He was deep in conversation with Barden and Porflax who, for some reason, were speaking in hushed tones.

Ballorn nudged Hunter and nodded toward the trio, "What do you think that's all about then?" he asked.

Hunter shrugged his shoulders, "Probably trying to figure out how you go about besting a fifty-foot dragon."

"Easy," said Stitch, "you get somebody else to do it!"

Ballorn held up his hammer, "They've already figured that one out," he sniffed. "Why get a seven-foot Thedarian to face a dragon when you've got a five-foot Nibrilsiem you can sacrifice instead?"

"I don't think they intend to sacrifice you, Ballorn," laughed Hunter. "The fact that you *are* the Nibrilsiem is the reason why you must be the one to face Grimbarr."

"Still doesn't seem fair to me," grumbled Ballorn.

"Here, Ballorn. Have you looked closely at the Thedarians?"

Ballorn frowned, "Closely enough," he replied. "Why?"

"It's their skin, it fascinates me! You see how it sparkles, it's like they're covered in tiny little feathers that catch the light."

"And how is that little gem of an observation supposed to help us?"

"Well, if you could do what they can do, it would be a great help!" Stitch replied excitedly.

"What can they do?" asked Hunter, curiously.

"They can make themselves invisibled!" Stitch whispered.

"There's no such word as invisibled," laughed Hunter.

"Alright then, vanished. They can make themselves vanished," hissed Stitch, "I was watching one of them last night. He was standing by a big oak tree then, as he turned to the side, he was just gone!"

"Last night?" sighed Ballorn. "You mean when it was dark?"

"But it wasn't dark, Ballorn! There were torches burning either side of him and I could see him as clearly as I'm seeing you! I'm telling you, it's something to do with their magic skin!"

"Fine! So they've got magic skin. How does this help me exactly?" asked Ballorn.

"Well it doesn't, but it would if you had skin like theirs."

Ballorn sighed.

"Am I mistaken," said Hunter, quietly, "or are we going back the way we came yesterday?"

"No, you're not mistaken," replied Ballorn. "But we're not sure where it is we're going are we? I wouldn't fret, Hunter, those three seem to know what they're doing. At least, I hope they do."

Hunter was right and it was not long before they neared the edge of the trees. Staring out at the vast expanse of ice, Stitch's heart sank. "Oh no," he groaned. "We're going back out into the cold again!"

"What are we doing back here?" Ballorn called to Volknar.

"We are here because this is where we will find Grimbarr," replied Volknar.

"And if you're lucky, Ballorn, this is where you'll face him," added Porflax.

"How's that lucky? One good swing with my hammer and I'll end up on my backside on the ice!"

"It's lucky because dragons can't stand being cold. It slows them down, something that will give you a major advantage," said Barden.

"And what if he's not lucky?" asked Stitch.

"Then, I'm afraid he'll have to search for him in the caverns," said Volknar.

"And how long will it take to reach these caverns? I don't know if you've noticed," said Ballorn, pointing across the ice, "but there's not so much as a hillock around here, let alone a mountain there could be caverns beneath."

"We're already here," replied Volknar. "Well, almost. See that slight bump in the distance? About a mile away? That's the entrance to the caverns."

"Well they can't be very big then," scoffed Ballorn. "Shouldn't take long to find him in those."

Volknar turned and looked at Ballorn, knowingly, "How far would you say Ellan-Ouine stretches from end to end, Nibrilsiem?"

Ballorn shrugged his shoulders, "Oh, I don't know, hundred and fifty miles or so?"

Volknar nodded in agreement, "Well, in that case, that is also the expanse of the caverns. They are directly beneath us and stretch from end to end and side to side of Ellan-Ouine."

"But it could take Ballorn days to find Grimbarr down there!" exclaimed Stitch. "Even a dragon could easily hide in a place like that!"

"Oh, trust me," said Volknar, grimly. "Grimbarr has no intention of hiding, he knows that his destiny is to face the Nibrilsiem. Unfortunately, possession of that knowledge also dictates to him that it is he who will need every advantage if he is to survive that encounter."

Stitch was flabbergasted, "Wow!" he breathed. "You mean the dragon's actually afraid of Ballorn?"

"No, he's not afraid of Ballorn," said Porflax. "However, *he is terrified of the Nibrilsiem.*"

"I'm confused," said Stitch, rubbing his face. "How does Grimbarr even know about Ballorn being the Nibrilsiem?"

"All you need to know, Stitch, is that he does. Dragons live for thousands of years. Imagine the knowledge one can obtain in such a lifetime," said Volknar. "Things that are long forgotten by others are never forgotten by dragons. Just be thankful in this case that, for whatever reason, Grimbarr knows why he fears the Nibrilsiem."

"Alright!" roared Ballorn. "We get it! He's big, nasty and horrible and he wants to squash me! Now do any of you geniuses have any idea of how we lure him up onto the ice?"

All eyes were suddenly drawn to the ground, each person hoping that someone else may have an idea. But none did.

"Grimbarr is many things, Ballorn, but foolish is not one of them," sighed Volknar. "I'm afraid you will have to enter the caverns and hunt him down."

"Right then," said Ballorn, confidently. Raising his hammer, he placed it on his shoulder and began to march forward onto the ice. "Let's go find a dragon!"

Hunter shrugged his shoulders and hurried after him, closely followed by the four wizards.

"Hang on!" cried Stitch. "Wait a minute, don't you want to get yourself prepared or something? Ballorn? Ballorn, I'm talking to you!" His shoulders dropped, "I'm going to regret this, I just know I am," he grumbled, as he begrudgingly shuffled after them. As he caught up, he caught sight of Ballorn's outstretched arm clutching his fur coat.

"Need this?" asked the Nibrilsiem.

"Thanks very much," mumbled Stitch, thrusting his arms into the sleeves.

Soon they were stood around the mound of snow. Ballorn gave the wizards a questioning look.

"Don't look at me!" said Porflax. "This wasn't my idea, I just joined in!"

"Nor me!" exclaimed Barden. "I thought I was just supposed to bring you to Volknar! I had no idea I'd be roped into your dragonslaying escapade!"

"Typical! Ask for advice and you can't shut a wizard up, ask 'em for an idea and they haven't a clue!" Ballorn raised his hammer.

"Wait, wait, wait!" cried Stitch.

"What now?"

"If you smash the ground beneath us we could all fall in and be killed! We don't know how deep these caverns are, couldn't you just give the ground a gentle tap?"

"We're not going to get in just by clearing the snow off the top, Stitch. I'll have to give it some welly if I'm going to break through."

"I know that," said Stitch, apprehensively, "I'm just advising you to hold back a bit and, thinking about it… that's what I'll do… I'll move back a bit."

With the others at a safe distance, Ballorn raised his hammer once more. Considering what Stitch had just suggested he struck the ground with little more force than the hammer's own weight. Other than disturbing the snow slightly, it had no effect. He glanced up at Stitch and rolled his eyes. "I'll give it another go."

"Remember, Ballorn, not too much," warned Stitch.

Ballorn's second strike had much more of an effect as the mound of snow began to sink. Slowly, it levelled out as if gently sifting through a colander. Ballorn believed that one more blow would do the trick, but even as he raised his hammer, the snow continued to sink. There was a visible dip that was getting deeper as they watched it.

"You must have made a small hole and all the snow is sinking into it," said Barden, but his expression changed as he realised what was actually happening.

A brilliant white light could now be seen penetrating what was left of the mound of snow as it melted away. A strange layer of pulsating light covered a perfectly cut hole in the solid rock. They moved forward simultaneously, standing around the edge and peering down, unsure of what they would see.

"Flippin' 'eck!" cried Stitch. "If we'd have fallen down there, we'd have been goners for sure! It must be a hundred feet deep!"

"Well, have fun down there, we'll see you when you get back," said Yello.

"You will be careful, won't you? We'd rather not have to come and sweep up the bits of you that are left if it all goes wrong," chuckled Emnor.

"What? You're not coming with us?"

"After all the hard work you've done, Barden?" smiled Yello, "It would be very bad form of us to be involved right at the very end and hog all the glory, don't you think?"

"Bloody wizards!" Ballorn mumbled under his breath.

"I knew this would come in handy sooner or later," said Hunter, unravelling a slender rope. "I just hope it's long enough to get us all the way down."

"Where did you get that from?" asked Stitch, "I've never seen it before."

"I always carry it, you just haven't noticed it," he replied, flinging it forward. He was shocked when it simply landed on the light that covered the hole and just lay there. "Ah, well I never expected that! How are we supposed to get down into the caverns if we can't even get through that shield thing?" But, even as he said it, the rope slipped through and dropped into the cavern below.

"It must be some sort of safety feature," suggested Yello. "You know, so that you don't fall in accidentally."

"We could do with something like that in Reiggan when he's trying out his spells," chuckled Emnor, pointing at Barden.

Barden raised an eyebrow, "Well you won't have to worry about that for the time being will you? You'll be up here, safe and sound."

"Not at all!" exclaimed Yello. "A fellow could catch his death out here, at least you'll be nice and warm."

"A bit too warm, if you get too close to that dragon," laughed Emnor.

"Have you two quite finished with your comedy act?" asked Ballorn, drolly. "Only there's something I'm sure we should be doing."

Hunter, having quickly tired of their banter, had already taken the initiative. Turning, they were amazed that, not only was he already standing in the middle of the light, but also beginning to sink into it. Holding the rope tied to a batch of arrows that he had driven deep into the ice, he winked at them cheekily. It amused him that they had not even noticed what he had been doing, "I'll see you down there."

Barden was next to venture through the light, but it was slightly more difficult for one as advanced in years as Porflax. Ballorn persuaded him that it would be far easier for him to carry the old wizard on his back, but Stitch was a different proposition entirely. Ballorn remembered how Barden had enchanted him when it was time to ride on Keldenar's back and, with hindsight, wished that the young wizard had not already descended into the caverns.

"Just give me a minute. I'll be fine. No, really, Ballorn, I can do this. After all, it's only a rope. You go first. That way if I fall, you can catch me."

"You're not going to fall, Stitch, you're far braver than you give yourself credit for. Now, take hold of the rope, that's it… now, move towards the hole. A bit further, no, further than that. Stitch, you're moving sideways, you're not getting any closer to the hole. Now you're going the other way, you need to move back. Good grief, we'll be here all day at this rate." His patience got the better of him and he grabbed Stitch by his lapels. Lifting him off his feet, he marched forward and placed the tailor in the middle of the light. "Just keep hold of the rope," he advised, backing away.

Stitch had his eyes tight shut and knew nothing more until he felt the tug of gravity once had passed through the light. He opened one eye and peeped down. "OH, MY DAYS!" he cried. "I'm going to die! Somebody get me down, I'm stuck!" Just when he thought his predicament could not be worse, the rope started to shake. "It's going to break!" he exclaimed.

"It's not going to break, Stitch. It's just me coming to help you."

Peeping down, Stitch saw Hunter below him, "Put your feet on my shoulders, but don't let go of the rope. I'll lower us down but you have to move your hands, okay?"

A minute later, they were safely on the ground. Stitch looked very pleased with himself, "See," he said proudly, "I told you I could do it."

Once Porflax and Ballorn had joined them, they gazed at the wonderous beauty of the cavern. Tiny pinpricks of light were embedded in the walls, diamonds that had formed there over countless eons.

"If Dannard was here, he'd be wanting to collect some of these," grinned Stitch. He glared at Barden, "But he's not, is he, 'cause you killed him!"

Barden rolled his eyes, "I never killed anyone, he wasn't even real," he protested.

"He was real to me!" shrieked Stitch. "But you…"

Barden's head dropped, "Will somebody please try to explain it to him?" he begged.

Ballorn puffed out his chest, "Grimbarr!" he called, mockingly. "Where are you, Grimbarr? I'm coming to get you."

Porflax took a few steps towards Ballorn and held up his hand, "Do you really think that teasing him is a good idea? Perhaps stealth would be a better option."

"That won't do us any good," said Barden. "He already knows we're here."

Their blood ran cold as they heard a deep, menacing growl. The expanse of the caverns amplified it as it echoed around the walls. They were in no doubt that it was a warning from Grimbarr, but for now he was choosing to remain hidden.

Ballorn glanced at his companions, "I'll go on alone," he said grimly. "It's me he's waiting for. You lot just wait here until I return."

"Hah," laughed Hunter. "That's not going to happen!" Standing next to Ballorn, he placed his arm around the Nibrilsiem's shoulders and whispered in his ear, "He won't expect to have more than one target. That may just give us an edge."

Yello and Emnor watched their escapades from above.

"Bit of a shame, don't you think, Emmy? We're part of one of the greatest adventures of our time yet, once it is done, we must never speak of it."

"Well, not to anyone else anyway. But that doesn't mean we can't speak to each other about it."

"And what if someone overhears what we've said?"

A mischievous grin appeared on Emnor's face, "We could just zap 'em a bit!"

"Emnor, surely you're not suggesting that we could alter someone's memories?" chuckled Yello.

"Why not?" said Emnor. "We've done it before, or should I say *you've* done it before."

"He deserved it, robbing swine! Nothing could justify the prices he…"

"He was an innkeeper, Yello! It's hardly ethical to erase someone's memory simply because you don't want to pay your bar bill!"

"Oh well, what's done is done," chuntered Yello. "We must focus on the present. There may be more than one person who needs zapping before today is done," he added, pointing into the hole.

***

"We're getting nearer," whispered Ballorn, "I can feel it."

"Perhaps we should split up," suggested Barden.

"Good idea," Stitch agreed. "The wizards can go that way, you and Hunter go that way, and I'll go back the way we came," he added, turning and trying to slink away.

"You get back here!" Ballorn ordered. "What are you going to do if you come face-to-face with Grimbarr by yourself?"

"I've got a plan," Stitch told him.

"Which is?" asked Hunter.

"Run like the clappers!" Stitch replied nervously.

"You'll stay with us where we can keep you safe," Ballorn informed him. "Just do what I say when I say it and you won't come to any harm."

Hunter considered what Barden had said. *More than one target*, he thought.

They were travelling through a narrow part of the caverns but noticed that the next chamber ahead of them was even larger than the one into which they had descended. It differed greatly with faint smoke filling the air and a distinct smell of burning. Even before entering, they could feel the heat coming from it.

"He's in there," Ballorn growled.

"Makes sense," Barden agreed. "The warmer the better for a dragon."

"Hunter, see if there's anywhere you can climb once we get inside the chamber and the wizards can make their way to the opposite side," said Ballorn.

"What about you?" asked Hunter.

"Well I've got the armour and the hammer," replied Ballorn. "They'll keep me safe if you can distract him for a second or two. *Then I'll be going straight for his throat!*"

"That won't do you any good, Ballorn," Barden told him. "You need to target the crystal."

"You need to go for his legs," suggested Porflax. "Bring him down so that you can reach it."

"Great!" exclaimed Ballorn. "I've got to face a fire-breathing dragon and your advice is to stamp on its foot!"

"Well it's either that or jump fifty feet into the air! I'm sure even you can't do that, Ballorn," muttered Porflax.

Hunter surveyed the walls as they entered the chamber, "There's nowhere to climb, Ballorn, these walls are far too smooth! There's not so much as a foothold to be seen."

Ballorn sighed as he stared at the billowing smoke at the far end of the cavern. "I wouldn't worry too much if I were you, Hunter. It's too late anyway."

The gout of flame and deafening roar could mean only one thing:

They had found Grimbarr!

Ballorn gestured for the others to move away from him. The wizards hurried to the right whilst Hunter went left dragging poor Stitch with him.

"What's this!" roared Ballorn. "Even now you choose to stay hidden from me, Grimbarr. The terror of Pordan, hiding like a frightened child!"

There was another roar and gout of flame, proof that Grimbarr was concealed by the dense smoke. "You should not have come here, Nibrilsiem. All that awaits you in this place… is death!"

"It'll take a bit more than a cloud of smoke to finish me, Grimbarr. Why don't you show yourself and we can get this over with."

Slowly, the dragon emerged, wisps of smoke drifting from its nostrils. Its scaled hide was unlike any other, charcoal grey, sparking and fizzing like tiny lightning strikes.

"So you're what everyone's scared of?" laughed Ballorn.

"I do not recall a sense of bravado when last we met, Nibrilsiem," replied Grimbarr, calmly. "More a sense of dread. I know not how you eluded me that day, but I will not allow you to escape me again."

Not wanting the dragon to see, Ballorn placed his hand over his face and glanced to see if the others were clear. Hunter had already placed an arrow against his bowstring and the wizards had pulled up their sleeves. It seemed that they were all as ready as they could be for the battle that was about to commence.

Ambling forward, Ballorn wagged his finger at the dragon, "If your plan is to talk me to death or keep me here long enough so that I die of old age, you're doing a good job," he groaned. "So what say we do this the old-fashioned way? You bare your teeth and breath fire, and I'll smash your face in with my hammer!" he bellowed.

"How do you expect to defeat me when you know so little, Nibrilsiem?" asked Grimbarr, advancing slowly. "I am no mere fire-breather, I have harnessed the very power of the heavens within me. I am the power, I am the storm, I am the wrath that exists to cleanse this earth of infestations such as you!" He lowered his head as the sparks around his body began to arc. *"You cannot win!"* he roared.

Ballorn had heard enough. He charged forward, hammer raised, and he too roared.

Grimbarr had not expected the Nibrilsiem to be so headstrong and stood his ground, waiting. Baring his teeth, he basked in how glorious it would feel to tear his foe apart. However, his illusion was short lived as silver arrows and spells rained down on him. He roared in anger, blinded momentarily by pain, something he had never felt before.

It was the distraction that Ballorn needed, and he swung his hammer with all his might. *Surely that will bring him down*, he thought. But he was mistaken.

Grimbarr stumbled backwards but did not fall. Slashing wildly with his claws, he caught Ballorn a glancing blow. Ballorn fell backwards and was barely quick enough to roll out of the way as Grimbarr attempted to stamp on him. Rolling back, Ballorn swung his hammer again, striking Grimbarr in the same place as before. The frantic confusion was difficult for him to cope with as the sparks emanating from Grimbarr's scales were reflected off his armour, blinding flashes hindering his sight and loud cracks that were deafening. He clambered to his feet and charged again. His second blow had had more of an effect and the dragon was visibly limping but still able to mount an attack of its own. Its head swooped down, ready to eviscerate Ballorn but the Nibrilsiem thrust his hammer into the air, smashing it into the dragon's jaw.

Ballorn turned and scowled at Hunter, "Watch what you're doing, you berk!" he bellowed as an arrow narrowly missed him. "Or was it something I said? Ooh, bugger!" He ducked just in time as Grimbarr took another swipe at him. *Now that was a bit too close*, he thought, resuming his attack.

"Wait until he's weakened it, then we can finish the job and get rid of those three at the same time," hissed Porflax.

"Excellent idea," panted Barden. "Any idea how long that'll take?" he asked, sarcastically.

"I don't like admitting it," confessed Porflax, "but, you seem to be a lot more powerful than I am, so you finish off the dragon and the Nibrilsiem and I'll take care of the other two. Then we can take the crystal!"

Barden gave him a sideways glance. There was no way he was going to allow the old wizard to get his hands on his prize. "Fine," he said, coldly.

Hunter was running low on silver arrows, "If Ballorn doesn't bring that dragon down soon, he'll be on his own!"

"He'll be alright, Hunter, he's still got the wizards helping him," Stitch said, trying to raise his spirits.

"Hardly!" exclaimed Hunter. "I'm far more accurate than they are, and I've nearly hit him a couple of times. The way they're blasting away, they'll do the dragon's job for it!"

Ballorn continued dodging and weaving but was beginning to grow weary. Each blow he struck had less effect than the last and the dragon was beginning to connect with more of his own. He lunged at the Nibrilsiem and swung his claws as hard as he could. Ballorn jumped to the side and Grimbarr cleaved a huge lump of rock from the ground which sailed through the air toward the wizards.

It smashed against the wall, many of the larger pieces striking Porflax and sending him reeling. A few shards caught Barden, slicing his cheek and brow but not harming him significantly. *This was his chance.* Making out that his wounds were far worse than they were he pretended to fall, but not before blasting the wall with a spell directly above Porflax. The rock above the old wizard exploded and the falling debris crushed him, killing him instantly. *One problem solved,* he thought. Staggering to his feet he stumbled toward the rubble in which Porflax was buried. Too engrossed by his own act, he was not paying attention and as he neared the wizard's corpse, more debris from the broken wall crashed down. He was struck on the side of the head, sending his eyes reeling as he swayed back and forth before collapsing in a heap.

"Oh no!" cried Stitch, "Hunter, look! The wizards, I think they're dead!"

"I think we'll be joining them soon, Stitch," Hunter said, angrily. "I'm out of arrows and Ballorn can barely stand." He smiled at Stitch, "Nice knowing you," he said, patting Stitch on the back and drawing his hunting knife. "I think I'll give my friend a hand," he laughed and sprinted toward Grimbarr.

The dragon knew he had won and was now simply toying with Ballorn. The nemilar could barely support his own weight and as he stumbled around tears welled up in his eyes as he saw Hunter racing toward them. He held up his hand and implored his valiant friend to flee, but he did not.

With one swift upward stroke, Grimbarr impaled Hunter on a single claw. He looked down, almost resigned to his destiny. He lived long enough to look into Ballorn's eyes, smiling briefly before the light left his.

Stitch watched as the dragon tossed Hunter's lifeless body aside and menacingly began his approach toward Ballorn. The tailor was angry. He glared at the scene before him and felt a rage that he had never experienced before.

"You leave him alone!" he bellowed. He shocked himself. It wasn't the meek tailor shouting at the dragon, it was something else. He felt stronger, confident and unafraid. A pain surged through his body and he fell to his hands and knees sweating and shaking. He stared at his hands as they began to grow. His fingers were thicker, his wrists were stronger, and the sleeves of his jacket started to split as his forearms doubled in size. He raised his palms and was about to cradle his head but found it difficult as his jacket had become so tight, but it did not encumber him for long as his swelling body shredded it. He fell forward as his body was wracked with pain once more. His palms slapped against the floor and he dug his fingers into the ground, creating deep gouges in the solid rock. The pain stopped and he rose slowly to his feet. He looked straight into Grimbarr's eyes.

Striding towards the dragon, he pointed at him, "I'm going to kill you!" he growled.

Grimbarr backed away slightly, unsure of what was happening.

Stitch leaned down and took his friend by the arm, "Go," he said, "I've got some business to finish." As he watched Ballorn stagger away he stooped down and took hold of the silver hammer. "*My turn!*" he roared, and charged forward.

Grimbarr planted his feet and swung at Stitch. The tailor leapt into the air, using the dragon's own claws as a stepping-stone. Soaring past the dragon's open jaws he took a huge swing and struck the crystal with all his might. Grimbarr roared and fell backwards, shaking his head as blood red droplets began to ooze from the crystal. A loud crack echoed around the chamber as it split and fell from the dragon's brow and Grimbarr crashed to the ground taking his last breaths.

Felidan took no pleasure in the dragon's suffering, quickly remembering the promise he had made to Volknar. Sprinting to his shredded jacket, he uncovered the hideous crown, then dashed back to the dragon.

Kneeling next to Grimbarr's head, he placed it on the ground beside him. "I'm really sorry, Grimbarr. I never wanted this, none of us did."

The dragon now had a gentle look in his eyes, "Do not apologise little one, you have done a good thing today. You have not taken my life, you have given it back to me. I have been used to do terrible things, things that should never be repeated."

Stitch held up the crown, "Volknar said that this will save you, I only hope he's right."

"Perhaps," said the dragon as his eyes closed, "but he is only a child."

A golden mist drifted gently from his mouth, lingering for a split second before swirling around Stitch and eventually being absorbed by the crown.

"So, now we know who the real Nibrilsiem is."

Stitch shuffled around to see Yello smiling at him. "What!"

"It's you, Felidan. You are the true Nibrilsiem."

"But, but I can't be! I'm not brave or courageous or any of those things! Ballorn is the Nibrilsiem."

"No, Felidan, the true Nibrilsiem comes forward, he is not chosen or informed by another that he is the one."

"I wish I'd have known earlier," Stitch said quietly as he started to sob. "Hunter's dead and so are your friends. We nearly lost Ballorn too."

"Hunter was a brave nemilar, I'm sure he wouldn't have wanted to live into his dotage anyway and Porflax was very, very old." He glanced over at where the two fallen wizards lay. "Unfortunately, Barden survived, horrible little git, he can't even die when he's supposed to!"

As Stitch reached for the crown he did not see Yello palm the smaller piece of the crystal and quickly thrust it into his robes, "I suppose we'd better get this back to Volknar and see if it worked," he said, quietly.

Yello pointed at the larger piece of the crystal, "I think you'd better bring that with you as well," he advised. "The senior wizards from Rciggan will be coming for it and I'm sure they'll want to thank you personally."

Stitch picked it up and stared at it, "Everything we went through, all the friends we lost… for this!" he sighed. "It doesn't make sense!"

Yello shook his head, "Things very rarely do when magical forces are involved, my friend."

Stitch tried to put the crystal shard in his pocket, but it was far too large to fit. Noticing the bag he had made for Ballorn, he picked it up, "I'll be able to carry this as easily as Ballorn did," he said, studying his biceps. "Mind you, I've thought of a better name for it. As it's used to pack things away, I'm going to call it a *'backpack'*."

EPILOGUE

Gelbran stared lovingly at Grubb who lay in his crib. Three years had passed since they had descended Muurkain. Their new village had taken shape surprisingly quickly, each family having their own warm, comfortable cottage. Occasionally they were visited by Asdor and Cordain and were only too pleased that they were the only dragons they had seen since they had been forced to abandon their hunt for Grimbarr.

There was a gentle tapping on the door. Gelbran smiled as he glanced across at his wife, who sat snoozing in the chair next to him. "Just a minute," he called gently as he rose from his seat.

He opened the door to see Fellis standing there, a look of deep concern on her face. Taking her arm, he steered her inside and quietly closed the door, "Fellis, what is it, what's wrong?"

Fellis seemed reluctant to answer.

Gelbran placed his finger under her chin and looked into her eyes, "Come on, girl," he said smiling, "it can't be all that bad."

A tear welled up in her eye as she spoke, "Oh, Gelbran, I'm so sorry. I didn't want to be the one to tell you, but I had to."

Mark of the Nibrilsiem

"Tell me what? Come on, spit it out," coaxed Gelbran.

Tears now flooded down her panic-stricken face, "It's the dragon," she sobbed. "The dragon's back!"

Without a word, Gelbran flung open the door, startling his wife and son, who began to cry. "EVERYBODY OUTSIDE!" He roared.

The light from the cottage doorways flooded the ground around him as he stood, breathing hard, waiting for the other vikkery. One by one, they joined him in the cool night air.

"Gelbran, what on Pordan is all this?" asked one of them.

"I've just been told that our old friend the dragon's back," he growled. "I say we go and put his fire out for good. Who's with me?"

The vikkery clamoured around, some grabbing weapons as they transformed. Fellis lead the way, sprinting ahead as Gelbran and two others followed, Gelbran ordering most of the vikkery to stay behind and protect the village.

Reaching the only large cave in the area Fellis pointed, "Look," she whispered. "He's in there."

Gelbran frowned, "You saw him go in there?"

"I didn't see *him*," she replied, "but look at all the sparks coming from the cave. The last time I saw anything like that, it was coming from *him*."

"This isn't right," whispered Gelbran, "there's no tracks or anything outside. If he was in there, his footprints would be all over the place."

"We have to look into this," Fellis urged, "whether he's in there or not."

Gelbran nodded and the four of them approached slowly. Suddenly, one of the vikkery cried out in pain as an arc of lightning struck the sythe he was holding. "Bugger, bugger, bugger," he yelled, trying to shake the pain from his hand. Now on the ground, there was a second strike to the sythe.

"Drop your weapons!" Gelbran cried, "It's going after *them*."

No sooner had they hit the ground, than they too were struck. The metal was instantly blackened and the handles charred.

"Alright then, if that's the way you want it!" snarled Gelbran as he grew. "Looks like it'll be teeth and claws that put you down, dragon!"

All four charged toward the cave. There was a blinding flash of light, and they all vanished…